Ice Cold Liar

Ice Breaker Cold Case Romance
Book 14

Cynthia Eden

She is beautiful, charming, and guilty as sin.

Ebenezer "Eb" Jones is in the mood for deadly payback. He knows that Naomi Romano killed his friend and former CIA partner. The cops suspected her, the DA wanted to charge her, but the woman was far too smart for them. She slipped away from justice. Or so she thinks. He's about to make certain that she pays for her crimes. A life for a life. He will absolutely wreck her life. Promise made.

He's dangerous, conniving, and cold-blooded to the core.

Lying is second nature to Eb. Pretending to be someone else is as easy as breathing. So he works to slip past Naomi's guard. To learn her secrets. And he will learn those secrets. Even if he has to seduce them all from her beautiful, lying lips. Does that make him cold-blooded? Guilty as charged. It's a dirty job, but someone has to do it.

Another enemy is stalking *his* prey.

Eb isn't the only predator who wants justice. Naomi is being hunted, and Eb has to step in and shield her from a series of deadly attacks. Everywhere she turns, Naomi faces danger. He pretends to be the good guy, the savior that she needs. She breaks before him, desperate for help, and Eb realizes the woman is either one very fine actress...or maybe she's not the killer he thought.

Now she believes he is a hero and doesn't know that he is someone she should fear.

Eb succeeded in his mission of getting close to Naomi. Except now, his careful control is unraveling. He begins to want her. To need her with a desire that is more savage and primitive than any he's ever felt before. Two options—Naomi is the best liar he has ever met in his life...or Eb has made a fatal mistake. He's betrayed a woman who might own his heart, and if he's not careful, a jealous enemy closing in on them may rip her from his world.

She also might wind up hating him forever once she learns just how deeply his betrayal runs...

Passion can be lethal. And love? It will make heroes turn into monsters.

Author's Note: Time to solve another cold case with the Ice Breakers! Except...this case is far too personal for Ebenezer Jones. And when things get personal, rules will be broken. Control will be lost. And a man with an ice-cold heart may find himself lying—and falling for—a woman who is not meant to be his. A master of disguise, Eb can pretend to be anyone, anytime. Getting the truth from Naomi should be easy. Falling for her? That should not be part of the plan. Yeah...his plan is about to explode.

Oh, Monica? This one is for you.
Have I told you that you are the most observant person ever?
Because you are. And I appreciate you!

Wishing you joy. Adventures. And lots and lots of books!

Prologue

HER BODY JERKED, TWITCHED, SHUDDERED. HER HEAD hit the floor even as her hand flew out blindly.

"What do you need?" He crouched in front of her. Handsome. Charming. The devil in the flesh.

She couldn't speak. He would know that, of course. He knew so much. Had made her the object of his intense study. What she'd viewed as interest, attention—and, God forbid, *love*—all of that had been a lie. A carefully orchestrated trick so that she'd fall ever-so-willingly into his web.

"I can't hear you, sweetheart," he murmured, his voice so tender and caring. "Why don't you try again?"

Such a bastard. Her teeth snapped together. Her fingers tingled as the shaking continued. It would get worse. She knew exactly how this would end.

And he would just keep watching.

"Do you have regrets?" He stroked his chin. "I bet that you do. I bet that you regret ever bringing up the past. Ever doubting me."

She regretted ever having met him.

Her twitching fingers stretched more. Had she reached the knife that she'd dropped earlier?

He didn't even look at her hand. His brilliant blue eyes —electrifying eyes—remained locked on her face. She could see the sick excitement in his gaze. He liked her suffering.

That was only fair. She'd like his, too.

In the distance, she could hear the frantic barks of a dog. The dog wanted inside. Desperately. But the dog couldn't get past the locked door.

The dog's claws scratched against the wood of the door as the barks turned into a long howl.

"Tell me what you need." His hand stopped stroking his chin. "I can give you everything in this world. You know I have that power. The connections. I can do so much for you. Haven't I helped you already? Didn't I make your nightmares vanish?"

He was the nightmare. Not the knight in shining armor. Those jerks didn't exist. If you wanted to be saved in this world, you had to save yourself. Basic truth.

Had she managed to grab the knife? She wasn't sure. The tingling in her fingers was worse. The back of her head rapped against the hardwood floor.

"Oh, darling." His hand slid beneath her head. "You are going to hurt yourself."

No, she was going to hurt *him*. Even if it was the last thing that she ever did.

A headache throbbed—then pierced—behind her left eye. When she looked up at his handsome face, she could have sworn she saw a golden aura around his head. Almost like he was an angel.

Not an angel. He's the devil, and I will send him to hell.

"What do you need?" he demanded.

The beautiful stranger above her was relentless. The stranger—her husband.

"Who do you need?" His voice dropped to a tender caress.

A tremble rocked her entire body. "Y-you..."

He began to smile.

But the smile died when her hand lifted, and she drove her knife right into his side.

I need you to die.

Chapter One

The first time that Ebenezer "Eb" Jones saw Naomi Romano...she was dancing in a fountain. In Vegas. Her pale blue dress had been utterly drenched as it clung to her like a second skin. Her long, dark hair had been wet, trailing over her shoulders, and utter delight had lit her face as she laughed.

She'd been the most beautiful woman he'd ever seen.

The second time that Eb saw Naomi...she'd been standing at a small chapel. Not Vegas this time. Baton Rouge. And she'd been wearing a white dress. Long and made of satin. Her hair had been carefully styled around her head. She'd clutched blood-red roses. Her face had been solemn as she repeated her vows...and married his former CIA partner, Hudson Wyatt.

She'd still been the most beautiful woman he'd ever seen.

The third time Eb saw Naomi? Well, she'd been in Baton Rouge once more. Not in a chapel, but at a graveside. Wearing all black. A dress that skated over her curves. Black heels. Her hands had been fisted in front of her. No tears had slid down her cheeks. She'd stared straight at the gleaming casket. A casket surrounded by so many flowers. Roses. Carnations. Orchids. Lilies. Her husband had been in that casket. She'd watched, expressionless, during the entire graveside service. Ice cold.

Whispers had surrounded her. Judging eyes.

His hard gaze had been on her the whole time, but she'd never once looked his way. Had she even known he was there? She'd seemed oblivious to everyone. Utterly lost in her own world. But, even then, surrounded by the mourners, with her eyes completely dry, he'd looked at her and thought—

*Still the most fucking beautiful woman…*Even though he'd understood then that beauty could hide the very worst evil in the world.

Murderer.

Despite all the suspicions, the DA had recently dropped the charges against her. They'd bought her story about a home invasion gone wrong. About her husband being caught by surprise while she'd been out during the night. But Eb had seen all the holes in her story. He knew Naomi for exactly what she was.

A killer.

And now, for the fourth time, he had his eyes on her. He'd been trailing Naomi as she left her place in Baton Rouge and darted across town in an old, blue, pickup truck. One that bounced and weaved down the dark road because the shocks on it must be worn to hell and back. He'd been curious about her destination initially, but as she'd continued her trek into the night, the curiosity had turned to unease.

She'd stopped in front of a sprawling, rundown bar. One that had a graveled parking lot lined with motorcycles of every type. High-end rides. Some tricked out with modifications that must have cost thousands. Others looked like barely sputtering, scarred-up bikes. The bald bulb near the entrance to the bar cast faint illumination over those motorcycles, and he saw the club colors on them. Not like he'd needed the colors to know he was staring at an outlaw motorcycle club.

But why was Naomi paying a visit to this location? You had to be looking for trouble to visit a place like this bar.

Naomi exited her truck, and she walked straight toward the bikes near the entrance. Her hands went to her hips. She stared hard at the bikes. Particularly the big Harley right beside the bar's entrance. A fancy, gleaming ride that Eb knew cost far, far too much money to be left outside of a dump like this one.

He slid from his own car, shutting the door with the softest of sounds. Music drifted in the air. Loud and hard. Voices rose and fell. A drunk guy stumbled from the entrance of the bar and barely gave Naomi a second glance.

She kept right on staring at the motorcycles. Then her head swung toward the bar's entrance.

And then back to the line of motorcycles.

A smile spread across her lips. One easily seen thanks to that bare bulb. That smile of hers was absolutely diabolical.

Eb tensed and hurried from the shadows.

But he didn't hurry fast enough. Naomi lifted one booted heel—black boots. She wore faded jeans, a black shirt, and kick-ass boots—and she drove one of those kick-ass boots straight into the side of the big, expensive Harley.

Nothing happened.

Her smile dimmed.

Then she kicked it again.

Again.

And—

He grabbed her arm. Hauled her away from the motorcycles and toward him before she could cause some serious chaos. "What in the hell are you doing?"

She blinked. Tilted back her head so all of that long, thick hair tumbled over her back, and she locked the deepest, darkest eyes in the world on him.

Fuck me, she's still the most beautiful woman I've ever seen.

Even knowing what she was, even knowing what she'd done, the sight of her was like a punch straight to the—

There was a screech behind her. A groan. Ragged. Metallic. Then...

Crash. A long and loud crash and another screech as the expensive Harley toppled and slammed into the ride beside it. Together, the two motorcycles hit the graveled lot.

Naomi glanced over her shoulder. "Dammit." A sigh of disappointment. "I was hoping that one falling bike would send them all knocking down."

No such luck. The big Harley and the gleaming ride near it were the only two that had fallen.

"*Ivan!*" A frantic roar from the open door of the bar. "Hey! Hey! Some prick just knocked down Ivan's ride!"

I didn't do it. She did. But, clearly, he was about to take the blame. Probably what he deserved for stepping in and trying to stop her. Had he not already learned that no good deed went unpunished in this world?

"In the movies, one toppling bike would create a domino effect and take down all the others. It would have been dramatic and beautiful at the same time." Another despondent sigh from Naomi. "Oh, well, at least I got his attention..."

His attention? "What the hell are you doing, Naomi?" Eb breathed.

Her gaze returned to his. Her gorgeous smile stretched her full lips, and he was pretty sure savage glee filled her face. "Getting back what belongs to me. Desperate times call for desperate measures, isn't that the saying? I'm desperate, and I don't care what I have to do in order to achieve my end goal." Grim intent filled every low word.

Yep, this lady is not the sweet ray of sunshine I originally believed her to be. Hell, no. She wasn't sunshine. She was a short walk straight to hell.

Naomi slowly blinked as she studied him. Then she inched a bit closer. "Ebenezer Jones." A shake of her head. "Of all the biker bars in the world...are you really sure you want to be at this one right now? With me?"

No, he did not want to be there. He wanted to be back home in South Carolina, sitting on a beach and laughing his ass off with his twin brother. He wanted to be listening to the soothing sounds of waves hitting the shore. He wanted to be playing poker with his ex-partner, Hudson.

But he couldn't.

Because Hudson was cold in the ground. Courtesy of the lovely Naomi. And Eb was there to get his pound of flesh from her.

Footsteps thundered behind him as men erupted from the bar. Lots of angry shouts thickened the air. Colorful cursing.

"You should probably run," Naomi advised.

Eb's jaw locked. This night was about to get really shitty. As if it had not already been shitty enough. But, for the record, "I never run."

One delicate eyebrow quirked. "I'll remember that about you."

"What in the hell is happening here?" A bellow. Then a hard hand grabbed Eb's shoulder and wheeled him around. "Asshole, you just made the worst mistake of your life!"

Eb found himself staring straight into angry, glinting eyes. A tall guy, wide, too. But not with muscle. Mostly fat. Thin hair. Big neck. Lots of tats stretching out beneath the dirty t-shirt that he wore.

The big bastard raised his fist and got ready to take a swing at Eb.

"*He* didn't make a mistake," Naomi declared, her voice very loud and clear for all to hear. Then, after making that blasting statement, she was there, ducking in front of Eb. Putting herself between him and the bastard with the beefy fist.

The guy let go of Eb, but he kept his fist raised.

He will not fucking hit her.

Eb would not allow that. Naomi would go down for her crimes. But no one would hit her.

"I'm the one who not-so-accidentally knocked down your bike, Ivan. Took quite a bit of effort, I must confess. But after several hard kicks, I did succeed in sending that precious Harley of yours slamming into the ground."

"Uh, Naomi?" Eb cleared his throat. "Maybe you should back away right now." Because the crowd was closing in. A very pissed crowd. Eb noted the tattoos they wore. Tigers. Stars. Medals. Skulls. They were in trouble. Big trouble. The name *Ivan* had rung unfortunate bells for him.

Ivan leaned his big, glaring face toward Naomi. "You want to die?"

Hell. Eb had to step in or else he'd be watching a

murder scene up close and personally. He reached for the gun he'd tucked beneath his shirt after exiting his ride—

"No, I don't want to die. I want Henry back, you jerk! And if I have to wreck every single motorcycle here, if I have to wreck your bar, if I have to wreck your *life* in order to get him, I'll do it!" A passionate declaration. Sightly unhinged, but passionate.

Eb's mouth tightened. *Who the fuck is Henry?*

Ivan glared at her. Glared long and hard and then he... laughed. Heaving, wild bursts of laughter rang from him.

Naomi did not laugh back. Her hands fisted at her sides.

Ivan's fingers rose and curled under her chin. "Pretty little killer..."

Oh, yeah. He knows exactly who—what—she is. They were on the same page. Nice to know.

"I will give you thirty seconds to get out of here," Ivan offered. "If you don't flee, I guarantee you will be meeting your husband again by dawn."

The bastard had just threatened to kill her. "I don't think so." Eb let go of his gun, for the moment. But only so he could curl his hands around Naomi's waist. "I'll take care of her."

"Who the hell are you?" Ivan demanded.

The faintest hint of Russia slid beneath his words. Making them rougher. Deeper.

Like I didn't already know you were Russian mafia. Eb was staring straight at Ivan Sokolov. The guy had been in the US since he was sixteen—that was why only a trace of his accent remained. Ivan had a rap sheet a mile long. He'd been linked to all sorts of crimes, both in the US and abroad, and he'd sure as hell been on the CIA's radar. He'd have to be on their radar, considering that he was a confidential source for them. Eb had never worked directly with the guy.

Ivan had a reputation for being a volatile prick. But Eb's partner Hudson had been Ivan's main contact on plenty of cases.

"I'm a friend of Hudson's," Eb replied.

Ivan's gaze flickered. "Don't know that name."

"Hudson Wyatt," Eb enunciated slowly. He got that Ivan was pretending not to know the guy in front of his crew. Not like the big Russian could admit to being an informant. Not admit it, and stay alive, anyway. "He's her dead husband."

Ivan's jaw hardened. "You mean he's the husband she killed? I do watch the news. I know her pretty, murderous face."

Naomi tried to lunge for Ivan, but Eb tightened his hold on her. When she kicked back, aiming perfectly for his shin, Eb swore at the impact. Then he just lifted her up and held her in the air as those booted feet of hers kicked aimlessly.

Ivan laughed.

"I'll take care of her," Eb promised. "Was on my way to see you when I caught her playing with the bikes." No, he hadn't been going to see Ivan. But he could lie very, very well.

Right now, I need to get Naomi out of here before this crew rips her apart.

"I gave her thirty seconds." Ivan crossed his flabby arms over his chest. "I figure that time is up."

"She's gone." She *would be* gone. "I've got her."

Naomi twisted and tried to surge for Ivan once more. "I'm not leaving without Henry, you sonofa—"

Eb tossed her over his shoulder.

Naomi let out a guttural scream. A truly powerful one that blasted in Eb's ears. He kept one arm around the back of her thighs as he began walking very determinedly toward her truck. One arm was around her, and his other hand had pulled his weapon. Just in case any of the gang members decided to attack.

Naomi slammed her hands into his back. "Let me go, *now!*"

"Do you want the Russian gang to rip you apart?" he asked her, voice pleasant. They were almost at the truck.

Almost. And there had been no attack...yet.

"They aren't even all Russian!" she snapped back. "Ivan is. Maybe three others. His cousins. The rest are just posers who flock around him. Dammit, put me down before I have to hurt you!" Naomi heaved hard against him.

Hurt? The woman truly thought she could hurt him? Almost amusing.

And they were finally at her truck. So he put her down and immediately caged her between his body and the metal frame of the vehicle. "Listen to me. Carefully." His voice was very, very low.

The gun was in his right hand.

A hand that was lodged between their bodies.

Her eyes widened. Then they dipped down to the gun. She swallowed. Slowly, her gaze came back up to meet his. They were far away from the lone exterior light, though, so he couldn't read her expression clearly. But he thought fear might have flickered on her face.

"Ebenezer?"

"Do you want to die tonight?" He didn't hear footsteps behind them. Not yet.

She didn't respond.

So he pushed and questioned, "Eager to join your loving husband?"

"He wasn't loving. And I don't consider him my husband."

"Funny. I could have sworn I heard you take vows." Shit. Had a hard edge just entered his voice? It had. An edge that absolutely, under no circumstances, could be jealousy. "Pretty sure you promised to love and honor him forever. But he wasn't even cold in the ground, and you'd ditched your wedding ring." Yeah, he'd noticed the ring had been gone at the funeral.

Because I notice far too much about Naomi.

"I am not talking about this with you." A hard, negative shake of Naomi's head. "Get out of my way, Ebenezer."

"*Eb.*"

"Yeah, well, if I was named after the mean old guy from *A Christmas Carol,* I'd want people to call me something else, too." Her chin notched up. "Get out of my way, *Eb.*"

He did not. He lowered his head. He crowded in closer. He got even more in her way. "That guy you just pissed off? He's Bratva." Would she even know about the Russian criminal underworld?

"Please. That guy is wannabe Bratva."

Okay, so she knew about Bratva, but she was wrong in thinking Ivan wasn't a dangerous threat. He was the real deal. Ivan should terrify her. But maybe nothing terrified Naomi. Maybe she didn't have the capacity to truly fear anyone or anything.

"Ivan has something that belongs to me, and I'm getting it back," she declared. "If I have to wreck his bar in order to get what I need, I'll do it."

The woman was impossible. "If I hadn't carried you away, you could be dead right now." Maybe she should try showing a little gratitude.

"Yeah, and why would you care?" Zero gratitude. Just a whole lot of kiss-her-assitude.

He blinked.

She heaved another sigh. "You hate me, Ebenezer. Oh, sorry, my bad. *Eb.* Like everyone else, you think I am a cold-blooded killer. Well, goody for you."

"You have no idea what I think." *But, yes, I absolutely think you are a killer. Cold-blooded to the core. You didn't even shed a tear at Hudson's funeral. Not one.*

Naomi huffed out a hard breath. "I don't know why you're here. I don't know why you're in my way. I don't know why you saw the need to *carry* me from my target. But here's a word of warning…" Her chin notched up. "Stay out of my way."

"Or what?" Eb had to ask. Her scent teased him. Not some sweet scent. This woman did not smell like candy. Or cinnamon. She was sensual. Sultry. Bold. Amber. Jasmine. A wild, warm—

"Seriously, you want an 'or what' answer from me?"

Yeah, he did. Thus, the question he'd just asked. "If I don't stay out of your way, are you gonna shove a knife into me the way you did Hudson?"

She stiffened.

He'd probably gone too far. The way to get close to the woman, the way to get her to reveal every secret she possessed, it was *not* to become her enemy and to have her hate him from day one. The hate could—would—come later. After he'd locked her hot ass up in a jail cell. For now, he had to try another technique. *So get your control back in place, man. Put on the mask you wear so well.*

"Is that what you think?" Zero emotion entered her voice. "You gonna join the crowd who believes I murdered my husband and then set up the scene to look as if an intruder came in to kill him? You think I'm that diabolical?"

Hudson was a trained CIA operative. Getting killing close to him would be tricky. Your average home intruder would never get the drop on him. But Hudson would be fooled by someone he trusted. Someone he loved. Someone he loved could easily get close enough to kill him.

And Hudson had loved his beautiful wife very, very much.

The autopsy had shown zero defensive wounds on Hudson's body. He hadn't fought back at all against his killer. Probably because he hadn't expected his beautiful, delicate, and deadly wife to attack him.

Eb swallowed. He took a step back. But her sensual scent followed him. Had his nostrils flaring as he tried to pull in more of her intoxicating scent. Intoxicating? Hell. *Do not lust after your dead partner's wife.*

Yeah, right.

Do not lust after the woman who murdered your partner.

That should have been an easy enough rule to follow. Unfortunately, Eb was a bit twisted on the inside and the truth of the matter was that he'd always lusted for Naomi. From the very first moment he'd seen her dancing in that fountain, he'd wanted her for himself.

He and Hudson had spotted her at the same time. Eb had planned to introduce himself. To talk to the woman with the beautiful laugh and the carefree spirit.

But...

Tragedy had struck. Eb's sister had needed him. He'd left Vegas without ever meeting Naomi.

And Hudson had wound up married to her.

Eb swallowed. "Crowds aren't really my thing. Never cared about fitting in with them. I'm more the loner-type." He glanced over his shoulder. Some guys were picking up Ivan's bike. Inspecting it for damage, but most of the crew—including Ivan—had gone back inside. That was a win, for the moment. "He worked with your hus—with Hudson," he corrected. "Ivan did. I'm in town to close out some old cases. Talking to him was on my to-do list." Total lie. Hell, Eb wasn't even officially with the CIA any longer. His departure was need-to-know info. Naomi did not need to know about it.

"Why the hell would the CIA care about a small-town thug like him?" she asked.

"Because Ivan isn't small town. I told you, he's Bratva." Had she missed that part? He turned his head back toward her. "He has connections you wouldn't believe. Just because he surrounds himself with local talent, it doesn't mean Ivan can't be an international player."

That should terrify her. Or, at the very least, give her a pause.

"He's an international pain in my ass, that's what he is."

So, uh, yes, she was not scared. Not of Ivan. Not of his gang. Was she not understanding basic facts of life? Maybe he needed to break this down even more for her. "Mess with Ivan, and he will hurt you."

"I *will* hurt him."

Eb laughed.

She glared.

Oh, wait, had she been serious? "You're five-foot-five. He has to clock in at six-three." Because he and Ivan had been eye-to-eye. "Pretty sure he could bench press you with one arm. And *one* of you will stand zero chance against him and his crew. So I don't know who the hell this Henry is..." *Probably a new lover, when Hudson is cold in the ground.* "But he's trouble. You need to forget him. If he's cast his lot in with Ivan's crew, you don't want that kind of trouble in your life." Naomi had plenty of trouble to handle on her own without adding bonus content to the mix.

"I'm not leaving Henry. I think he's in that bar. Probably in Ivan's back office."

What, was Henry like…Ivan's accountant or something? Might make sense. A good accountant could make dirty money vanish—

"If he's not in the back office, then Ivan must have him stashed at his home." She shimmied around him. Yanked open the door to her truck and hauled out a bat. A baseball bat.

He blinked at her. "Uh, slugger? Just what are you planning to do with that?" *And, yes, this makes you seem extra murdery, sweetheart.*

"Whatever needs doing."

He raised his eyebrows. "A little birdie told me that the DA only recently decided to drop the charges against you." He paused. "You really think going into a bar, swinging a bat, won't make the DA rethink his idea that you're innocent?"

She dropped the top of the bat to touch the ground. "First, the DA doesn't think I'm innocent."

Neither do I.

"He just doesn't have enough evidence to prove I'm guilty."

That's why I'm here. I'm looking for evidence to lock you away.

"But I don't think he'll really care if I break a few doors at Ivan's place. Not like the DA and Ivan have some fantastic relationship." She lifted the bat. Moved to stroll right past him.

Sighing, Eb wrenched the bat from her and tossed it into the bed of the truck. When the bat hit, it made a loud clang.

Her hands immediately went to her hips. "Why the hell did you do that?"

"To save your life." The same reason he picked her up—yet again—even as she squealed in outrage, and he dumped her in the driver's seat of the truck. "Forget the new boyfriend. Get your—" *Homicidal. Nope, can't say that. Can't say…Get your homicidal ass back home.* So he settled for, "Get your gorgeous ass back home." He stood right next to the driver's seat, with the open door at his side.

She grabbed the steering wheel, but turned her head toward him. "What new boyfriend?"

"Henry." A disgusted shake of his head. "Lady, you have enough problems without worrying about some dumb asshole—"

"Henry is not my boyfriend. He's my *dog*."

Her what?

"Ivan stole him while I was being held in jail. You know, back when the DA thought it would be super fun to lock me away for ages even though I'd been convicted of zero crimes. I was being held for murdering my husband, held without bond, even though I told everyone who would listen that I wasn't guilty." She sucked in a deep, shuddering breath. "A neighbor was supposed to be watching Henry. Ivan *stole* my dog."

"Get a new dog. You'll stay alive that way." He started to back up.

Her hand flew out. Curled around his wrist. "Please." Her voice broke.

Something in him seemed to break, too. *Wait. What the fuck is happening?*

"I love that dog," she said, and damn if it didn't sound like the woman—the same woman who'd been ready to go swinging with a bat a few moments ago—was about to cry.

She hadn't cried at her husband's gravesite, but she was on the verge of tears over a dog. "I *need* him. I-I can't explain but just, dammit...that dog is mine. *Mine.* I have to get Henry back."

She let go of his wrist and dashed a hand across her face. The interior light was on in the truck, shining brightly down on her, and Eb realized she was dashing away actual tears.

Now she cried. *Now.* Outside of a bar. Over a dog. Check.

He whistled. Okay, maybe she was the best actress he'd ever seen. Maybe this could explain why the DA had caved and dropped those charges. *Did you pull the teary routine with him, too? Turn on the grieving widow waterworks and the DA thought the jury would never convict you based on the circumstantial evidence he had?*

"I will do anything to get my dog back. Break some bikes? Fine. Done. Pound a bat into a door in order to make those jerks pay attention to me? *Done.*"

She could not be serious. "You're gonna die for your dog? Is that on your to-do list?"

"I don't plan on dying." She drew in a shuddering breath. "I want my dog back. He's all I have." Her head bowed forward.

Shit. "You're seriously doing all of this...for a dog?" He could not quite wrap his mind around what was happening. Too surreal.

Her head whipped toward him. "He's a special dog, all right? *I just want my dog back.* And I will do anything, I—" She stopped. Her hand flew out and curled around his wrist once more. "You know Ivan."

Not really. Knew *of* him. They were not buddies.

"You probably read his CIA file or something like

that. You can convince him to give me back my dog." Now she jumped from the truck. Her body brushed against Eb's because he sure as hell wasn't about to retreat. "If you can get my dog back, I would be so grateful to you!"

Just how grateful?

She'd already said that she'd do anything...

He stared down at her.

"Please." She bit her lip. Then, "Please, I am begging here, Eb. I get that you don't like me. But that dog is special. I need him. And if he stays with Ivan—look, I think Ivan only took Henry to hurt me."

"And Ivan wants to hurt you because...?"

"The same reason all of Hudson's friends want to hurt me. Because they think I killed him." She swallowed. "Isn't that why you want to hurt me?"

His gut tightened. "What in the hell makes you think I'm here to hurt you? Told you, I was just meeting with Ivan to close out old business with the agency..." Total lie. He was there to obliterate her world.

Her eyes were big and deep. Those eyes would suck in a normal man. Convince him that she was weak and innocent. In need of protection. The princess who needed some kind of knight to ride fast to the rescue.

Screw that knight bullshit. He was more of a destroyer than a savior. She'd learn that, eventually.

Besides, she was no innocent princess. If this was the fairytale, she'd be the villain. The wicked witch who poisoned her own true love—or rather, stabbed him right in the heart.

If she'd ever even loved Hudson. Eb doubted that she had. With Hudson's death, she'd inherited all his assets.

So why the hell is she driving that old pickup truck?

"If you aren't here to hurt me, then help me. I will owe you."

He'd wanted an opportunity to get close to her. Earning her trust would be paramount in this game. Eb just hadn't expected the opportunity to be handed to him on a silver platter. But, then again, his twin Jake had always said that Eb was the lucky one.

"I'll help," he said, making the words sound grudging. He put away his gun. For the moment. "But you have to do exactly what I say, understand?"

She threw herself at him. Curled her arms around him and wrapped him up in that sultry scent of hers. "Thank you!"

He should not—a thousand times, *should not*—have responded physically to her, but he did. The dark truth was that he'd always responded physically to her. Even when she'd been walking down the aisle to marry his friend, his dumb dick had been saluting her. He'd even entertained a fast and *wrong* fantasy about stealing his friend's girl. Running with her from that chapel.

But he hadn't moved from his position. Hadn't said a word when the officiant had asked if anyone objected to the wedding. He'd stood in silence.

I lusted after my friend's bride.

And now I'm going to wreck her world.

His hands slowly closed around her. She was warm and soft against him. Deceptively delicate. No wonder she'd been able to slip past Hudson's guard. She didn't look like a killer.

His head moved near her right ear. "You have to get back in that truck, and you have to go home."

She stiffened against him. Began to pull back.

He kept his grip on her because he wasn't done. "That

gang will erupt if they see you again. So do what I say. My plan, my rules. You get in the truck. You go home. I'll get the dog." How the hell was he gonna pull off that magic trick? Eb didn't know yet. But he'd always been pretty good at figuring shit out in the heat of the moment. "I'll bring him to you. Then you pay me back. Deal?"

He heard the whisper of her breath. A second or two later, he felt the movement of her head as she nodded.

Slowly—more reluctantly than he should have—Eb released her.

"What does the payback entail?" she asked.

"Does it matter?"

Naomi's head tilted to the side. "Perhaps."

"We'll start by saying that you let me crash at your place. Staying in a guest room at your place will be better than me having to find a hotel room for the night." *I need to get in your house. I need to search every inch of the property. I need to be close so that I can learn your secrets and catch you when you slip up.* Because, sooner or later, she would slip up.

Criminals always did.

Laughter sputtered from her. The sound was warm and rich, and it caught him completely off guard.

"You have clearly never seen my place if you think it's better than a hotel room. Not in its current state, it's certainly not better. Despite the dreams I once had. But, sure, I'll be happy to give you a place to crash." She brought her hand up between them. "You give me back my dog, and I'll give you a crash spot. Plus, whatever else you add to our deal later."

He closed his hand around hers. "No more questions?" He didn't buy that. "What if I want things you're not prepared to give?"

"Just what sort of things would you mean?" Her hand was soft against his.

I want everything you have. All that you are. "I want the truth." Shit. Clusterfuck. He had not meant to make that stark statement.

"The truth about what?" Careful, now. She began to tug her hand back.

He let her go. "The truth about you. The truth about Hudson." A pause. "I want you to help me find your husband's killer."

She backed away fast and rammed into the side of the truck. "*What?*"

"You're not guilty. That's what you've been claiming all along, right?"

"I've been saying that, yes." Slightly breathless.

"Then I'm offering you a team-up. After I finish my business with Ivan, you and I will find the real killer. Because what I want—most of all—is to make certain the killer is captured." He nodded. "Deal?"

The silence ticked past.

"*You* think I'm innocent?" Naomi finally asked, voice husky.

"Aren't you?"

She rocked forward. "Get my dog, and we have a deal."

Hell, yes. "Get that ass into the truck, get out of here, and *then* we have a deal."

She climbed back into the truck. Slammed the door. Cranked the engine. Well, on the third, sputtering try, Naomi cranked the engine. Only instead of driving away, she lowered the window. "I have a confession."

Already? Damn. He'd expected more resistance. Eb put his forearm on the side of the door. Leaned in toward her.

"I always thought you were far too damn sexy, Ebenezer Jones."

What. The. Fuck?

"And I always wondered...what would have happened if I met you before Hudson? Just how different would my life have been?"

Shock froze him.

"Better step back," she advised, voice sugary sweet. "I'd hate to run over your foot on my way out of here."

He stepped back.

She rattled off an address. Not like he needed it. He had her address saved on his phone. Imprinted on his brain.

"See you soon," his prey told him. All merry and bright. Like they were planning to meet up for tea or some shit. All signs of tears were gone.

In silence, Eb watched her drive away.

I always wondered...what would have happened if I met you before Hudson? Just how different would my life have been?

How different would his own life have been?

Would he be the dead one lying in a cold grave?

Eb waited until her taillights vanished, then he turned and stared at the rundown bar. After a moment, he squared his shoulders and headed for the entrance.

He wondered how many bastards he'd have to fight in order to get back one dog for a lady who looked like pure temptation but had a heart of absolute ice.

* * *

NAOMI WAITED until she rounded the curve and...

She hit the brakes. Then whipped that truck around.

Ebenezer Jones, I don't trust you for a second.

What did he think? That she'd been born yesterday? Hell, no, she wasn't just going to drive away like a good little girl while he took care of business.

She'd tried to be good. Too many times. That routine didn't work for her.

These days, she didn't take orders from anyone.

And she was getting her damn dog back.

Eb could be the distraction in the front of the bar.

She'd sneak in the back.

Game. On.

Chapter Two

THE MUSIC STILL POUNDED, BUT EVERY EYE IN THE place was on him.

Eb stood just inside the old bar's doorway. As soon as he'd crossed the threshold, heads had whipped toward him. Several goons jumped to their feet. Their hands were fisted, and it was clear that they were just waiting on the order before they attacked him.

Yep, he was gonna have to take out far too many bastards in order to get back one mangy dog. Such a pain in his ass. He didn't even like dogs. *That's provided that the story about the dog is even true.* He half-feared she was just setting him up for an ass-kicking.

But if that was the case, Naomi would discover he could more than hold his own in a fight.

"Who's gonna be first?" Eb wanted to know. He lifted his right hand and waved two fingers in a come-and-get-some motion.

One tattoo-covered man with a shaved head and a face full of piercings took a step forward. Right. Why not start with the biggest guy in the place? Figured. Eb rolled back his shoulders. "Okay, so are there gonna be any ground rules?"

A giant fist came at his face. Eb dodged the blow, lunged to the right, then immediately plowed his fist into the attacker's stomach. "Guess there are no ground rules." He shoved the prick into a table. "Good to know."

Someone grabbed Eb from behind. Thick, hard arms closed around him and tried to squeeze the life from him. Eb just slammed his head back at his attacker and drove his foot back at the SOB in the same instance. When those grabbing arms let go, Eb spun around and delivered an uppercut that had the biker stumbling back.

Two more attackers came at him. *Dammit.* Eb had started to breathe a bit harder. He grabbed the first attacker, but the second managed to slam a fist into Eb's side. Eb kicked the fist-slamming bastard in the dick. Hard enough to have the man howling, and then he took out the other jerk with two fast punches. Eb scanned the room and saw that plenty more attacks were about to come his way. *Fine. Bring it. Let's get this show over.*

They advanced.

"Stop!" A hard order from Ivan.

The goons stopped advancing.

"Really? The fun is ending so soon?" Eb rolled back his shoulders. "And here I was getting good and warmed up."

Ivan strolled right up to Eb. He barely spared a glance for his injured men. Instead, he raked a stare over Eb. "You took care of the woman?"

"Yes." For the moment. "She's long gone."

Ivan grunted. "Then we talk. In my office."

But Eb didn't move. Not yet. Suspicion crystalized in him. "You know who I am." Not just that he was a *friend* of

Hudson's as Eb had said before. The Russian understood exactly who—what—Eb was.

A shrug. "After seeing those punches, I figure you have to be Eb. Always heard you had a killer punch."

Ah, so Hudson had definitely mentioned him to the Russian. Good to know that Ivan was holding lots of secrets.

Ivan turned and began to stalk through the crowd. Of course, the crowd parted instantly for him.

Not so much for Eb. He had to shoulder and shove his way past the jerks.

But after a few moments of shoving, he found himself in front of a black door. Ivan swung it open. They marched inside and—

Growling.

Huh. How the hell about that? There was a dog, after all. So he wasn't just chasing a bullshit story from Naomi. Good to know. "I think the dog's owner wants him back—" Eb broke off, stunned.

Because they'd just made it fully inside of Ivan's private office. An office that had been locked because Ivan had *unlocked* the door before he swung it open. The dog was inside the office—a big, grinning Golden Retriever with a blue collar waited in a black cage near Ivan's desk. Only the dog wasn't alone.

Naomi crouched right next to him.

A Naomi he'd seen drive away moments before.

"Sonofabitch," Eb growled. He kicked the door shut behind him.

"What the hell is this?" Ivan bellowed. And then he reached for his gun.

Naomi had one hand shoved through the bars of the cage, petting the dog's head, and the other hand had been poised over the latch in front of the cage. When she saw the gun, her eyes widened, and her lips parted to scream.

Eb grabbed Ivan from behind, and he shoved the bastard as hard as he could toward the desk. The gun fired, the blast echoed around them, but it didn't hit Naomi. Or the dog. The bullet just thudded into the wall. Ivan tried to come up and aim that gun again, but Eb was on him. He slammed the bastard's hand into the side of the desk. Two slams and the gun dropped to the floor.

Ivan snarled and pushed at Eb, but Eb was not in the mood to be pushed so he just pinned the Russian against the desk.

"Who's a good boy?" Naomi cooed. "Not just a good boy, but the best boy in the entire world!"

For fuck's sake. "Naomi!" Eb thundered.

He heard the frantic thuds of footsteps rushing for the office door.

Ivan started laughing. "You're both dead. Dead—for a damn dog." More laughter.

Eb backed away from the laughing bastard, but he just retreated so he could pull out his own weapon and, when Ivan faced him, Eb aimed the gun dead center at the gang leader's chest. "Weird. I feel oddly alive."

The door began to swing open—

"Tell them to stay out or I fire," Eb ordered, voice low.

"Or even better," Naomi murmured, "why don't you just tell them that their boss is an informant. Then his own gang can kill him and handle the dirty work for you."

"*Stay out!*" Ivan roared to his men. "Out! My gun just misfired. Everything is *fine* in here." Then he was rushing toward the door and slamming it fully closed himself. Then locking it.

"Boss?" A fist pounded into the door. "Boss, you sure?"

"Get the fuck away from my office," Ivan ordered as spittle flew from his mouth. "*Now.* I'm handling business in here. You know I don't like to be disturbed when I'm handling my business."

Naomi had opened the cage door, and the dog bounded right into her arms. She crouched beside him as the Golden Retriever sniffed her neck, then butted its head against her.

Thank you, she mouthed to Eb. She looked all grateful and relieved. Her beautiful face practically glowed.

Screw that.

"I just saved your life," he snapped at her. "*After* you lied to me. Believe me when I say...I get more than just a thank you." But for now, he kept his weapon aimed at a glowering Ivan. "You stole her dog." Talk about a dick move.

"That's my dog!" Ivan argued. "Mine!"

Eb spared a glance for a still crouching Naomi. "The dog that is currently cuddled against her is *your* dog? That's the story you're going with right now?"

"Henry, here!" Ivan boomed.

The dog placed its body in front of Naomi. Sat down. Stared at Ivan.

"Henry, *here!*" Ivan's voice broke a bit around the edges.

Henry did not move.

Behind the dog, Naomi rose. Her fingers skimmed over Henry's head in a brief caress. "I'll be taking my dog now. And you'll be staying the hell away from us both."

Ivan's eyes narrowed. His head swung from her to Eb. "Not so fast, Hudson's partner. I know all about you. So many details." He smiled. "We can make a deal. Same kind of deal I had with Hudson. I figure you'd be coming around, sooner or later. Actually took you a bit longer to show up than I'd originally guessed."

Unease slithered through Eb. "What kind of deal did you have with Hudson?"

"Oh, the usual."

There was no usual deal.

"You make sure my life stays nice and easy," Ivan said. "In return, I make sure you get all the inside info that you need. Simple enough, yes?"

Nothing was ever really simple.

"But why are you pointing that gun at me?" Ivan asked. His bushy brows lowered. "It should be on her. We both know what she did."

A low whine came from the dog.

Eb's gaze jumped to the big Golden Retriever. He saw that the dog had glanced back at Naomi. Once more, her fingers skimmed over Henry's head.

"You should have let me shoot her," Ivan continued, a definite note of petulance in his voice. "I had a clear case of breaking and entering. The DA probably would have thanked me when he found her body." Ivan grunted. "It could still happen. If we play the scene right."

"Uh, Eb?" Naomi seemed worried.

She probably should be. The Russian wanted her dead.

"I am happy to do the job." Ivan tapped his chin. "Or... or do you just want to kill her yourself?"

Silence.

"You have to be pissed," Ivan added. His accent deepened just a little in those words. Half-forgotten. "She murdered him. Took a knife and carved up Hudson. I *liked* the guy, and I don't like many people in this world."

Everyone had liked Hudson. He'd been open, friendly, easy-going. And rich as hell.

"Turn the gun on her." Ivan stepped away from the door. "I can be your witness. I'll claim it was self-defense.

One quick squeeze of that trigger, and we both get the vengeance we want."

Eb stalked toward Naomi.

The dog shifted, instantly alert as it stood on all four feet.

"You didn't follow orders," Eb told Naomi. He'd specifically told her to go home. Had he said to break into a bar? To sneak into a Russian criminal's private office? Nope.

She grimaced. "It's a character flaw I have. A distinct inability to follow orders."

"You lied to me."

"That's another character flaw I have. I do tell the occasional lie." A nod. "Do you want me to apologize?"

He wanted to get her the hell out of there without utter chaos erupting on them both. One wrong shout from Ivan would have all his goons breaking down the door. Ivan's fear of being revealed as an informant was the only thing currently keeping the wolves at bay.

Ivan grunted again—he seemed to do that a lot—as he swaggered closer. "What about being a killer, pretty lady?" Ivan asked. "That a flaw you want to confess about having, too?"

Her deep, dark eyes didn't leave Eb. "You aren't going to shoot me."

"At the moment, no, it's not on my agenda."

"*Why the hell not?*" Ivan exploded. But the explosion of words was apparently not enough for the man. He barreled straight at Naomi.

The dog growled.

So did Eb. "Because I have other plans. Now, get the fuck away from her." He put his body between Naomi and the dog...and the pissed-off Russian.

Ivan's furious gaze dropped to the gun in Eb's hand.

"Our friend Hudson would be so disappointed in you. Choosing her...bad decision." His lips pursed. "Or is it that you are *fucking* her? Is that what happened? Perhaps you were involved all along and when Hudson was shoved into the ground—"

"I came for the damn dog," Eb said. "Don't steal someone's dog. That's a real shit move." He tucked the gun in the back waistband of his jeans. "Now we're going to leave. You're going to keep breathing, Ivan. And that will be the end of things."

"That's not the end for me," Ivan told him flatly.

"Fine. Then come after me. I'll probably shoot you. Or maybe I'll—"

"I'll tell your gang buddies that you're an informant," Naomi chimed. "Do not test me."

Ivan peered around Eb so he could see Naomi. "Hudson told me to take the dog. A week before he died, he said the dog had to go. Like the good friend I am, I simply followed orders." His attention shifted back to Eb. "Are you a good friend? Or are you the kind of friend who fucks a dead partner's wife?"

Eb smiled at him.

Ivan blinked. Then looked nervous. Good. He should be nervous.

"I'm the kind of person you don't want as an enemy," Eb informed him. But those words were for Naomi, too. *You don't want me as an enemy, but that's exactly what I am.* "Stay out of my way. And stay *away* from Naomi." Because Ivan would just screw up Eb's plans if he interfered.

"There's a back door to the bar," Naomi said softly. She grabbed Eb's hand. "Come with me."

He went with her, and, sure enough, there was another door *inside* that back office. One that led directly outside, to the rear of the bar. The dog stayed at her side, and Ivan followed them out. But he didn't shout for backup. Didn't say anything at all until—

"It will be your funeral next," he warned Eb.

Then Ivan retreated and slammed the rear door shut.

Hell. Eb sucked in a long breath. "We need to haul ass, now." Because that sure had sounded like a threat to him. Her truck waited about twenty feet away. The tricky woman had circled behind the bar and crept inside while he distracted the gang. Damn cold of her to use him that way. Sneaky and cold.

She ran for the truck. Hauled open the driver's side. The Golden Retriever shot in before her. She jumped into the seat, then turned her head toward Eb.

"Go!" he snarled at her.

"Get in! Jump in the back!"

No, his business was not finished. But with the truck's driver side door open, he did lean in close to her. "Don't lie to me again."

"*Will you get in the truck?* His men could come storming out any minute!"

His gaze fell to her mouth. That delectable mouth. The mouth that had teased and tormented him. And he—

Fuck.

He kissed her.

His lips slammed down on hers in a fast, frantic kiss. One that he had not intended. This was not the place. The grimy alley behind a Russian gang leader's rundown bar was not the place for a first kiss. This was not the time.

And he should never, ever be kissing her.

But he was.

She tastes as good as she smells.

He wanted to taste her everywhere. *Hell.*

Eb pulled back before he could give in to the absolutely savage need that knifed through him.

"Wh-what was that for?"

"For the audience that's watching." He was sure Ivan had eyes on them. But, no, the kiss actually hadn't been for that bullshit reason. The kiss had been because he'd walked a knife's edge of desire for Naomi for far too long. "Now get the hell out of here. I *will* see you at your place."

"Don't you dare get shot." She touched her lips. Then caught herself and let her hand fall. "Or bruised. Or damaged—or beat up by a gang—"

"Really? Now you care about what happens to me? Where was the concern when I was being used as your distraction?"

"*Would you just get in the damn truck?*"

"Drive away, Naomi. Follow that order. And I'll see you at the house."

"I told you already, I have a character flaw when it comes to following orders." But she shifted into drive. "Dammit!"

And she drove away.

He watched her go. Just as he'd watched previously. He wondered if she'd stop a bit down the road. Then circle back as she'd done before.

He waited a beat longer and then...

Then he returned to the back door of the rundown bar. He hauled it open and came face-to-face with Ivan. He'd figured the other man was waiting for him.

"If shooting her isn't part of your plan..." Ivan's head cocked to the side. "Then what is?" His arms were crossed over his chest.

"I don't kill women. But I have no qualms about sending a murderer to prison for the rest of her life."

"Huh. You're playing a game with the pretty woman."

"I don't play games. What I am doing is dead serious."

Ivan pursed his lips. "You pulled a gun on me."

"You did that crap first. I was simply defending myself."

Those bushy brows beetled again. "You took out three of my men."

"I took out four of your men." He waited a beat. "I would have taken them all out if you hadn't stepped in to rescue them." Okay, probably not. But so what if he stretched the truth? He would have beat the crap out of as many men as possible.

Ivan sawed a hand over the stubble on his jaw. "Are we going to have a problem, you and I?"

"If you get in my way, damn straight, we will." He hadn't jumped into the back of Naomi's pickup truck because Eb never ran from anyone. So he stepped right up to the Russian. "Get in my way, come at me again, and we will most definitely have a problem."

Ivan didn't blink.

"You stay away from Naomi—and her dog—from here on out, got it? I'll be handling her and any punishments she gets."

"Because you're going to send her to prison. And not just save us all time and kill her instantly."

No one will be killing Naomi. "Because I'm going to make sure that Hudson's killer gets the punishment that fits the crime."

"A bullet to the brain would be faster."

In his mind, Eb could see the jerk raising his gun to fire at Naomi. And if Eb hadn't been there, if the Russian had been alone in the small office with Naomi, that was the exact scene that would have played out. Now he understood exactly what the Russian had been doing. "You took the dog in order to lure Naomi to you. You wanted her on your turf. Wanted to be able to say she broke into your place. You planned to kill her when she came for her dog."

The Russian's hand fell back to his side. "That was one of my options. But you got in my way."

"I'm still in your way. Hear me again. One final time." His words were flat. Hard. Brutal. "Naomi is mine. Her punishment is mine." *She is mine.*

"You just want to fuck her."

Yeah, guilty. But he also intended to get justice. "Like I can't fuck and punish at the same time." What was this, amateur hour? "You don't touch her. You try to hurt her again, and maybe you'll be the featured star at the next funeral."

Ivan sniffed. "You don't sound like an agent."

"Oh, my bad. Didn't I mention that I'm retired?" Now Eb smiled. "I'm not playing games. Not following orders. I'm doing whatever the hell I want. So there will be no one to stop me from coming after you if you cross the line."

"She pays for what she did. She pays and that's all I want."

"Don't send your guys after her. Don't come at her again. Or it will be a fatal mistake for you." Not a threat. A promise.

Then he turned and walked away. He could feel the Russian's eyes on him, but Eb didn't look back. He rounded the building. Headed back to his car and—

Sure the fuck enough, a pickup truck waited by his ride.

Naomi had turned off her headlights, but the truck's engine idled.

He went straight to the driver's side of the truck. Rapped on the window. Prayed for patience with her.

She rolled down the window. "Fancy seeing you here," Naomi greeted him.

Fancy, his ass. "You can't follow orders for shit," he told her.

"Pretty sure I mentioned that character flaw to you before." She cleared her throat. "I didn't want to leave until I was sure you weren't going to die tonight."

He squinted inside the vehicle. The dog sprawled on the seat beside her. On its back, belly in the air. Eb pulled his gaze from the dog and sent it back to Naomi. "Why would you care if I died?"

"Because you saved my dog. Now that good deed means I owe you." She pointed to his car. "Get in. Follow me home. You're spending the night with me."

Hell, yes, he was.

"Then you're explaining why you kissed me." Naomi exhaled on a ragged breath. "Because I know you hate me. I know you think I killed your partner."

Ex-partner. And most of the town believed she was guilty as sin.

"I don't see you as the type to be turned on by hate," Naomi continued.

He leaned closer. "So you want to know what turns me on? Is that what you're trying to discover? If so, just ask directly, sweetheart." Eb used the endearment deliberately. Mostly to piss her off. Also to see what reaction it would have on her.

Her hand rose. Slid against his jaw. For some reason, he felt the impact of that small touch explode throughout his whole body.

"Ebenezer..." Naomi sighed his name. The name he'd always hated. But when she said it, he didn't mind so much. "I don't have to ask. I already know what turns you on."

"Oh, yeah?"

"Yeah." She poked her head through the window. Pressed her lips to his ever so fleetingly. Teasingly. Tormentingly. "I do."

Fuck. "Yeah, you do." Grim.

She sucked in a breath. "How about we get the hell out of the Russian gang's parking lot while we're both still living, huh?"

Great plan.

But first...

"I think I turn you on, Naomi." Because she was still touching him. She'd just been the one to kiss him.

"That's the thing." She let him go. Put both hands back on the steering wheel. "You do. Now, watch the foot."

She drove away. Barely, in fact, missing his foot.

You do.

That woman was trying to work a serious mind-fuck on him.

Too bad for her, when it came to mind-fuckery, he excelled.

He was smiling as he drove from the lot.

Chapter Three

"I'm evil. Wicked. Cold to the core. I murdered your partner. Set the whole scene up to look like a B&E gone wrong, and then I convinced the DA—using my wily charm, of course—to drop all the charges against me." Naomi made sure to dramatically bat her lashes as she made her confession. "If you're not careful, you'll be my next victim."

Eb quirked one brow even as he made himself more comfortable on her couch. He didn't look particularly concerned about the danger he faced. Instead, he asked, "With all of Hudson's money, why are you living in this shithole?"

Her teeth snapped together. "The home is a work in progress."

His gaze swept the den. "It's in the progress of falling apart."

As if on cue, part of the ceiling fell down and landed with a loud *plop* right near her feet.

Henry rolled over, snuggling in his bed and ignoring the

chaos. The way he always did. For a moment, her gaze lingered on the dog.

I am so glad you are back. Eb didn't understand how important the dog was to her. He didn't know about her secrets. She'd worked hard to hide as much of her life from others as she could.

But Hudson...he'd known.

That heartless bastard had absolutely known.

"I'm going through a renovation project. When the place is finished, it will be a killer bed and breakfast." Or, hell. Her shoulders slumped. *Maybe not so killer any longer.* "That had been the original plan. Until news got out that—"

"That you are, indeed, a killer?" he finished.

Her eyes narrowed on him.

Ebenezer Jones. Eb. The man, the myth, the big, bad-ass legend. Hudson had been in awe of his partner. Talked about him all the time. Practically from the moment they'd met.

He'd admired Eb.

Wanted to emulate him.

Hudson had also envied him.

And, she was about ninety-nine percent sure, Hudson had secretly hated Eb.

So much for friendship.

Her chin had lifted at Eb's mocking words. Hardly the first time that someone had called her a killer. The last few months had been basic non-stop accusations. She'd gone from being the beaming bride one day to being the hated villain the next. No one had stood by her. There had only been accusations—whispers, at first. Then louder cries. Angry shouts. Harassing phone calls. She'd even had a few bricks tossed through her windows because...why not?

She was the villain, after all.

Then came the actual arrest. Getting locked up. Denied bail. Even as she'd screamed her innocence. Time had ticked by.

She'd discovered just how small a jail cell could be.

But the charges had been dropped. She'd been released. The nightmare was supposed to be over.

Only she'd gotten back her freedom and immediately discovered that Henry had been taken. Naomi had known that she would do anything necessary to get her dog back. Even if she'd had to use her bat and take a few swings at a bar.

"Being a killer might actually attract guests for you," Eb mused. "I suspect there is a whole true crime crowd who would jump at the chance to stay at your B&B."

"Pretty sure that I haven't been convicted of anything." She smiled sweetly at him. She was good at sweet smiles. Good at not letting anyone know when she hurt. "I believe in this country we are all presumed innocent. Since the DA isn't trying me for any crimes, I certainly don't qualify as a killer."

He didn't even blink. Just continued lounging on her old—but comfortable—brown couch, with one muscled arm extended along the top of the cushions and his long legs spread out before him. He didn't look like a guy who'd just taken on half a bar of gang members. His thick, dark hair was barely mussed, and his strong jaw was clean shaven. His eyes—such a warm, rich topaz, shot with lots of gold and brown—remained locked on her.

I kissed him. He kissed me. Probably two mistakes. But...

Well, hardly the first time in her life that she'd made a mistake. Not the first time, and certainly not likely to be the last, either. "I thought you said you were here in Baton Rouge in order to find Hudson's killer. As in, the actual killer. If you are just locked and loaded on me, then you are going to be wasting your time. Just like the DA wasted his time."

"Hudson died on this property."

Goosebumps rose on her arms. She paced toward the window in the front. The window she'd had replaced last week after brick number three had come hurtling into her home. "Yes, he did die here. In the guesthouse, actually." She pushed aside the curtain, and her hand touched the hard pane of glass. "Such a shame I wasn't there to save him."

"Is it?"

Swallowing, she let the curtain fall back into place. Naomi turned to face him.

"Some women wouldn't want to stay on the property where their husbands were brutally murdered. They'd want to get the hell away from such a grisly scene." His gaze swept over the interior of the house. The wall on the left side of the den had been freshly primed. Paint cans waited in a corner. The wall on the right still had a massive hole in the middle of it. And, yep, a few chunks from the ceiling littered the floor. "Especially when the home is damn well falling apart."

Was that anger rumbling in his voice? He was mad because her house was falling apart or because he thought she was a murderer? Maybe both?

"I poured every cent I have into this place." Now she stalked toward him. Stopped just a foot away from the couch...and him. "I have no place to go. If I leave here, I'd be sleeping in the truck." She'd slept in a car before. Not like life had ever been particularly easy. She didn't want to do it again, thanks. "I'm renovating. This property will look great when I'm done." Truly, she had gotten the historic property and the massive acreage for a steal. Hudson had helped her negotiate the real estate deal. Back when he'd been trying to charm her.

Or, as she now realized, back when he'd been trying to manipulate every aspect of her life and make her completely dependent on him.

Her shoulders squared. "If you have a problem with my home, you can certainly go stay in one of the hotels you mentioned previously."

Lazily, he rose. A ripple of muscle. Casual grace. Then he stood in front of her. Towered over her. So close their bodies brushed, and, yes, a spark of electricity snaked through her.

True story? She'd never felt that spark with Hudson. No matter how hard she'd tried. He'd seemed so perfect. Naomi had thought the flaw must be on her side.

Stop it. Do not go down that path right now.

"I'm staying with you." His voice was deep and rumbly. Sexy as sin. "In case you missed it, we pissed off a Russian gang tonight."

"Hard to miss that highlight." Why was her voice so husky? "But thanks for pointing it out to me."

His lips almost quirked at her response. Almost. But... "You also have zero security here. Unless that sleepy golden of yours is some sort of secretive attack dog, then someone can break in here and you'd be completely defenseless."

"Again, thanks for noticing and pointing it out." She tilted back her head. The better to stare up into those gleaming eyes of his. "I'm afraid that hiring a lawyer drained my accounts. I put new locks on the doors, and I have one of those doorbell cameras at the front—and back—of this house." And at the entrance to the guesthouse. "But that's all I could manage." Her savings account had twenty-seven dollars and forty-eight cents left in it.

The faint lines near his mouth deepened. "I'll get a system installed first thing tomorrow."

Nope. He would not. "Unnecessary—"

"If you're going to make a habit of pissing off gang leaders, then, yes, it's absolutely necessary."

"I had to get my dog back." She glanced toward Henry. "Not like I was just doing it for fun."

Henry's head lifted. He stared at her.

A shiver slid over her body.

Eb's fingers caught her chin, and he gently turned her face back toward him. "Why is the dog so important to you?"

Keep your secrets. But… "How much do you already know about me?" Naomi backed away from him. Being too close to Eb was dangerous. It made her feel—too much. "Mr. Big, Tough, CIA Operative. I bet you have all kinds of access to classified intel. You probably peek at the secrets people carry all the time." She paused a beat. "What do you know about me?"

She knew far too little about him.

"Being CIA is supposed to be something that one keeps quiet," he said. "You don't go around announcing your job to everyone you meet. Ivan already knew what I did, thanks to Hudson. Same thing with you. Hudson revealed the truth to his bride. Otherwise, I never would have told you about my work."

She raised her brows. "That cat has been out of the bag for a while regarding what you do. Right after he proposed, Hudson told me that you two were partners, that you worked international cases." A delicate pause. "He also revealed a few other details about you with me. So why don't you share what you know about me…and I'll share the details *I* know about you."

"Hudson always talked too much."

Adorable. You think that was Hudson's worst trait? His big mouth? You have no clue.

Or, maybe he did know the truth, and that was the part that scared her the most. Because what if she'd just let another monster straight into her life? Into her home?

And they were all alone. He was much bigger than she was. Much stronger. He could overpower her in an instant.

No, no, he's not like Hudson.

But she still retreated. Made her way casually toward the set of tools she'd left spread out after doing some repairs that morning. A hammer waited to the left. A weapon to use in a pinch if she needed one.

He didn't follow her, but Naomi felt his gaze on her as he said, "You grew up in the foster system. Have no close family. Your juvenile records are supposed to be sealed, but you did enjoy going on a joy ride or two back in the day, didn't you, Naomi?"

Her spine stiffened. "I didn't steal cars when I was a kid." That had just been a lie told in order to get her transferred from one foster home to another. She'd been painted as the villain so someone else would be safe.

It never pays to be good.

She eyed the hammer. Did she need a weapon?

"You put yourself through college by waitressing. Got a degree in business. You were working as a manager at one of the fancy hotels in Vegas when you met Hudson."

"Vegas is great. It hides all the sins in the world beneath a glossy surface." She'd thought about going back to Vegas. Maybe if she got the property fixed up well enough, she'd sell it and not go with the bed and breakfast dream any longer. That dream sometimes felt like a weight around her.

"There was no more law breaking once you hit eighteen. In fact, you were quite the upstanding citizen in Vegas."

Had she been? Maybe she'd gotten too boring for a time.

"You loved the party circuit. Were seen with plenty of movers and shakers. The rich and the elite."

"Those were the people who visited my hotel." She turned away from the hammer. "It's called networking. A necessary part of the job."

His head tilted to the side as he watched her.

"That's all you know about me? Truly?" Naomi tsk-tsked him. "Very disappointing. And here I thought you'd have something dark and deep to share. Some earth-shattering details about my torrid past. You've just disappointed me."

He strode toward her. Again, moving with that casual but dangerous grace. A predatory grace.

When he stopped before her, his scent teased her nose. A slightly woodsy, definitely masculine scent. She might have liked that scent a bit too much.

"Do you have something dark and deep buried in your past?" he asked.

She did. "Doesn't everyone?" Now her hand rose and pressed to his chest. Instantly, that spark was flaring through her again. Dammit. "Don't you have something dark and deep that you hide?" She knew he did. "How many people have you pretended to be over the years, Eb? How many personas have you adopted in order to bring down your targets?"

He blinked. "Hudson told you about that?"

Hudson had told her plenty. "You're the master chameleon. You can adopt any accent. Become any person. Good. Bad. Everything in between. He told me that you speak five languages."

"Six."

"Wonderful for you." She kept her hand over his chest. "You slip into hellholes. You dance with princesses. You can be anything and anyone. And you are relentless. You don't stop until your goal is achieved."

"I do like to be goal oriented."

"What's your goal now?" She wet her lips. "You've been staying away, you've barely spoken to me during our entire acquaintance—even when I stood at Hudson's grave, you didn't say a word to me. No sympathy, real or fake. You just watched me. Watched and didn't speak."

"Didn't realize you even knew I was there."

"I felt your stare on me." Hard to explain, especially with so many other judgmental eyes on her. But there was something about Eb. His stare almost burned it was so intense. She'd felt it at her wedding. Felt it at the grave. Felt it *now*.

"You're mad I didn't approach you at the funeral."

Mad wasn't the right word. She was hurt, shattered, that not one person had stood at her side. Everyone had already been suspicious. So certain she was evil. What happened to the whole innocent until proven guilty bit?

"What did you want me to say?" His hand lifted. Not to cup her chin this time. But to slide over her cheek. His fingers slid into the thickness of her hair and his palm pressed lightly to her skin.

"Oh, you could have said the usual. *So sorry for your loss.* I think that's what people are supposed to say at times like that. Only, well, no one said that to me at all. Instead, they whispered, and they gossiped. And I stood alone." Anger breathed in those words. A mistake. Naomi hadn't meant to let the anger out. She backed away from him. One step. Two. She—

He caught her hand. Pulled her back against him. "So sorry for your loss," he told her. Only Eb didn't sound particularly sorry. He sounded...*pissed*.

And the anger that she'd been battling blazed to life. The anger—no, the rage—as everyone judged her and felt such sympathy for Hudson. Hudson the absolute *bastard*. "You didn't have any really good secrets on me. How about I give you one? I'll be generous and share a killer secret with you."

His eyes narrowed.

She pushed onto her toes. Tugged him closer toward her. Her mouth went to his left ear. "I'm glad he's dead," she whispered. Her lips feathered over his ear lobe. Her tongue gave him a quick, sensual lick. "Glad."

His hands locked around her hips. Tried to. She slipped away. Took several steps to put needed space between them.

"Have a good night," Naomi added. She was pleased that her voice now sounded normal. No huskiness. "You can take the room at the top of the stairs. It's the one I've already renovated. Nothing but the best for Hudson's partner." Her smile felt brittle. She tapped her leg, and Henry instantly moved to her side. "I'll be in the room next door to yours." She and Henry headed for the stairs.

Eb moved into her path. Of course, he would block her semi-dramatic exit. Leave it to him—he'd ruined her scene.

"You're *glad*? Glad your husband is gone?"

She hadn't stuttered when she made the confession. *Glad.* "I wasn't with Hudson when he died because I was leaving him. If he'd lived, our marriage would have been over."

"You weren't even married for twenty-four hours before he was found dead!"

True.

His gaze whipped around the house. "Why were you even here, on the property? Why not go to some lush honeymoon suite? Why stay at this rundown place?"

"This rundown place was going to be our home. We—I—wanted to spend the first night of our married life in the home we'd build together." She swallowed. "Some dreams suck. My mistake."

"No." Adamant. His probing stare returned to her. "No. No, you don't go from wanting to build a home with someone to wanting out of the marriage after one night—"

"You do if it is one horror show of a night." She rubbed her hand over Henry's head. Such a warm, steady presence. She'd missed Henry so much. He was not just a dog. Never that. He was the reason she was alive. So, yes, oh, yes, she would walk through hell to get him back any day of the week. She'd face off against a dozen gang members if she could get Henry back. "I'm keeping up my end of the deal. You helped me get Henry, and now you can crash here. Done."

A muscle flexed along Eb's clenched jaw. "I told you I was in town to find Hudson's killer."

"You did mention that." Carefully cool.

"Don't you want to find the bastard? Don't you want to work with me to make the person who killed your husband pay?"

"Not particularly. But I could send the guy a thank-you basket."

He blinked. "You aren't serious."

"I've moved on. You should, too. Let the dead rest." She skirted around him. Henry shadowed her movements.

"You...hate him."

She reached for the banister. She'd fixed that banister last week. The wood was smooth. Freshly stained a dark mahogany. Parts of the massive house were falling apart, yes, noted. But other parts showed such promise. "Is there a point in hating the dead?" She climbed two steps.

He snagged her arm.

She turned to face him. "Look, unless you are about to offer me unbelievable sex, I'm going to sleep."

His hold tightened. "You talk about murder and sex in the same breath."

"Some people are turned on by murder." Twisted but true. "Tell me, secret agent man, what turns you on? You said before that it was me. You'll have to excuse me if I don't quite buy that answer. Perhaps you're turned on by adrenaline. Or maybe it's danger. Thus, your occupation. I mean, you only take high-risks jobs in this world if you're into the whole life-or-death scene, am I right?"

His fingers stroked lightly over her skin. "You want to know what turns me on? We're back to that?"

"Like I said, it's obviously adrenaline and danger." She'd thought about this a lot on the drive home. No way could he actually just want...her. "We had both of those tonight. So maybe that's why the powerful heart of yours is racing wildly. Because of the rush." Not because of the way he felt about her. Certainly, not that.

Her heart also raced wildly. Was it from the events of

the night? Or because Eb was touching her? Or maybe because she was just at the end of her rope?

He leaned toward her. One hand on the banister. One hand still holding her. "Answered you before. You. You're what turns me on."

He'd been...serious about that? No, no, she would not believe him. Could not. Eb was drop-dead handsome. He could have any woman he wanted with the crook of a finger.

"You turn me on." Each word from him was bitten off. "And how fucked-up is that? To be turned on by the woman married to my partner? I fucking *know* I should keep my hands off you."

Her heart raced even more now. Hello, palpitations.

"But all I want to do is touch you everywhere."

Yes. Do it. Great idea. Let's forget all the reasons this shouldn't happen and have wild, dirty sex all night long. Oh, the temptation.

A dangerous temptation.

Because he was a dangerous man. One who could wreck the world that she was struggling to rebuild. "I'm not married to your partner."

"No, you're his widow. The Wicked Widow."

At that moniker, Naomi tensed. That had been the name given to her by the local press. And picked up by the people online who were out for her blood.

Why?

Because they thought she was a killer.

"Do you want to fuck a killer, Eb?" She thought it was a fair question.

"Do you?" he returned.

Goosebumps skittered over her body. "What's that supposed to mean?"

He smiled and that lethal grin stole her breath. Holy

hell, he had a dimple. Talk about an unfair and potentially lethal secret weapon. Even as she was adjusting to the reality of that dimple—this was her first time to fully appreciate it—Eb told her, "I don't play by typical rules. I'm not *nice*. I've gotten my hands bloody plenty of times over the years. Fuck me, and there will be no going back for you."

Right. She did not need to, ah, fuck anyone. No matter how tempting Eb might be. But, because he was right there, and her position on the steps put her at the perfect level with him, she reached out and curled her arms around his shoulders. "It's *nice* to be with someone who doesn't pretend with me. I'm sick of lies." The lies she told. The lies others told her. "Hudson was a straight-up bastard. Sadistic. Twisted."

A furrow appeared between Eb's brows.

"He made my life hell. I am glad he's dead." The truth just kept pouring from her. It felt freeing. "You won't believe me, of course. Everyone thought he was so perfect. And he was your friend. Your partner. He would tell me all about your great adventures together."

"What do you mean...sadistic?"

She put her mouth on his. The kisses before had been rushed. And maybe...maybe she thought that she could kiss him, and a *real* kiss would show that the passion wasn't truly there between them. That the sparks she felt when they touched wouldn't ignite into a blaze. Instead, they'd fizzle out with a real kiss.

His lips were open.

So were hers. Her tongue dipped into his mouth. Stroked. Teased. And he—

A growl tore from him. His hands flew to curl around her hips as he hauled her toward him. He took over the kiss. His lips, his tongue—he took. He tasted. He claimed and the spark didn't fizzle. It erupted. A wildfire that pulsed through her veins. She opened her mouth wider. Her fingers sank into his powerful shoulders. She knew this was wrong.

But Naomi didn't care. She hadn't kissed someone and felt this soaring passion in…in…

Ever.

She'd never kissed someone and felt this way. This consuming, lightning-fast need was what happened in movies. Books. Not real life. Certainly not her life.

Henry bumped into her leg.

Reality surged back. She pulled her head away from Eb. Her mouth.

"I want to fucking devour you," Eb growled.

Same.

But then he was the one retreating. And something that could have been guilt…maybe even horror…came and went on his face in the blink of an eye.

A knot settled in her belly. "He'll always be between us, huh?"

His jaw hardened.

"Good night, Eb." She darted up the stairs. Henry followed her every movement. She turned at the top of the landing and headed toward her room.

"Tell me that you didn't kill him."

She looked back down at Eb. "I didn't kill Hudson." Easy words.

He frowned at her.

"Turn off the lights when you're done down there, will you?" She could still taste him. "I'm trying not to have high electric bills." An exhale. She put one foot in front of the other and got to her bedroom. Naomi shut the door once Henry was inside with her.

She could *still* taste Eb. Still feel him.

She could also hear her own words replaying through her mind.

I didn't kill Hudson.

Did he think she was a liar? And why did what Eb thought matter so much?

Chapter Four

HUDSON WAS A STRAIGHT-UP BASTARD. SADISTIC. Twisted. He made my life hell. I am glad he's dead.

Eb peered up the staircase. The door to Naomi's room had shut with a soft click of sound, but her words seemed to blare through his head on megaphone level, on a near endless loop.

Why would she call Hudson sadistic? Twisted? The guy had been an honored agent. He'd fought for his country. Sure, he'd had contacts that were more than slightly shady—case in point, the Russian—but in their business, all the agents had shady contacts. That was just a way of life.

The wind howled outside. In the distance, Eb thought he caught the roll of thunder. A storm was coming their way.

Sadistic. Twisted.

He'd made contact with his prey. He'd succeeded in getting close to her. He was in Naomi's house. Would sleep in the room right next to her own.

I kissed her and meant it when I said I wanted to devour her.

57

Did he feel guilty for lusting after his partner's wife? His *dead* partner's wife?

Hell, yes.

Guilty and angry and so freaking horny. He wanted her. Had wanted her from the first moment he spotted her in the fountain. He'd damn well *told* Hudson...

I think I'm fucking in love. Mocking words. Because Eb had never been in love. He'd come close once...a long time ago, but that woman had wound up becoming his best friend. Not the love of his life.

And now she's my sister-in-law. A different story.

He'd never looked at someone and instantly craved the way he did with Naomi.

Not love at first sight. Lust. The kind that will eat you up and consume you. The kind of lust that would make a man break every rule that he possessed.

Eb backed away from the staircase. He did a sweep of the house, making sure all of the windows and doors were locked. The security was truly shit, and that annoyed the hell out of him. Hudson had possessed plenty of money. His first priority should have been making certain Naomi was safe. The house should have been secured.

Sadistic. Twisted.

He pulled out his phone. Didn't call anyone yet. Just listened intently to the sounds around him for a few moments first. The howl of the wind. The creaks of the old place settling.

After a time, he made his call. It rang once, twice and then...

"Are we having fun on our latest adventure?" Hunter McQueen asked him. That was the man's greeting. No hello. Typical.

As for the response to Hunter's question, Eb supposed

that would depend on a person's definition of fun. "I knocked out four gang members earlier."

"Dammit, why didn't you invite me?" Real envy flashed in Hunter's voice. "I told you, I've been bored as hell lately. Do you know how dull my boss is now that he's settled into wedded bliss with your sister?" A long sigh. "Why do you get to enjoy all the excitement and I just sit around looking for trouble?"

"I may need help." There was no *may* about it. Eb was calling because he needed a favor. The slightly illegal sort.

"Okay, now you are talking my language. I can be on a plane in two hours."

"Don't go packing your bags just yet."

A disgruntled sigh was Hunter's response. "You know I always have a go bag at the ready."

True. They all did. It paid to be prepared. "Will you get Declan to work his tech magic for me?"

"Shit. If you want Declan's help, then call your brother-in-law. Not me." Definitely disgruntled. "And why the hell would you need his tech help? Don't you have the CIA at your beck and call?"

Not exactly. "I want to know if there were ever any red flags with Hudson Wyatt. Things that the CIA might have kept from me."

Silence. Then, "I thought this guy was your friend."

"Friends can have secrets. And the CIA happens to be very, very good at keeping secrets. Even from its own agents."

"Shit." Hunter whistled. "The woman must be seriously pro-level skilled. You're barely down there a day, and you're already doubting your partner. She convincing you that he was evil so soon? What's next, is she going to be justified in killing him?"

"Stop being an asshole."

"Why? It's who I am. Who you are, too."

"*Get Declan to dig for me.*" Declan Flynn was a billionaire, Eb's brother-in-law, and an absolute tech genius. Most of the tech that the government used came from Declan. So if there was a backdoor way to get access to confidential bits of data from the CIA, Declan would be the one holding the key to that treasure.

Declan was also Hunter's boss and best friend.

"I need Declan's help," Eb said quietly. No getting around it.

"*Then call him yourself.*"

"I can't." Thus, the late call to Hunter. "Marley told me I couldn't call him again after midnight. One of her rules. So I'm calling you, and you can tell him for me."

"Oh, sure. Because it's cool for you to call me after midnight. Not like you're disturbing my beauty sleep. Here's a fun idea...why don't you just call during daytime hours? Did you consider that option?"

Yes, he'd considered the option and discarded it. "I'm spending the night with Naomi, and while she's sleeping, I'm using the time to call so she won't know what the hell I'm doing."

"Whoa, whoa! Stop and back up. Are you staying with your prey? Like, in the same house? Damn, same *bed*? On night one? Shit. Okay, you get that she's trying to trick you, right? Trick you, use you, fuck with your head and your body?"

His grip nearly shattered the phone.

"You called her a cold-blooded murderer yesterday," Hunter continued. "I saw her pics. I get that she's hot. But don't let your dick lead you straight to death. She'll fuck you and stab you. Hey, did you ever see *Basic Instinct?* An oldie but a goodie with Sharon Stone. She fucked the guy and killed him right during the big orgasm moment, and you don't want that shit to happen to—"

"Shut the hell up," he groused. "This is not *Basic Instinct*. I'm also pretty sure the killer used an ice pick in that movie and not a knife."

"Ah, so you are familiar with the classic. My bad. Ice pick. Check."

He glanced over his shoulder. The staircase was dark. Silent. When Naomi had climbed the stairs, he'd noticed that step four and step nine both creaked. Good to know for future reference. "I need you and Declan to dig into the CIA's files."

"Sorry. Repeat that. Pretty sure you just asked me to commit a felony for you."

"I have to make sure they aren't covering up anything about Hudson."

"And you would think they are because...?"

"Naomi called him sadistic. Twisted."

"Now you want to rip his life apart. Check. The dead man. The victim. You want to rip his world apart because the suspected killer said he was sadistic. Uh, huh. So, personal question. Ahem. Are you thinking with your dick or your brain?"

His dick was certainly still up because of that kiss with Naomi. "You didn't see her when she said it, okay? There was real emotion in her voice and on her face." So much for thinking she was cold as ice. First, she'd been crying over her dog. Then that hard mask of hers had cracked when she'd spoken of Hudson. He'd swear she'd even been afraid in that instant.

"Real emotion. Uh, sure, unless—and I'm just throwing out ideas here—unless the woman is just a really good liar.

Then it was fake emotion. Because people can do that. Fake emotions. But, yeah, fine, I'll dig for you. I'll commit a felony. In case you missed it before, I am bored. But, hey, while I'm ripping into the victim's life, should I be taking a harder look at your new girlfriend, too?"

"She's not my girlfriend." Eb kept his voice low.

"Tell me you don't want her to be. Tell me you are being one hundred percent professional with this whole vendetta investigation you have going on in Baton Rouge."

How about I tell you that I was kissing her ten minutes ago? Nah. He should not reveal that info to Hunter. "Her juvie files were sealed, but I got data that told me she'd gone for some joy rides back in the day. Nothing major." He sucked in the side of his cheek. "Dig into her life," he said and ignored the way guilt suddenly twisted in him. It felt as if he was betraying her. He wasn't. He was looking for the truth. *And betraying her, dammit.* "See if there is more in Naomi's past." More than the bits he'd gotten courtesy of the CIA.

"The more you know, the better trap you can set," Hunter told him, but the man's voice wasn't mocking any longer. "You need backup on scene? Or is that twin of yours already lurking around someplace?"

His twin was not lurking anywhere close by. "He's at home with Wren." His twin brother Jake had finally gotten the woman of his dreams. A long-term obsession had become reality for Jake, and the last thing Eb wanted to do was tear his brother away from his current moment of happiness. Jake hadn't known a lot of happiness. Darkness clung too tightly to him.

And to me.

But Eb was good at acting like he fit in with everyone else. He could wear the mask and pretend to be normal.

Jake? Not so much.

"If your twin isn't there, then you need backup on the ground. I can take Declan's private jet and be there before the sun rises."

"No, not yet, I don't need backup. I need intel. Deliver it for me, will you?"

"You could always ask the CIA directly."

He could. If he trusted the people there completely. He did not. "If Hudson went off the rails at any point, and they covered it up..." *Sadistic. Twisted.* "Then they aren't going to confess that to me. He would be a problem that they just wanted eliminated." And wasn't that an option he had not considered until this moment? *If Hudson did something wrong on a mission, the CIA would need to cover up the mess. They would need to make the problem totally vanish.* Surely...surely, the CIA would not kill one of its own agents.

But they've done it before.

Fuck. The web was getting more tangled by the moment. Eb also knew that he was searching for other options because he just didn't want Naomi to be a cold-blooded killer. He wanted her to be innocent.

He wanted her.

Lust is fogging my brain. Hunter is right. I'm thinking with my dick on day one. Eb knew better than to let his emotions cloud his judgment.

"You worked closely with Hudson." Hunter's musing voice pulled Eb back to the conversation. "You ever see any signs that he might go off the deep end?"

"No." No, he hadn't. But then again...

No one knows just how dangerous I really am, either.

"Okay, I'll dig for you. Felonies for friends and what-not. But you are going to have to pay me back, and I mean a major payback. I don't even know what I want yet, but believe me when I say it's gonna be big. Giant."

"Yeah, yeah, whatever. I have to go."

"You have to go and get back in bed with the prey. Gotcha."

His teeth snapped together. "I'm not in bed with her. I'm in the bedroom next door to her." *Dick*.

"Ah, but where do you want to be?"

In bed with her.

When he didn't immediately reply, Hunter's laughter boomed over the line.

Eb hung up on him. He blew out a long breath and turned for the stairs. But he paused before advancing. Just stared up at that darkness. So much could wait in the darkness.

Sadistic. Twisted.

He grabbed the travel bag that he'd brought in earlier and slung the strap over his shoulder. Taking his time, Eb began to climb the stairs. He skipped stair four. And stair nine.

He walked right past the room she'd indicated would be his. Instead, Eb stopped in front of her door. Her closed bedroom door. He reached for the knob.

Hunter—the laughing bastard—had been right. Eb did want to be in her bed. Even better, he wanted to be in *her*.

He lusted for the woman who might have killed his friend.

How screwed up was that?

How screwed up am I?

* * *

A DOG WAS BARKING. Sleep and confusion pulled at Naomi as her eyes fluttered open.

The barks came again. Louder. Sharper.

She surged upright. The past and present tangled all together for her as she struggled to see in the darkness. Shadows were everywhere. Covers weighed her down and—

Something moved. Someone. Her eyes adjusted to the dark, and she saw the powerful form of a man coming toward her. Her hands flew up. "Don't hurt me!" A desperate cry.

The dog barked again. Henry. Henry was barking. He was—

"I'm trying to save you, not hurt you." Eb's disgruntled voice. "Can you tell the dog to stop barking? We all have to get out, now."

What?

Naomi shook her head, frantic. Her heart raced in her chest, and the ghost from her past kept pulling her under. "Where's the knife?" She had to protect herself.

"Fuck if I know." He threw the covers back. "Cops never found it, remember?"

Henry kept barking.

"I've *got* her, okay?" Eb snapped to the dog. And he did have her. He scooped Naomi right into his arms.

The last of her confusion vanished when he hauled her up against him.

Eb. Eb is taking me out of the bedroom. He's...saving me?

She didn't need saving.

Did she?

"Let me go!" Naomi shoved against him.

His grip tightened on her. One hand pressed hard to her thigh because, yep, her legs were bare. She wore an oversized shirt. Panties. And that was it. Not like she'd been planning to entertain in the middle of the night.

"Do you smell the smoke?" Eb gritted as he turned for the door.

Henry barked and bounded toward the open door.

"Your house is on fire. I'm getting you and your precious dog out of here so you can both keep living."

"Fire?" Naomi repeated as her eyes widened. An old, never-forgotten terror clawed at her insides.

They were in the hallway. Then rushing for the stairs. And, yes, she could smell the smoke. He'd flipped on one of the hallway lights and she could even see the smoke drifting lazily in the air. Not too strong, not yet.

He flew down the stairs with her still cradled in his arms. She coughed because the smoke was so much thicker down there.

My home is on fire. Her home. The only thing she had left. Her future. Her head whipped around as her hands suddenly clung tightly to his neck. The flames were coming from her den. From the area where she'd had all her paint. But the fire—it wasn't *too* bad. Not yet. Not as bad as it could be. Not as bad as she'd seen it before. "Stop!"

He didn't. He barreled for her front door. Only when he got there, he had to put her down so he could unbolt the door, and she used that time to break away from him and run toward the den.

"Naomi!" He grabbed her from behind and hauled her back against him. "We don't run *toward* fires. We are not firefighters. We get the hell away from them!"

"*We* try to save our house!" She twisted and turned in his grip. "Get my dog out. *Please!*"

"I'm getting you and the damn dog out!"

"He's not a *damn*—" Naomi stopped. Sucked in a

breath and tasted smoke. "I have a fire extinguisher in the closet." How bad were the flames? Big and twisting, but... *manageable. Still manageable.* Hopefully.

They were wasting time. Every second was vital. And if he opened that front door, he'd introduce more oxygen to the scene. The flames would flare higher. "Let me go!"

"Naomi..."

She tore from his arms. Grabbed for the closet door. The one right near the entrance to the sprawling house. Her desperate fingers closed around the fire extinguisher. She grabbed it and rushed for the flames. "Get Henry out of here!" His barks haunted her.

The fire wasn't too big yet, was it...?

The flames chased up the side of the wall. They ate at the couch.

Okay, yes, they were big. They were terrifying. They reminded her of the past she'd never escape.

She pulled the pin on the fire extinguisher. Aimed the extinguisher at the bottom of those twisting, heaving flames. She squeezed the handle. A white cloud shot from the fire extinguisher, and she yelled in surprise because Naomi hadn't been expecting such a powerful burst. For a second, she almost lost her grip on the extinguisher, then she tightened her hold and swung it from side to side as she tried to hit all the flames.

And—

Another fire extinguisher began spraying.

"You don't listen for shit," Eb told her. He sprayed at the flames. Flames that were flickering and dying.

Where was her dog?

They sprayed. Kept battling until the fire extinguishers were empty. Until the flames sputtered away. When her extinguisher stopped shooting, she let it drop to the floor. Eb sprayed longer, hitting the flames that lingered on the edge of her curtains.

In the distance, she heard the shriek of a siren.

Smoke lingered in the air, and she coughed.

He dropped his extinguisher and immediately reached for her. "Now we're getting the hell out."

The fire had stopped, hadn't it? Wearily, she nodded. Tension held her shoulders in a tight grip as Naomi stumbled for the door. She'd barely taken two steps when Eb scooped her into his arms.

This time, she didn't fight him.

They made it outside. She sucked in fresh air. Henry wasn't barking, but he was right with them. The stars glittered overhead.

Eb lowered her onto the grass. Henry licked her face, and she put a hand on his head. "I'm okay," she told him.

"No, you've got a fucking death wish," Eb fumed. "That is not okay. Not in any world."

She looked up at him. Way up because he was still standing.

That siren shrieked again in the distance. "You called for help." Had thunder just rumbled, too?

"Not like I'm just going to let you burn." His hands fisted at his sides. "Next time, don't you dare run *to* the fire."

"But I put it out, I—"

"*You could have died. Right in front of me.* What the fuck?"

"The flames weren't that big. There was still time." She felt what could have been a raindrop hit her cheek.

"Oh, right, because you're some fire expert and you know. You know that there is still time when—"

"It was nothing like the fire that took my parents." She hadn't meant to say those words. She hadn't. Because she didn't talk about that time. Not to anyone. So why did she pull Henry closer and tell Eb, "This one was smaller. There was still time to stop it. The flames weren't rolling up the wall and onto the ceiling. The smoke wasn't so thick that you couldn't even see your hand in front of your face. The heat didn't lance your skin and make every single breath hurt."

He dropped to his knees right in front of her. "Naomi?"

She held Henry tighter. "I didn't have to get thrown from the second-story window by my dad because it was the only way out." A brutal toss that had saved her life but broken both her legs. She hadn't been able to run to the neighbor's house for help. Her dad had wanted her to get help, but she'd only been able to crawl. To crawl and scream and scream and...

Oh, shit. She'd just said all those words to him.

"Fuck, baby." He hauled her toward him. Her and Henry because she wasn't letting go of Henry. And Eb...Eb hugged her. "Baby."

She shuddered against him. And, over his shoulder, she stared at her darkened house.

No flames erupted. She'd stopped them.

This time.

Another raindrop fell.

And a tear slid down her cheek.

Chapter Five

"The fire's out, for now." The firefighter tipped back his helmet as he studied the house. His crew still fanned out. Half inside. Half near the idling firetruck. "Always have a chance of rekindling, so we want to check the scene as thoroughly as we can." His gaze slid back to Naomi.

A quiet Naomi. A Naomi who wore just that oversized shirt. An oversized shirt wasn't supposed to be dead sexy. But this was Naomi. Her long legs were bare, the shirt just skimming the tops of her thighs. She didn't have a bra beneath it. The tight edges of her nipples were clear to see.

Lightning flashed overhead. More raindrops drifted down on them. Just great. What did Eb need now? For Naomi's t-shirt to get drenched and stick to her like a second skin.

"Ma'am, I am happy to help you in any way you need," the firefighter told Naomi as he took a step closer to her.

Yeah, Romeo could slow the hell down. Eb yanked off his own shirt and stepped in front of Naomi. He shoved his shirt over her head. Then yanked her arms through the sleeves. He pulled that shirt down as far as it would go—

"What are you doing?" Naomi asked him as she swatted at his hands.

Covering her up. Keeping those tight nipples away from anyone else's eyes. "You're cold." Thus, the tight nipples. "I'm warming you up." He tugged the hem of the shirt as far as it would go. There. Mid-thigh. Better than before. Satisfied, he nodded.

She shook her head. "Now you have no shirt. And it's probably going to full-on rain soon."

Yeah, he was shirtless, but the firefighter wasn't ogling him. So, win. He turned back toward the firefighter. What was the guy's name? Saul? Paul? "How did the fire start?"

"Hard to say. You'll need the fire investigator out here in order to make a determination like that. But I did note a lot of paint cans and flammables in the den..."

Yeah, there were plenty of those cans. A recipe for disaster. And Naomi had stayed to *fight the flames*. When the whole thing could have erupted like crazy at any moment. Rage seethed inside of Eb. "Mind if I check the scene?" He wanted back in there to get an up-close look for himself.

"Not safe to go in, not yet." A pause. "I'd advise finding another place to stay for the night."

Not like there was a whole lot of night left. Maybe a few hours. But, yeah, not going back into the house that had been *on fire* seemed like a good plan to Eb. The home would reek of smoke. Plus, some of the firefighters had been spraying water in the den. In other words...

We aren't going to be staying in that house for a while.

"We can bring some clothes out for you," the firefighter offered. "Do you have another place to stay?"

"Yeah, I do. There's actually a small guesthouse at the edge of the property." Naomi waved to the right. Past the line of giant oak trees that lined a small trail. "I can, um, bunk in there." A shiver skated over her body.

He understood the shiver. Because Hudson hadn't been killed *in* the main house. Back then, the place would have been even more of a renovation wreck. Instead, Hudson had taken his bride to the guesthouse.

The first place to be renovated.

The place where he'd died.

"You can go to a hotel," Naomi told Eb as she squared her delicate shoulders. "You don't need to stay in the guesthouse with me."

Oh, he absolutely did need to stay in there with her. He'd been dying to get inside, and, well, Hudson had actually *died* inside. "My clothes are in the main house, too," he told the firefighter. "Second level. First room. My bag is at the end of the bed."

Someone called out for the firefighter. *Saul.* Not Paul. Definitely Saul. Eb made a mental note of the correct name.

Saul hurried away.

Naomi reached for Eb. Her fingers slid over his abs, then she jerked back, as if she'd been burned.

Oh, sweetheart, it was a very near thing. Those flames had come entirely too close to her precious skin, and he'd come entirely too close to a complete freak-out.

"Take your shirt back," she whispered. "I do not need it."

"I could see your nipples. Saul could see your nipples. Trust me on this, you need the shirt."

She immediately crossed her arms over her chest. "Sorry you have a problem with my sleep attire. When I went to bed, I didn't exactly plan to entertain the whole fire department tonight."

"Next time I tell you to get that sweet ass out of a burning building, you do it." This whole scene bothered him. Especially with her past.

I knew a fire had taken her parents. But he hadn't known that Naomi had broken her legs when her father tossed her to safety. He hadn't realized she'd been thrown from a second-story window.

His chest ached.

"This burning building is all I happen to have left! Don't you get that, Eb? It's my future. If it goes up in flames, what will I do?" Her chin jutted up. "The fire was still at a level where it could be contained. There was still time. So I tried to save my property."

"Fires can spread in an instant." Something she should know. "Don't play with your life, not ever again. Wood and bricks aren't worth you dying."

She edged closer to him. "Aw, Eb. When you talk like that..." Now her hand rose. Curled carefully around his arm. "It seems like you care about me."

His back teeth had clenched. "Your smoke detectors didn't go off."

Her head tilted to the right. Her hair trailed over her shoulder. "What?"

"After a fire took out your family, you expect me to believe you don't have working smoke detectors? You had a closet with *two* fire extinguishers."

"I have fire extinguishers all over the house. I have one every forty feet."

One every forty feet. "And no working smoke detectors?" He knew she *had* smoke detectors. He'd seen them on her ceilings. When a chunk of plaster had fallen in the den shortly after his arrival, Eb had looked up. Spotted the first smoke detector.

"They should all work." Her hand tightened on his shoulder.

"They didn't, baby." *Baby.* Why the hell had he called her that? It wasn't even the first time the endearment had slipped out. "Not a single one went off. I was awake." Awake and using his laptop to dig deeper into the mystery that was Naomi. "I smelled the smoke. Then I went to get you."

But what if he hadn't been awake?

A new Naomi fact that he'd discovered...she truly slept like the dead. When he'd rushed into her room, she'd been out hard. Then she'd been confused. Afraid.

Don't hurt me!

That cry had pierced right through him.

Of course, she'd followed up that desperate plea with a very demanding...

Where's the knife?

And he couldn't help but think of Hudson. Who'd been found stabbed three times. Twice in the side. Once in the heart. The knife had never been recovered.

Where's the knife...indeed. It was the question every cop and the DA had certainly wanted to have answered. But when he'd been in that bedroom with Naomi, Eb hadn't seen a killer.

He'd seen a victim.

He didn't buy that the blaze tonight was an accident. Not with the smoke detectors failing. "I'm checking the scene." He had to get in that house.

"What?"

"Stay here." He looked to the right. "Henry, guard her."

The dog just watched Eb with his steady, dark gaze.

The dog had been remarkably well-behaved during all the chaos. Even now, he didn't rush toward any of the firefighters or bark to get attention. He just waited with Naomi, a constant presence at her side.

"He's not a guard dog," she muttered, disgruntled. "And I'm not a dog, either, so how about you drop the *stay* commands, huh?"

The woman was going to be the death of him. Eb was increasingly convinced of that fact. "Naomi, will you *please* stay here? I need to search your house." Not an easy task considering the massive size of the place. Over six thousand square feet.

"I'll come with you," she immediately offered. "Not like I enjoy sitting on the sidelines."

Yes, he'd noticed that about her. Naomi was certainly not a sideline sitter.

But before he could convince her to stay out of the still smoking house, a police cruiser rolled onto the scene.

"Crap." She exhaled. "Now it's gonna be a real circus."

Like it hadn't already been? "Stay here. Try not to piss off the cops."

"Oh, I make zero promises on that score. I think I piss them off just by breathing."

But she turned to face the patrol car and the exiting officers even as Eb hurriedly slipped away. This whole scene bothered him and before it got wrecked anymore, he needed to do a bit of investigating.

Wrecked anymore? It's already been burned, sprayed, and had half a dozen firefighters stomping through the place. Any good evidence of an intruder was probably already long gone.

Eb rushed around the house. The front door had been locked when the fire broke out. He'd secured all the doors before bed. *He'd* been the one who unlocked the front door.

What about the door at the back of the house? Had it still been locked when the firefighters arrived? Or had someone perhaps broken in through that door and set the fire?

Eb hurried to the rear of the house. Bounded up the porch steps and moved toward the door. Still closed. He reached for the knob.

It twisted easily in his hand.

Eb yanked out his phone. He'd tucked it into his pocket right before he'd hauled ass to Naomi's room. He turned on the phone's light and pushed the glow toward the lock.

Scratch marks.

But were those old? New?

"Hey, buddy, you shouldn't be back there!"

Eb turned toward an approaching firefighter. "Did any of your crew open this door?" Maybe he was just being a suspicious SOB.

"Hell if I know," the firefighter replied. He lumbered toward Eb. "You need to get away from the structure. The scene isn't secure yet. Incident Commander hasn't given the all clear."

A young guy. Barely looked twenty-one. One long and bushy mustache covered his upper lip. A very impressive mustache. The kid still wore his full gear, minus the helmet and face mask.

"I need to check the smoke detectors inside," Eb explained. The faulty detectors were his red flag. The detectors, and, of course, the big red flames that had burned in her den.

"What?" The firefighter hunched his shoulders.

"The smoke detectors. I need to check them. They

didn't go off. Either let me in to check them or you go and check them. Find out why the hell they didn't work."

Because Eb had a very, very bad feeling about this scene.

Someone could have slipped in the back door. Set the fire...

And waited for Naomi to burn.

If she'd been alone, without the smoke detectors to alert her to the fire's presence, she *would* have burned. She would have died.

* * *

NAOMI DIDN'T KNOW what she was supposed to do with a hero.

One who'd literally given her the shirt off his back.

Her arms remained crossed over her chest as she waited for the cops to close in. Familiar figures. At this point, most of the police department members were familiar to her. But it wasn't the officers in uniform who had her tensing. It was the detective who walked behind them. The man who'd pulled up in his predictably dark SUV. A guy in jeans and a half-buttoned shirt who'd clipped a badge to his belt and had a holster beneath his left arm.

Detective Clark Anderson. He'd been particularly driven to get her locked away for the little matter of her husband's murder.

"Naomi." A shake of his head. "Causing trouble again, are you?"

Henry remained sitting at her side. "If by causing trouble, you mean...did a fire break out and nearly destroy my home? Yes. That did happen. But I'm safe. Thanks for your concern, Detective Anderson. Always glad to know you are looking out for my well-being."

He stopped a few feet away. His gaze raked over her. And, yes, fine, she was suddenly grateful for the double shirts. It took all she had not to dramatically call out...*Who does a woman have to kill in order to get full clothing around here?* But, no, that question would not be appreciated. She got that. Her dark humor would be inappropriate.

Still...

She was so on edge that she almost blurted it out. Almost.

"What happened?" Clark asked. The two uniformed officers flanked his sides.

"A fire." Shouldn't that be obvious based on the fire truck at the scene? And the firefighters? But then again, she hadn't found him to be the sharpest tool in the box during all of their previous interactions, either.

He'd been too intent on locking her away. Or, even better...as he'd once told her...getting her the death penalty. *A life for a life.* Naomi swallowed. "Why are you even here? I get the firefighters. I even get uniformed cops. However, I hardly think a detective should be at this scene in the middle of the night."

"Heard the call go out. Recognized the address." His hands went to his hips. "Knew I had to come immediately."

How wonderful. Not.

"You start it?" Clark asked.

Her gaze narrowed on him. "Are you seriously asking me if I just tried to burn down my own home?"

"Well, only fair, isn't it, given that you murdered your own husband?"

She took a lunging step toward him.

Strong hands closed around her shoulders. "Sweetheart, are you going to introduce me?"

Shock rolled through her. Had Eb just called her *sweetheart*? She'd thought she heard him call her *baby* earlier, but that had been in the heat of the moment. A possible auditory hallucination given the fire around her and the stress but this time...

He did it. He called me sweetheart.

He pulled her back against him. Back against his warm, strong, bare chest. And one arm moved down so that his forearm slid over her chest while his fingers brushed lightly over her shoulder. His breath blew over her skin. *"Play along,"* he whispered. Or, she thought he whispered the command. The order was so incredibly soft. A bare breath of sound against the shell of her ear.

"This is..." Naomi cleared her throat. "Detective Clark Anderson. And Officers Kennedy Willow and Aziah Burch." Yep, she remembered them all. Hard to forget because Kennedy and Aziah had cuffed her at this same location. Ah, memories. They'd cuffed her even as she'd loudly protested her innocence.

"Who the hell are you?" Clark demanded as he glared at Eb. The officers remained silent. Watchful.

"Eb Jones." He kept her pinned against his body. Kept right on holding her, too.

"Eb Jones?" Clark took a step closer. "As in, Hudson's former partner?"

"Guilty as charged," Eb said.

She flinched. Dammit, he did not need to go around saying stuff like that. If she didn't get to use dark humor, then neither did he.

Clark closed in even more. "You're the partner...and

you're here?" His gaze dropped to the arm that Eb still had curled around Naomi. "With her?"

"Looks that way," Eb responded. "You are observant."

"Where is your shirt?" Clark wanted to know. His tone had flattened.

"Sir." Kennedy stepped forward. Her hair was pulled back into a tight bun, even in the middle of the night. "It appears she is wearing the shirt, sir."

Oh for goodness... "Yes, I'm wearing it. Excellent deduction." Naomi lifted her hands and curled them around Eb's forearm. She tugged. Casually.

At first, he hesitated, then he let her go.

"I'm the victim." She stepped to the side and waved back toward her house. The still smoking house. The smoke could easily be scented on the wind. So could the coming storm. "My house caught on fire tonight, but I'm good. No need for the cops to get involved, I am—"

"There's a need," Eb cut in to say. "It's a good thing they are out here."

Wait, it *was?*

"This is my new friend, Jeffrey Lee."

A young firefighter stepped forward. One that, in the swirl of lights, she could see sported a very large mustache.

"Jeffrey did a bit of checking inside the structure for me," Eb continued. "Jeffrey, will you tell the cops what you found?"

Jeffrey bobbed his head. He clutched a helmet in the crook of his arm. "The smoke detectors didn't have batteries."

Naomi sucked in a sharp breath.

But Clark just shook his head. "You took out your own batteries, huh, Naomi? Trying to get an insurance claim, were you? Did you think that if you—"

"She was asleep, dumbass," Eb snapped.

Clark stiffened. "What did you just call me?"

"I had to wake her up. Carry her down the stairs. Then she insisted on fighting the blaze with fire extinguishers that she had in her closet. A woman who sets her house on fire doesn't stop to try and put out the flames. A woman who survived a fire as a child doesn't set herself up again to face that same hell." Rage vibrated in Eb's words. A carefully controlled rage.

That was the thing about Eb. He knew how to control his emotions. She struggled in that regard. In that very moment, it felt as if her emotions were close to ripping her apart. It took all of her energy to hold herself together.

"You're saying someone else set the fire?" Clark rocked onto the balls of his feet.

"That's exactly what I'm saying. Thanks for following along," Eb gritted out. "I think someone could have broken in via the back door of her place. Got inside, started the blaze, and slipped out while Naomi slept."

"And when would this genius arsonist have taken the batteries from her smoke detectors? Oh, wait, let me guess. Right before he started the fire?"

"The smoke detectors upstairs and downstairs didn't go off. She had them throughout the house." Eb's flat response. "None of them alerted us to the fire."

Eb was right. She did have plenty of smoke detectors. They'd been the first thing she installed after buying the property.

"No one got upstairs. I would have known." Eb was adamant. "So that tells me the batteries were removed *before* tonight. As in this was a premeditated attack."

The officers shifted a bit uneasily and glanced toward the house.

Clark kept his gaze on Eb. "So you're a fire investigator? Here I thought you and Hudson were just government pencil pushers."

A pencil pusher? Really? Was that the story the CIA had fed to him when the detective had been poking around about Hudson's job?

"I'm telling you that someone just set up Naomi to either die or get seriously hurt. Now *you* should act like a cop and investigate." Eb glanced at Naomi. "You ready to get away from here?"

More than ready.

"I have clothes for you, ma'am," the firefighter with the impressive mustache told her. He extended a bag toward Naomi. Grateful, she took it from him and realized that Eb had a bag resting close to his feet, too. She hadn't even noticed it until that moment.

"She's not leaving. I have more questions!" Clark puffed out his chest. "Questions for you both." His right hand rose, and he jabbed his index finger into the air. It went first in Naomi's direction, then in Eb's. "First, are you screwing your dead partner's wife?"

Naomi opened her mouth to snap out an angry response.

"Yes," Eb announced before she could reply. "Though I don't think of it as screwing. I'd never be so crass with her."

What was happening?

"Making love. That's what we do," Eb clarified.

"You're *fucking your dead partner's*—"

"That question has been asked and answered." Eb took the bag from Naomi. "I'll carry it for you." He spared a glare for the detective. "What else do you want to know?"

"Why the hell are you in town? I was told that you worked outside of the country most of the time. And when you were in the US, your home base damn well wasn't in Baton Rouge."

No, it wasn't. Hudson had told her that Eb's home was in Hilton Head, South Carolina.

"I'm here for Naomi," Eb told him. "Thought that was obvious when I answered the previous question. I came for her. I'm staying for her. And if you won't do the job and find out who is threatening her, then I will do it for you." A brittle pause. "Any other questions?"

"Yeah. Plenty of them." Clark bared his teeth as the emergency responder lights swirled around them. "Just who would hate Naomi so much that they'd want her to burn?"

Chapter Six

WHO WOULD HATE NAOMI SO MUCH THAT THEY'D WANT *her to burn?*

The question pierced right through Eb because, when he'd first started this hunt, all he'd felt had been twisting, seething hatred for his target.

Don't lie to yourself. You hated her, and you lusted for her. Hate and lust. A dangerous combination.

"What do you want?" Naomi demanded as her hands flew into the air. "A list? Fine, you hate me, detective. You're enraged because you think I snuck my way out of a trial."

The detective didn't even try to argue with that assertion.

"I'm pretty sure I pissed off a Russian gangster and his wannabe mob tonight."

Now the detective did a double take. "What?"

"Ivan Sokolov. He's on my list. He stole my dog. I got him back."

Everyone looked at a quiet Henry. He stood at attention near Naomi.

"That is a one gorgeous dog," the female cop said as she

reached out a hand toward him. "I bet he'd like a big old pet—"

"No." The sharp reprimand came from Eb's new buddy, the ever-so-helpful-firefighter who'd introduced himself as Jeffrey Lee before he went to check the smoke detectors. His mustache twitched in annoyance as the bright lights from the emergency vehicles swirled around them. "Don't you know better than to interfere with a working service dog?"

Eb did a double take. "Service dog?" Naomi had never mentioned a word about Henry being a service dog. But he'd never seen a dog stay so quiet and focused like Henry. The dog had been Naomi's shadow since they'd taken him from the bar.

"Can we get back to my hate list?" Naomi inquired crisply. "Ah, yes, we should also add Hudson's only living family—his cousin Jaxon. Jaxon is getting me tied up in legal knots and refusing to honor the will. Because, you know, he thinks I'm a horrible villain. And, it would be remiss of me not to mention, there's Eb." Her head ducked toward him. "The new, ah, boyfriend?"

Wait...

Hold the hell up.

Had she just listed his name?

His head jerked toward her.

"I think you hate me, too," she said, and Naomi seemed sad.

He didn't speak.

"No denial." A nod from her. "But while you may hate me, you aren't trying to kill me. You're saving me. Have I thanked you for that?"

Eb's lips parted.

"Wait just a damn minute!" Clark exploded. He

pointed his right index finger at Eb. "How do we know that he didn't set the fire? He was in the house. Close proximity. And he could have taken the batteries out of the smoke detectors! Maybe he's guilty as sin, and he's trying to throw suspicion off himself."

That dick could not be serious. "I just told *you* about the batteries. I got her *out* of the house. If I wanted her dead, why do that? Why not just let her burn?"

"Because where is the fun in that?" Clark asked, voice dropping to a low and considering tone. "Because there is getting your revenge on someone...and then there is making sure the person suffers. A quick death is too easy. Far better to rip someone's world apart, don't you think?"

Naomi barely appeared to be breathing. She'd gone statue-still, with one hand reaching out to touch her dog's head. That hand had frozen mid-air. Henry moved, stretching up, and his head pumped into her palm.

Eb's gaze flickered to the watchful detective. "You're dark, man. Dark. You get that, don't you?"

Clark hummed. "I just understand how vengeance can twist you up. Eat you from the inside out. Your partner is dead. Did you come to town in order to get some payback? Fucking and hating at the same time? Now, *that's* dark."

Eb's focus shifted back to Naomi.

She shook her head, and she took her hand away from Henry. Only to then press that hand to Eb's side. "He's here for justice." Clear. Flat. "Eb came to town because we're working together and we're going to find Hudson's killer. As in, the real killer. Not me. Because I told you—over and over —the murderer wasn't me. I didn't kill Hudson. Eb believes me. He's not here to hurt me. Not here to rip apart my world." She smiled at Eb. The kind of smile that hit a man with the same impact as a punch to the gut. "He's here to give me my life back."

* * *

"THERE'S ONE BED."

Eb had just crossed the threshold into the guesthouse when Naomi made that announcement. He shut the door behind him. Okay, fine, he slammed it. Slammed it way harder than he should have. He dropped their bags and flipped the lock in place.

She spun toward him. "I'm *not* asking you to share the bed with me. Just stating a simple fact. There is only one bed in this guesthouse." She waved toward a small hallway. "Bedroom is in there. With a queen-size bed."

"Your marriage bed." He bit off the words.

Naomi's little pink tongue swiped over her lower lip. "I didn't fuck him on my wedding night. So, no, not technically my marriage bed."

What? He was pretty sure his jaw hit the floor.

"It's not the same mattress from that night, either. Just FYI. That mattress was evidence. It was also covered in blood, so not like I wanted to keep it around. New bed. New mattress. New sheets. New everything." She shoved back a lock of hair that had tumbled over her cheek. "There is also a perfectly good sofa right here." A dip of her hand toward the mini-den area. "You can crash on it. Or you can go get a hotel room. There is no reason why you have to stay here with me."

Eb rested against the wood of the door. "Plenty of reasons. Reason one is that someone tried to kill *us* tonight."

She grimaced. "Pretty sure someone tried to kill me.

You were probably collateral damage. If that's any consolation."

"It's zero consolation."

Naomi retreated a step. "I need to get changed. Actually, I need to shower and then get in bed." Her hand stretched for her bag.

He caught her hand. The better to stop her from retreating any more.

Henry whined.

It was the first sound the dog had made since they'd entered the guesthouse. Eb spared him a glance. "You know I'm not going to hurt her."

"Does he know that?" Naomi's low question. "Do *I* know that?"

Eb's gaze jumped back to her. "You put me on your freaking hate list for the detective." Right after he'd gone to all the trouble of trying to set up a cover of them being a couple.

"Didn't realize I was supposed to lie about how you felt." She rolled one shoulder. "Out of curiosity, just how much do you hate me?" A soft question.

He wasn't answering that careful query. "You said you didn't kill Hudson."

"That's not a response to my question." She bit her lower lip. Tugged it between her teeth for just a moment.

"Why didn't you fuck him on your wedding night?"

"Because I realized that I'd married a monster." Naomi spoke as if that answer should have been obvious. "Some people are particularly adept at hiding a dark side. Hudson hid his until I was legally tied to him. Then, surprise, surprise..."

He frowned at her.

"Did you know that Hudson was born and raised in

New Orleans? That he spent the first eighteen years of his life there?"

What in the hell did that have to do with anything? But, yes, he knew all of that.

"His grandparents lived in Baton Rouge. And after their death—since his parents were gone by that time—he inherited their property and fortune. I think that pissed off his cousin Jaxon, by the way. The fact that Hudson got everything and Jaxon wound up with nothing. Some might even say that was a motive for murder. But, hey, what do I know? I'm just the Wicked Widow."

"Naomi."

"Hudson moved here a few years ago. Well, I don't know if *moved here* is the right description. He sort of used the location as a home base as he went back and forth on all his super-secret missions."

Eb wasn't sure where she was leading him with this story.

"You ever heard of the Ice Breakers?"

Now he blinked. "Yeah." He'd actually heard plenty about the Ice Breakers, and not just because they'd been in the news a lot lately. They were an online team. Came from all kinds of different backgrounds. They were former law enforcement, one was a reporter, another a bounty hunter. They were bankrolled by billionaire Archer Radcliffe, a man who had once been suspected of murder himself. Only the Ice Breakers had cleared him of that pesky suspicion.

Fun fact? Eb's sister worked with the Ice Breakers. Marley was one of their new recruits. She loved working with the team. Their goal was to solve the coldest of crimes. To bring justice to the forgotten. Or so Marley had proudly told him at least three times.

"On my wedding day, a man named Memphis Camden came to see me. Said he was an Ice Breaker."

His thumb stroked along her inner wrist. He felt her pulse jump.

"Don't do that," she chided immediately.

His thumb stilled. "Don't like it?"

"I like it too much. I like it far too much when you touch me."

Her honesty left him speechless.

"I don't respond normally to you. It's more like I'm in overdrive when we touch. It's been a wild night, and I am hanging on by a thread. Push me too much—touch me too much—and I'm not real sure my control will last with you."

His hold tightened.

"You saved my life tonight. I guess, technically, you've saved me twice. You helped me at that rundown bar, and you stopped me from burning to death in my own house. I have to confess, I'm not quite sure how to handle a hero."

"I'm not a hero." Guilt twisted in him. He'd been lying to her.

"Fine. I'm not sure how to handle a cold-blooded bastard who occasionally does a good deed. Better?"

He wanted to keep touching her. No, he wanted to do far more than just touch. *Take, take, take.* "Did the story about Memphis have a point?" He let go of her wrist.

The dog remained close. Watchful.

"Memphis believed he was on the trail of a serial killer." A little bubble of laughter came from her. Would have been a musical sound, if it didn't hold the note of desperation. "Turns out that back when Hudson lived in New Orleans, a girl he dated went missing."

Now Eb nodded. "I know. Mary Fontenot."

Her lips parted. "He told you about her?"

"Mary was his high school sweetheart. It devastated him when she vanished. Said it changed his whole life." Her disappearance had been the reason his partner wound up in the CIA. At first, Hudson had been bound for the FBI. He'd wanted to stop violent criminals, but then the CIA had recruited him. Stolen him right from under the FBI's nose.

That tended to happen a lot.

"It devastated him, huh? Interesting." She nodded. "According to Memphis, Hudson was a major suspect in Mary's disappearance."

Eb's shoulders tensed. "Romantic partners are always suspects." No big surprise.

Another laugh slipped from her. One tinged with more desperation. "Tell me about it."

His lips thinned.

"Memphis thought Hudson was tied to other disappearances, as well. *Two* other disappearances in New Orleans. Females who had a similar appearance to Mary. Victims who vanished while Hudson lived in the Big Easy."

This was bullshit. It was—

"Hudson began working with the CIA after those disappearances, and it became harder to track his movements. You know how you secret CIA guys are. Always slipping in and out of countries. New identities each time. But Memphis believed that he had managed to uncover a few concerning patterns. That Hudson might have been tied to the disappearance of a woman in the UK. Then another one in Spain."

The pounding of Eb's heartbeat seemed far too loud as it echoed in his ears. "Some guy—a total stranger—appears on your wedding day and spins a story about your groom being a serial killer and you...you what? Just buy it?" This was unreal.

"Memphis had no proof. No concrete proof. Just his suspicions, but he said he had to tell me. That he thought I deserved to know because he believed I could be in danger."

"What did you say to Memphis?" Eb asked. He didn't know Memphis personally, but the name had clicked for him. He was well aware of Memphis Camden's reputation. A former bounty hunter, Memphis was rumored to be completely relentless. He had a real knack for tracking killers. According to the stories, his prey never escaped him.

"I told Memphis to screw off, of course. I wasn't marrying a killer. Surely, I wouldn't make the mistake of falling for a man who was a real monster? I mean...no way." Her fingers lifted and curled around the wrist he'd held moments before. "Hudson was always kind to me. Incredibly caring. I'd never had anyone pay so much attention to me. He seemed to know me better than I knew myself."

The fingers of his right hand tightened into a fist.

"He made sure I always had my favorite dessert when we went out to eat. Those amazing chocolate lava cakes." A full smile came and went on her face. "He found this property for me because he somehow knew that my dream was to open my own business. My own bed and breakfast where I could make my guests feel at home. So very welcome. He knew about that dream before I even told him. Just like he knew where I had always hoped to vacation. He knew the movies I liked. He knew the jewelry I thought would be the prettiest. He knew me sometimes..." A faint click as she swallowed. "He knew me better than I knew myself. And he promised me that my life would never be the same once we married. That he could give me everything I wanted in this world." An exhale. "So on my wedding day, when a stranger appeared and told me that the man who loved me, the man who had always shown me nothing but care—when a stranger appeared and told me that man could be a serial killer, I told *him* to get the hell out. I told Memphis Camden that he was wrong. And I walked down the aisle to marry Hudson."

Eb had been right there. And he'd never seen any doubt on her face. No fear. "Is that why you killed him?" Eb questioned, wondering if he was about to get the confession he needed. "Because Memphis made you doubt him? You snapped that night, and you attacked? You should have told the cops the truth. You should have—"

She surged toward him. Didn't quite touch him. Almost. He could feel her warmth all around him. "I thought you believed I wasn't the killer. Didn't you say we were going to team up to find the real murderer? Haven't we been over this?"

I lied, sweetheart. You understand that, don't you? Because you've been lying, too.

"Hudson was a very good liar. He had to be, didn't he? That whole CIA business means that he had to lie all the time. I didn't even know he was CIA, not until after he proposed."

You didn't just go around announcing the truth of the job all the time. It was something that was definitely need-to-know. The local detective only knew because Hudson had been freaking murdered. The truth about his job had to come out for the investigation. But the higher ups at the agency had spun a tale about Hudson and Eb just being pencil pushers. Good old data crunchers.

Bullshit.

"Hudson always said you were better at the job than he

was. That you blended better. That you could become anyone in the blink of an eye. He called you a chameleon."

Blending was Eb's specialty.

"I think that means you're probably far better at lying than he ever was." Now she backed up a step. "Do you know how much that terrifies me? Because he was very, very good."

Time to recap. "You're standing here, telling me that my partner was a serial killer. And I'm just supposed to buy this?"

Her lips curled in a humorless smile. "You sound like me, when I was talking with Memphis." The smile vanished. "No bodies have ever been found. Those women just disappeared, seemingly without a trace. It's hard to prove the crime without the victims. I told you, Memphis had no proof. Just his suspicions. He said he had to tell me before I went through with the ceremony..." Her words trailed away.

"You married Hudson anyway."

"I had a chapel full of people waiting. A caterer who'd been paid." The words were mocking. Her sad gaze was not. "And you, standing there and glaring at me the whole time. I have to know, curiosity compels me to ask, did you start disliking me from the first moment you saw me? Or was it before we ever met?"

"No, I *wanted* you from the first moment I saw you dancing in that fountain. Hate had nothing to do with it."

Her lashes flickered. "What...fountain?"

"The one in Vegas. When you were wearing the pale blue dress and laughing after midnight. You looked carefree and so beautiful, and all I wanted to do was scoop you out of that water, pull you into my arms, and kiss you."

She took three frantic steps back.

Henry let out a low whine. He stood at attention.

"No, no. I-I didn't meet you in Vegas." A frantic shake of her head. Her hand rose, and she tucked a lock of hair behind her ear.

His gaze sharpened. Were her fingers trembling?

"I met Hudson there, not you. You were not in Vegas."

"I was there. Heard you laughing and headed for the fountain. Saw you. Wanted you."

Another negative shake of her head.

"But I got called away. Family business." What an understatement for the hell that had wrecked his family. "Before I left, I told Hudson that you were going to be mine." Something broke inside of him. He surged toward her. *Don't touch. Don't touch.* She'd said she felt too out of control when they touched.

How the hell did she think he felt? Anger and need twisted and seethed inside of him. "*I* saw you that night." Such a long-ago night. Another lifetime, almost. Because when he'd gotten called away, that had just been the start of the battle he had to fight with Marley. He'd even wound up going undercover, living in hell for a time, because he'd wanted to eliminate the threat to her. *All that time. All that effort.* Only for Marley's now husband to swoop in and steal Eb's vengeance.

During all that time, when Eb had been distracted, when he'd had to become someone else, Hudson had been working to slowly seduce Naomi. To get her to fall for him. It hadn't been some rushed, head-over-heels wedding. It had been a long time coming. When she'd said that Hudson had given her everything she'd wanted, the man had. Like a careful, strategized plan. *A plan that never should have been put in motion because I wanted you first.* "I said I wanted you. But he got you because I fucking wasn't there." Gone far too long. Living in a hell she would never understand. "He took you...and now you're standing here, telling me some BS serial killer tale? You married him, and if you murdered him, just *say* it!"

"I told him what Memphis said," she blurted. Her hand flew out. Gestured wildly around the guesthouse.

Henry padded closer to her.

"Told him right here. He'd carried me over the th-threshold..." Her eyelashes flickered again. "Barely put me down. I-I don't know why I..."

Henry bumped into her.

"Back away, Henry," Eb growled.

Henry didn't. He bumped into her again. His nose pressed to her, and he whined. Then barked. The dog seemed to *push* her.

"I...feel dizzy." Her breath came in and out. "I should g-get to bed."

Henry nudged her. Carefully. Gently?

"Henry?" What in the hell was the dog doing? "Henry, back off."

But the dog ignored his command and pushed Naomi again.

Naomi stumbled for the couch. "Closer..." Her breath heaved. "Can't believe this is...happening *now*."

"What's happening?"

The dog was at her side. Completely alert. Naomi sank onto the cushions of the couch. She put a trembling hand to her head. *Definitely trembling.*

Alarm flashed through Eb's body, and in an instant, he was on his knees beside the couch. "What is happening?" he repeated, throat tightening.

The firefighter had said Henry was a service dog.

"Just...need a little while," she rasped.

Her skin seemed paler.

"Why don't you...take the...ah, bedroom? I'll stay here." She spread out on the couch. One hand flew toward Henry. "Good boy," she whispered. "I'm okay."

She didn't look okay. A savage surge of worry rolled through Eb because he could have sworn a hard tremble just shook her whole body. "Naomi?"

"Don't hurt me," she breathed.

"I won't." *Not fucking ever*. He bit back those words. Barely.

Another tremor shook her. Harder.

"Naomi?"

Her body jolted against the couch.

Henry barked. Loud. Sharp. Again. Again.

Her eyes rolled.

Shit. Eb grabbed her shoulders. "Naomi!"

Another jolt. A shudder.

"What do you need?" Eb demanded. "*What do you need?*"

* * *

NOT NOW. Not now. *Notnownotnownot-nownotnownotnow*. A frantic, terrible refrain in her brain. But her brain and her body weren't listening. They'd never listened. She'd fought so hard for control. She'd tried so hard over the years.

But sometimes, there was no control. Sometimes, she lost herself.

Her arm jerked. Her leg flew out to the left.

"Naomi!"

He was over her. Big, strong. With shadows chasing over his face and...a golden halo just peeking behind his head. She'd thought she was absolutely crazy the first time she'd seen one of those halos.

But everyone had said she was crazy back then. That she'd had fits, even as a child.

They aren't fits. Someone, help me. Help. Me!

Her teeth snapped together.

The dog was barking. Her Henry.

The man was over her. Dark and dangerous, and his words were the same. She was in the same house. The guesthouse. The same terrible place.

And he was saying the same words to her...

What do you need?

Her arm jerked again. Her fingers squeezed into a fist. But there was no knife in her grip.

"What do you need? Tell me how to help you!"

Not the same voice. That wasn't Hudson's voice. Hudson's voice had been taunting. Falsely sympathetic. Smug. All of the—

"Naomi!"

Eb's face was right before her. His topaz eyes were worried. A bit wild. So was the expression on his face. Wild and almost desperate.

Did he care? Was that another lie?

She couldn't hide this secret. Her body had betrayed her.

Her dog was barking again.

"I'm calling nine-one-one," Eb said.

There wasn't much the EMTs could do for her. They'd load her up. Take her to the hospital. Everyone would know her secret.

She'd been taking her pills. Prescribed by a doctor in another town. She tried to keep her secrets. Always.

Why was this happening now? At least, it wasn't too bad. She could still process. Still think—

"What do you need?"

Her arms and legs jerked. Time vanished. Hell returned. Fear blasted through her. Deja-vu.

Did this before. Been here before. Same place.

But, no, different man. Different—

Fear consumed her. Awareness drifted. "Help..."

Nothing else. There was no more. She was lost.

Gone.

Help.

Chapter Seven

"I NEED AN AMBULANCE!" EB BLASTED INTO HIS PHONE. "My—" *What is she? What is Naomi to me?* "My girlfriend is having a seizure, and I need help right now! We're in the damn guesthouse at..." Eb fired off the address as quickly as he could and heard the instant promise from the nine-one-one operator that help was coming.

Help needed to hurry the hell up.

Naomi's body seized again. The dog barked.

Service dog. The firefighter had been right about that score. The dog Naomi had wanted back so badly, the dog that Ivan had stolen from her had been an *epileptic service dog*. The sonofabitch had taken a lifeline from her.

The dog had known before Naomi's seizure began. Henry had known it was coming and tried to get her to a safe spot so she wouldn't fall and hurt herself.

He was going to buy Henry every treat in the world. *After*. After Naomi was okay. After her seizure had stopped.

How long had it been? Two minutes? Three? Three

damn minutes that lasted forever in his mind? His heart raced and sweat slickened his back, and Eb wanted to make it *stop*. He knew from previous emergency responder training that five minutes was the time when he *should* have called for an ambulance. That he should have waited because most seizures didn't last longer than that time period. But—

Screw that. He hadn't waited five minutes. He'd called for help because he felt frantic. He didn't know Naomi's history. Didn't know how bad things could get for her.

How do I not know? The CIA had given him lots of intel on her, but there had been no notation of any health conditions.

Really, CIA? Gonna actually obey HIPAA rules?

He'd removed anything close to Naomi that might cause any sort of accident. Not that much had been close.

He'd turned Naomi onto her side. Made sure her airway was clear.

He hovered over her. "Naomi, you're going to be okay." Eb tried to sound soothing, but the truth was that fear filled him. Fear and fury.

She was too vulnerable this way. She could be hurt. Couldn't defend herself from an attack in this state.

Henry edged closer to her. He sniffed her. Barked.

"I've got her," Eb promised. How long had it been? Four minutes now? Her breathing seemed labored. Her eyes had sagged closed. "Naomi?"

She'd asked for help. Tried to ask for help, anyway. He'd do whatever she needed.

The seconds ticked past. Another hard jerk of her arms.

Five minutes? The ambulance had better be flying to them. *Come on, come on...*

More precious time ground past. His heart thudded. He watched her, utterly helpless and hating that he could do nothing for her. Eb didn't do well with being helpless.

Not at all.

Her body stopped jerking. Did her breathing ease? He thought it did. His fingers skimmed over her cheek. Her eyelashes fluttered.

"Naomi?"

Her body seemed to go slack. She'd been tense before but...

She softened against the couch.

He wanted to scoop her into his arms and hold her tightly, but he was afraid. *Can't hurt her. Won't hurt her.*

Her lashes fluttered once more.

"I'm here. Help is coming." The ambulance needed to hurry.

She...moved her head. A no.

"Yeah, well, too damn bad, sweetheart. An ambulance is on the way. You're getting checked out because you just scared ten years of my life away." Did she understand him? He knew confusion could follow a seizure.

Her hands fluttered, as if she was trying to get up. Her body shifted against the couch cushions.

Cute. "No. Stay where you are." He was adamant. "You just had a seizure. But you're safe."

"N-no..."

"You are safe," Eb repeated. Her voice had been slurred. Hell, yes, that slurring alarmed him. Too much. "I'm with you, and you are always safe with me."

A tear trickled down her cheek.

"Did you hear me? You will always be safe with me."

"*Liar...*" A breath.

Eb swallowed. He also stared hard into the tear-filled darkness of her eyes. "You will always be safe with me." That wasn't a lie.

It was a vow.

Chapter Eight

"The trip to the hospital was completely unnecessary." Naomi sniffed. "Like, do you even have any idea how expensive the ambulance ride alone will be for me?" As if she needed an extra expense to add to her current troubles.

"I'll take care of any bills," Eb growled.

They stood in the hospital's parking lot. Dawn was coming, sending streaks of red across the sky. For a moment, she got lost in that redness. Looked like blood. What was that old saying? Her dad used to quote it every time he saw that tell-tale red...

"Red sky at night. Sailor's delight. Red sky at morning. Sailor take warning..."

Her father had grown up along the Florida coast. She'd lived there, too. Had spent so many days jumping into those gorgeous, emerald waters when she'd been a little kid. She'd been happy back then.

But things had changed.

"When a seizure lasts for five minutes, a trip to the hospital is absolutely necessary."

"I'm sure it wasn't that long. Not like you were counting." Her whole body felt bone weary. The responding physician had tried to keep her for observation. She'd refused. Again...*expensive*. She would also *not* be letting Eb foot any of her bills.

"I was watching you every moment."

Yes, she knew it. He'd seen everything. No hiding. Did he have any clue how vulnerable she felt when the seizures hit? When her body jerked like a puppet on a string and she could do nothing to control the desperate movements?

"You told the doctor you'd had seizures all your life."

Of course, Eb had heard that part. He'd been beside her every single moment. "Yep. Started when I was a kid. Hoped I'd grow out of them. Some people do, you know." She hadn't been one of the lucky ones. Her parents had tried to take care of her. But, when they'd been gone...a few of her foster families had freaked over the seizures. One lady in particular had thought Naomi had been possessed by the devil when her eyes started rolling back in her head. "They don't come that often." *And maybe I do have a bit of the devil in me.*

"When was the last one before this episode?"

Episode? Naomi snorted. Not like it was a TV show. "Where is your car? I know you followed the ambulance in it. If you could just drive me back to the guesthouse..." Though, frankly, she hated the thought of staying there. "If you could drive me back, I'd really appreciate it." There. Had that been polite enough?

"My car is this way." He caught her hand.

At his touch, that same, wild charge went right through her. A charge, an awareness that should not be happening. She was dead on her feet. *Ha. Let's not imagine that.* Exhaustion pulled at her, as it always did after a seizure.

She wanted to tumble into the comfort of sleep, but this wasn't exactly a safe sleep spot.

"You need to rest," he murmured.

"Tell me something I don't know." She let him lead her to the sidewalk and toward the car that waited. Blessedly, not too far from them. The nurse had wanted to wheel her out in a chair. Naomi had balked. The nurse had argued. Been adamant about hospital protocol.

In the end, they'd compromised. The nurse had wheeled her to the sliding doors in the lobby. Then Naomi leapt out of the chair.

"I could have brought the car to you," Eb said.

"We're already here." And they were.

"I mean...you didn't have to *walk* out. You could have been wheeled to the exit and then straight to my car and—"

She turned on him. "I can walk on my own. Don't you dare start pitying me." Her hand snatched from his, but mostly just so she could jab an index finger into his chest. A chest that was covered by a soft, black t-shirt. "I had a seizure. Thousands of people have them every single day. Don't you start treating me like I'm going to shatter at any moment. I am *not*."

"No shattering. Noted." He looked down at her poking finger. "When was the last time you had a seizure before this one?"

She pulled her hand back. "Why do you have a classic car?" She eyed the ride. Black, sleek, and beautiful. "At first, I thought it was a '67." He'd brought clothes for her, thank goodness. Not like she wanted to rush around in those two t-shirts forever. Now she wore jeans, a gray blouse, and sneakers. The sneakers made no sound as she padded across the pavement. The wet pavement. Because while she'd been rushed to the hospital, the threatened storm had finally erupted. Now the storm had passed, and all that was left were the wet puddles on the pavement.

After dodging a few of those puddles, Naomi reached the passenger side of his ride. An impressive ride, she'd give him that. "Like I said, at first, I thought it was a '67. But the '67 has a bumper that's flatter. In the front and back, it's flatter." She eyed his classic car. Such a thing of beauty. "This one has a more streamlined front. The corners of the grill meet the bumper." A critical assessment, then, "And the hood is a wee bit longer. Definitely a '68 Impala. Not a '67." She nodded. "The corner pieces of the grill are the big tell."

He unlocked the car. Opened the passenger door for her. "So in addition to everything else, you're a classic car expert."

She had to laugh as she slid inside. The laughter felt oddly good after the night from hell. "Actually, I'm a *Supernatural* expert."

His brows shot up. "What?"

A sigh escaped her as she leaned back against the seat and closed her eyes. "Get in the car."

He shut the door. A moment later, she heard the driver's side door open and felt him slide into the Impala with her. Her eyes remained closed as he started the car.

"What kind of expert are you again?" Eb asked.

"A *Supernatural* one. As in, Sam and Dean from the unforgettable TV show." Her life-long bad-boy addiction had made her fall for Dean instantly. "The main character, Dean—he drove a '67 Impala. So I may have learned a bit about the car."

"Sounds like you learned more than a bit."

Horror sank through her. "Oh, no." Her eyes flew open. Her head swiveled his way as she gaped at him. "Do you have a brother?" Hudson had never mentioned much about Eb's family.

"Actually, yeah, I do have a brother."

Again... "Oh, no."

"Why is that a problem? I happen to love my brother."

She tugged at the seatbelt she'd pulled over herself. "Of course, you do. Because you're too much like freaking Dean and that may explain why I have the urge to jump you."

Eb cleared his throat. "You're gonna need to explain more. Especially about the jumping me part."

No, she should not explain more. Instead, she should end the conversation before things were said that she could not take back with her currently loose lips. "I'm tired." Way more than just tired. "I am not thinking clearly. I have none of my usual control. I will be collapsing ASAP." A worry rose, making her heart race. "Where is Henry? Tell me that he's safe—"

"Relax."

"You relax," she snapped right back even as her whole body ached, and she wished that she could relax. Oh, if only.

"Jeffrey has Henry."

"Who in the world is Jeffrey?"

"The firefighter? The one with the impressive mustache? The one who realized right away that Henry wasn't just an ordinary dog? Jeffrey Lee."

She sniffed. "There will never be anything ordinary about Henry." That dog was her superhero.

"Jeffrey was on the scene when you were hauled out of the guesthouse."

Her memories of that scene were pretty foggy. Eb had

been shouting orders. And demanding that she be okay. He'd gripped her hand until she'd been loaded into the back of the ambulance. *That* part she remembered quite vividly. One of the EMTs had pried her hand from Eb's.

"Jeffrey agreed to watch your dog."

"I'll have to thank your new firefighting best friend for his pet sitting service."

Eb turned the wheel. His long, strong fingers flew over the surface.

She swallowed. Why was it oddly sexy to watch those powerful fingers spin that wheel?

"He knew before you actually *had* the seizure. Henry knew, I mean."

"Now you get why I wanted him back so badly. That dog is worth his weight in gold." She just wanted to curl up into a ball and crash. To know that she was safe and didn't have to worry for a while. "Had to get him back." She'd been so desperate. "Golden Retrievers have a great sense of smell."

"That's how he knew the seizure was coming? He could smell the difference with you?" A whistle. "That's freaking amazing."

"That's Henry." She loved that dog. "A friend helped me get him in Vegas."

"Hudson knew that Henry was your epileptic service dog."

She pressed her lips together. Epileptic service dog. Seizure alert dog. Seizure response dog. Lots of names that all equaled the same thing. Her superhero dog, Henry.

Naomi had discovered that, in this world, you couldn't trust a man. He'd let you down. But a dog? Again, *worth his weight in gold.*

"Why would Hudson tell Ivan to take your dog, knowing how important he was to you?"

"Probably because your partner wasn't the superstar that you keep believing him to be." Hadn't she told him about Memphis's visit? Naomi was pretty sure that she had. But things were a bit blurry thanks to the seizure. "Did you miss the serial killer part?" Maybe she should review it for him.

"I get that Memphis Camden is an Ice Breaker, but he was dead wrong. Hudson isn't—wasn't—a serial killer. I think that kind of thing would have popped up in the agency's psych evaluation. They have the best shrinks in the world there."

"They also have the best actors in the world. People who know how to become someone different in the blink of an eye." Naomi studied his profile. "People like you."

"I'm confused." Actually, Eb sounded stiffly polite as he asked, "Did you just imply that I'm a serial killer?"

"Are you?" Naomi tossed right back.

"No." His grip tightened on the wheel.

"Good to know." He had a great profile. Strong nose. Hard jaw. Square and perfectly cut. Lined with stubble now because they'd spent all night together. Mostly together, anyway. "What's your brother's name?"

"What?"

"Your brother." Going back to her *Supernatural* obsession. "What's his name?" She could almost imagine Eb saying—

"You seriously want my brother's name? Now?"

Seriously, she did. It was why she'd asked. Naomi bit her lip, then just had to question, "By any chance, is his name Sam? Sammy?"

"What?" Again, the same bark. Then, "No. His name is Jake."

A tough, strong name. "Are you older than Jake?"

"Yes. By all of two minutes and forty-three seconds. Dammit, why are you so interested in my family all of a sudden?"

Her eyes widened. "You have a *twin*?"

"Sure do."

"As in, identical? Or fraternal?" No way. No way could there be someone else walking about with that gorgeous, but oddly dangerous and intent-looking face. That would be too impossible. Too amazing.

"Identical. But you should be warned, Jake doesn't have my easy-going personality."

Laughter spilled from her.

He seemed to tense. "God, that's a gorgeous sound."

Could a sound be gorgeous?

"A real laugh from you. I like it." He'd braked at a stop sign. "But I wasn't bullshitting. Everyone always thinks that Jake is the dark and intense one. I'm the fun twin."

"Well, everyone is wrong. You're clearly extra dark and intense beneath that killer smile you enjoy tossing around like confetti. The bigger the smile, the darker the soul. And that dimple is just damn deceptive. Makes you look all sexy and fun when you're clearly the opposite deep inside." A hard exhale. "The bigger the smile, the darker the soul," she repeated.

He accelerated. "I don't think that's a thing."

"It's one hundred percent a thing." She yawned. "Hudson said he hadn't killed them." Sleep tugged at her. How much sleep had she gotten that night? Maybe an hour before the fire? If that long? Add in the hard toll the seizure had taken on her body...

I am crashing...

"Naomi?"

She jumped. Her eyes fluttered open.

"Hudson told you he wasn't guilty?"

"Yes. But he was lying." Her eyelids sagged closed.

"How do you know?"

Her breath whispered out.

"Naomi."

Her lashes fluttered. She was confused. Disoriented. And...still in the car? She fumbled and pushed against the seatbelt. Had she fallen asleep for a moment?

"When was the last time you had a seizure? The doctor asked, and *I* asked but you didn't say. How long was it before this one?"

"My wedding night." Another yawn. Couldn't the man just let her sleep?

She heard a curse. Her eyes had fallen closed again. "Wake me up when we get there," she murmured. The words tumbled out all at the same time. *Wakemeupwhen...*

"You had a seizure on your wedding night? Did Hudson help you? Did you lose consciousness? Is that what happened? You lost consciousness and never saw the killer and you just gave the cops some story about being gone and an intruder attacking him?"

Her eyes reluctantly opened. Her stare locked on his profile once more. He gripped the steering wheel far too hard. Poor Eb. He thought he'd just solved the big mystery. She hated to disappoint him, but he needed to understand who his friend had truly been. "Hudson didn't help me. He watched me suffer. Wanted me to beg. I didn't beg."

"*Naomi.*"

"The mask fell away. He didn't love me. He wanted to

control me. He wanted to hurt me. He *did* hurt me. But now Hudson can't hurt anyone."

Stunned silence.

"Believe me or not. Your choice." Her breath drifted out on a sigh.

Eb didn't ask any other questions. Good. Because she didn't have more answers to give.

Naomi let her eyes drift shut once more.

Chapter Nine

He parked the car. Turned his head to look at the passenger. Naomi's eyes were closed. Her lips slightly parted. Still no good color in her cheeks. Still looking far, far too fragile for his piece of mind.

She was just...not what he'd thought.

She didn't seem cold-blooded. Calculating.

She was vulnerable. But strong. So very strong. With her past. With her present.

And with every moment that he spent with her...*I don't feel hate for Naomi.*

Maybe he should stop lying to himself about that shit. Because he did not hate Naomi. Far from it. He killed the engine. Unhooked his seatbelt and exited the vehicle. He strode to her side, opened her door, and then unhooked Naomi's seatbelt. She barely stirred.

His hand lifted and softly touched her cheek. "Naomi?"

Her breath rustled from between her lush lips. Her eyes remained closed.

No sense waking her up. She'd basically gotten zero sleep the night before. Neither of them had gotten much sleep. Eb wanted to crash, but he needed to make sure she was secure first. And there were other plans that he needed to put in place.

Carefully, slowly, he lifted her from the car and held her in his arms. He used his hip to shut the door and then carried her toward the guesthouse.

He didn't like the guesthouse. They would not be staying in it after today. Other arrangements would be made. Changes had to occur.

Her safety would come first for him.

They'd almost reached the entrance to the guesthouse when she gave a quick gasp. He felt the sudden alertness in her body even before her eyes flew open.

"Easy," he soothed. "You're safe. I've got you." And, with a bit of skill and dexterity, he managed to unlock the door and keep carrying her. Good thing he'd swiped the keys to the guesthouse before racing after the ambulance.

"Why...why do you carry me so much?"

He crossed the threshold. Shut the door. "Do I carry you a lot?"

"Yes." A whisper. She curled one arm around his neck. "You can put me down."

"Sure." But he didn't. He carried her to the small bedroom. Spared a glance for the bed. "You never slept in this bed with Hudson."

"No." Sleepy.

"Good." He put her on the bed. Pulled off her shoes and socks and tossed them away. Even tucked her under the covers. His hands lingered for a moment on her. "Go to sleep, Naomi. We'll talk more after you've rested." Time to back away. Only his hands kept right on lingering.

"I don't...like that you saw me that way." A quiet admission.

He sat on the edge of the bed. Still not leaving. Still not backing away like he should. "What way?"

She swallowed. "Helpless."

His hand rose to brush back a lock of her dark hair. Then, of course, his fingers decided to linger once more. This time, against the silk of her cheek. "If you can't be helpless in front of a friend, who can you be helpless in front of?" A mocking question to try and lighten the sudden tension in the room.

"You're not my friend."

"No? Then what am I?"

"I'm scared that you might be my enemy. It's terrible to be helpless in front of an enemy."

He leaned toward her. "I'm not your enemy."

"You're Hudson's friend. His partner."

She needed to understand this. "I'm not your enemy."

Her gaze searched his. Dark shadows lined her eyes. Still no good color in her cheeks. Even her lips looked too pale. Plump, gorgeous, but pale. "If you're not my enemy, what are you?"

"How about I be *your* friend?"

"I don't have a lot of those. People in town...the few friends I'd made, they turned on me." Quiet. Tired. "People don't like to be friends with murderers."

"But you're not a murderer." Wasn't that what she kept telling him?

A soft exhale. "I need to sleep. You need to sleep."

"Yes." He went right on lingering. Lingering might be his new favorite hobby. "I'm going to watch over you."

A little furrow appeared between her brows. "Does that mean you're going to watch me sleep? Because that's creepy."

His mouth curled. "I don't want to be creepy."

"Then no watching me sleep." Again, that deep gaze of hers searched his. "You feel sorry for me." A negative shake of her head against the pillow. "Don't. I was helpless in that moment, but I'm not weak. I won't ever be weak."

"Wouldn't dream of thinking that you were. Quite the opposite, in fact." For him, there was nothing sexier than strength. An unbreakable spirit. "I don't know you well enough. That's my mistake. I believe in learning from my mistakes. I will discover your secrets, and you'll discover mine."

"And we'll be...friends?"

Not exactly. "Full disclosure, I don't usually want to fuck my friends."

Her eyes widened.

"You can't be surprised. You had to know I want you. Pretty sure I give the secret away every moment when my gaze locks on you. Surely you see the hunger in my eyes." But now wasn't the time for this big talk. It also wasn't the time for fucking. She needed rest and care, and she was going to get both. "Go to sleep, Naomi. You have nothing to fear while I'm close."

"That's different."

"What is?"

"Not having to fear when a man is close." Her lashes flickered. "I wish I'd never married him."

I wish the same thing.

"More, I wish I'd never met him. Wish I'd met you first."

I saw you first. I wanted you first.

And, deep inside, didn't he sometimes worry...

Did he take you away, just because I wanted you?

No, no, impossible but...

Her eyes had begun to close, but suddenly, they opened and zeroed right on him. "Ebenezer is an unusual name."

"Yes." He'd thought she was drifting away, and now this question?

"You're the only Ebenezer that I've ever met."

"I prefer Eb." His fingers slid down her cheek.

"Sure you do. It's tougher, stronger. More you."

He leaned over her. "I was named after a heartless bastard. You know him, most people do. The one and only Ebenezer Scrooge." His lips crooked up. "You even called me on it before. *A Christmas Carol*, remember?"

The darkness of her eyes lit up. She smiled. A gorgeous grin that shot straight through him because it was a real smile.

"You aren't serious," she said. Then, immediately, "Please be serious. Please really be named after him and don't let it just be a coincidence."

"I'm dead serious. My mother loved *A Christmas Carol*. I'm Ebenezer, my twin brother is Jacob, and my sister is Marley."

"That's fantastic."

"Really? You try being named after the miser who turned away love."

"But he didn't." Her hand lifted. Pressed to his chest. No, pressed right over his heart. "In the end, he found out what mattered."

"He'd already lost the woman he loved. There was no going back from that." In the old story, Ebenezer had been more concerned with collecting his money.

And I've been focused on vengeance. His whole life, the "eye for an eye" mentality had ruled him.

"You don't know that he lost her completely. There was still time. He got his Christmas when the book ended. Who knows what happened after that?" Her eyes gleamed at him. "I like your name."

"You haven't heard my full name yet."

"What's your full name?" Softer. Sleep clearly pulled at her once again.

"My mom wasn't just a fan of *A Christmas Carol*. She was a hardcore admirer of the author. So Jake and I were also named after him." He paused. "He's Jacob Charles Jones. I'm Ebenezer Dickens Jones."

If possible, those incredible eyes of hers widened even more. "Stop."

"It's true. My brother tells me that I'm a real dick all the time."

Her laughter rang out. Husky and beautiful. He loved that sound. Drank it up greedily.

But then she stopped. Looked around. The laughter had vanished, and no smile lingered on her lips. "I can't believe I'm laughing...*here*."

"Want me to get you out of here? We can go to a hotel. Jeffrey has Henry at the fire station. We can get him later and—"

"Talking to you is kinda taking all my energy. A confession I did not want to make. Like I said, I don't like being helpless in front of you." A whispered admission. "I'll sleep and...then figure things out."

He'd have her another place ready to go before she woke up. "Close your eyes," he told her. "You don't have anything to fear."

"Sure, I do." But she closed her eyes.

"You don't have anything to fear from *me*." And he would protect her from any threat that came her way.

Only once again, she said, "Sure, I do."

His chest tightened. "Naomi?"

"I think you could break me. Because I think...I think I could fall for you. If I'm not careful."

She had not just said those words to him.

He didn't speak. Didn't leave, either. He stayed until her breathing eased into the rhythm of sleep. Made sure she was comfortable, that she didn't immediately wake up, scared.

He didn't like it when she was scared.

I am so fucked.

When Eb was sure that Naomi was resting deeply, only then did he finally slip from the bed. He padded silently from the room. Went back to the small den-slash-kitchen area. Hauled out his phone. Made a quick call. It rang once. Twice.

"You just can't quit me, can you?" Hunter grumbled. Sleep roughened his voice. "Look, I am going to do your digging, if you'd give me a bit—"

"I need help."

"Yeah, I know. Got the previous phone call. But I don't work miracles, so I need time—"

"Hunter," Eb cut through his grousing. "I need you. I need backup on the ground."

"*What's happening?*" Instant alertness.

"So many fucking things. But let's start with this... someone tried to torch Naomi's house last night. With me and Naomi in it."

"What?"

"I have to get a secure place to stay with Naomi, stat. Her place has zero security and feels like a death trap." Probably because it was.

"Can we go back to the torching?"

"I also need to talk with my sister. She's working with the Ice Breakers." Something that had not initially thrilled him, given Marley's past and the pain she'd endured, but he could sure use her ties to the cold case solvers. "I'll have to get my sister to set up a meeting between me and Memphis Camden."

"Uh, why do you want to do that?"

"Because I have to find out if my partner—if Hudson was a serial killer or not."

"Shut the hell up," Hunter fired back. "Wait, for real? You are actually telling me that the dead guy could have been a serial? How the hell did you get to that suspicion? We talked less than five hours ago! You mentioned none of this to me. None. Zilch about any potential serial connection."

"It's been a big night." He glanced back toward the hallway. The bedroom. "I think I was wrong about Naomi."

"You *think* you were wrong? Back up. Is this your mind talking, your heart talking, or your dick talking?"

"Someone is trying to hurt her. That can't—won't—happen on my watch."

"I'm coming down there. Consider me your backup. I'll be there as soon as I can get that jet wheels up."

"She needs protection. She needs help." A low exhale. "She needs me."

"Wait, wait, wait. *Think with your head, man.* You were the woman's executioner."

He flinched. "No."

"Bad choice of words, but you were the one who was going to bring her down. Less than twenty-four hours after arriving, you're shouting her innocence and proclaiming your partner's guilt? Dude. Slow down. Don't get taken in by a beautiful face. I figured you'd be better than this." Hunter cursed. "Yeah, I'll be borrowing Declan's private plane. Definitely. Getting my ass down there ASAP because you clearly need me. Should I call in your brother, too? Maybe he can talk some sense into you."

"Did you miss the house-torching part? Someone is after her."

"Yeah, *you* were after her, like, yesterday! She has enemies because people believe she is a killer!"

He had been after her the day before. Had arrived in town with plans to wreck her world.

And now...

Now he wanted to keep her safe. To make her smile again.

Yeah, okay, I am seriously compromised.

No, compromised probably wasn't the right word.

He finished talking to Hunter. Made more plans. Even hauled out his laptop from the bag he'd snagged with help from his new firefighter buddy, Jeffrey. Then he went back to the little bedroom. Opened the door. He needed to check on Naomi, after all. Make sure she was okay after the seizure.

She slept peacefully. She'd turned on her side. One hand curled under her chin.

He headed for the bed. Not quite a big enough bed for him.

But he still slid onto the mattress. Got right beside her as exhaustion swept through him, too. In order to keep her safe, he had to rest. Not like he could continue running on fumes. And he could have slept on the couch, provided that he didn't mind his ass half hanging off it.

There was also the option of sleeping on the floor...

"Eb..." Naomi rasped his name. Her hand reached out. Curled around him.

Yeah, his ass was staying right there. In bed. With his target.

She's not the target.

He kicked off his shoes. Kept on the rest of his clothes. Settled more comfortably against the bed.

She drifted closer.

"It's okay," he told her. "You're safe."

No, she was not the target, but he might be the one in danger because Eb damn well knew he was becoming obsessed with her.

Chapter Ten

Fatal mistake.

She was in bed with the enemy.

Only, he didn't feel like the enemy.

Naomi's eyes had opened and immediately locked on Eb. Eb who was sleeping right beside her in bed. Eb who had thick, tousled hair, a stubble-covered jaw, and almost ridiculously long eyelashes. He slept beside her, seemingly at total ease, and one of his arms rested around her.

The man was dangerous and intense when he was awake. When he was asleep and all that lethal energy that cloaked him had quieted, he was drop-dead gorgeous. And far too sexy.

It had been six months since Hudson's death and funeral. Six months since she went from a bride to a widow to a murder suspect. She hadn't been involved with anyone in that time. How could she hook up with someone new? The Wicked Widow hadn't exactly attracted a throng of eager admirers.

Not that she'd been interested in anyone. Her body had locked down into what felt like cold storage after her nightmare of a wedding night. In order to get involved with someone new, she'd need to be able to trust the person. She'd made a mistake with Hudson, and Naomi had been terrified that she'd be wrong about a new lover, too.

You had doubts before that terrible night with Hudson. Don't lie to yourself. You thought he was too good to be true. She'd stood in her wedding dress, staring at her reflection in the mirror of her dressing room as guests waited in the chapel, and she'd felt doubt.

Even before Memphis Camden had barged his way into the dressing room, she'd felt doubt.

Hudson had wooed her for a long while. Yep, *woo*. That was how she thought of it now. He hadn't come on too strong, not at first. Not back in Vegas. He'd taken his time. Slowly pulled her in. Hadn't rushed her.

At the time, she'd been grateful that someone wanted to take things slowly. No pressure. No rush. The months had slipped by. He'd continued to be charming. Continued to always seem to know exactly what she wanted even before she knew herself.

With his job—the job he'd first said was some sort of international public relations gig, but later she'd learned had actually been with the freaking Central Intelligence Agency—Hudson had been gone often. Sometimes, he'd vanished for weeks or even months at a time. But he'd always come back. Always picked up their relationship.

Eventually Hudson had told her that he was switching jobs. That he'd be stateside. That he wanted to be with her, forever.

Then had come the engagement. Again, not rushed. They'd moved to Baton Rouge. Found property that would be perfect for her dreams. Planned the wedding.

With every step, she should have been deliriously

happy. She'd finally gotten a partner who swore he loved her more than anything. That he would do anything for her.

It was just that, sometimes, Naomi thought she'd seen cracks. Small flashes of anger. Tense moments. She could have sworn she felt secrets.

Then Memphis had appeared. The personification of rain on her wedding day with his suspicions and gruff voice and his worries. She'd listened to him. Her stomach had knotted.

But she'd still gone through with the ceremony. Why?

Hudson was offering me everything I ever wanted. And she'd thought, surely Memphis had to be wrong.

She'd fallen for a handsome liar. He'd offered her a perfect life on a silver platter, but it had all been a lie. The truth had come out when she was helpless.

No, even moments before that. The truth had come out when Hudson pulled out the knife. When he put it to her throat. When he told her he could do anything he wanted and no one could stop him. When he'd hurt her, driving his fist into her stomach. Not just once. When he'd seemed to enjoy her pain.

When he'd pulled the blade of the knife down her body...

And then the seizure started. She'd been too terrified. Too desperate. The seizure had swept over her, and Hudson had loved the power he had as he watched her be so helpless. He'd even let go of the knife. The better to just relax and enjoy her suffering.

Now she was in bed with another man. One who had saved her. One she knew suspected her of murder. But...

Eb wasn't lying. He wasn't pretending.

For her, he was real. What she saw with him—that was

what she got. Growly, rough, unpolished, suspicious, and fierce. Not perfect. Far from it.

Naomi had discovered she hated perfection.

He got my dog back for me. He got me out of bed when the house was burning. And when she'd been at her absolute most vulnerable, as tremors had wracked her body, he'd held her hand. He'd stayed with her. He'd gotten her help.

He hadn't made her beg, the way the man who'd professed to love her had done.

Her gaze lingered on Eb's handsome face. If only she'd met him first...

But there was no changing the past or erasing the sins that we committed in this world. All we could do was move forward. Speaking of moving forward...

She needed to get out of that bed before she made a very bad mistake. A mistake that might feel so very good.

Sex with Eb.

Nope. She should not. Should not think about it. Fantasize about it. Most definitely, Naomi should not give in to temptation and actually do it.

But I want to. I want Eb.

Time to get out of the bed.

First, though, she needed to slip out from beneath his arm.

"If I don't get to be creepy and watch you sleep, it hardly seems fair for you to watch me." His eyes opened. Totally aware. Completely awake. "Morning, beautiful."

She felt the impact of his stare all the way through her body. Those eyes of his—they stared at her with almost...a possession. No, she had to be wrong about that. Didn't she?

He blinked, and this gaze was just steady. Intense.

I was wrong. "It's not morning." Her voice was too husky. Naomi cleared her throat and tried again. "The light coming in the window tells me that it has to be late afternoon." At least.

His lips kicked into a grin. "Feel better?"

She did. No longer hollowed out and on the verge of collapse. "Thank you." Another clearing of her throat. "For looking after me. You didn't have to do that." She had to get out of the bed. Naomi shot up and away from his warm arm. She was grateful to see that she still wore her clothes. Minus her shoes and socks. When had she lost them? Didn't matter. Naomi scrambled for the side of the bed.

He caught her wrist. "Of course, I had to do it. You think I'm so much of a monster that I'd let you risk death alone?"

"My husband was a monster who watched me and wanted me to beg." There. Done. She was *done* keeping secrets and tiptoeing. Maybe Eb would believe her. Maybe he wouldn't. She'd been dropping details about Hudson and spilling the truth bit by bit. Why not just go all-in? "But you probably think I'm lying about that, don't you? About him being a monster? Surely your friend couldn't be a monster. Except, he was." Naomi tugged on her wrist. "Let me go."

"I'm setting up a meeting with Memphis Camden. I want to know exactly why he suspected Hudson."

Well, she hadn't expected that news. "Excuse me?" She did a double take. "The detective thought that story was bullshit. As far as I know, Clark never even called Memphis!"

Eb sat up in bed. He was still dressed, too. And she found that disappointing. Would it have killed him to take off his shirt before he climbed into bed with her? She didn't think so. And, um, "Why are you in bed with me?"

"I wanted to be close in case you needed me."

That was... "Kind," she whispered.

A furrow appeared between his brows. "There's not a lot that's kind about me."

"I disagree."

The furrow deepened. "Some women would be really pissed that I entered their beds without an invitation."

What if I said you always had an invitation? Her lips clamped together so she would not say those words out loud. Because they would be a mistake. Right? "Some women haven't just had seizures. I appreciate you looking after me."

His gaze burned. His thumb slid over her inner wrist, just along her pulse. Her pulse immediately raced.

She needed to get back on track, stat.

"Naomi."

She liked the way he said her name. All deep and rumbling and sensual.

"Naomi, you *told* the investigating detective about Memphis and his claims—and the guy did nothing?"

As far as she knew, yes, nothing. "Clark said I was making allegations against the dead. Allegations that had no way to be proven."

"Did you tell the DA? The press?" Then Eb shook his head. "No, no press. I would have read about the story if you had."

"The press already had their villain. They were already twisting everything I said or did. What would be the point in giving them more fuel for the fire?"

He let go of her wrist. She sprang away from the bed.

Jaw locking, he rose, too. "Are you keeping more secrets? If so, tell them to me, now."

"What do you want? For me to make some big confession to you right now?" She backed away. She really, really wanted to confess all to him. Wouldn't it feel great to share her burden with someone else? But she was so afraid to make another mistake. "What will you do?" Naomi asked. "What will be your big plan? Hmmm? If I were suddenly to confess to you—to say that Hudson was hurting me. That he pulled out a knife on our wedding night. That he put it to my throat and then dragged it down my body and told me he could do anything he wanted to me. That he punched me in the stomach over and over and laughed when a seizure had me shaking and shuddering on the bed."

All of the color seemed to leave Eb's face. His eyes narrowed to slits of fury. "*What?*"

But she kept speaking, rolling right along feverishly because she almost could not stop right then. "He wanted me to beg, and I was sure that I was going to die. But even as the seizure had my whole body shuddering, I knew that I had to fight back. So maybe..." She licked her lips. "Maybe I grabbed the knife he'd dropped. Is that what you want me to say? Maybe I was able to reach it." Her heart pounded. "What would you do if I told you *all* of this really happened? And that maybe I had to take the knife and stab him? *If* I confessed to stabbing Hudson, what would you do? Would you immediately rush to Detective Anderson and the DA? Would you personally shove me in a cell?"

He stalked toward her. His eyes glittered at her. "Is that what happened?" His hands tightened into hard fists. "Tell me. Tell me the truth."

"What would you do?" Because if he turned on her...

The cops will be back at my door. The detective with the angry eyes who hates me. The DA who wanted to lock me away. She could lose her freedom and her life. All by putting her trust in the wrong person.

Been there, done that before. So maybe she needed to slow down. To put some needed distance between them before she made another mistake. "I have to shower," Naomi said before he could answer her question. "I need to get dressed. I need to find out who torched my house."

He stopped advancing.

"We spend the night together, and you think I'm going to wake up and make some big, dramatic confession?" Naomi let her eyes widen. *Shit. I just did that very thing. Mostly.* "I swear, that detective grilled me once for nearly twenty-four hours straight. I didn't break then or during any of our other marathon interrogation sessions. I kept to my story. I'll repeat it for you now." *Don't you dare slip up just because you're thinking this man is some kind of hero, Naomi! Just because you woke up and felt safe and protected and you thought about having mind-blowing sex with him. Get it together, woman.* "I had a fight with my husband. I left in the middle of the night because I needed air. I went for a long walk with my dog. I got lost outside. The property stretches and stretches and I'm not familiar with everything. Especially in the dark, things get confusing. I got confused. When I finally got back, when I came in the guesthouse..." She looked over at the bed. "I called out for Hudson. He didn't respond. I found him dead on the bed."

"Here's another scenario." Eb remained rooted to the spot. "And it includes the *real* story that I think you just gave me minutes ago. Only that story doesn't include all of those '*maybe*' uses that you were throwing around."

She swallowed the lump in her throat and lifted her chin.

"Hudson was bigger than you. Stronger than you. He had training provided by the government that would mean he knew how to inflict maximum pain. He could cause you so much pain that you would be begging him to stop, and while he was doing that, he would not even leave a mark on you."

A shiver slid over her. "Guessing you had that same training?" But Hudson had left marks on her. Her stomach had bruised from the punches.

"I had more."

She backed up. *Not* what she needed to hear.

"Don't." Low. Rasping. "I will not hurt you, Naomi. You never need to physically fear me."

"I'm going to shower. I'm not running from you." Her chin kicked up even more. "Just trying to get clean." She whirled away.

"Some sins can't be washed away."

His words had her stilling.

"Hudson was bigger than you. Stronger than you. You fought. You were seizing and he wasn't helping, and you were afraid...so you grabbed a knife, and you stabbed him. Maybe your hand jerked. See what I did? I just used the word '*maybe*' for you. Here, let's do it again. *Maybe* you didn't intend to kill him, but you can't control yourself when the seizures hit, can you?"

I did exactly what I intended to do. Her control was back. The temporary weakness or insanity or whatever it had been—that was averted, for the moment. She looked back at Eb. "I am glad he's dead. Take that statement however you want to take it." With those words, she marched into the small bathroom. No dramatic door slamming. Instead, Naomi just closed the door softly behind her. Her gaze slid to the mirror. To her reflection. She stared into her own eyes. Didn't flinch. "I'm glad," she whispered again.

* * *

THE SHOWER HAD TURNED ON. He could hear the water thundering out.

Eb wanted to be in that shower with her. Not going to happen, of course. So what if he'd woken up, aching for her?

Twenty-four hours. He hadn't even been back in her life that long.

She didn't trust him.

She didn't want him to fuck her.

And she doesn't know that I came to this town intending to fuck her over.

If he had his way, she'd never know that particular truth.

* * *

"YOUR TURN."

Eb's shoulders stiffened, and he glanced back. Steam drifted from the open bathroom doorway. Naomi stood there, her body wrapped in a towel. Her wet hair slid around her shoulders. Her cheeks had color, and some of the shadows were gone from beneath her eyes.

Beautiful.

"Figured you'd want to shower, too. And, uh, there is some extra toothpaste by the sink. You can borrow the toothbrush there, too. I opened it. It was a fresh one I'd stocked. I used it, and um...Well, just do whatever you want." She hurried forward and waved behind her toward the open bathroom. "It's all yours."

All yours.

His gaze was on her legs. Those long, sexy legs that he could too easily imagine wrapped around him. Or thrown over his shoulders as he drove as deep into her as he could go. Eb swallowed. Very, very slowly, his gaze rose. Drifted over her. Lingered where the towel had been knotted between her breasts.

I will devour her.

"Eb?"

He didn't say a word. He couldn't. He stalked into the bathroom. Shut the door just as softly as she had done before. Moving by rote, he grabbed the toothbrush and toothpaste. Used it. Grabbed for the faucet in the narrow shower stall. Not warm water. Ice cold because that was what he would need.

Ice. Cold.

His dick shoved hard against the front of his jeans.

*   *   *

THE WAY he'd just looked at her...

Naomi's breath shuddered in and out. She'd forgotten to take fresh clothes into the bathroom with her. She'd been in such a hurry to escape that she'd just gone straight in there with only the clothes on her back. Sure, she could have just put her previous clothes on again. She hadn't. She'd gone with the towel. Maybe she'd wanted to see his reaction.

Eb had looked at her as if he wanted to eat her alive.

As she'd seen that heated look, her nipples had tightened against the soft cloth of the towel. Her sex had quivered. Yep, an actual quiver. And she'd yearned.

But he'd walked right past her. Hadn't said a word. Had gone straight into the bathroom.

When she inched toward the now closed door, she could hear the thunder of the water. Her tongue snaked over her lower lip. Should she ask if he needed anything? Like...

Me?

Do you want me, Eb? Want to have fast, hot sex that sends us both hurtling straight into an unforgettable orgasm? Sex that doesn't mean anything but feels so very good? Sex that lets us forget—for a few precious moments—how incredibly screwed up everything else is? So very tempting.

But, no, she could not do that.

Twenty-four hours...

He'd only been in Baton Rouge with her for less than twenty-four hours.

During that brief time, he'd helped her get her dog back. Saved her from a fire. Held her when she'd been helpless.

Less than twenty-four hours.

Could a whole life change in that time?

She reached for the top of the towel, for the part she'd tucked between her breasts.

The bathroom door opened.

Eb stood there. Filled the doorway with his broad shoulders. Shirt gone. Chest bare. Muscles so tense and hard. And, jeez, how many abs did he have? Like she didn't look at the man and immediately want to lick him.

All over.

Stop it.

"Do you, ah, want something?" Naomi asked carefully. Maybe he'd forgotten his clothes, too? Naomi realized that she didn't hear the thunder of the shower. He'd turned off the water.

His eyes were on her. The gold in his topaz eyes burned.

"You want fresh clothes?" Her voice had gone extra husky.

A negative shake of his head.

"Towels? I, um, think towels are in the bathroom. Some soap is in there, too. Nothing fancy, but—"

"No." Almost guttural.

Okay, this was awkward. Mostly because her gaze kept dropping to his chest. Then back up. Then down again. "What do you want?"

"You."

Her knees almost buckled.

Chapter Eleven

WHAT IN THE HELL WAS HE DOING? WHY WASN'T HE under the icy cold water? Why had he just made that confession?

Oh, right.

Because I fucking want her. I want to rip the towel away. I want to taste every single inch of her, and I want her coming and screaming my name while I'm buried as deep into her as I can go.

Gentlemanly? Nope. Rational? No, not that either.

But honest?

Yes.

"You...want me." Naomi's words were halting.

"Tell me no." That was all she had to do. Say that simple word. One word. Easy.

Her lips parted.

He tensed.

"Yes."

He hadn't heard right.

"Yes," she said again, louder. Stronger. "Yes, I want you,

and it doesn't mean anything. It *won't* mean anything. It's just sex. Just desire. A physical attraction. But I want you so badly. I want—"

He was on her. Kissing her fiercely. Thrusting his tongue past her lips and taking and taking what he wanted. Her fingers curled around his arms. Her nails bit into his skin. She moaned against his mouth, and he greedily drank up the sound.

Want her.

Take her.

He lifted her up. Carried her. Dropped her on the bed and yanked away her towel so that he could stare down at her. See every single inch of her.

Perfection.

Full, round breasts. Tight nipples. Flaring hips. A sex that had been groomed bare. Fucking *delicious.*

He went right for her core. Grabbed her legs, pushed them apart, and feasted. His tongue dipped into her folds as he licked and sucked and worked her until she was moaning and arching wildly for him. Mouth. Tongue. His fingers. He drove her hard toward a release because he wanted to feel her come against his mouth. He wanted her taste on his lips and tongue. And, oh, what a taste. Wild. Spicy. Sensual.

Incredible.

"Eb? Eb!" Her hips surged up against him. "I want you in me! *You! I want you!* But, oh, that feels so good....I-I can't wait, I can't—*Eb!*" Naomi came, quivering.

He lapped her up. Then he eased back. Stared down at her. Saw the rapid rise and fall of her breasts. The flush on her cheeks. The wide eyes that peered back at him.

Mine. Every single inch. Mine.

His wallet was near the bed. He'd tossed it there before crashing in the bed. Without a word, he grabbed it. Took out the condom from inside. In seconds, he'd stripped completely. Had rolled on the condom. Then he climbed onto the bed with her. Crawled over her.

Her hands rose to hold his shoulders. Her gaze collided with his.

She'd said it would mean nothing. Casual sex. Fine. She could say that. To him, it meant everything.

It meant no going back. It meant *taking her*.

"Eb?" The faintest hint of fear. "Don't hurt me."

"*Fucking never*." Then he drove into her. She was tight. So freaking tight. She squeezed him and surrounded him, and he almost lost his mind because she felt too good around him. The sweetest heaven. The hottest hell. Everything he'd ever wanted. *His*.

His hands slammed into the mattress on either side of her as he made sure to keep his weight up and off her. He tried to give her time to adjust to him—

"Don't you *dare* stop!" Her legs locked around him.

Stop? Ha. He pulled back. Drove into her. She urged him on with her moans and the frantic dips and slams of her hips against him. There was no slowing. There was no build-up. There was just a frantic passion. A lust that overtook them both. His right hand flew down to wedge between their bodies. He stroked her clit. Fast and hard. Pressed with his fingers and his thumb and she bucked beneath him when she came.

Orgasm number two.

She didn't shout his name. That would have been fucking fun. Instead, her head turned, and the edge of her teeth rasped over him in a sensual bite.

Fucking fun.

The final thread of his control ripped away. He pounded into her. Felt her muscles clamp so perfectly around him. Felt the aftershocks of her orgasm as he thundered toward his own release. When it hit, he was the one to shout. To bellow her name as he came on the most powerful release of his life.

With the woman he should have never touched.

* * *

THE MAD DRUMMING of her heart slowly eased. Her breathing stopped being so ragged and pant-intensive. Her fingers fluttered over Eb's shoulders. Those, big, powerful shoulders.

His head lifted.

His eyes immediately met hers.

He didn't say a word.

Neither did she.

Slowly, he began to pull out of her.

Her breath hitched. He stilled.

For a moment, she wanted to clamp her legs around him and hold on. But that wasn't the way this scene would work. He probably already regretted what he'd done. She'd gone off like a Fourth of July rocket, coming as soon as he'd put his mouth on her. The orgasm had been incredible. Unbelievable. Until that moment, she'd never responded so completely and quickly to someone.

"Gonna tell me this was a mistake?" His voice was rough. Gravelly.

She held his shoulders. She needed to let go. "Is that what you think it was?"

"I shouldn't have touched you."

Yet one of his hands still curled around her hip. Possessively. She wet her lips. "Then why did you?"

"Because I've wanted you since I saw you dancing in

that fountain. Told you that already." He pulled out completely. Rose to stand beside the bed. He stalked to the bathroom. Shut the door.

Cold, lost, uncertain, she grabbed for the covers. She'd wanted that wild rush. Wanted the thrill of a powerful orgasm but Naomi hadn't counted on the *after*.

The way she'd feel when they were done.

The way she'd ache.

The way she'd still want him.

The way her heart would hurt when he just walked away and left her naked in the bed. Like what they'd done didn't matter. Like she didn't matter. Like—

The bathroom door flew open.

Her chin had tipped down, but now her head whipped back. Her eyes widened as she saw him standing in the doorway. Correction, glaring in the doorway. "Now what the hell am I supposed to do?" Eb demanded.

She rose from the bed. Pulled a sheet with her because she was far too vulnerable in that instance and would not stand naked before him.

"I had you, and I still want you. I had you, and I want to come inside you again and again." A muscle jerked along the side of his jaw. "Am I supposed to act like this didn't happen? That you didn't just squeeze me so tightly with that hot pussy of yours that I nearly lost my mind?"

"I—" Okay. This was intense. He was intense.

And was she supposed to pretend that she hadn't just come harder for him than she ever had in her entire life?

His eyes glittered. More gold than anything else in that moment. Normally, the topaz swirled. Right then, it blazed a truly golden fire.

"Tell me it was a mistake," he dared.

She clutched the sheet tighter. Was that what he

wanted to hear? Too bad. "That was the best orgasm of my life."

He surged toward her. Caught himself. His hands fisted at his sides.

She could see the hunger on his face. The lust. He wasn't unaffected as she'd feared. Wasn't walking away like the sex had meant nothing. Instead, he was just as wrapped up and lost as she was.

That made Naomi feel better. Infinitely so.

She wanted to jump him again. But she was already sinking fast and hard under his spell. She knew a time for a strategic retreat when she saw one. The delicate ache of her inner muscles also told her she needed to slow way down. Someone was out of practice when it came to hot, hard sex. That someone? Her.

"Thank you," she told him sweetly.

His eyes narrowed.

"Now, shall we go and find out who tried to kill us last night? It's sort of important, don't you agree?"

Eb growled. "Fucking you again is important."

She held her breath. For a moment, she thought that he might pull her into his arms again and, heck, yes, she wanted that. She was down to—

"Find the killer. Hell, yeah. That's what we have to do." Now his nostrils flared. "I will fuck you again."

When? She bit back the question.

"But it's not gonna be in this damn guesthouse. Not on this damn bed. We're getting out of here, and we aren't coming back." He spun and stomped into the bathroom.

Her breath shuddered out. She looked down at the sheet. Then over at the bed.

OhmyGod.

She'd just had sex where her husband had been murdered. Eb had just taken her where Hudson had died.

And...

OhmyGod.

She'd been so lost to Eb that she hadn't even cared about where they were.

Chapter Twelve

SHE'D THANKED HIM FOR THE BEST ORGASM OF HER life. A very polite and well-mannered thank you while he'd just wanted to grab her, lift her up in his arms, and thrust hard and deep into her until they both hurtled straight into a mind-blowing, body-shaking release. He'd wanted to fuck her endlessly, and she'd *thanked* him.

His hands gripped the steering wheel.

I also fucked her in what was supposed to be her marriage bed.

Only she'd replaced the mattress...so, not technically the marriage bed but still...

Her husband died in that room. And I fucked her there.

A fucking. A...claiming?

Yeah, maybe he should apologize. Only he didn't exactly feel sorry for what he'd done. More like, he wanted to take her again at the first opportunity.

"Who's a good boy?" Naomi cooed beside him.

His hands gripped the wheel even tighter.

"You deserve all the treats in the world. You are the best boy. The smartest, the bravest. I adore you."

Okay, hell, now he was getting jealous of her freaking *dog*. She kept cooing at Henry, and she'd given the dog a ton of treats since they'd picked him up from the fire station. And the damn dog *was* good, Eb would give him that. Better than good.

Rock star status.

But…

"Could you get back in your seat?" Eb snapped at her. "I'd prefer for us not to have an accident where you wind up decapitated."

She huffed. Patted the dog again as he sat in the backseat, then slowly twisted back around and resettled in the front passenger seat. "How about you drive safely, and I won't get decapitated? Hmmm? How about that?"

He was working on it but… "When your ass keeps rubbing against me, it's fucking distracting." She had a world-class ass.

"Oh, was I doing that?"

Fake innocence. He'd bet his life on it. "Naomi…"

She hummed. "We both agree that Ivan is suspect number one for the arson at my property. Goes without saying."

"You gave me and the cops a bullshit list of your enemies. I need a real list." How could he investigate when she just kept holding back on him?

Now she gasped. Okay, dramatic Naomi was in full effect. Damn if it wasn't almost…cute for some weird-ass reason to him.

"That list was not bullshit!" Naomi declared. "I gave you and the detective an actual, real, honest-to-God list of my enemies."

"You listed Ivan."

"Right. Yes. And he remains at the top of my list. He's a

seriously shady criminal who had tight ties to Hudson. The man stole my dog. Hours after we get my dog back, my house is magically set on fire? Come on, we can both connect those dots."

Magic had nothing to do with it. When they'd picked up Henry, Eb's new firefighter contact, Jeffrey Lee. had let slip that arson was definitely suspected. Surprise, surprise.

"All signs point to Ivan for me," Naomi continued determinedly. "But we can't forget Hudson's cousin Jaxon. He thinks I killed Hudson and am trying to make off with Hudson's money and family assets. The man called me a murderer straight to my face."

Yes, he would be investigating Jaxon. "You also listed me on your list."

"Yes, yes, I did." Just that.

He fired her a quick glance. "I fucked you today."

Her brows shot up. "Like you can't fuck someone and hate them at the same time? I'm pretty sure there is a name for that. It is literally called a hate-fuck. Are you really not up on the lingo?"

He almost slammed on the brakes. "Did you hate-fuck me?"

"I don't hate you at all. Why would you think that?"

He had to ease his grip on the wheel. "We're going to Ivan's bar." He needed to get this conversation on track. *Do not focus on hate-fucks.*

"Figured we were heading to his place. I know this is the road that leads to that destination." Another little hum. "So did you hate-fuck me?"

The woman was driving him crazy. "Did it feel like I hate-fucked you?"

"It felt incredible."

The car lurched a bit to the right. He got it back on track. Immediately.

"I don't want you to hate me," Naomi revealed. Her voice had gone a bit husky.

"I don't." Gritted. And...truth. He did not hate her. Sonofabitch. He was all twisted up. *I don't hate her. I don't.* Maybe he...never had. Shit.

"Good. Then there was no hate-fuck involved." Now she seemed satisfied.

"Naomi..."

"Not too far to go before we get to the bar, huh?" Her voice was way too falsely bright.

She was right, though. They didn't have much longer to go. Ivan's bar had been Eb's intended destination from the moment he'd picked up the dog and Jeffrey had said the investigator called about signs at Naomi's place that pointed to arson. As far as Eb was concerned, yes, Ivan was the most obvious suspect. They'd tangled with the Russian and his men and then, the exact same night, her house got lit up? Nah. Eb didn't believe in coincidences. Especially those that involved near-death experiences.

"Hudson's cousin is convinced I'm a gold-digging murderess. You know, like the rest of the town." Music played lightly from the car's radio. Classic rock. She'd picked the channel and had been singing along every now and then. Despite the fact that she'd had her house torched, been nearly murdered, and had a seizure that scared the hell out of him, Naomi seemed to be in an oddly good mood. "And, expanding on my list of enemies, we have to include Detective Clark Anderson. The man truly can't stand me. Clark wants me tossed into a cell for the rest of my murderous days."

Wasn't that what Eb had wanted, too? So, when had his plan changed?

"I need to thank you."

His head shook. "No, you don't." Where was this coming from? Hadn't he told her not to thank him before? When she was all nice and polite and showed *gratitude* to him, it just made Eb feel like a real sonofabitch because he was lying to her.

I came to town because I was just like everyone else. I thought you were guilty as sin. I wanted you locked away for the rest of your life. Your punishment was my mission.

It...still was. Right? *Right?*

"I don't think you want to hurt me," she said. Her voice had softened even more. Turned thoughtful. "So you don't belong on my list of enemies. I mean, if you wanted to hurt me..." A faint click as she swallowed. "You could have done it while I was helpless."

When she'd been jerking on that couch.

"Instead, you saved me. Thank—"

"Do *not* thank me again." He didn't want her gratitude. Whenever she said *thank you*, it felt like she'd just stabbed a knife into his chest.

Nope, that is what happened to Hudson.

"You don't consider me to be your enemy any longer, do you, Eb?" she asked carefully.

He spun the wheel, got the vehicle off the road, and had them sliding into an empty parking lot. The gas station had long since been shuttered, and dust and dirt flew up in the wake of his sudden turn. He threw his arm along the back of the seat, his fingers skimming her shoulders, and Eb locked his eyes with hers. "Am I *your* enemy?" he asked her. Jealousy heaved and stirred within him. A jealousy he'd been trying to fight but couldn't. "Do you always fuck your enemies?" Because she'd been ticking off names on her list of enemies, and she'd better not be screwing those men.

She'd hooked her seatbelt back once she stopped petting the dog. Now, though, Naomi unhooked it. With her gaze never leaving him, she inched forward. Then confessed, "I haven't fucked anyone since Hudson died."

His back teeth ground together. *You shouldn't have been with him. You should have been with—*

"I am very choosy about who I do and do not fuck. But I'm not asking you for a recap of your previous lovers, so how about we stay in the present, shall we?" She'd painted her lips a slick red. He'd retrieved her makeup from the main house for her. The makeup and her seizure medicine. The den had been a soggy wreck, and the whole house had reeked of smoke.

No way would they be staying there for a while.

And we won't be in the guesthouse, either. Too many painful memories for her there.

She wanted to be in the present. Well, check. Presently, he wanted to fuck her. Right there in the car. There would be enough room in the front seat. He could spread her out or just lift her over his hips while he remained in the driver's seat.

"You don't want to hurt me."

No, he wanted to fuck her until she couldn't move. Taking her at the guesthouse had been a phenomenal mistake. Because there was a fantasy—imagining what sex with her could be like. And then there was reality—knowing just how mind-blowingly good the orgasm would be...and wanting that explosion again and again like an addict who'd just taken his first hit.

"You want to fuck me," she whispered.

Yes.

"I'm not hearing a denial, Ebenezer."

He should unclench his teeth and say something—

"I want to fuck you, too," she confessed. "I wasn't prepared for how strongly I responded to you. Full truth be told, I'm not prepared for you at all."

He was not prepared for the honesty she was giving him.

"I don't really know what to say or do with you. I don't want to mess this up. Whatever *this* is." She motioned between them. "I don't want you to hate me. Because if you hated me while I was all twisted up over you and over what we've done together, that would just make everything a million times worse."

I don't hate you. He finally unlocked his jaw so he could say, "I'm not your enemy." *I'm your lover.*

But sometimes, a lover was an enemy.

Her smile came again. One that lit her eyes. Made her even more gorgeous. Hell. He had to take control of the situation. Stat. "We need to get to Ivan's."

She eased back against her seat. Reached for the seatbelt once more. "Right. Check."

"I want you to stay in the car with Henry when we get there. I'll go in and grill Ivan." It was still late afternoon/early evening. The full crew of wannabe thugs shouldn't be at the place yet. Actually, maybe *no one* would be there, and if that was the case, then Eb might do a wee bit of breaking and entering so he could search Ivan's office.

"Didn't you try to get me to stay in the car once before at Ivan's place?" Naomi batted her lashes. "How did that work?"

Horribly. Hell. "If you're not waiting in the car, then you *stay* with me, every moment, got it?" Yeah, he wasn't really fighting on the stay-in-the-car bit because he would feel better if he had his eyes or his hands on her at every moment.

The better to protect her, of course.

Not because he just liked having her close.

Keep lying to yourself.

"Every moment," she agreed.

He sucked in a breath and got them back on the road. Soon they were pulling into the lot of Ivan's bar. An empty lot. No long line of motorcycles. No music playing.

Nothing but silence waiting for them.

"I have his home address," she told Eb when he killed the engine.

"Of course, you do." Why wouldn't she have a gang leader's home address? This was Naomi, after all.

"You don't have to be all judgy about it. I was getting Henry back." She reached into the rear seat and gave the golden a soft rub on his head. "Either Henry was stashed here, or he was at Ivan's home. I started here at the bar and got lucky when I found you."

She thought she'd been lucky? Oh, so wrong. "I'm searching the bar." While the place was deserted, he'd have the perfect chance to nose around.

"Ohmygosh, *yes*. Let's do it."

Why was he not surprised that she immediately agreed to a B&E?

"I can show you how I got in last night," Naomi offered. "Easy as pie."

"Maybe don't confess to B&Es so quickly. Just for future reference."

"But my confession is just going to make it easier for you. Come on." Just like that, she was out of the car, with her dog padding obediently at her side. Given no choice in the matter, Eb followed. Because, sure, why not commit a little felony with a dog in tow? That was his life now, apparently. No more secret spy biz. Just teaming up with a suspected murderess to break into a Russian gang leader's club. With a grinning Golden Retriever. As you do.

Naomi looked back at him. The sun hit her hair, igniting the highlights hidden in the depths. She smiled. Smiled before committing their B&E.

He caught her arm. "Me first."

Her gaze trapped him.

Dammit. He had to get his shit together. So she'd been an amazing fuck. *Focus.* He huffed out a breath. "I go in first. I'm the one with the gun."

That incredible gaze of hers widened. "You have a gun? Since when?"

"Since five seconds after you jumped out of the car and I took it from the glove box." She hadn't bothered to look back. "Now, *behind me.* You and Henry."

Henry moved behind him. Gazed soulfully and expectantly at Naomi.

She shuffled behind Eb, too.

Good. They all crept to the back of the bar.

"I came in that door," Naomi told him as she poked at his spine. "I can pick the lock for you, if you want."

He glanced back at her, offended.

"What? I'm trying to *help.*" Her voice was a bare whisper.

"I can pick a lock myself." Did she think he had zero skills? Insulting. He advanced, then immediately stopped.

She bumped into him. "Eb?"

No lock picking was going to be required. He was close enough now that he could see the back door hung slightly ajar. Tension immediately gathered between his shoulders.

He gripped the gun in his left hand and slowly pulled the door fully open.

More silence. But…

Henry started to whine.

Immediately, Eb's head whipped back toward the dog and toward Naomi, wanting to make sure that she was all right.

But Henry's gaze wasn't fixed on Naomi. Instead, the Golden Retriever stared hard at the open door. His body had completely tensed.

"This isn't good," Naomi whispered.

No, it wasn't. "Sure I can't get you and the dog to head back to the car?"

"No," Naomi said, voice barely above a breath. "You and I are a team. Teams stick together."

Henry advanced. Bumped against Eb's leg.

"All three of us are a team," Naomi corrected.

Hell. He gave the dog a quick pat. "I'm going in first, buddy." And he did. With his gun up. With his body way too tense with adrenaline as he hunted for danger. The place felt as still and quiet as a tomb around him. A far cry from the way the bar had been the first time he'd visited.

He took a few steps inside. This door had led straight into Ivan's back office—

Sonofabitch.

Henry whined behind him.

"Eb?" Naomi's soft voice. "What's happening—*Oh, my God!*"

Yeah. He slanted a fast glance over his shoulder at her. "Do not touch *anything.*"

Her horrified gaze wasn't on him. Her gaze was on the body sprawled over the floor. Ivan's big body. His blood-soaked body. Blood on him. Blood beneath him. The Russian's body had been beaten to hell and back.

"Eb." She grabbed his arm, hard. "Eb, I think that's my bat."

He'd already seen it. Already thought the same damn thing. Hard to mistake the bat, after all, seeing as how it had her initials on it. *Blood-stained initials.*

He hadn't noticed the initials the first night. It had been too dark. But now, in the office that reeked of blood and violence, light drifted through the window, and he saw the very distinct, white, cursive NR on the barrel of the bat. The white letters were splotched with red. Wet blood.

Naomi scampered forward and bent near the body.

"What in the hell! *Naomi!*" He grabbed her shoulders to pull her back. "What part of '*do not touch anything*' confused you?"

"I'm trying to make sure he's actually dead! He, um, kinda feels warmish."

"His brains are on the floor."

"*OhGod.*" Her fluttering fingers had almost touched said brain matter.

"And I know dead bodies." He'd seen more than his share. "Ivan is gone."

Her fingers still went to Ivan's throat. After a moment, she swallowed and darted back. Her foot kicked the edge of the bat. The blood-stained bat had been used to beat the Russian to death, in his own office.

"We need to get out of here, now," Eb ordered. There would be no searching the scene. There would only be getting the hell out of there and trying to figure out who had used Naomi's bat to beat the gang leader to death.

The last time Eb had seen that bat, *he'd* thrown it into the back of her truck.

Fantastic. My prints are going to be on the murder weapon and so are hers.

Sonofabitch.

"My initials are on the bat because..." Naomi's halting voice. "I...I played high school ball. Was MVP. They called me the home-run queen."

She had a killer swing. Double sonofabitch. "Back out. *Now.*"

They backed out. They didn't touch anything else. Henry was tense and alert, and so the hell was Eb. They went straight for the back door, with him being the last to exit Ivan's office. He covered Naomi's six, looking for threats and evidence. The bar was so quiet. So still. His instincts told him that the killer wasn't inside. *But that doesn't mean he isn't still close by.*

Before he could call out a warning to Naomi, she darted through the open rear door of the bar. Dammit! *What if the killer was waiting?* Alarm surged through him. "Naomi!" He bounded right on her trail.

And Eb saw that, this time, she'd been the one to come to a sudden, dead stop. Naomi had gone statue-still a few feet from the bar's back door. Her hands were in the air. Her dog protectively crouched right in front of her.

"*Freeze!*" At that loud bellow, he understood exactly why Naomi had frozen.

A swarm of armed men and women seemed to explode around Eb and Naomi. Their guns were held tightly in their hands. Their gazes were sharp. Assessing.

The woman leading the group had been the one to blast the loud order to freeze. A woman with short, black hair. Bright green eyes. A slightly pointed chin. And an expression that said if you tested her, she would bring hell your way.

Her green gaze darted over Naomi and locked onto Eb. That green gaze sharpened. Hardened.

"Eb Jones," she barked. "What in the hell are you doing here?"

He still had his gun. He should lower it. Especially considering that he was surrounded.

The woman took an aggressive step forward. She also motioned for some of the armed group members to enter the bar. Two men—both in plain clothes but who moved with a lethal grace that told Eb they had black ops experience— immediately dashed inside the bar.

Eb cleared his throat. How to play this scene? Hmm. He'd try friendly first. Why not? "Hi, Madeline." He flashed a smile and knew that his dimple would wink. The dimple could occasionally be disarming. Though, based on extensive experience, he knew it was very hard to disarm Madeline. "As always, it's a pleasure to see you." It actually was not. Quite the opposite. "FYI, the men you just sent in? I feel I need to warn you that they're going to find a dead body inside the bar."

Naomi glanced back at him in surprise. "You're just going to flat out *tell* her that detail? Announce it as calm-as-you-please?"

Madeline Desalt shook her head. She also holstered her weapon. "He'd damn well better tell me what's happening. Kinda part of the package. After all, he's working for me."

Naomi flinched.

Eb didn't correct Madeline's words. Even though he was not, in fact, still working for Madeline at the CIA. He was too busy trying to figure out why a ground team was swarming a rundown bar in Baton Rouge. Not exactly typical spook behavior.

Madeline's hands went to her hips. "I'm Eb's boss," she added, in case Naomi just couldn't connect the dots. "And you two are in a world of trouble."

Chapter Thirteen

"I TOLD YOU TO STAY OUT OF THIS CASE," MADELINE told Eb as she paced in the small police station at the edge of town. They were currently in one of the interrogation rooms, a tight and narrow space with a long mirror positioned along the left wall.

Eb thought that having him in interrogation was more than a bit of overkill, but, hey, if she wanted to put on a show for the locals, who was he to argue?

She'd flashed some official-looking government paperwork to the police chief and basically taken over the station. The only cop who'd tried to stand up to her had been a very loud and vocal Detective Clark Anderson. But he'd quickly been ordered to stand down by his chief. After all, when the CIA rolled into town, you didn't get to argue with them. You just had to back the hell away or else they would mow right over you.

"I don't remember you saying that, exactly." Eb kept his own voice cool as he continued to recline in the chair near the old, scratched table in the middle of the room. A wobbly table. One leg didn't seem to match up in height to the other three. "You told me that the DA wasn't filing charges against Naomi for the murder of her husband."

"I told you that this case was not related to our work. Not our jurisdiction. Not our wheelhouse."

And, yet...here they all were. Right in the wheelhouse.

"In case you need a translation, when I said all of that? It meant don't get your ass involved." She stopped pacing. Exhaled—fine, she let out a long sigh. Her hair skimmed her jaw as she shook her head. "You were supposed to stay the hell out of things in Baton Rouge."

They'd separated him from Naomi. Something Eb did not like. But he was trying not to show just how much the situation pissed him off. What happened between him and Naomi was their business. No one else's.

"You came down here to prove the widow was guilty as hell, didn't you?" Her hands were on her hips. One of her favorite poses. A pose that was reflected in the one-way mirror near her.

Eb had only glanced briefly toward that mirror once. He wasn't particularly in the mood to see his own reflection. "That was the original plan I had, yes. I think I told you before that I'd handle things when it came to her." When she'd called to tell him that the DA had dropped charges, he'd told Madeline—specifically told her—that he'd be handling Naomi.

So why is Madeline here with a ground team? What is really happening?

Madeline sucked in her cheek. "How is that working out for you? The, uh, handling of things?"

"Got to admit, things are not necessarily going according to plan." His plan had not included him being separated from Naomi. Was she being grilled in another interrogation room? Probably. But who was doing the grilling? A local cop or a trained CIA interrogator?

He still couldn't believe that Naomi's bat had been used to beat the Russian to death. What a clusterfuck.

Madeline strode toward him. She didn't bother pulling out the other chair, though. Instead, she hopped on the edge of the wobbly table. It tilted beneath her weight. Her high-heeled feet swung lazily. "Not according to plan, huh? Then you did not *mean* for the chief suspect's house to nearly go up in flames?" She rocked back and forth, testing the table as it wobbled beneath her and her swinging feet. "The chief here should really spring for some new furniture."

He doubted that the chief gave a flying flip about the wobbly table. With minimal effort, Eb kept his relaxed pose. "Are you asking me if I set fire to Naomi's home?"

"Did you? Did you set the fire so that you could play hero and get her to trust you? Smart move, if so." Admiration entered her voice. "There is no faster way to gain a perp's confidence than to convince the individual that you are a savior. A confidant. A friend." A pause. "Maybe even a lover?" One dark eyebrow quirked.

He smiled at her. He didn't know Madeline's age, and he damn well would never ask. No wrinkle lines gave her away. Not so much as a hint of gray appeared in the darkness of her hair. She was beautiful and smart and had been working for the Agency before he'd ever been recruited. As far as he knew, she hadn't done much field work. Madeline enjoyed manipulating from behind the scenes. She'd been his handler and Hudson's. Sometimes, she'd been their only point of contact in a world that seemed to have gone straight to hell.

She'd always been there when they needed her. She'd

never abandoned them. She'd also never told them the full story about many of their missions. Such was the way of the Agency.

"Did you find the evidence you needed?" Madeline asked him with a bob of her head. "Did you get proof that Hudson's wife is a cold-blooded killer?"

* * *

ICE POURED through her entire body. Naomi stared through the glass. She waited for Eb to throw back his head and laugh at the woman who sat so casually in front of him. If not laughter, a good denial that he'd never intended to prove Naomi was a murderer would have been outstanding.

Instead...

"Still working on it," Eb admitted with a roll of his shoulders.

A roll of his shoulders.

Henry sat on Naomi's right foot. His warm body pressed against her leg.

"But you're gaining her trust?" The woman—*Eb's boss*—pressed. "That's the first step of your master plan?"

The drumming of Naomi's heartbeat seemed terribly loud as it echoed in her ears.

"You don't spill all your secrets to someone if you don't trust them." Eb seemed almost bored with the whole scene. "Isn't that the first thing that the Agency teaches recruits? You have to become anyone necessary in order to get the job done. In this case, I decided to become Naomi's hero. I *played* the hero for her."

She wanted to back away. Or to raise her hands and pound against the thin glass and tell Eb what a bastard he was. Her insides twisted and her heart ached, and she could not believe that she'd actually been letting herself fall for a liar...a second time.

First Hudson.

Now Eb.

What was wrong with her?

Fool me once, shame on you.

Fool me twice...shame on me.

She hated that old saying. Almost as much as she hated Eb in that moment.

"Thought you might like to hear what they had to say," Clark told her. He'd been the one to pull her from holding in the back of the station—that particular holding cell had certainly been familiar to her, almost like a second home—and to haul her to the small observation room. As if she didn't know that plenty of cops and the DA had watched her from this very perch during her marathon sessions with Clark.

Only this time, she wasn't the one sitting at that interrogation room table. The table with one short leg that made the whole thing wobble. She was the one watching.

And getting my heart broken.

No, no, her heart could not be breaking. There was no way that she was in love with Eb. Not so soon. Absurd. She'd just—she'd fallen into his web. Not fallen *for* him. A huge difference. She hurt this way because she didn't like being played for a fool.

I had sex with him. She'd trusted him enough for sex. The best sex of her life. And he'd been playing her the entire time.

"You real sure you were with that man every moment, Naomi? You absolutely sure you had eyes on him at all times?"

"I told you already." She had said this before, but she'd

say it again. "I had a seizure last night after the fire. Eb insisted that I go to the hospital. When I returned to the guesthouse, Eb stayed with me. He was still with me when I woke up." *When we had insane sex.* "He was with me when we found Ivan's body. We went in the bar together." Eb was her alibi. She was his.

"But you had to sleep, didn't you?"

Her eyes were on Eb. She wanted to hear what he had to say. Hard to do with Clark chattering away in her ear. "Yes, I had to sleep."

"How do you know that he didn't sneak away while your eyes were closed?"

"Sneak away and beat Ivan to death with a bat?" She didn't buy it. "Eb hardly seems the type to do that."

"You just never know about someone, do you?" His shoulder brushed against her arm. "Will he alibi you the way you just alibied him? Or will he turn on you?"

He's already turned on me. The truth was that he'd been against her from the very first moment, and she just hadn't realized it. No, no, unfair. She'd suspected the truth. From the very first moment. After all, he'd been Hudson's partner. But Eb had said he didn't hate her...

Liar, liar. "Of course, he won't turn on me." Now she slanted a glance at a watchful Clark. "How many times do I have to tell you? I'm not a murderer."

"Pretty sure your initials are on the bat that was used to beat Ivan Sokolov to death."

"Huh. How about that?"

* * *

Madeline's feet swung lazily. "Just how hard are you working on it?"

He stared back at her. "Why are you in town?"

"Business."

"What kind of business?"

Her gaze slid to the one-way mirror. She smiled at her reflection. "The kind that is confidential."

Sonofafuckingbitch.

His teeth snapped together, and in an instant, he was on his feet. "You didn't." He spun for the one-way glass. The stupid fucking mirror. His furious expression glared back at him. "*Naomi!*"

She was there, just beyond the glass, he knew it. Knew it with absolute, soul-destroying clarity. His own boss had just set him the hell up. He surged straight for the glass. Could imagine that he saw her behind it. Could all but feel her pain reaching out to him. "Naomi!"

Madeline had been talking plenty, but the instant the conversation turned to CIA matters, she'd clammed up. Only one reason for her to do that…

The room is not secure. Someone else is watching.

His sinking heart told him exactly who that someone was.

* * *

"I THINK that's our cue to leave." Clark's hand curled around Naomi's shoulder.

Henry growled.

Clark's hold tightened. "Get the dog to settle down."

"Henry is always settled. He just doesn't like it when hands are put on me. Got to confess, I don't like it, either." Her gaze never left the glass. Or rather, never left what was right behind the glass. Eb. A furious, glaring, breathing-too-hard Eb.

He'd shouted her name.

She'd flinched.

Clark jerked his hand away from her. "It's time for you to go. You've been wanting to bust out of this station ever since we dragged you in. Can't believe you aren't running for the door now that I gave you the all clear."

She wouldn't run. She'd walk out nice and slowly. With her dog at her side. "Will there be a throng of local reporters waiting outside the station? Will they scream questions at me? Or has the CIA worked their magic and convinced you and your chief to keep all this quiet?" Naomi would like to be properly prepared for whatever new, fun adventure waited.

"Guess you'll find out when you go outside."

"*Naomi!*" Eb shouted her name again.

She released a long breath. A breath that she hadn't realized she'd been holding. "I don't have a car. My truck is still out at my property." Eb had been the one to drive them to the bar.

"One of the uniforms will give you a ride back to your place."

Great. Fabulous. A cruise in a patrol car. "I'll just call a ride, but thanks for the offer. I'll use one of those apps." She forced her gaze off Eb. "Come on, Henry."

He walked by her side as they exited that little room.

"Oh, something you might want to know!" Clark called out.

Correction, they'd almost exited that little room. At the door and at Clark's quick words, she glanced back.

Clark had shoved his hands into the pockets of his blue pants. "You probably want to be glad that Ivan is dead."

Her lips pressed together. Was this another trick? She was so tired of the games. Of the cops always testing her to see if she'd slip up and make a mistake. "I don't think you're supposed to be glad when people die. Bad form. Bad karma. Bad something."

"Yeah, well, in this case, like I said *you* probably want to be glad. Because, see, we found out that he'd put a hit out on you."

She whirled to fully face the detective. "Excuse me?"

"A hit. On you. Ivan did it late last night. Found the texts on his phone when we were collecting evidence today."

When they'd been collecting evidence and just leaving her in holding for ages.

He sniffed. "But, seeing as how dead people can't pay for hits...probably a good thing for you that he's gone, am I right?"

Not necessarily. "Does the hitman know that Ivan is dead?"

He rocked onto the balls of his feet. "Guess you'd better hope so, huh?" The words were a taunt and a cold smile tipped up the edges of his lips.

She had to snap her gaping mouth closed. Then, "You are a terrible cop. You get that, don't you? Like, horrible at this job. You don't tell grieving widows that hits are on them and that they'd just better go out and...hope for the best."

His thick brows beetled. "You're not a grieving widow."

"And you're not hoping for the best." Her mind spun. "Did the hitman have anything to do with my burning home? Am I walking straight into danger when I leave here?" In other words, did she have a giant target painted on her back? Sure felt that way to Naomi.

"The lady in there with your new boyfriend said she'd take care of the hitman."

The lady who knew Eb so well. His boss.

Naomi had recognized her, of course, because the woman had also been at Hudson's funeral. Back then, she'd introduced herself only as Madeline. They'd shaken hands. Madeline's fingers had been so cold, and she'd looked at Naomi the same way everyone else had. As if she'd already judged Naomi and found her guilty.

Naomi had known Madeline was connected to the CIA. She hadn't asked questions, had just made a point to stay away from Madeline because the last thing she'd wanted to do was attract more attention from that particular direction.

And, now, Madeline had appeared again. At a murder scene.

Naomi's gaze darted beyond Clark to the one-way mirror. Madeline stood behind Eb. The other woman put her hand on his shoulder. Eb immediately turned toward her.

Naomi swallowed. Her shoulders straightened.

It felt as if Eb had carved her heart right out of her chest. But Naomi would be damned if she let him see her pain. Determination poured through her veins. She wasn't going to run away. Lick her wounds. Sob and be broken. Oh, hell, no. She hadn't broken when everyone in town called her a killer.

She wouldn't break just because one more person thought she was guilty. Or because that one person had lied, betrayed, and seduced her.

He told me to say no. I didn't. I did have the best orgasm of my life.

Time to confront the treacherous, amazing-orgasm-giving bastard. Time to show him that she would not be broken. Not by him. Not by anyone. She tapped her thigh. "Let's go, Henry."

Henry was only too happy to ditch the detective with her.

"Don't worry about seeing me out," she tossed over her shoulder. "I more than know my way around this place." Oh, she definitely did. Only she wasn't going out...

Instead, Naomi marched down the hallway.

Took a left.

Then another turn.

And...*Hello, destination.*

"You can't go in there!" A shout erupted from behind her. "Stop!"

Well, if she shouldn't be going in, then the door should be blocked. It wasn't blocked. So...

Naomi threw open the door. Perhaps she threw it open a wee bit too hard because it slammed into the wall and bounced back toward her. She hurriedly raised a hand to halt its progress before it could fly right at her, then Naomi shoved the door again, only less hard this time. Less ragey.

Eb whirled toward her. His eyes widened. First with alarm, then with relief.

What a world-class liar.

It takes one to know one.

He rushed toward her. Staggered to a stop inches away. "Naomi!" His hands lifted, but he didn't touch her. Caught himself just in time. "I was afraid you'd seen..." His words trailed away.

Henry slipped past her and bumped into Eb. Rubbed against him. She almost called her beloved dog a traitor, but, no, she held that back. "Afraid I'd seen what?" Naomi asked, all innocence. "Eb, I've been looking for you."

Relief definitely flashed in his eyes. Then his hands reached for her. He pulled her against him. The stupid electricity surged through her veins. So much for that attraction dying. Even knowing what his real intentions were with her, the physical reaction Naomi had to him was the same.

Well, not quite the same. The electricity was there.

But it also felt as if her heart was shattering.

Dammit. Fine. So you could fall for a person far too quickly. One of her many mistakes.

"Naomi!" Clark thundered. "You can't be in here!"

She heaved a sigh. "I came for my ride." Making sure her expression was controlled, Naomi eased away from Eb. Her brows lifted. "After we were, uh, detained at Ivan's bar, I was driven here in the back of a patrol car." She rose onto her tiptoes and peered around him—at the watchful Madeline. "But I think your connected friend let you drive your own vehicle to the station, right, Eb? Nice to have perks, huh?"

Madeline pursed her lips.

Naomi glanced back at Eb. "You're my ride or die." *Emphasis on the die.* "Will you take me back to the guesthouse?"

He opened his mouth to respond.

"Are you done interrogating the suspect so quickly, Detective Anderson?" Madeline asked, voice brisk. "Thought you'd be busy longer."

Ah, so Madeline had been involved in making sure Naomi knew Eb was just using her. Such a fun setup. Was she supposed to be grateful to the other woman for ripping away the blinders? Was she supposed to be a beaten ball of mush? What was the end game?

"We're not going back to the guesthouse," Eb told Naomi. "I have a safer place for you."

Safer, hmm? Henry had backed away from Eb. Come to her side. She gave him a little pat even as she said, "Good. I need a safer place." And an actual hero on her side. "Especially with the hitman out there."

"Hitman?" Eb seemed to choke. "What hitman?"

She craned around him once more. "Didn't you tell him?"

Madeline blinked.

Naomi jerked a thumb over her shoulder in the detective's direction. She could practically feel Clark breathing down her neck. "My buddy informed me that Ivan the Terrible placed a hit on my head."

"I am *not* your buddy," Clark denied. "Not. I am not your friend. I am not your buddy. I am not—"

"It's cool, buddy." She smiled at Madeline. "He also said that you would be taking care of the hitman for me."

"*What hitman?*" Eb's voice had gone lethally soft.

"Again, the one Ivan hired to kill me." Wasn't this obvious? Eb really seemed to have trouble following along. "The cops found info about the hit on Ivan's phone. Seems Ivan was super pissed after our visit, and he called for an end to my life. Some people just can't handle their emotions well. They explode. Attack." She felt like doing some attacking, but Naomi was holding tightly to her control.

"Ivan put out the hit. Yet Ivan is the one who died." Madeline's heels tapped on the floor as she closed in on Naomi. "Funny how that worked out."

"Hilarious." She wanted out of there. She wanted away from Madeline. She wanted away from Eb.

No, she wanted Eb to pull her close. To hold her and tell her that he'd been lying—lying to Madeline. *Not to me. I don't want him to be lying to me.* She wanted him to say that he didn't trust Madeline. That he'd been playing a role in front of the agent. As impossible as it was, Naomi wanted...

I want him to be on my side. I want, for once, for

someone to actually be on my side. Was that asking for too much? She didn't think so.

Henry rubbed his head against her thigh. Not an alarmed motion. Soothing. Comforting.

Her fingers stroked lightly over him. Okay, so she did have someone on her side. "I didn't kill Ivan." Just so everyone could be clear. "Eb didn't kill Ivan."

His jaw hardened.

"But whoever set the fire at my place could have. It would have been easy enough to set the fire, then grab the bat from the back of my truck. While we were all scrambling at my place, the arsonist could have gone to Ivan's bar. Slipped inside. And took some swings." Her words came out all flat and calm. Pretty amazing given the way her insides were twisting and heaving.

"Interesting." Madeline tapped her chin. "Do you think this mystery arsonist is the same person who killed your husband all of those months ago?"

"Certainly a possibility." A cool retort.

"Anything is possible in this world," Madeline agreed.

She thinks I'm guilty too. Must be really hard to be so certain that another person was a killer, but to have zero hard evidence. Naomi was just so—*done.* "Did you know he was a psychopath?" Naomi asked, her voice still just as calm as could be. "Did you know it all along? I mean, what— you're the boss, isn't that correct? Hudson's boss? Eb's boss? So maybe you knew. Maybe you knew that Hudson was a twisted killer, and you didn't care because he was your weapon. *Your* killer. You aimed him, you pointed him, and you got him to take out anyone in your way."

All traces of mild amusement fled Madeline's face. She bounded forward. Grabbed Naomi's hand and jerked her close.

A hard growl filled the room.

Actually, two growls. One from Henry. Sweet Henry.

The other from Eb.

Madeline immediately let go of Naomi. Blinked. A calm mask slid over her features. "Detective..." She slanted a glance toward Clark. "You need to get out of here. Shut the door. Make sure we are not disturbed."

"But—" Clark began.

"And no fucking watching from the room next door. I think we've had more than enough of that, don't you?" She shooed with her hands. "Go."

Grumbling, swearing, he did.

Even as the door shut behind him, Madeline pulled out her phone and made a quick call. Into the phone, she barked, "Get eyes on the detective. No one sees or hears what is happening in this room. Make certain we are secure." She hung up. Slapped the phone down on the table. Madeline rolled back her shoulders. "I hate dealing with locals. Always such a pain in my ass." She marched toward the one-way mirror. Squinted.

Why was she squinting? Naomi was pretty sure there was no way to see through the glass, at least, not from this room. "I'd like to know if a hitman is on my trail. Then I'd like to know if you knew Hudson was a psychotic killer. Two very important points."

Eb growled again. "I want to know about those points, as well."

"Simple questions," Naomi continued determinedly without glancing his way. Her focus remained on Madeline. "You can answer them with a yes or with a no."

Madeline spun toward her. Said nothing. Did that count as a maybe response? Or just a general *fuck you*?

"Are you going to respond?" Naomi pushed.

"Did you kill Hudson?" Madeline asked. "You confess first, then it can be my turn."

Yep. She did not like this woman. Fact established.

"I'm getting Naomi to a safe house," Eb said. "She's the one in danger. She's the one I'm protecting."

"Oh?" Madeline's delicate brows climbed. "And here I thought she was the one you were going to send to jail. You'll have to excuse my confusion." Her gaze was considering as it swept over Naomi. "Must have been some, ah, intense get-to-know-you session that you and Eb have recently shared. I am dying of curiosity. How do you get men so wrapped up in you?"

"My magic vagina," Naomi returned without missing a beat.

Eb choked.

Madeline's jaw almost hit the floor.

"Or maybe—just maybe, and go with me on this...*I'm not guilty of murder!* Maybe Eb is considering that truth. Maybe the fact that some psycho set my house on fire, stole my bat, and used it to beat a Russian gang member to death makes Eb feel like he could have been wrong about me." All of those factors had better make the man reconsider. "As far as the safe house is concerned..." She honestly did not hate the idea. Because staying in the guesthouse again? Yeah, no. She'd prefer the safe house, thanks so much. "I'm in." He could give her the address, and she'd find a way to get to the location.

"I expected more of an argument," Eb muttered.

"Then you expected the wrong thing. Tell me the house is ready right now." The sooner she got there, the better. Though Eb could find his own place to stay. Either he was on her side or he needed to get the hell away.

He nodded. "I have a friend who has already arranged things for us." He took her hand.

Very deliberately, she tugged her hand away from him. A friend, huh? Wasn't she staring at his *friend*? "I think your friend is here. She's standing a few feet away from you."

"Let's cut through the BS."

"I would love to do that. Grand idea."

He swallowed. "You heard everything I said, didn't you?"

"I heard. I saw. Pretty sure that was her plan." *Do not dare shatter in front of him.* "And your plan—just so we are all on the same page—was to get my big, bad confession. You were even willing to seduce it out of me, hmm? Talk about taking one for the team."

"*Eb!*" Madeline's sharp voice.

His expression turned stark. No, wrong word. Savage. "You think that's what I did?"

"I know it. I know—"

"Yes, there's a hit on you." Madeline pushed between them. Faced Naomi with blazing green eyes. "And I'm the hitman." She yanked out her gun. Aimed it right at Naomi. "Guess what? Bang. You're dead."

Chapter Fourteen

Eb grabbed the gun in a blink and snatched it right from Madeline's fingers. "What in the hell are you doing?" He quickly positioned his body right in front of Naomi's. "That isn't funny."

"Good. Because I'm not laughing. Stop this bullshit lover's quarrel and focus." Madeline grabbed for her gun.

He didn't let it go.

Her brows shot up. "Eb?" She tugged on the weapon. "I'm giving you an order. Release the gun."

"Did you forget?" A silky reply. "I don't take orders from you or from anyone else at the Agency. Not any longer. *And you don't ever fucking aim a gun at her.*" That shit had not been funny. *Bang. You're dead.* What. The. Fuck?

Half of Madeline's mouth kicked into a smile. "Ah. I see that you've fallen to the same affliction that took Hudson. Be careful. You might wake up with a knife in your chest."

Okay, now he was really pissed the hell off. *Naomi knows that I lied to her. She knows that I came here to get her locked away.* Shit, shit. Talk about a clusterfuck. He should have remembered just how good Madeline was at manipulation. His old boss probably thought that seeing a fresh betrayal might lead Naomi to crack.

Only...

Eb glanced over his shoulder.

Naomi stared back at him with dry eyes and a lifted chin. Grim determination—and a quiet fury—cloaked her. She was not a woman about to crack. Not even close.

A rumble came from Henry.

His gaze dropped to the dog. Those golden eyes of Henry's didn't seem particularly warm in that moment.

"He doesn't like you anymore," Naomi informed him way too enthusiastically. "It's a feeling he and I both share."

Sonofabitch. The dog was mad at him, too? But he liked that dog! "Let me explain."

"Give me back my damn gun!" Madeline tugged harder. "It's not loaded! I took the bullets out before I came into interrogation. After that agent got his ass shot that time in Boston, with his own weapon, you know the rule is to keep bullets *out* of our sessions!"

He was well acquainted with the rule.

He let the gun go.

She shoved it back into her holster. Looked disgruntled.

What the hell ever. He was more than a bit disgruntled, too. "That *bang* bullshit was ridiculous."

"I was trying to refocus you two. The fact that a hit was placed is the big deal, don't you think? Not the BS between you two?"

The BS between him and Naomi was important. To him. *I need to get Naomi alone. I have to explain.*

Except, explain what? That he had planned to trick her? Maybe even seduce her if it got him what he wanted?

"Ivan had become problematic," Madeline suddenly

announced. "With Hudson's death, he stopped cooperating with the Agency. Started being far too secretive. I suspected something big might be in the works with some of his old partners—Bratva still in Russia. So I had some tech guys piggybacking on his communications. When I received word about the hit on Naomi, I stepped in. The Agency was the one responding to Ivan, not the jerk he was actually trying to reach. Then I assembled a team, hauled butt down here to make certain Naomi kept breathing—you're welcome for that, by the way, Naomi. Only what did I discover? You two, standing over the dead man. And her initials on the bloody baseball bat."

"FYI, it's a softball bat, not a baseball bat." Naomi cleared her throat. "And we weren't standing over him. We were outside his bar. And the bat was stolen. So, there's all that."

Madeline huffed out a breath. "I *watched* you enter the bar from my vantage point in the woods. My team was in the process of approaching the perimeter when you two sashayed up."

His shoulders tensed. "I damn well did not sashay." He'd approached carefully and cautiously.

Madeline rolled her eyes. "Please. You took a *dog* to a crime scene. Hello, amateur hour. And to think, I once called you the best of the best. Now this. How the mighty have fallen. Just so you know, your performance reflects poorly on me."

Did he give a flying flip? "Didn't know it was a crime scene at the time," he pointed out grimly. But, yeah, Henry had been watching his six. So what? The dog was damn good at sensing threats.

"You went in, and you found the body."

"Right." From Naomi. He could practically feel her

simmering. With anger. With pain? "We found the body," Naomi confirmed. "As in, we didn't kill Ivan. You know that. We know that. Inform Detective Anderson, then everyone will know. And I can leave. Get to this promised safe house and figure out a life plan for myself."

He reached back and curled his fingers around her wrist because he didn't want her rushing away. *Can't let her get away from me. I have to explain—*

What? The truth? He had to explain the truth to her?

Unfortunately, the truth was a whole lot more complicated than him just lying to her.

"I can't tell Detective Anderson that you're innocent. I don't know one hundred percent that you are. Could be that you are just a really fine actress," Madeline mused. "Maybe you snuck away from Eb and you went to the bar and you swung that bat—one that happens to have your initials engraved on it, by the way—"

"Well aware," Naomi muttered. "Why does everyone keep harping on that fact? Can't we focus on the part where I said it was a *stolen* bat?"

"You swung the bat, and you killed the man who'd taken your dog." Madeline's head cocked as she peered down at Henry. "He's quite a beautiful dog, by the way."

Henry winked at her.

Deliberate? Random?

Madeline smiled at the dog.

Eb locked his jaw. "Naomi didn't sneak away. She had a seizure after the fire."

Madeline's gaze remained on the dog. "Service dog." A nod. "You're worth your weight in gold, aren't you, boy?"

"She was wiped out after the seizure," he continued through clenched teeth. "Naomi slept when she got back to the guesthouse. She didn't go out and beat a Russian criminal to death."

"She slept for every moment?" Madeline seemed doubting as her gaze slowly rose to crash with Eb's. "I think it's possible that—with her in one room and you in the other —she could have crept away without you realizing what she'd done. You need to give her more credit. Since Hudson's death and the DA's absolute refusal to prosecute, I have been doing a deeper dive into her past."

"I'm right here," Naomi snapped. "Stop talking over me."

Madeline fired him a sharp smile. "If you try hard enough and you happen to know just the right people, you can unseal all sorts of old documents. You can also get people to share details that were supposed to remain quiet when you flash official-looking government ID." She put her hands on her hips. Ah, the favorite pose again. Madeline stepped to the right. The better to see Naomi. "There is more to you than meets the eye, isn't there, Naomi? Just how old were you the first time you killed a man?"

What in the hell kind of question was that? *"She didn't creep away. I was in the same bed with her the entire time. I would have noticed her absence. Naomi didn't kill Ivan."*

Madeline didn't look shocked. More like... disappointed? But she nodded. "The same affliction that plagued Hudson." A soft sigh. "Be careful, Eb. I really don't want to lose two agents."

Fuck this. "Was Hudson a killer?" *Don't think about what she said regarding Naomi's past. Not now.*

"Ah, come on. Don't play the faked shocked role with me. This is the CIA." Madeline's gaze flickered toward the one-way mirror. "We're all killers." Low. Mocking.

There was a difference between cold-blooded murder

and stopping someone who was about to detonate a bomb and kill dozens of people. Or stopping someone who was running at you with a freaking machine gun as he fired wildly and took out innocents in a crowd—

"Tell yourself whatever you have to in order to sleep through the night," Madeline added. "But at its core, you know the job. You know agents have to do things that push them to the edge. And sometimes, beyond that edge. It takes a certain personality type to handle the job. Otherwise, guilt would eat you alive." Her gaze flickered over him. Then shifted toward Naomi. "Every employee at the Agency is given a personality assessment. A deep psychological analysis. We have to make sure that people are in the positions that fit their individual talents."

"Yeah." Annoyed, from Naomi. "Was Hudson's individual talent his ability to kill women? Because I've been told by someone with a pretty damn good bit of knowledge about killers that he did, indeed, have a talent for—"

"Memphis Camden is wonderful at tracking down runaway criminals," Madeline cut in to say. "He's got a knack for understanding the dark motivations of killers, but he is far from infallible."

Eb sucked in a deep breath. "Memphis came to you. He told you about his suspicions."

She tipped her head forward. "Memphis came to me. *After* Hudson's murder." A quiet admission. "But I informed him that he didn't have a full picture of Hudson. Or of what he thought Hudson was doing with the, ah, international victims, that Memphis had compiled." A shake of her head. "One person's victim is another's monster who must be stopped. Things are not black and white, and

Memphis should have realized that much, much sooner. Especially with his own past."

Shit. Eb's heart slammed into his chest. "They were sanctioned kills." The international victims that Memphis had tried to link to Hudson hadn't been part of a serial killer's twisted bloodbath. They'd been targets that the CIA had wanted eliminated. So Hudson had eliminated them.

Madeline stared back at him. Not confirming. Not denying. Just as the silence stretched a bit too long, she finally said, "I think we've shared enough in this police station, don't you? Let's head to a different location." A quiet clearing of her throat. "Memphis was made to see the error of his profile regarding Hudson. Memphis is not, after all, a professional when it comes to creating profiles on killers." A wave of her hand toward the one-way mirror. "Memphis actually had told his story to Detective Anderson. A very inconvenient tale. I closed down that line of investigation because there are some things that my bosses at the CIA refuse to be allowed public."

Damn. Hudson had definitely killed some of those women, but it seemed that he'd done it under orders from the CIA?

"Don't look so judgmental, Eb," she chided. "You've had similar orders. You know evil comes in all shapes and sizes."

His back teeth ground together. The people he'd taken out had been the worst of the worst—and they'd all been moments away from destroying innocent lives. Sick, sadistic torturers who—

Naomi called Hudson sadistic. Twisted.

And now she probably thinks I'm exactly like him.

"If it's any consolation to you, Hudson didn't kill the girl from his teenage years. Memphis was wrong about that situation. Hudson loved Mary and mourned her for years." Madeline's tone was brisk. "The real killer from that time period was eliminated ages ago. *By Hudson.* Now, as I said, it's time to leave this station. Any other reveals will have to wait. Or rather, just not happen at all. Naomi, frankly, you don't have clearance for more. And, Eb, seeing as how you just reminded me moments ago that you no longer work for me...well, you don't have clearance, either. It's the end of the road for you both. As far as CIA intel is concerned, that is."

He didn't need clearance. He had shady-ass friends like Hunter and Declan who would help him retrieve the information he needed.

"The CIA will be heading up the investigation into Ivan's murder," Madeline announced. "The locals will understand that we are in charge."

"Uh, yeah, the CIA *has* no law enforcement function," he reminded her because this was absolute bullshit, and he wasn't some deluded local cop to fall into line just because some government official intimidated him. "Our job is to focus on intelligence gathering."

"Right." She winked at him.

"We only do domestic intel collection on a limited basis." An extremely limited basis. "Our primary work is international." That was why he'd bounced from country to country and why his ability to pick up new languages had been so important to the CIA. "You don't have the power to take over this case. Even Detective Anderson will realize that."

"Ivan Sokolov was an international criminal. Wanted in four countries. He had valuable intel to offer to us, particularly regarding organized crime, arms deals, narcotics, and even terrorism. I can assure you, his murder—

correction, his assassination—falls within our jurisdiction. A call to the governor of Louisiana will make sure that he has my back on this."

Yeah, Eb was sure the governor would back her up. The CIA always got backing.

"If you should change your mind and want your old job back, then perhaps I will be able to share additional intel with you, but until then..." A shrug of her delicate shoulders. "How about you stay away from baseball bats—sorry, softball bats? And you be very, very careful with the company you keep." Her gaze darted to Naomi. Lingered. "Because some people can just be absolutely killer."

* * *

THERE WASN'T a crowd waiting outside. The soon-to-be-setting sun was bright. Blaring. And when Naomi left the police station, she wasn't immediately greeted by shouting reporters.

So Ivan's murder—and her link to him—hadn't been shared by the cops yet. Or by Eb's CIA buddies. Great to know.

She marched toward the sidewalk with Henry close to her side.

Eb wrapped his hand around her shoulder. "My car is this way."

"Fantastic. Go jump into it. I'll message a driver and find my own way home." Or she could find her own hotel. No, scratch that—she didn't have enough money for a good hotel room. *Let's circle back to the safe house idea...*If Eb would cough up the address for the place, she'd get there on her own.

His hold tightened on her. "I'm not letting you go."

"You don't have me." Anger broke free, for just a moment, as she whirled toward him. Back in that interrogation room, as she'd listened to Madeline spill details that had made her very bones seem to shatter, Naomi had been shell-shocked. She'd gone dead silent at times, something not like her at all.

But it's not every single day that you learn your husband was a killer for the CIA.

And your new lover? He just happens to kill for them, too.

Her new lover was a killer. And a liar. And he'd hurt her. Made her start to believe in heroes, damn him. "You sonofabitch." Low. Her whole body quivered. "You fucked me."

"We fucked each other." He leaned in close. "And it was the best fucking of my life." He'd slapped sunglasses on his face, so she couldn't read the expression in his eyes, but that jaw of his was tightly clenched. "We're not having this fight right here."

Uh, seemed to her that they were. Right there. Right then.

"They're watching us. You really think Madeline's interrogation ended the moment we walked out of that room? She thinks one of us killed Ivan. Or maybe she thinks we did it together."

"Because you're afflicted?" Naomi asked, voice sweet. "You and Hudson are suffering from the same affliction?" How freaking insulting had that been? *I am not an affliction.* She really, really did not like Madeline. At all.

"She thinks I might have helped you kill Ivan because she believes I'm just as obsessed with you as Hudson ever was. When the truth is that *I* saw you first and you should have been mine."

Shock rolled through her. What? "I'm not a *thing*, Eb. You don't get to see me and call dibs. So how about this? You stay the hell away from me. Just get away." She put several important steps between them.

He shook his head. "That's what she wants. Basic divide and conquer. The CIA uses that technique all the time with suspects. It's why she had you in that observation room so you could hear us talking. I should have realized what was at play sooner." His shoulders squared. "Get in the car with me, and I'll explain everything, I promise."

What was his promise worth? "Better idea," she tossed out. "Get in the car by yourself. And drive away. Again, by yourself. I have other plans." She turned on her heel and began marching forward. Her phone was in her bag. They'd given her the bag back before she left the station. It had been taken by the cops and searched but she had it now. The bag and her phone. She'd use one of the apps on her phone and get a driver to come and pick her up. She did not need Eb. Or his safe house. The sooner she was away from him, the better. Then she'd be able to think more clearly. Maybe breathe without feeling like a weight was on her chest. "I'll find my own way home."

"Don't go back to the guesthouse."

"Go screw yourself," she suggested without looking back.

But the pad of his steps told her that Eb wasn't taking her helpful advice.

Fumbling, she pulled out her phone and began tapping on the screen.

"Madeline made sure they took your phone so that she could have access to your email and your texts and everything else you have on the device."

Now she stopped and peered back at him. "The CIA just bugged me?"

"It's a whole lot more complex than them bugging you. FYI, they did the same thing to my phone."

"That's not legal." Talk about a major invasion.

"Yeah, that's the CIA. Ivan is apparently a BFD so they will go balls to the walls on this."

Her eyes narrowed.

"Big Fucking Deal—"

"I *know* what a BFD is."

"Right. He's a big deal to the CIA. Or else a whole ground crew wouldn't be in your town right now. They swarmed the bar. Only someone beat them to Ivan. That someone is now going to be hunted by a very elite team."

"A team you belonged to. Until you...what? Quit? And decided to go all vigilante because you wanted to bring me down?" The anger within her quaked again. She stepped toward him. Dammit, why had she just stepped toward him? "So Ivan's murder is a BFD, but Hudson's death wasn't?"

"Hudson wasn't tied to organized crime, arms deals, narcotics, terrorism—"

She held up her hand, stopping him. "I heard the list she gave. You don't have to go through it again."

"Ivan had ties that the CIA wanted to use. With his death, they'll have cases in jeopardy of imploding. They are going to dig and dig to uncover as much as they can on his killer—and to try and salvage cases under investigation."

Wonderful. So the CIA would be swarming the city. Another problem to wreck her life. And, speaking of a life being wrecked... "Do you always fuck women you believe have committed murder?" She hadn't meant to say that. Had she? Maybe.

He smiled at her. An angry, tough, and, damn him, sexy smile. The dimple was in full force right before he revealed, "No, you're special."

Her mouth dropped open.

"That came out wrong, didn't it?" He lost his smile and the dimple and raked a hand through his hair.

"How did you want it to come out? Did you want it to seem like you just admitted you think I'm a cold-blooded killer?"

"I wanted you to know that you're nothing like any woman I've met before."

"Because I'm a cold-blooded killer. Check. Got it."

"No, I've met plenty of those before. You're not like them." His hand fell to his side. "I wanted you. I knew I shouldn't cross the line, but I didn't care. I told you to say no. I warned you—" He broke off. "Get in the car, will you? Eyes are on us."

Like she didn't know that? Again? "You seriously think I want to be anywhere near you right now?"

His nostrils flared. "In the car."

"Why don't you just—"

He scooped her into his arms. Tossed her over his shoulder. The same damn way he'd done at Ivan's bar when he'd carried her away after she'd knocked down Ivan's motorcycle. For just a moment, absolute rage held her still. And then, her fists pounded relentlessly into his back. "Let me down, *now!*" They were in front of a police station for goodness' sake! Where was a cop when she needed one? She was being abducted right in front of the entrance doors!

"Stop this!" Naomi snarled at him.

"You are in *danger!* You leave me, and who the hell knows what could happen? You might be pissed as hell at me," he tightened his hold, "but believe me when I say that I will stand between you and danger."

"I don't want you standing anywhere near me!" A hard heave against him. Only he didn't let her go. Bastard!

"Well, this is new." A man's voice. Mocking. Not overly concerned. "Not every day that you see a woman being carried off so close to a cop station. Takes a lot of balls—and probably not a lot of sense—to pull this move."

Her hands shoved into the base of Eb's powerful back, and she levered herself up. She found a tall, broad-shouldered male staring at her and Eb with raised brows. He looked bemused when he should have been looking horrified. Dammit, were there truly no heroes left in this world? "Are you going to help?" she snapped to the stranger.

He blinked.

"Yeah, *help*," Eb emphasized. "Stop standing there like a prick, Hunter, and open the door for me. In case you missed it, she's trying to get the hell away from me."

"It's really hard to miss." He leaned against the side of the Impala and made no move to open the door. "I do a lot of things to help out you and your brother," he continued, voice turning thoughtful. "I dig up classified intel, I bend some laws here and there, I face down killers—because you know, I do hate to be bored."

"Sonofabitch, Hunter!" Eb surged forward, scrambling to hold her and open the door at the same time.

"But I think I have to draw the line at kidnapping a woman in broad daylight—right in front of a police station. I mean, we all have our limits, you know?"

Eb had no choice but to put her down. He tried to open the door when he released her. Naomi used that opportunity to whirl and aim a vicious knee right for his groin.

He realized her intent and dodged back. Mostly dodged. She made a hit because she heard the sudden inhalation of his breath.

"Naomi!"

"Figured it was her," the stranger noted. "I don't remember the masterplan being to kidnap her, but hey, maybe I've missed a few steps."

Her breath heaved in and out.

Eb straightened and stepped toward her.

"Don't even *dare* try to touch me again," she warned him.

The stranger—had his name been Hunter?—whistled. "Dude, do not do it. She is *pissed*."

Henry trotted over to stand in front of her, taking up a guard position. She spared him a glance. *Glad someone finally decided to get on my side.* Would barking at Eb have been too much to ask? Maybe even a bite on the leg?

"I am trying to keep you safe," Eb gritted out. "You walk away alone, and I'm afraid of what could happen to you."

Uh, huh. "Right. Because you care so much about what happens to your dead partner's wife."

"I care about you! Damn straight, I do!"

If she hadn't discovered what a phenomenal liar he was, Naomi would have believed those words. They actually sounded truthful.

"She doesn't have to leave alone," the stranger offered. "She can leave with me."

Her head whipped toward him. "Who in the hell are you?"

He extended his hand toward her. "Hunter McQueen.

You can call me Hunter. You can call me Mac. You can call me—"

"The jerk who just *stood there* and didn't help me?"

A nod. "That will work, too." He cleared his throat. "But I am actually offering help now. I've got a safe place lined up for you to stay. One that isn't bugged by cops or CIA asshats. You can decompress there. Come up with a plan of attack."

"My current plan is to get the hell out of this town." Because nothing good happened there. At least, not to her. The dream she'd had—Naomi knew it had gone up in smoke. There wasn't going to be some bed and breakfast. She wasn't going to own her own place and welcome her own guests. She needed to get back to Vegas. To the lights that hid every sin. To the visitors who tumbled in—one after the other—looking for adventure and magic. The perfect escape.

She needed to escape. To get far, far away from Eb.

"Running will make you look guilty," Eb warned her.

Her hands flew into the air. "Everyone already thinks I'm guilty! Including you."

Since she hadn't taken Hunter's offered hand, he dropped it. But mostly just so he could let Henry sniff his fingers. "Hi, there, fellow. Aren't you gorgeous?"

"I don't need a ride from either of you. I can call a driver and get the hell out of here on my own." She didn't look at Eb. Couldn't. She was too angry. Too hurt. Staring directly into his eyes—*no. Don't do it.*

"Ma'am..."

At that drawl, her gaze did whip toward Hunter.

"I get that you don't know me. But I am not here to hurt you. Eb asked me to find a safe house for you, and I did. You don't want to stay in this parking lot, you don't want the reporters—uh, they are just minutes from here, by the way— you don't want them closing in while you're standing on the corner waiting for a driver to appear."

"How do you know the reporters are close?" Her head whipped toward the road. She didn't see them. Her head snapped back toward him.

He smiled at her. "I have my ways, I'm resourceful like that. They're coming. You're going to be standing out here like the perfect prey, and they will surround you." A pause. "Unless you let me give you and your dog that ride I offered."

"She can ride with me," Eb growled.

"In your dreams." She turned fully toward Hunter. "How do I know you aren't some crazed killer? After all, you appear to be friends with Eb. Hardly a ringing endorsement."

"Oh, I am a killer." He nodded. "Guilty."

Her gaze darted over him in a fast assessment.

"Former Army Ranger," Hunter murmured. "Current troublemaker. It's what I am and what I do. Not gonna pretend I'm some good guy. I won't ever be. But I'm also not going to slice you into pieces and wear your leftover skin, so, there's that."

Stunned, her gaze came right back to his face.

"Hunter..." Eb's voice deepened even more in warning.

"What? I'm being honest with her. Maybe it's time someone tries that tactic."

Her chest burned.

"Hunter McQueen," he said his name again. "I fight viciously. I fight dirty. But I am not about hurting innocents. Not who I am or who I ever will be."

"Eb doesn't believe I'm innocent," she told him. It

actually hurt to say the words, and even more so to add, "No one does."

"I like to make my own opinions about people."

"And what have you decided about me?"

"Still working on it."

Her breath heaved out. "Give me that ride."

"*What?*" An explosion from Eb. "Why the hell would you choose him?"

She spun toward him. "Because he's being honest with me." *And I think that means the reporters are coming.* Actually, crap, behind Eb's massive shoulders, Naomi caught sight of a white news van barreling toward them. "I could use some honesty in my life."

"I am *sorry*," Eb said, voice rumbling.

"For fucking me?"

"*Oh, damn,*" Hunter rasped. "Damn."

"Or fucking me over with your lies?" she asked sweetly.

"That's a news van," Hunter told them. "How about we take this chat to a new location?"

She was more than ready to leave. Nodding, she sidled toward Hunter.

"*Naomi.*"

A shiver slid over her. There was an odd note in Eb's voice. An ache. A plea? No, no plea. Eb would never plead for anything. Certainly not for her.

Not. For. Her.

She left Eb and didn't look back. Not like she really needed to look back, though.

She was one hundred percent sure he'd be tailing her and Hunter to the safe house.

Naomi settled into Hunter's SUV, with Henry making himself comfortable in the backseat. Her head leaned back against the headrest. Hunter cranked the vehicle.

They didn't drive away.

Her head turned toward him. She found him staring at her. The kind of intense, focused stare that told her he was trying to figure things out in his mind.

"You don't look like a cold-blooded killer."

Great to know. "You do."

He smiled. "I know."

They drove away.

Chapter Fifteen

IT WAS A FUCK-UP ON A COLOSSAL SCALE. HE SHOULD have known how Madeline would operate. Should have known the minute she separated him and Naomi that his former handler was working one of her games. Fun random fact about Madeline? According to the CIA grapevine, the woman had been some chess prodigy back in her teen years. She was always fifty steps ahead of most people. It was one of the reasons she'd been recruited by the CIA at such a young age.

Sometimes, I think they brought her in when she was a teen. Not like the CIA would ever admit that, though. Not like the CIA admitted much at all. It was very much a cover-your-own ass situation there.

He'd made it to the safe house. More like safe mansion. He slammed his car door and glowered up at the stylish, sleek structure. One that stuck out like a sore-thumb in front of the massive oaks with their swaying Spanish moss and the dark bayou that waited in the distance.

"I know," Hunter said from the porch when Eb approached him. "It's a lot, ostentatious as hell, but the

194

owner is a friend of Declan's, and I can guarantee you that it has the best tech in the world. Cameras all around the property. Locks that no one can pick, not even your talented self. A security system that was installed by the infamous Wilde group. If you want safety, you've come to the right place."

He grunted. Safety wasn't what he wanted. He wanted Naomi. Only he didn't see her.

"She's inside." Hunter jerked his thumb over his shoulder. "Her and the dog. The lady marched in without a word, with that dog of hers right at her side. Figured I'd stay out here so you and I could talk."

Fabulous. He climbed up the two steps that led to the porch.

Hunter immediately blocked his path. "Looks like that master plan of yours didn't go so well."

"She knows I came to take her down."

"Uh, huh. Figured that. At what point did you decide *throwing her over your shoulder* was the way to go? Truly curious about that one. I wrongly thought you were the level-headed twin."

Hell, no. He wasn't. Definitely not level-headed when it came to Naomi.

"Or, at least, I assumed you were the one not likely to commit a kidnapping with cops just watching."

Eb's hand rasped over his jaw—and the stubble growing there. "I'm trying to protect her."

"That what you're doing now? I thought you were trying to get her tossed into a cell. Or are we multi-tasking? Protecting her *and* getting her locked away? Hey, maybe she'll be *safe* locked away! Is that the thought process you're having?"

"Hunter..."

"Or have you decided that she's innocent?"

The front door opened. Naomi stood there, and the breeze hit her, coming from those trees with their swaying moss and sending her hair blowing gently. He drank her in. The fury in her eyes—he understood that. But it was the pain he saw that gutted him. He'd *hurt* her. And you could only be hurt if you cared.

When had Naomi started to care for him?

He'd been wrong about her. She wasn't cold. He was starting to think that Naomi might feel far too much. She tried to put up a wall of ice between herself and the rest of the world because she needed a shield to block others. Only he'd smashed that weak shield to pieces.

"I don't think she's innocent," he said the words deliberately. Naomi had chosen Hunter because she wanted honesty. Fine. He'd give her honesty. Not like she could hate him more than she already did.

Or, hell, maybe she could?

Her chin notched up at his words.

"I don't think she's innocent," he continued because he truly did think she'd killed Hudson. But he also... "I think Hudson might be guilty."

Guilty as hell.

"Yeah, me, too," Hunter revealed. "And so does the guy waiting inside."

Wait. Hold the hell up. Some guy was waiting inside? There was no other car near the house.

"Memphis Camden," Hunter revealed. "Former bounty hunter. Current Ice Breaker, cold case solver. I believe you wanted your sister to arrange a meet and greet with him? Well, consider it arranged."

Damn. Someone had sure moved fast.

"You'll have to thank her ridiculously wealthy husband

for Memphis's private flight over from Texas. And my flight, too, because Declan wanted you to have backup on the ground, ASAP."

"Declan's your best friend."

"He's a pain in the ass most days, but he can also sure come in handy. I think we can both agree on that score."

A man appeared behind Naomi in the doorway. Tall. About Eb's own height. Dark hair. Calculating gaze. Intense attitude.

"You're the partner," Memphis said as he studied Eb. "The one seeking vengeance."

"You're the bounty hunter," Eb returned without missing a beat. Was everyone trying to block him from getting Naomi alone? Clearly, they were. "The one who tried to stop the wedding."

"I should have listened to his warning." Naomi hauled a hand through her hair. "The next time a man appears at my wedding and says I'm marrying a serial killer, I *will* listen. Be sure of that." She turned away. Headed fully inside with Memphis.

"Ahem." Hunter had just done an overly loud throat-clearing. "Did she say the *next* time someone tries to stop her from marrying a serial killer? Jeez, does the woman have a type or what?"

Eb stalked into the house.

I am her fucking type.

She was sure as hell his.

* * *

THE HOUSE FELT COLD. Correction, icy. Goosebumps rose on her arms. Maybe it was because of the contemporary architecture style of the house. Too clean lines, a minimalist style. No ornamentation but massive windows everywhere you looked. The house felt imposing. Stark.

Or...

Maybe it wasn't the house.

Maybe the chill Naomi felt came from the three men in the den with her. Three men who all seemed to carry danger and raw power. Hardly the easy, friendly type. More like the...

We-can-kill-a-man-and-never-blink type.

"So, Memphis, according to the brass in charge at the CIA, your allegations against Hudson are BS." Eb hadn't sat down. Neither had she.

Naomi stood near a fireplace, one that wasn't on, and Eb had taken up a position near one of the windows on the right.

Memphis sat on the couch. Hunter sprawled in a brown leather chair.

Eb and Memphis had done their weird version of an introduction, then they'd just dropped straight to business. *Your allegations against Hudson are BS.*

She wrapped her arms around her stomach, the better to fight off that chill, and shot a quick glance over at Henry. A massive dog bed had been waiting in the den for him. He'd settled comfortably in it, but she wasn't surprised to see his eyes were on her.

Naomi inclined her head toward him. *I'm okay. I've got this.*

Fabulous, now she was lying to herself and mentally fibbing to her dog. Naomi hurriedly darted her gaze toward Memphis.

Memphis nodded in response to Eb's flat statement. "So I've heard before. I was personally informed by Madeline

Desalt that my suspicions about Hudson Wyatt were incorrect." He rolled his shoulders. "In fact, I was given a lovely song and dance about how my international victims were not going to be discussed at all. Not investigated even a bit. I was told that every person who seems to be a victim may actually be something far different. Then I hit the full-on CIA stonewall, and there was no more discussion." His hands hung loosely between his spread knees as he lounged on the couch. "I can read between the lines. I understood that I was being informed Hudson was a government assassin who took out individuals who were deemed a threat. I'm sure you CIA types do that far more often than the world believes."

So, Memphis was just casually saying that...Hudson *and* Eb were assassins. And Eb wasn't arguing.

Eb's voice remained tense and hard as he noted, "*I* was also told the deaths you tried to link to Hudson from here in the US were attributed to someone else. Someone who Hudson had stopped."

Memphis quirked an eyebrow at Naomi. "Heard you had one hell of a wedding night."

"Quite unforgettable, I assure you." No matter how hard she would like to forget.

"I came back to town after that night, just so you know. I told my story to that arrogant detective."

Her hands fell to her sides. Madeline had mentioned that Memphis had talked to the detective. *And Madeline shut down that line of investigation.*

"Also made sure the DA heard me out. Couldn't get to you at the time because you were in lock up, and they weren't allowing you visitors."

Ah, yes, her lovely isolation period. Another bonus stage in her life.

"But I wanted them to know your husband wasn't some man of the year."

Oh, she certainly understood that Hudson had not been that.

"The CIA told me that I had everything all wrong. They wouldn't provide me any evidence. Just wanted me to take what they were saying at face value. I'm not real good with doing that."

"Did you find proof that Hudson was guilty of Mary Fontenot's murder?" Eb asked, voice darkening with intensity.

Memphis's focus slid to him. "You and your sister have vastly different personalities."

"Stands to reason. We're vastly different people."

"Siblings often are." Memphis settled back against the couch a bit more. "Family, oh, family can be such an interesting biological trick. All those genes, spinning around and around. Always fascinates me to see what traits are inherited and which ones aren't. Marley and I actually have this friend—" He broke off. Beetled his brows at Naomi. "Have you met his sister Marley?"

She shook her head.

"You'll like her," Memphis assured her. "Everyone usually does. I mean, she thawed the cold, cold heart of Declan Flynn, so that has to tell you the woman has skills. Seriously, though, she's a great profiler. Total asset to the team. Hate that business that she had to endure with Sebastian Glass. Fucking demented SOB."

Sebastian Glass. The name rang a very distant bell for Naomi.

"He was on death row," Memphis continued blithely. "He liked to cut up his victims. Break them. You might know him better as *Broken Glass*. That's what the press called him. Because by the time he was done carving up his victims, they looked like they were—"

"You've painted enough of a visual, thanks," Eb cut in tightly. "Don't really like to talk about the bastard who tried to murder my sister, if you don't mind."

Her mouth dropped open. *Broken Glass.* Yes, yes, she knew the story. The guy had been a real-life monster. Movies were being made about him. And the thing was...

He'd recently died. A brutal end in prison. He'd been attacked in the prison yard. Beaten. Stabbed with a shiv by the other inmates.

Eb stalked closer to her but stopped when he seemed to catch himself.

"I like connecting dots," Memphis suddenly admitted.

"Someone give the man a cookie." Eb did not seem impressed.

Naomi's stomach growled. Damn. She *could* go for a cookie. How long had it been since she'd eaten?

"Funny thing about you, Eb, is that you have some glaring holes in your past." Memphis exhaled on a long sigh. "Big holes."

She forgot about the cookie.

"Holes happen when you work for the government." Eb didn't seem concerned. "Sort of a need-to-know lifestyle that you live."

"Right. But there is one hole in particular that I don't think is related to that CIA life of yours. After your sister's attack, you seemed to vanish completely. No trace of you at all. Obviously, you were working an undercover mission, but just where was that mission? Some far distant country? Or...perhaps somewhere closer to home?"

Eb stiffened. "It doesn't matter. That particular mission wasn't successful."

What was happening? "Could you two stop talking in code? If you have something to say, spit it out." They were giving her a headache. And Hunter wasn't speaking. Just listening intently. Was he as clueless as she was?

Memphis waited a beat, then, "Let's just say that I believe Eb has a long history of seeking vengeance. Going to extremes in order to get that vengeance. Maybe when I leave, he can tell you more about Glass. And what it's like to spend months in a maximum-security lockup."

Okay, her goosebumps got way, way worse. "Why would Eb know what maximum security is like?"

"Because I spent time there." Eb's voice held no emotion. "This isn't relevant. Can you get back on track?"

Might not be relevant, but it certainly was terrifying. *Eb had been in a maximum-security lockup? Why?* "What did you do?" she breathed.

His eyes blazed. "Nothing." Grim. "But sometimes, to stop a killer, you have to become one."

Broken Glass had been killed in a prison riot. Stabbed with a shiv. And...Eb had been *in* prison.

"Did you kill him?" The question burst from her.

"No." Hunter's quiet response. So, yeah, he did know what was happening. Not so clueless. "Something that I think still pisses Eb off to this day. Eb really hates it when his prey gets away from him. Or, worse, when someone takes that prey away. All that time wasted..."

Her temples throbbed. "I don't understand—what does this have to do with—"

"Eb wasn't around to hold Hudson in check," Memphis told her. "During that period of time when Eb went dark, he had no contact with his partner. He couldn't keep him controlled. You see, I think Eb did that, probably far more than he realized."

A muscle jerked along Eb's jaw.

"Eb vanished because he was taking care of some family vengeance. He was off the radar, couldn't be contacted, and Hudson used that time to get close to you, Naomi. As far as I can tell, Hudson had not allowed himself to get close to any woman, not since Mary Fontenot's disappearance so long ago. Sure, he had flings. Hookups. But nothing permanent. Not until he met you."

She kept thinking that Mary was the key. "When you came to me on my wedding day, you told me that you believed he'd killed her."

"Yes."

"Do you still believe that?"

"I...can't be sure."

What in the hell? She had to pick her jaw up off the floor. "You were so certain before!"

"So were you. You were dead certain that Hudson was innocent that day." He rose from the couch. A ripple of strength. "And because you were so certain, I dug more. Deeper. Families are a bitch, aren't they?"

She wouldn't really know. She'd lost her family a long time ago.

The intensity deepened in Memphis's eyes. "Did you know that Hudson's mother died when he was seven years old?"

She nodded. "Yes, she was attacked during a mugging."

"Hudson's father died during a mugging the year after Hudson started working for the CIA."

Her heart shoved hard into her chest. "That's tragic."

"Sure. It's also convenient."

Losing your parents was convenient? Uh, no. It certainly hadn't been for her. It had been life-altering. Heartbreaking.

"And when I dug more..." Memphis continued because she was coming to see that he only operated in one mode—relentless. "When I dug more, I realized that maybe Hudson wasn't guilty of the crimes in New Orleans that I'd tried to connect to him. The evidence was there. But the evidence could also be framed another way. Because... perhaps Mary wasn't the first victim. Maybe the first victim had actually been murdered a long time ago. When our killer was still learning. Still honing his craft. Maybe that first victim had been claimed all the way back when Hudson was just a kid. If that was the case, then he wasn't the killer I'd been after. He couldn't be the killer."

She shook her head. No, no, Memphis could not be saying—

"Families," Memphis murmured. "Like I said, I'm fascinated to see what traits are inherited and which ones aren't. All those genes, spinning around and around and around. Where they'll stop...well, who knows? Got a friend, Sloane, and she's doing research specifically related to the children of serial killers. Some kids, of course, are completely normal. They're horrified and embarrassed and so ashamed of what their parents have done. But others... others have their own dark sides that they try to hide."

She couldn't speak.

Hunter could. And he did. "You're saying Hudson's old man was the killer? You got it wrong? The father was the serial, not Hudson? Dude. You probably should have shared that sooner. Like, a lot sooner."

"I'm saying...I got Mary's death wrong." Crisp. Annoyed. "Or rather, the identity of the man who abducted her. Mary's body was never found. For that crime, I was looking at the son. I was focused on Hudson. I should have seen the father."

Hudson didn't kill Mary. Did he kill the others? Did he—

Nausea rose. She slapped a hand over her mouth.

She could feel the watchful weight of the men's stares on her.

"You said you trusted him," Memphis recalled. "You said he was a good man."

Tears pricked her eyes. You had to trust the man you were going to marry, didn't you?

"So I dug deeper. With Mary...I don't think Hudson was to blame. With the vics in New Orleans who vanished shortly after Mary—I think they can also be tied to Hudson's father. But he's dead. Hudson's father is dead. Hudson is dead. It's doubtful we will ever learn anything for certain."

Wrong, wrong, wrong. Her lips trembled. The words wanted to burst out of her.

Who will believe me?

No one.

No one believed a liar.

Henry rose from the cushy, dog bed. His ears tilted back.

"Naomi." Eb was right in front of her. "Baby, look at me."

She turned her head. Stared into his eyes. The topaz swirled. Burned.

"Talk to me," he urged her.

But she couldn't. He wanted to lock her up. To shove her into a cell. He'd fucked her as a means to get close. He didn't really care about her.

"I believe Hudson knew what his father had done." Not her words. Memphis. Still talking. Still shattering her life one word at a time. "He was in town when his father was stabbed and killed in the course of that mugging. A mugging with no witnesses. With a knife that plunged straight into the victim's heart. Such a fast, brutal kill. Almost like a professional hit, wouldn't you say?"

Eb wasn't saying anything.

Neither was Hunter.

And Naomi didn't dare speak.

"Eb...I've got to ask, just what sort of hits did your friend perform while he was in the CIA?" A pause from Memphis. "What kind of hits did *you* perform?"

Assassin. No, no, not possible. Eb—

I played the hero.

A dull ringing filled her ears.

Henry padded closer toward her.

Eb grabbed her hands. "Naomi?"

She wanted to snatch them away from his grip. His touch sent that treacherous charge flooding through her veins. "I'm not having a seizure." But she sure felt as if she was breaking apart on the inside. "Don't worry about me."

"You've lost every bit of color in your face. Your body is trembling. Your breathing is too shallow. I damn well *am* worried. I'm worried you're about to faint on me."

She tried to pull in a deep breath. "I'm not fainting." She wouldn't. Would not.

"Uh, so..." Hunter heaved to his feet. "We just discovered that—let me make sure I'm following along here okay—Naomi's husband killed his own father because the dude was a serial killer. His dad had killed both Hudson's mom and Hudson's girlfriend?" A loud whistle.

Henry's head jerked toward him, but Henry didn't leave Naomi's side.

Hunter nodded. "Yep, if you find out that your old man killed both your mom and your girlfriend, that would piss you off. Make you all kinds of homicidal. Add to that, Memphis pretty much suspects that it's a whole like-father-like-son situation, so Hudson probably killed a number of people over the years. Vics we can't tie to him because he was one of the CIA's assassins and they are covering their sins and burying them all deep in the ground. Sure, why not? Check, check, insanity check."

"My friend Sloane thinks that some killers deliberately try to make their children become like them." Memphis tilted his head to the side as he studied Naomi. "They'll do whatever it takes to grow the darkness inside their own family members. Maybe that's why his father attacked Mary all those years ago. To turn on that darkness in his son. Or, hell, maybe he just coveted what his son possessed. Some people get like that, you know. They want what someone else possesses, and they will do whatever it takes to acquire that possession."

"Fuck." Eb's seething voice. "*Fuck me.*"

She already had. She'd planned to do so again. Then she found out that he was hell-bent on destroying her. No more fucks, thanks.

You are such a liar. You want him right now. His touch is sending electricity pulsing through your veins. His touch was also—oddly enough—steadying her. Naomi no longer felt as if she would shatter apart at any moment.

"Your friend Sloane seems interesting," Hunter allowed.

"Um." Memphis sauntered closer. He'd shoved his hands into the pockets of his jeans. "My wife was targeted by a serial killer." Casual news. Like he was saying it was sunny outside.

He'd basically delivered everything in a casual tone.

Except there was nothing casual about the expression in his eyes. Fury smoldered.

"Serials are a different breed," he stated without batting an eyelash. "Most don't seem to feel the normal range of emotions that everyone else does. They are smart, diabolically so, and they can obsess in ways that most people will never understand. They see something they want, and they take it. They crave it. They will do whatever it takes in order to keep their possession."

The way he was looking at her...

Possession.

But she wasn't a possession. She was a person.

She finally succeeded in yanking her hands from Eb's. "What...happened to the serial killer who went after your wife?"

"I can obsess, too," he revealed as his gaze continued to hold hers. "I can crave. I can also burn down the world if it means protecting the woman I love. There are no threats to my Eliza any longer. I've eliminated them all."

Okay. *Scary. Intense.*

Memphis's gaze finally left her. Only to then head straight to Eb. "Can you understand that? The necessary elimination of threats? With your job and your past, I would think so."

"I get what you're saying," Eb snapped.

"Thought you might. Thought you also might really understand that we all need to do what's necessary for survival. Vengeance is never black and white." A roll of Memphis's shoulders. "The Ice Breakers are not involved in the investigation of Hudson Wyatt's death. He's not one of the cases we will ever be working to solve. The dead can rest." His stare swung back to Naomi. "The song always said there was no rest for the wicked. I don't happen to agree with that. Sometimes, the wicked have earned their rest, too." Memphis dipped his head toward her. "Time for me to go. I've got a plane to catch. My wife is waiting at home for me. I don't like for my Eliza to ever wait." With that, Memphis swung on his heel and headed for the door.

"Yeah." Hunter huffed out a breath. "I'll just follow him out. Make sure there aren't any other details that Captain Dramatic just forgot to drop on us." He hurried after Memphis.

The wicked have earned their rest, too.

She was the Wicked Widow.

And, like so many others, Memphis Camden thought she was guilty as hell. He just didn't particularly care because he believed her husband was scarier and more evil than the devil.

He was right about her husband. Hudson had been scary. Evil at his core.

But...

He was wrong about her.

"I didn't kill Hudson." Words she'd said over and over again, and no one had ever believed her. No one would believe her. She'd always carry the weight of everyone's suspicion and the judgment would follow Naomi wherever she—

"I believe you."

Shock blasted through her at Eb's low, deep words, and Naomi took a staggering step back.

Chapter Sixteen

A HARD, VEHEMENT SHAKE OF NAOMI'S HEAD. "No, you don't. You're just lying to me. Again."

"Tell me you didn't kill him."

"I *didn't kill him!*"

"I believe you."

"I *didn't kill Hudson.*"

"I believe you." Eb would say it over and over again. As many times as necessary, he would say it. "You chose Hunter because he was being honest with you at the police station." Like that choice hadn't cut like a knife. "Baby, I've been so many people over the years that, sometimes, I forget who I really am. I forget how to be honest, even with myself. But I'm going to fix that. Starting now. With you." A hard nod. "I believe you."

Did she get what he was saying? Probably not because he barely understood himself. Things were moving way too fast between him and Naomi. His emotions were not locked down the way they should have been. Everything was out of control. "I believe you." Harder. Rougher. But he swore...

It felt the same as saying...

I love you.

Impossible. But...

I love you.

He'd fucking fallen the first time he saw her in the fountain. Love at first sight? What a crock of BS.

Except...

I knew it was real when she was on the couch, her body jerking and twitching and I would have traded my soul if her pain could stop.

"I stabbed him."

He didn't let his expression change at that stark admission from her.

"I was shaking and jerking, and he wanted me to beg. He was a monster. Telling me that he held all the power. That he could do anything he wanted. That I could die and no one would ever question him. That others had died and nothing happened to him. *Nothing.* He wanted me to hurt. He...he switched out my medicine."

Now he couldn't control his expression. "*What?*"

"I found out later—after Hudson had already been buried—that my medicine had been changed. *He* must have done it. Maybe he wanted to see me helpless. On our wedding night, *I* was helpless. Because of the medicine change or the terror or just horrible luck, I was *helpless.* When the seizure hit me, Hudson smiled, and he watched. That was, after, of course, he played around with his knife and thought it would make for extra fun to drive his fist into my stomach. All of that was true, by the way. The story I told you before? *It happened.* My wedding night was a true nightmare. No *maybe* BS about it. A real nightmare."

He'd called Hudson a friend. A partner. He'd fought right beside him.

And...

If Hudson had been there right then...

I'd be the one killing you, you bastard.

"I have no idea how long I'd been taking the fake medicine. I didn't even notice the change until I got a new bottle after the burial. I'd taken the medicine so long and..." Her breath shuddered out. "I reached for the knife. He'd put that knife to my throat. Did I tell you that part? I did, didn't I? That he'd put the knife to my throat. Then pulled it down my body. I could feel the blade skimming over my skin."

Now he understood exactly why she'd called Hudson twisted. *Why did you do this to her? What in the hell was wrong with you?* And why hadn't Eb seen the monster hiding behind his friend's smile?

"Hudson told me that I should never have questioned him about Mary. That the past would stay dead and he—" A shuddering breath. "I was jerking. He was laughing. I-I begged. Cried. *He watched, and he smiled.* I married him. He promised to love me forever, and he smiled as I begged."

His hands curled into fists. Everything he'd believed about Hudson had been dead wrong. He'd seen the truth in the interrogation with Madeline. The faint sweat on her forehead. The brief flicker of her lashes. Small tells, but because he'd worked with her for so long, Eb had spotted them. She'd been holding back about Hudson. *She knew he was a killer.*

Now Eb did, too.

And he wished, he *wished* that he'd been there for Naomi when she needed him.

But I will be with her from here on out. He'd protect her. Fight for her. Make damn sure that she was never hurt again.

"I grabbed the knife he'd dropped, and I plunged it into

his side. I did it twice, and he got off me, and I managed to make it outside with Henry. I fell. The last thing I remember was Henry trying to drag me away and when I woke up..."

The front door slammed. "Well, he's gone." Hunter strode back into the den. "Not exactly sunshine and rainbows, is he? But at least we got intel we can use." He strolled forward, only stopping when he was right in front of Eb and Naomi. His gaze swung back and forth between them. A faint line cut between his brows. "Everything all right in here? Because I swear, I was only gone for like, two minutes, three, max. But you two seem, ah, extra intense."

Eb's hands remained clenched into powerful fists. "I need to talk with Naomi alone." He had to get the rest of the story from her.

"Like...as in now? Because we should really all talk—this whole little group we have going, cute dog included," he waved toward a watchful Henry, "and come up with a game plan. Because, clearly, someone in this town wants Naomi to suffer. First the house fire, then the frame-up job. You've got a very serious enemy," he told Naomi.

"I know," she said, and her stare was locked right on Eb.

Dammit. He advanced toward her. Their bodies brushed. "I am not your enemy."

She stared straight into his eyes. "Bullshit."

She was the most beautiful woman he'd ever seen. And he'd shattered her growing trust in him.

Naomi swiped away a tear that had leaked down her cheek.

An actual tear.

Another knife in my chest.

"You need to very much consider us one and done." Her brittle declaration. "I don't like to repeat my mistakes."

"Oh, shit," Hunter rasped. "You're a mistake, bro. That has to hurt. Savage."

Yeah, it did hurt. "I heard her, Hunter. No need for the repeat." Hadn't he asked to speak with Naomi alone?

Her eyes glittered. "If you two will excuse me, Henry and I are heading to the kitchen."

What? "We need to finish our talk!" She didn't get to just drop a bombshell about stabbing Hudson and leave Eb hanging without telling him the rest of the story.

"I need to eat, and I am hoping like crazy there is something semi-edible in this house." Her head swung toward Hunter. "Point me in the direction of the kitchen?"

"Yeah, sorry, but you're not gonna find a whole lot in there." A wince. "How about I order some pizzas?"

How about Naomi finishes telling me the damn story about Hudson's murder before I lose my mind?

"I want pepperoni," she said.

* * *

"You screwed up."

Eb stared at the remains of the pepperoni pizza. They'd torn through two and a half boxes of pizza. Turned out that they'd all been famished.

Naomi had eaten. Then she'd vanished upstairs to her room. She had not dropped any other major bombshells on him.

"You're wearing regret like a second skin."

He slanted a glance toward Hunter. The other man slouched on the back porch of the house. They'd eaten outside. Sunset had come and gone, turning the sky a deep, dark red before the growing darkness had started to spread out like hungry tentacles. The insects chirped now, their calls getting stronger with every moment that passed.

"Did you apologize to her? Maybe try a bit of groveling? I've heard some women really go for that." Hunter brought a beer bottle up to his mouth. Took a sip. "You came down here so big and bad. So determined to wreck her world. Now she has you wrapped around her pinky finger. That was a fast fall, got to say."

"Thanks for that, buddy, appreciate it." He brought his own beer up to his mouth. A practically full beer.

"Anytime."

He put the beer back down, no sip. "You made any progress on the psych files?"

"Dude, you said your old CIA handler was in town. That she was the one interrogating you and Naomi at the police station. Why don't you just ask her directly about the guy's psych history?"

"Because she'll lie. Madeline is even better at lying than I am." She'd been the one to train him and Hudson.

A grunt. "If she's such a world-class liar, then how do you know the other stuff she's told you is the truth? That part about Hudson offing the real serial killer? Maybe that was BS."

Maybe it had been. Except... "One rule you learned early on at the CIA was that the best lies were based in a kernel of truth. Made it easier to tell them. Made it easier for you to pass polygraphs because part of what you were saying was the truth."

"You're telling me that you can lie and pass a lie detector test." He saluted Eb with the beer bottle. "Impressive."

"No, it's not." It just meant he'd gone so far down the

rabbit hole that his conscience didn't tend to bother him any longer. At least, not most nights.

This night, it bothered him.

"Who do you think set the fire at Naomi's place?" Hunter wanted to know.

"Thought it was Ivan. Then we found him beat to death."

"Huh." Hunter turned his head and stared into the night. "Huh." His head tilted to the right.

In the distance, thunder seemed to rumble. The chirps of the insects grew louder, but even over their calls, Eb could practically hear Hunter's thoughts grinding along. "You got something to say?"

"I'm not some fancy profiler. Don't have a fistful of degrees. I'm just a former soldier who knows how to kill really well." A shrug. "Guess we all have our talents, am I right?"

"You're right," Naomi responded from behind Eb.

Eb had known she was there. He'd heard the faint opening of the back door. The squeak of the porch beneath her feet. And as crazy as it might seem, he'd felt the charge in the air shift the moment she'd joined them.

Thunder rumbled again. Sounded closer.

"We do all have our talents," she agreed. "You two are apparently talented when it comes to protection and keeping people alive. After some careful consideration, I've decided that means we should all work together."

They both turned toward her.

"Uh, Naomi," Hunter began, voice amused, "you're already at the safe house with us. That means we *are* working together."

"I debated leaving right after the meal. Sneaking over

and hot-wiring the Impala while you two were out here throwing back beers."

They were not throwing back beers. He'd had maybe three sips and Hunter's bottle was three-fourths full.

"I have experience hot-wiring. Did it back when I was a kid."

"The joy rides," Eb said. His gaze drank her in. She'd changed clothes. Put on leg-hugging jeans. A top that flowed lightly over her breasts. Sneakers. All clothes that had come courtesy of Hunter because the guy had gotten bags prepared for them both. Bags that had been waiting at the safe house.

"I'm not surprised that you dipped into my past to learn all my naughty secrets," she retorted, voice tight. "I'm also not surprised that—when it comes to me—you only learned part of the truth."

He leaned his hip against the porch railing. The thunder came again. Louder.

"I stole a car when I was fifteen. Had to do it. The foster home I was at—there was this real jerk named Paxton who also lived at the place—he liked to sneak into my bedroom at night."

Eb lunged away from the railing. "What?"

"He was two years older than me. The *real* kid in the family, you know? The biological one. I was just the extra they'd taken in. Paxton didn't get why I wasn't totally into him. Girls had always liked him. Fallen at his feet. I didn't fall."

"Naomi..."

"Guy didn't take rejection well. So he'd come in, he'd scare the hell out of me, and he'd try to touch me." Flat words. Fast words. "I wasn't in the mood to be touched, so I swiped a knife from the kitchen. I kept it with me. One night, he came in again, and I sliced his hand. He screamed, and I ran, and I jumped in that car and..." She walked toward the railing. Didn't look at Eb or Hunter as she stared into the night. "It was easy for the parents to just tell everyone I was a troublemaker who'd taken the car for a joy ride. Better to say that than to reveal that their precious high school quarterback son was a creep who'd had a finger nearly sliced away when he touched someone that he shouldn't have touched."

Paxton. Eb would not forget the name. He'd be finding the creep.

"I was the villain back then. I'm the villain now. Played the role a few times actually. Because it's all about the story that gets the most attention, isn't it? It's about who gets to tell the story first, too." She slanted a glance his way. "By the way, I made sure to wreck that car. It was Paxton's. It really pissed him off when he found it slammed into a tree."

He wanted to reach out to her. Wanted to hold her and make everything better, only he was one of the people making life worse for her.

Thunder quaked once again. Still distant but...

"Must be one hell of a storm coming," Naomi murmured. A long sigh. "Detective Anderson found out about Paxton. Told me I had a history of using a knife on my lovers. Just made me look guiltier."

"Paxton talked to Anderson?" Hunter asked.

She nodded. "He came to town."

"Fuck," Hunter breathed. "Hello, suspect."

Her hair slid over her shoulder. Her focus had shifted away from the darkness of the night and onto Eb. "You're not saying anything."

Because rage choked him. He wanted to get his hands

on Paxton. Teach the SOB that you didn't touch what did not belong to you.

"Guess you don't believe me, huh? Think I'm just spinning some other wild story to cover my own guilt?"

"I think I want to break both of Paxton's hands."

He heard the sudden sharp inhalation as she sucked in a breath. "What?"

"I believe you," he said. He would keep giving her those words until she understood exactly what they meant. "No secrets. From here on out. Not for me. No secrets. No lies. You might not like the truth I have for you, like the fact that I am one hundred percent serious about breaking that jackass's hands, but I will be honest. You have my word."

Silence.

But she was weighing him. Studying him. Judging him?

Aw, baby. Don't do that. I'll fail when you judge me. Because he knew exactly what he was. What he'd done. He also knew that he should never have put his blood-stained hands on her.

The tension in the air thickened as they stared at each other.

"Okay." Hunter drummed his fingers on the wooden porch column. "I'm still standing here. Feeling like a third wheel, so I'm just gonna try and get us all back on track. That cool?"

Eb didn't glance his way.

"Like I was saying a few minutes ago, I'm no profiler. But I have chased down enough predators in my time that I know how a lot of them think. I can see where you two were figuring that the fire and the attack on Ivan were linked—that they could have been done by the same person. Maybe you even suspect the bat was left there to frame Naomi."

Naomi nodded.

Eb agreed. They were both thinking—

"That's certainly a possibility. But...all of this? There's another scenario that can play out here, too. What's happening might not be about hate. You have to realize that. Love can twist you up just as much as hate can."

Now Eb's gaze flew to Hunter. They'd turned the porch light off when darkness fell. The better to not attract the million bugs out there, so Hunter's form was a big shadow. "What are you talking about?" Yeah, Eb absolutely felt twisted up.

"Maybe Ivan did set the fire. Maybe he was pissed at Naomi. Maybe he'd been pissed at her for a while, and he got one of his guys to go in and disable the smoke alarms at her place."

Eb had told him that detail earlier. The disabled alarms bothered the hell out of him because they showed premeditation. *Someone planned for Naomi to burn. This was no spur-of-the-moment attack.*

"But I figure Ivan likes a personal touch. So maybe his men set the groundwork. Then he went in—all pissed because Naomi had taken Henry back—"

Henry had flopped on the porch after Naomi came outside. But at the sound of his name, his big head lifted.

"So Ivan comes out to start the fire himself. Only he doesn't count on being seen at the house while the fire is raging."

Eb shook his head. "We didn't see him."

"Not talking about you. I'm talking about the person who was watching Naomi's house. The person who saw Ivan, got pissed as hell at what he'd done, and grabbed Naomi's bat to go and punish him."

His muscles tightened. "Say again?"

"You told me a few minutes ago that the bat was in the bed of her truck."

Yeah, he had told him that. While they were doing a rundown of the case after eating.

"So go with me here a moment, would you? Let's just say this guy didn't like what he'd seen. Didn't like that Ivan torched her place with Naomi inside. He was pissed. He grabbed the bat and he went for his vengeance. Got there and beat the hell out of Ivan. Instead of the attacks being linked, we're looking at two separate events. One, the fire—potentially set by Ivan. Two, the beating that Ivan got by our unknown perp. A perp who did it not to set up Naomi but because he didn't want anyone hurting her." He took a quick swig from the beer. "Just a theory. But sometimes, it helps to look at something from a different perspective. Maybe not everyone in this town believes that she is a villain. Maybe someone out there thinks she needs protecting. Maybe that's what he's been doing all along. Protecting her. I mean, if she didn't kill her husband, then just *maybe* the person who did was trying to protect her from Hudson. To eliminate the threat Hudson posed."

"That's one hell of a protector." Or a completely obsessed psychopath. Or—

An alarm started beeping.

Hunter pulled out his phone. "Speaking of eliminating threats...that wasn't freaking thunder that we were all hearing. We have company coming. Just passed the front gate." He cursed. "Not a pizza delivery guy this time. Got motorcycles. Coming in hot."

Eb could hear the thundering—*growling*—sound of the bikes. So much clearer because they were close. Dammit. He caught Naomi's hand instantly and hauled her into the house. Hunter was steps in front of him, and Henry was right behind him. Eb locked the back door. Made sure the extra bolts were in place.

"Eb!" Hunter called his name.

Eb turned and caught the gun that Hunter had just tossed to him.

"No!" A quick yell from Naomi. "Don't throw guns! Don't ever throw guns at each other! Let's make that a new rule, all right? Because you could drop the gun and it could fire and one of us could get *shot*."

He pushed the gun he'd just caught into her hand. "You know how to use this." A statement, not a question.

She blinked those deep, soul-stealing eyes of hers at him. "I know how to use this."

Of course, she did. "I want to kiss you."

"*What?*"

"Tell me no."

Her eyes widened.

"*Eb!*" An annoyed shout from Hunter. "We do not have time for bullshit. I'm counting seven bikes. Each with a pissed-off rider. There are two of us. Sure, I like the odds, but how about we focus on the attack and save everything else for later, okay?" He looked down at his phone. At the security feed that had to be showing on the screen. "Great. Now it's ten bikes. Dammit. They are out for blood. I think I'm about to have an up close meeting with Ivan's gang."

Eb backed away from Naomi.

Her left hand—the hand not holding the gun—flew out and fisted in his shirtfront. "You aren't going outside."

That was exactly where he was going. He was planning to snag another gun first, but, yep, outside was the destination.

"There are *ten* of them."

So he'd heard. "Their leader was just killed, and Hunter

is right—they're out for blood. They aren't going to leave." Not without their prey. And he knew he was looking at that prey. *Naomi*. "They'll either bust in or I can go meet them."

Her grip twisted in his shirt even more. "Then let them bust in! Let's call the cops!"

They could be dead before the cops arrived. He tore his gaze from her worried face. "Hunter, I know this place must have a safe room."

"Upstairs. Second room on the right," Hunter replied instantly. He was checking his weapon.

"Go upstairs," Eb urged as his head turned back toward Naomi. "Second—"

"I heard him," she tossed right back. "You come with me. You both come with me. We'll call the cops."

Wasn't gonna work like that. "If I don't go out, then—"

"Um, they have gasoline cans," Hunter announced.

Eb's head whipped toward him once more. Hunter was done checking his weapon and had returned to peering down at his phone screen.

"Pickup truck just arrived." Hunter glanced up. Shared a grim look with Eb. "Something tells me that if we don't go out on our own, they'll burn us out."

No one was burning Naomi. So...new plan. "We'll distract them." He hauled the keys out of his pocket. Took the delicate hand that Naomi had been twisting in his shirtfront, and he pressed his keys into her palm. "I moved the Impala to the back. Near the garage."

"I know where it is! I told you I considered hot-wiring it and leaving."

But she hadn't left. She'd come to him and told him about her past. She'd stayed.

And I will protect her. I'll do whatever it takes. "You wait until we have their full attention, then you and Henry haul ass. Get to the Impala. Get in it. *Go.* I'll find you when this is over."

How the hell had the gang found them so quickly?

He was sure they hadn't been followed when they left the police station. He'd been so very careful. And only Hunter had met the pizza driver at the edge of the property. Naomi and Eb hadn't been seen.

"You want me to leave you," Naomi said. Her nose scrunched. "While you face off with a gang."

"Yep, that's the plan." He sure as hell would have liked to kiss her once more, but—

She rose onto her tiptoes. The hand holding the keys looped around his neck and hauled him toward her. Their mouths met in a passionate crash. Lips parted. Tongues tasted. Lust flared. And—

"For fuck's sake!" Hunter's disgruntled exclamation. "I'm good, but I can't take out ten guys on my own. A little help, Eb, and a little less make-out time, got it?"

He got it. Eb backed away from Naomi.

Her breath heaved. "You're not supposed to be a real hero."

"I'm not." He grabbed a second gun. "Wait until we have their attention."

"Don't you *dare* get shot. Or burned!"

He planned to do the shooting. "Just haul that sweet ass as far from here as you can get."

Hunter cleared his throat. "There's a dirt path that cuts from the garage in the back. Get the car out, keep the headlights off, and just drive out that way. If anyone tries to give chase, Eb and I will stop them."

Henry circled Naomi's feet.

Eb gave the golden a brief pat. "Keep her safe."

The motorcycles roared louder outside, like the bikers

were deliberately flaring the engines to send a message...
probably because they were.

Come out, come out...

Eb spun on his heel and walked away from Naomi.
Because he had to. Because she had to be protected.

"They have kicked the wrong hornet's nest," Hunter
said.

"Damn straight, they have." They weren't going out the
front door. What were they, idiots? They'd open the door
and likely get shot.

Nah. A better plan was always at play. This was not
amateur night. The gang was about to learn that very
important fact.

"You weren't supposed to be a real hero!" Naomi
argued again.

He glanced back at her. Smiled. "I'm not, sweetheart."
The gang was about to learn that fact. "But I'm the best
assassin you'll ever meet."

Shock flashed on her face.

Chapter Seventeen

HUNTER AND EB HAD VANISHED. DRIFTED THROUGH the house like ghosts. She stood in the den, one hand gripping a gun and the other fisted around the keys Eb had given her. Henry sat on his haunches and stared up at her with his big, trusting eyes, waiting for a command.

She was supposed to run. Eb and Hunter were going to be the distraction. She'd sneak away. Take Eb's precious Impala.

Meanwhile, Hunter and Eb would...what?

I'm the best assassin you'll ever meet.

Her heart drummed far too hard and fast in her chest. The house had gone quiet around her. She didn't even think Hunter and Eb were *in* the house any longer. They hadn't gone out the front door, though, or the back. Had they snuck out a window? Was there another exterior door somewhere in this maze of a house?

They'd left without making a sound. All she could hear beyond the house was the snarl of the motorcycles as they circled in.

Yes, she was supposed to run. To wait for the distraction and save herself while Hunter and Eb faced the danger.

I'm the best assassin you'll ever meet.

She should have known she wasn't falling for a hero. She never had gone for that type. Not once in her life.

* * *

THE MOTORCYCLES SPUN IN CIRCLES. The engines howled and growled, and the truck had come to a grinding halt. Some guy was hauling out gasoline canisters from the bed of the pickup.

Eb waited in the darkness and surveyed the scene. He recognized several of the men—mostly because he'd kicked the shit out of them once already. Obviously, they'd come back hungry for a rematch.

The pyro jumped out of the truck bed, with an orange gasoline canister in each massive fist. A big guy—the biggest fellow there. When he stalked through the heaving bikes, the headlights hit him. Shaved head. Face full of piercings. *Hello, old friend.*

Though, they weren't actually friends. But that jerk had been the first to step up and fight Eb at the bar when he'd gone to collect the dog for Naomi. Probably meant the guy was next in line when it came to the pecking order for the gang. And without Ivan there...

The wannabe leader dropped the containers and let them fall at his feet. "Bring your ass out!" he bellowed as he glared at the house. "You're gonna pay for what you did to Ivan! *Get out, now!*"

Considering how much gasoline this gang had at the ready, it certainly looked as if they'd been responsible for the fire at Naomi's place. *So maybe Hunter's theory was right. Maybe Ivan did set the fire. Someone saw him. After the fire was out at Naomi's, the watcher went over for some payback.*

The bikes spun around the big bruiser once more before lining up near him. They all faced the house. Bikes and dumbasses.

Really? They never—not for one second—considered that their prey might be behind them?

"Send out the woman!" From the wannabe leader. "We want *her! Send her out first!*"

So he was delusional. Great to know.

The bikes started moving again. The gang members were shouting, blasting their voices and their bikes and wrecking the nicely landscaped yard. One guy sped toward Eb's hiding spot, then turned at the last moment. His bike's wheels slipped on the grass, and the rider had to grab the handlebars quickly to adjust and—

Eb just tossed him right off the bike. Then he knocked the bastard out with two fast punches while the riderless bike careened away. Someone had a glass jaw—plus that *someone* had made the mistake of not wearing a helmet. Didn't he know that was a fatal mistake? Such a poor life choice.

Another motorcycle crashed into a tree about fifteen feet away. A motorcycle without a rider. When Eb looked over that way, he saw that Hunter had just plucked the guy from the bike.

The crash into the tree had captured everyone's attention. The other motorcycles stilled.

All eyes went to Hunter.

They haven't even seen me. Because his attack had been one hell of a lot quieter than Hunter's. The former Ranger had so much to learn.

"Whoops!" Hunter announced and his voice was *happy*. "Did I interrupt your party? My bad."

The motorcycles immediately blasted toward him.

Hunter pulled out his gun.

So did Eb.

* * *

SHE WAS ALMOST at the Impala when she heard the first gunshot ring out. Naomi flinched at the sound, and she dropped the keys. She kept the grip on the gun—win!—but the keys hit the ground. Immediately, she crouched to her knees and scooped them up.

Henry bumped into her, urging her forward.

Forward, yes, to the car. To escape. To drive away and not look back but...

Another gunshot blast rang out.

I'm the best assassin you'll ever meet.

Such confidence. But...what if he'd been wrong? At last count, Hunter had said there were ten gang members out there. Ten against two. She hated those odds.

More than that, though, Naomi hated that Eb thought she'd run away without a backward glance and leave him.

Not happening.

She rose and rushed to the car. Hauled open the door. Henry immediately tried to jump inside. "No!" A sharp order.

His head swung toward her.

She bent and put her head against his. "Too dangerous," she whispered. "I love you, and I need you to stay here, in this garage. Understand?" She lifted her head. The light from the Impala's interior poured onto Henry.

He blinked up at her. Those sweet, trusting eyes.

"Stay here," she ordered again. "I'll be okay."

Then she got in the car. Put the gun in the passenger seat. Cranked the engine.

And drove.

* * *

His goal wasn't to kill. Not unless he had to do so. Eb already had enough blood on his hands, and he generally tended to avoid killing unless it was the only solution.

Wounding and incapacitating his prey? That worked for now.

He'd taken out three men. The first had been the idiot he'd knocked off the bike.

Two attackers had fired at him. Both dumbasses had missed because they couldn't aim and ride their bikes at the same time. One had crashed on his own. Putting him out of commission had been easy after that because he'd barely been able to stand.

Eb had fired at the other one's front tire. Sent him hurtling into the sky. Then the ground.

He was pretty sure Hunter had taken out about two guys, as well. Not that he was counting, but if he *had* been counting...

I'm winning.

Motorcycles howled around him.

"Eb!" Hunter shouted. A warning cry.

Like he needed the warning. He could hear the snarls and knew they'd all decided he was the main target. The bikes were coming at him but so was the big, wannabe boss. Swinging one of the gasoline containers right at Eb's face.

Eb dodged. Turned out, it was easier than one might expect because a gasoline container made for a bulky-ass weapon. When the slugger came at him again, Eb caught the base of the container and shoved back. The tattooed, pierced attacker gave a shriek and let go. He also fell on his ass.

Eb had a gun aimed on the bastard two seconds later. "You're gonna keep your ass right there," he ordered. "And you're going to tell me how the hell you found us!"

"You killed Ivan!" And the big bruiser ignored the gun and leapt at Eb.

Sonofabitch, the man packed quite a tackle. Since Eb knew the dead couldn't give good, quality answers, he didn't shoot. He went down beneath the big guy, kept the gun gripped with his right hand, and when the slugger pulled back to hit him, Eb reached up and ripped the piercing right out of the man's nose.

Blood flew. The guy screeched in pain and lurched upward.

And Eb took the opportunity to put his gun to the guy's chest. "I repeat, how did you find us?"

The man froze. Blood dripped from his nose.

The motorcycles roared around him. Their lights hit Eb. He didn't look toward them. Hunter was out there, hopefully taking out more of those jerks.

But the biker before Eb grinned with grim intent. "They're gonna tear you to shreds beneath their wheels."

The bikes roared.

The man above Eb yanked out a knife. *Dammit.* Eb whipped his gun to the side and fired a hole right through the guy's raised hand. The hand that had been clutching the knife. Then Eb rolled, jumped to his feet, took aim again—

Motorcycles rushed right at him.

And so did...

His Impala. It surged from behind the house with a

series of wild blares from its horn. It bobbed and heaved—*Dear God in heaven, my precious baby is bobbing and heaving*—and barreled right at the men on bikes. They scrambled. One raced down the driveway road and didn't stop. Another flew into the thick brush in an effort to get away from the Impala. A third...

The Impala hit the back of his motorcycle and sent both the bike and the driver hurtling into the air.

A fourth guy might have crashed into a bush. Eb stopped looking for him as the Impala screeched to a stop right in front of Eb and the biker who was clutching his bleeding hand and sobbing.

"Holy hell," Hunter exclaimed with possible admiration as he stepped from the darkness. "Did I just see that?"

Steam came from the hood of his Impala. Eb was pretty sure he had to blink away tears. *My baby is bobbing and heaving and...steaming?*

The door flung open.

"It was more than ten, for the record," Hunter announced. "That's why it took me longer to get to your side. They kept coming and coming, like ants crawling out of a mound. I think we got swarmed by the whole gang."

Naomi's head popped over the open door. "You good?" she called out.

Good had nothing to do with how he felt. Steam still rose from the hood of his Impala. And the prick with the bleeding hand and nose had suddenly stopped moaning. Probably because he'd seen Naomi, too. The guy used his uninjured hand to reach for the knife he'd lost earlier— when Eb had shot a hole through his hand.

The prick was intent on hurting Naomi. So Eb stomped his injured, heavily bleeding hand.

The creep's pain-filled howl filled the night.

Then Eb stomped on the other hand.

"Savage," Hunter rasped.

Oh, he could show the guy savage. But first... "Naomi, I told you to leave."

She slammed the door. Rushed toward him. Almost seemed to be about to hug him, but then she stopped and put her hands behind her back. "Pretty sure we covered that I had a distinct *inability* to follow orders—"

Henry bounded from the back of the house. Of course, Henry bounded out. He raced forward. Went right to Naomi's side. His tail thumped as he sniffed her, and, satisfied, he proceeded to plop down beside her.

"Henry! You were supposed to stay!" Naomi cried out.

So they both had that problem with following orders. Interesting.

"Do *not!*" Naomi suddenly snapped as if she'd read his mind. "I am not your pet to stay where you command." She scratched Henry beneath his ears. "And Henry is my *family!*" She slid her hand beneath his collar. Tickled him with her fingers. "I told him to stay back because I wanted him safe."

"Imagine that. Giving an order because you want someone to be *safe*. Earth-shattering idea."

She'd crouched to pet the dog, and she glared up at him. "Sue me for saving you."

Saving him? *Saving*—

"We have an easy dozen gang members who are down but not out completely," Hunter informed them before Eb could choke out a response. "The lover's quarrel can wait. We need to know exactly how they found us. *Now.*"

Eb was still stomping both of the big guy's hands. He also had his gun aimed at the man's forehead.

Huh, maybe his current pose was the reason Naomi

hadn't gone through with the hug he was sure she'd intended.

She came back to save me.

That meant she didn't hate him, right? She'd driven his car at gang members who'd been intent on running *him* over. That had to be a positive sign. If she'd hated him, surely, she would have just let the guys roll forward and crush him beneath the wheels of their bikes. Correction, try to crush him.

Eb could have handled them, of course. But, it was still sweet that she cared.

"Who's a good boy?" Naomi questioned in her sugary-sweet voice. Her fingers fluttered under Henry's collar once more.

"You told him to stay somewhere, and he didn't," Eb pointed out. "That's hardly a good—"

"Oh, no." Horror sharpened her voice.

He tensed. "Naomi?"

Her hand lifted. There was something small and white in her hand. His eyes narrowed as he struggled to see it better in the darkness.

She turned the object over in her fingers. "I think it's one of those tracking tags. It was tucked under his collar."

Hunter took it from her. "Hell. It was probably on the dog when you took him from Ivan's place."

Laughter boomed.

Eb glared down at the jerk who'd been leading the attack party.

"Always knew...knew exactly where she was...part of his plan..."

Ivan's twisted plan to make Naomi pay. "Ivan set the fire at her house."

The bastard flashed a killer grin at him.

Eb stomped down harder on the hand with the giant hole in it.

This time, the guy didn't laugh. He screamed.

"Let's try again," Eb said. "*Who set the fire?*"

"I did!" A shout. Spittle flew from his mouth. "I set it because he told me to do it! Ivan wanted her to suffer for what she'd done to his partner. So suffer, she fucking will! You stopped the fire before, but I'll make sure she burns. Sooner or later, those flames will get her. Ivan told me—said that fire was perfect for her! Hudson told him about how she'd almost burned as a kid, and it would be a fitting end for her." His gaze jumped to Naomi. "You don't screw over our gang and get away! We *will end you!*"

No, they wouldn't. Eb would make certain of that. He eased off the prick's hands. Stepped to the side.

The fool lunged up.

Eb kicked the bastard in the jaw. His prey crumpled, head sagging, body slack.

You come for her, and I will end you.

Chapter Eighteen

"LET ME GET THIS STRAIGHT." MADELINE PINCHED THE bridge of her nose and squeezed her eyes shut as she stood on the front porch of the safe house. "You and your new friend—ah, Hunter McQueen, I believe his name is—"

"That's me," Hunter drawled as he sat on the top porch step. His legs spread out in front of him.

Madeline cleared her throat. "You and your friend Hunter took out twelve gang members."

Eb surveyed the wreckage in front of the house. Plenty of the motorcycles had been smashed to hell and back. "Probably gonna need some tow trucks out here."

"Oh, you think?" she snapped back.

Yeah, he did think that.

"Already called them," she muttered. "Rest easy on that score."

Her agents—along with local cops—had also taken the bikers into custody. A lot of those SOBs had been whining and moaning about their injuries. Like Eb cared about blood and bruises. "They came out here to kill Naomi."

Naomi stepped forward from her position near the front

door. "I'm pretty sure they came here to kill us both, Eb." She motioned toward Hunter. "And I don't think they would have cared if you went down in the flames, too." She wrapped her arms around her body.

As always, Henry was a shadow close to her. Quiet, watchful.

"You said Brock Arison is the one who confessed?" A long sigh broke from Madeline. "And in case anyone is confused...Brock was the big bastard, the one missing a nose ring and sporting a bullet hole in his hand," Madeline elaborated. "Does that help?"

"Yep, he confessed to us." A flat reply from Eb. Tension still poured through his body. Adrenaline pulsed. Hunter had needed to pull him away from the creep named Brock because Eb had wanted to rip the man apart. Actually, he still wanted to rip him to shreds. The prick thought he'd hurt Naomi? Oh, hell, no.

"I'm going to interrogate him, thoroughly," Madeline promised with a nod, "once his injuries have been patched up. Would have been easier if you hadn't shot him."

What? Was he supposed to be sorry for that? Not happening. "I let him keep living. You're welcome for that."

Naomi sucked in a sharp breath.

I'm scaring her. Yeah, well, learning that he was an assassin, a cold-blooded killer, probably hadn't been the highlight of her night. Then again, having a gang of criminals come to *burn her alive* couldn't have been a thrill, either.

Madeline slumped her shoulders. "This is a clusterfuck."

"Brock admitted to setting the fire at my place." Naomi's voice shook a bit at the edges. Understandable, wasn't it? "He was at my house, so he had access to the bat that was used to kill Ivan. The guy was clearly relishing being the leader tonight. Maybe he saw an opportunity. He took the bat, he eliminated Ivan, and then he came to kill me so he could tell the gang that I was the one who'd taken out Ivan—and that they'd all just gotten vengeance. I was his scapegoat and victim all at the same time."

It was a story that Eb had already been considering, too.

Madeline nodded once more. "I'll be sure and find out if that's the way things played out. He'll tell me everything. One way or another." She strode off the porch. Made a quick gesture toward her team with one hand. They scrambled faster at the motioned order. "We'll get the bikes cleared away," she tossed over her shoulder. "There'll be more questions, of course. So expect another visit from me tomorrow." Her hands were on her hips as she surveyed the wreckage. "Twelve gang members." Her head angled back toward them. "Against you two men?"

"No." Eb moved to the side of the porch. *I should have ended Brock when I had the chance.* He didn't like loose ends. "It was twelve against three. Naomi came hurtling in with my Impala. She sent her share of men running." It had been a full-on team effort.

Hunter cleared his throat. "Pretty sure she sent one flying into a tree."

Yeah, she had.

Madeline turned fully toward Naomi. "Eb let you drive the Impala?"

"He gave me the keys," Naomi replied.

Eb snorted. "I told her to get the hell away. Hunter and I were supposed to be the distraction. The pricks arrived with containers of gasoline. I couldn't risk her staying here and getting burned."

"Yet here she is." Madeline's head tilted to the right.

"And the bad guys are all in custody. Funny how that worked out."

Eb didn't find a damn thing about the situation to be funny. Fury-inducing, sure. Funny? No.

"I wasn't going to leave Eb."

Those quiet words from Naomi pierced right through him.

"And it wasn't three against twelve," Naomi corrected. "It was four against twelve." Her fingers stroked over Henry's head. "He was supposed to stay put, but Henry was ready for action, too."

"That dog..." Madeline shook her head in bemusement. "He's quite something."

Naomi gave the Golden Retriever another loving pat.

Yep, okay, I am jealous of her dog once again.

One of the agents shouted for Madeline.

"Duty calls." She began to hurry away, but paused. Looked back again. "You don't have to stay here tonight. It's going to take a long time for cleanup. You can head back to your guesthouse. Or go get a hotel room."

Naomi shook her head.

So Eb said, "Nah, we'll wait." He wanted to watch and see everything that the agents and cops did on the scene.

Madeline gave him a brittle smile. "Of course, but, Eb, let's have a word, shall we? A private word."

Hell. "Absolutely." He ambled off the porch.

The agent called out for her again.

Madeline waved the man away. She strode to the side with Eb, maneuvering until they were close to his precious Impala. He spared the car a brief glance and realized he'd never forget seeing his ride hurtle toward him.

Naomi and that car had saved his ass.

"This could have been a bloodbath," Madeline groused

to him. "Do you know what a pain in my ass that would have been?"

"I am aware." Lights illuminated the perimeter. Bright lights from the cars that the local cops had driven. Extra lights that had been brought in and positioned for cleanup and evidence collection. "That's why they're all still breathing." Though he had been so very tempted to end that whole breathing routine with Brock. *Some people are better off dead.*

"You *shot* a man in the hand!" Her words were still hushed but definitely tense.

The gunshot wound was hardly a big deal. "He was reaching for a knife. Told you that already." Eb had told her that at least twice. Maybe three times. "These assholes rolled out here, they brought gasoline canisters, and they threatened to burn us alive. What else was I supposed to do? I had to fight back."

"You mean you had to protect her." A wave toward the porch. Toward Naomi.

Damn straight, I did.

"Because she was the target."

"She was the target," he agreed, voice rough and low. "Either because Brock believed she'd killed Ivan and he wanted his justice for his dead leader or because...maybe because Naomi was right back there—maybe Brock saw an opportunity for upward mobility. He took out his own boss and wanted to blame Ivan's death on Naomi. To shut her up —permanently—he came here. He thought with all the numbers on his side, we'd be easy prey." A roll of Eb's shoulders. "He was wrong."

"Of course, he was. You're never easy prey. You're probably the most dangerous bastard I've ever met. You fight dirty as hell, and you don't stop until your goal is achieved. Or at least, you don't usually stop."

Tow trucks had arrived. Three of them. A giant flatbed. Oh, those beat-up bikes really weren't going to be good for more than scrap.

"You still think Naomi killed Hudson?" Madeline's voice had dropped even lower. "Is your goal still to prove her guilt? Or, for the first time in your life, are you giving up on your agenda?"

"Naomi says that she didn't do it." He watched the tow trucks get into position. "I believe her."

"Seriously?"

"I believe her," he said again.

"Well...damn. Okay." She moved to stand directly in front of him. "If she's not our killer, then who is?"

"Maybe Brock can shed light on that for us."

Silence. Then... "While you had the bastard bleeding on the ground, did he say something that you want to share with me?"

He put a hand to his heart. "Madeline, are you suggesting I was torturing the man in order to get intel? I'm shocked. That's hardly the CIA way." His voice was deliberately bland.

The agent who'd been trying to get her attention for the last few moments shouted again. Madeline ignored him.

"He really wants to discuss something with you," Eb pointed out.

"Morris is a green recruit who wants me holding his hand every moment. Forget him. *Did you learn something you want to share with me?*"

He hadn't been able to interrogate Brock because after that creep's crack about ending Naomi, Eb's temper had gotten the better of him. "I knocked him out. Naomi and

Hunter insisted we call the authorities—that'd be *you*—so, no, he didn't share more with me. But if you'll give me a few moments alone with Brock in a room, I can get him to tell me every secret he's ever had in his life."

Soft laughter poured from her. "I don't think so. In case it somehow slipped your mind, you're not CIA any longer, remember? I'll be handling the interrogation from here on, but thanks." She patted his shoulder. "And I'll assume you'll keep staying close to the grieving widow?"

"She saved my ass. She could have walked away. Uh, driven away and never looked back."

Her inscrutable gaze studied him. "One good deed doesn't redeem a person. That's not how it works."

"Naomi said she didn't kill him. I believe her."

The nearest tow truck hoist groaned and shrieked as it began to lift one of the wrecked motorcycles.

"Of all the people in this world," Madeline mused, "you know there is just no redemption for some individuals. Sometimes we can try, but we can't ever wipe away our sins. They're permanent. Like scars or tattoos we will always wear."

The bike slipped off the hoist. Crashed to the ground.

"She saw you in action tonight." Madeline edged closer to him as the tow truck driver shouted angrily at his assistant. "If Naomi truly is innocent, do you think she's going to want to tie herself to a killer?" Her hand slid from his shoulder and pressed to his chest. "For plenty of people, you'd be a hard no." A pat against his chest. "Better get ready for her to leave you. It will happen as soon as she's cleared. We find the person who murdered Hudson, we lock that individual away, and you will never see Naomi again. Sucks, I get it, but that's life. In particular, that's *our* life. You know no one at the Agency ever really gets a happy ending in this world. We lie to everyone, even the people we want to love."

* * *

"THEY SEEM COZY," Naomi noted crisply. Yep, her words held an edge because she was pretty certain jealousy was slicing and dicing its way through her body.

"Who? The tow truck drivers?" Hunter rose from his relaxed position. "They seem kinda pissed if you ask me. And loud. They are loud as hell. It would probably help if they stopped dropping shit."

"You know I'm not talking about the tow truck drivers," she grumbled right back at him. "Stop being difficult. Eb and Madeline. Those two. They seem...cozy," she repeated. Too cozy. In fact, Madeline could stop touching Eb's chest at any moment.

Any old moment.

If Madeline wasn't going to stop touching him, then would it kill Eb to remove the woman's hand from his person?

Soft laughter. Then Hunter said, voice amused, "I don't think she's his type."

"She's beautiful, smart, and some kind of super spy. I'd think all of those things appeal to Eb." She hadn't asked him about his love life before they'd, ah, jumped into bed together. Oh, no. Naomi's stomach dropped. What if he was involved with Madeline?

Spies with benefits?

Naomi took a hard step back. Oh, no. No way. Naomi was not a side piece. She was the main piece. Dammit.

"I think..." Hunter's tone was musing. "Call it instinct, but I suspect Eb likes a different sort of woman. The type of woman who takes your favorite ride, aims it at your enemies, and guns it for all she's worth."

She barely heard him. Her gaze was still on Eb. And Madeline. And Madeline *patting* Eb's chest. Naomi's eyes narrowed.

"Personally, I've never really been jealous," Hunter continued. "Just never cared enough about someone to feel it. But, judging by your reaction and your glare, it looks like a real bitch. My advice? If you have a problem with what you see, go fix it. A doer like you should never sit around. I mean, aren't you the same woman who just plowed into a biker gang? You really gonna retreat and wilt? Or are you going to—"

She stalked past him and down the steps.

"Fight," he finished and sounded smug.

She kept right on stalking until she was beside Eb. And Madeline. They both turned their heads and frowned at her. Because every light in the city seemed to have been brought into the yard, Naomi could clearly see them.

And the hand that was still on Eb's chest.

Sighing, she reached out. Removed the hand.

"What are you doing?" Madeline asked her.

It should be obvious. But she'd spell it out. "Removing the hand."

Madeline gaped at her.

She ignored the other woman. But she did glare at Eb. "You should have removed it."

"*What is happening here?*" Madeline seemed to be choking.

Naomi felt a burn in her cheeks. Clearly, she'd let Hunter egg her into an action she should not have taken but —screw it. Too late to back away now. "Jealousy." A nod. "Hunter was right. It is a bitch." Naomi sucked in a deep breath. The tow truck hoist was grinding nearby and the sound grated like nails on a chalkboard. "Are you two involved?"

"No," Eb replied.

"*No.*" Adamant. From Madeline.

Naomi spared Madeline a glance. "Good. Keep the hands off." Another nod. "Now I'm going inside, and I'm going to bed." Before she did or said anything else that would be terminally embarrassing, Naomi prepared for a fast march away.

Only Eb's hand flew out and curled around her wrist. Electricity instantly surged through her. At this point, Naomi figured she'd always feel that particular surge whenever he touched her. A hazard of being around Eb.

"I wouldn't fuck you while being involved with someone else," Eb stated, his voice low. "*You* are the woman I'm involved with. Only you."

Good to know.

His thumb slid along her inner wrist. "Jealousy, huh?"

"I don't just ride to the rescue for anyone." A sniff. "Now, if you'll excuse me..." With her head up and her spine straight, Naomi walked right back to the porch.

"What just happened?" Madeline asked behind her.

Naomi didn't hear Eb's response. The pounding of her heart was too loud as it echoed in her ears.

Hunter smiled as Naomi approached. "Feel better?"

Actually...yes.

"Told you," he added with a half-shrug. "She's not his type. He's far too obsessed with you to see anyone else."

Obsessed. Obsessed wasn't the same as loving someone. But...no, they weren't talking about love. What was happening between her and Eb? It was lust. Passion. Need.

Obsession.

She tapped her thigh. Henry hurried to her side. They went in the house.

And she only looked back once, but when she did, Naomi found Eb's gaze locked on her.

* * *

"Be careful," Madeline urged.

Eb couldn't drag his gaze off Naomi. She'd just looked back at him.

She was jealous. She still wants me.

He was about to go insane with wanting her.

"Maybe she's not the cold-blooded killer we assumed, but...no way she's going to go after forever with you. It's just not in the cards."

He forced a smile as he finally glanced at his former boss once more. "Since when am I the forever type?"

What could have been sympathy came and went on her face. "Even tough agents can get broken hearts. Just watch yourself, that's all." She backed away. "Now I have to go handle Morris before he has a heart attack. I'll update you on my interrogation with Brock. You know, *after* he has medical clearance so I can talk to the man." Waving her hands in the air, she hurried away. "Morris, stop trying to help the tow truck drivers! You're about to get your ass crushed!"

Eb headed for his Impala. The steam had stopped pouring out, so that was a good sign. He touched the hood. Still warm, though.

"Are you going to keep her?" Hunter asked.

He wasn't the least bit surprised that Hunter had sauntered his way over to the vehicle.

"Of course, I'm keeping the car." As if he'd ever let go of

his baby. "Probably just some small problem from when Naomi was gunning it around the yard. You're supposed to treat my baby with care." But he wasn't mad at Naomi. He could overlook the gunning of his Impala. Actually...

It was hot the way Naomi saved me. Not that he'd needed saving, but, still...

You learned a lot about a person in dangerous times. Some people would break. Some people would panic. Some people...

They'd risk everything to save someone else.

"I wasn't talking about the damn car."

Yeah, he'd known that. But... "You don't get to keep people. They either choose you or they don't." Simple fact of life. You couldn't make someone stay. Not when the person just wanted to leave. Or worse, not when the person just didn't want you.

"She ran into a biker gang for you. Literally. Ran the car right at them. If that's not choosing you, what is?"

He wanted to believe that Naomi would choose him. So badly. "I fucked up with her." Stark. He'd lied. He'd tricked her. He'd intended to lock her sweet ass in a jail cell. Now, he wanted to do whatever it took to keep her out of a cell. To protect her, always. So, yeah, he'd done a one-eighty. It happened.

"Did you grovel?" Hunter wanted to know. "I told you it would be necessary. Women go for big grovels."

"There are some things that apologies don't fix." Some hurts that went too deep. He'd never been good at apologizing. Hell, his family could tell Naomi that fact. But for her, he was willing to try just about anything. Including the best grovel he could manage.

Or maybe I'll just find the real killer, beat the shit out of him, and tie him up with a bow for Naomi. When she gets her name thoroughly cleared, maybe she'll forgive me then. Maybe...

Or maybe Madeline had been right. And, in the end, Naomi would walk away from him.

"If it were me, I'd keep her."

Eb's head swung toward Hunter. Frustrated, he growled, "I told you, you don't get to—"

"Find a way. *Find. A. Way.* If she really matters, you'll do it."

Did she really matter to him? Hell, yes, she did. So, as far as keeping her, as far as finding a way...

I damn well will.

He'd start with the game plan already swirling in his head. Find the real killer. Beat the shit out of him. Tie him up with a bow...

Deliver him as a gift to Naomi.

Some women liked flowers. Not his Naomi.

She's going to get a killer on a silver platter.

Chapter Nineteen

The house was quiet. Naomi peeked out of her bedroom window. The wreckage had been removed. No more agents rushing around. No more tow trucks. No more crazed gang members looking to watch her burn.

The sun had risen. A new day.

She'd slept some, on and off, even with the voices and the chaos from outside. Each time she drifted to sleep, though, she'd dreamed of fire. The fire that had taken her parents. The fire at her house.

A fire here, at the safe house. Only she hadn't escaped the flames.

They'd been closing in on her. And then...

Eb had been there.

Hero. Villain. Maybe some combination of both. But what she knew with certainty was that when she needed him, he was there for her. Even in her dreams.

He'd helped get Henry back for her.

He'd fought the fire at her house with her.

He'd stood by her when the seizure had her shaking and unable to speak.

And he'd gone out to face a dozen bikers for her.

If he really hated her, he wouldn't do any of those things. As for her own feelings, hate didn't enter the equation when she thought of him. Something else did. Maybe it was time to stop hiding from the way she felt. To do something about it. To be honest with him.

Naomi threw on fresh clothes and her sneakers, and she hurried from the room. She darted into the hallway and pounded on the door right across from hers.

"Come in," a gruff voice ordered.

She swung open the door and barreled inside. "We need to talk because I still want you and you still want— *Hunter!*"

"Yeah, hey." Hunter sat up in bed, with the sheets tangled around his waist. A long, jagged line of scarred flesh ran from his collarbone down to those sheets. *I recognize the raised, angry scar from a fire when I see one.* Because over the years, she'd volunteered with plenty of burn victims, and Naomi knew when she was staring at the damage flames could do to skin.

"Eyes up here, sunshine," he chided.

Her eyes whipped up to meet his.

"I think you knocked on the wrong door." A long exhale from him. "Pity. But I'm guessing you're looking for Eb?"

"What happened to you, Hunter?"

"A nightmare. Same thing that happens to plenty of us. Lucky for me, my buddy Declan was there to help haul me out. He was also there to push me when I didn't want to keep living."

Declan Flynn. "I've read news stories about him." Only those stories weren't always the most positive. In fact, some of the stories just straight up said Declan Flynn was mob royalty.

And Eb's sister had married that man?

"Ah, but you of all people know not to believe everything you read." Hunter sawed his hand over the stubble on his jaw. "Declan is not the boogeyman. If he was, I'd be dead. Marley wouldn't have married him. And Eb wouldn't now have an extremely useful, exceedingly rich brother-in-law."

She gripped the doorknob far too tightly. "Where is Eb?"

"He slept downstairs. I think he was trying to put some distance between himself and temptation."

Naomi swallowed.

"Temptation...AKA, you."

Yeah, she'd gotten that part. But should she be insulted or flattered that Eb had put so much space between them? Insulted seemed to be the way she was leaning.

"If he's not sprawled on the couch, check the garage." A lazy suggestion from Hunter. "The man is a fanatic about his car."

She'd noticed that personality quirk, too. "Sorry to bother you." Backing up, she began to pull the door closed.

"Naomi."

She paused.

"He has a heart, too, you know. Try not to break it." With that, Hunter lowered back into the bed. "Beauty sleep." A dramatic sigh. "Why won't anyone ever let me get it?"

Quietly, she closed the door. Then she hurried down the stairs. Checked the couch. No sleeping Eb. So she went toward the back of the house because she knew the Impala had been moved to the garage. Henry brushed against her, then headed for his food bowl. While he munched, she slipped out the back door. Shaking her head, Naomi noticed that there was a doggie door cut in the bottom of that wood. It truly was a safe house that came with all the essentials.

The sky burned with reds and golds as she made her way to the garage. Her sneakers made no sound on the damp grass. Damp from dew, not rain. Birds sang in the distance, and the creaks and calls of insects teased her ears.

The garage door was open, so she slipped inside. Eb was at work, bent beneath the hood of his Impala. He wore jeans. Sneakers. A white t-shirt that stretched across the powerful muscles of his back as he leaned forward.

"You're up early."

His words made her jump because she hadn't realized that he even knew she was there. Even as her heart raced, Naomi managed to say, "Ah, so are you."

He eased from beneath the hood. Tossed a screwdriver into a tool box. Carefully lowered the hood of the Impala and turned toward her. Black streaks slid across the front of his shirt. His hair was tousled, and his eyes were as intense as ever. The thick stubble on his jaw just made him look rougher. More dangerous. Way sexier. "Couldn't sleep well," he admitted.

"Me, too." Low. She folded her arms over her chest.

"Every time I closed my eyes, I'd see that stupid gang coming for you."

Her breath caught. "I kept dreaming about fire."

His expression hardened as Eb took a step toward her. "I'm not ever gonna let you burn, Naomi."

"I believe you."

He gave a little jerk at those words. *"Naomi."*

She walked toward him. Her steps were probably too fast. Clumsy. Grace had never been her strong suit. Her hands fell back to her sides. "Sorry if I messed up your car."

"Don't apologize to me. You saved my ass."

Her fingers trailed over the closed hood as she stopped before Eb. "Thought you could handle things on your own. That you didn't need saving."

"You didn't know that when you came riding to the rescue. You came because you were worried about me."

Yes. She swallowed. "I dreamed of fire, and I dreamed of you. When the fire was closing in, you were there."

"I won't leave you to the fire. Not ever." His voice had deepened. Gone so much rougher.

His voice scraped along her body and soul in all of the very best ways. "Like I said, I believe you."

His jaw hardened even more. "Means something different to you..."

"What?" What was he talking about? What was different to her?

"Nothing." Eb cleared his throat. "I need to shower. I'm sure we'll be having a hell of a day." He started to walk by her.

But her hand flew out, and she caught his wrist. "Don't leave." Low. Careful. She moved closer to him. Pressed a kiss to his shoulder, right through the white t-shirt. "I need..." But her words trailed off. Her fingers slid along his inner wrist. When he touched her there, sensation fired through her blood. Awareness. Attraction. He probably didn't feel the same surge, though, so she should just stop stroking his inner wrist.

She let him go.

But in a flash, his hands had closed around her waist. "What do you need?"

Her lips pressed together.

"I will give you anything you need. Just tell me, Naomi. *Tell me*."

Was this a mistake? Did it matter? Especially when the mistake felt so good?

"Naomi."

Fine. But there would be no going back. "I need you."

He lifted her up. Turned her and put her down on the Impala's hood. Her eyes widened as her hands flew out and curled around his shoulders. "Eb?"

"Hunter is inside the house."

She nodded but didn't mention her accidental trip to his bedroom. No need to, ah, spoil the mood.

"No one can see us in here. And I want to give you exactly what you need."

His hands flew down her body. He tossed away her shoes. Then those fast fingers of his moved to her waist. He unhooked the jeans, lowered the zipper, and started hauling those jeans off her legs...*while she was on the hood of his car.* "Eb!"

"Trust me?"

Her breath sawed out. "The car is supposed to be so important to you. Aren't you afraid I'll dent it or something this way?"

"You already did dent it—when you ran it into the biker."

Oh, right. Her bad.

"And I can think of nothing better than fucking you right here, right now."

That did sound promising, she had to admit.

"But I think I'm supposed to grovel." He'd tossed her jeans and her panties to the floor of the garage. "So I should do that first." He hauled her to the edge of the hood. Spread her legs wide. "Can't say I have a lot of experience at groveling, so you'll have to tell me if I do it right."

"What?"

His fingers raked over her clit. "Sorry I lied to you." His thumb stroked her. He dipped two fingers into her. "Sorry I didn't tell you the truth from the very beginning." His thumb stroked harder. Swirled and he—

He bent and put his mouth on her.

She fell back against the hood, her legs widening more as he licked her and teased her with his tongue and his lips even as he worked those long, broad fingers into her again and again and again—

"Sorry I made you doubt me." A hard plunge of his fingers. His breath blew over her clit. "Sorry I made you cry." He licked her. A long, slow lick. Then his tongue was dipping into her core.

"Eb!"

"Sorry I wasn't on your fucking side..." She could *feel* each word. "From the beginning." He teased her. Plucked her clit. Strummed with a frantic rhythm. "But I am now. *I am now.*" His mouth took her again.

Her eyes squeezed shut. Her body tensed and shuddered, and an orgasm was close, she knew it was close. She knew—

"Sorry I hurt you. *Will never do it again.*" His tongue licked her clit. Lashed her. Wild and intense. Desperate. Both of his hands were on her thighs now as his mouth full-on took control. There was no stopping. There was no slowing. Her body had slid higher up on the hood, and he'd followed her and he was feasting and taking and she was coming against him. Coming on the car. Coming with her legs spread wide. Coming as his mouth licked and sucked and the release detonated inside of her.

Coming...on what had to be the best apology ever.

His head slowly lifted. His eyes met hers.

Naomi realized that she'd thrown out her hands and

that her palms had slapped down on the metal of the hood. Her breath came too fast. Her heart thudded too hard. And Eb looked at her as if he wanted to eat her alive.

Been there, done that. And, please, do it again anytime.

"I'm fucking you now," he told her.

Excellent plan. Brilliant.

"I want my dick in you, and I want you coming around me."

Fair. She had to swallow a few times before Naomi could manage to say, "I want your dick in me, and I want to feel you coming inside of me."

His teeth snapped together. He backed away. Left her spread out on the hood.

"Uh, Eb?" Talk about suddenly feeling vulnerable.

He stalked to the side of the car. Reached inside. Fumbled a bit. She pushed herself up. Sat on the hood and started to haul her shirt down to cover her bare sex.

"Condom was in the glove box."

Her head whipped up. He was back. In front of her. He was already rolling on the condom. He'd jerked open his jeans, and his thick, heavy dick shoved toward her. In a flash, the condom was in place, she was perched on the edge of the hood, and Eb was between her legs. His hands slammed down on either side of her body.

Then his dick was driving into her. Not fast, though. Not hard. Instead, he pushed in, one slow inch at a time. One thick, full, aching inch at a time. Her sex clamped greedily around him, squeezed hard, took him in. Craved more. More.

"You feel...fantastic," he gritted out.

She leaned forward. Her mouth pressed to his neck. She licked and sucked. Bit lightly with the edge of her teeth. "So do you."

He shuddered, and Naomi was pretty sure that she heard the sound of his control shredding. His hands flew to clamp around her hips. He withdrew, then sank in deep again. Withdrew. Drove into her. Over and over.

She licked him again. Kissed his neck. Caught his earlobe with her teeth and tugged.

He had her off the car. He'd yanked her into his arms. "Legs around me."

Her legs locked around him. He took two frantic steps and had her against the wall of the garage. He pounded into her. Fast and frantic. Deep and hard. He pinned her against the wall even as one hand snaked between their bodies. Pushed down to her clit. He tormented, pressed, and he—

Release. Naomi opened her mouth to scream as the orgasm erupted, but his mouth took hers. He kissed her with a wild fury even as his hips jerked and he emptied into her. The release held her captive as surely as he did. Pleasure poured through her body on wave after earth-shattering wave. She was pretty sure the whole world had just obliterated around her.

His head slowly lifted. His eyes met hers.

She still had on a shirt. At least, Naomi thought she did. Yes, yes, she did. Shirt, check.

Body-quaking orgasm? Check, check.

He still wore his t-shirt, too. And his jeans, mostly. Her legs were locked around his hips, and he was lodged inside of her.

"That was…" Naomi licked her lips. "Probably the best apology I've ever had in my life."

Laughter boomed from him. Deep and warm and real.

And the cold spaces deep inside? The spaces that she'd thought might never be filled? The ones that lurked in the hidden places of her heart…

They started to warm.

"Sweetheart…" He leaned down and lightly kissed her lips. "I can apologize all day long."

She was the one to laugh then. Against his mouth. To feel the warmth spread inside of her as she laughed and held him. Her thoughts were scattered. Hopeful. *Don't use me. Don't lie to me. Let this be real. Let us be real.*

"But how about we take this inside?" Eb suggested with a wide smile. One that had his dimple winking at her.

Going in was probably a great plan. She'd also never, ever be able to look at his Impala the same way.

Carefully, he withdrew. He lowered Naomi until her feet touched the floor of the garage. He ditched the condom. Tossed it into the trash and straightened his own clothes. With tender hands, he helped her to dress. His fingers twined with hers as they headed out of the garage.

They passed Henry. A Henry who sat near the exterior of the garage, with his paws over his eyes.

"I think we embarrassed him," Eb noted.

She felt heat burn her cheeks.

"Better get used to me being around her, buddy," Eb warned her dog. "I don't plan on disappearing anytime soon.

Naomi's steps stumbled. Did he mean those words? No, he couldn't. This wasn't for keeps. This was just— attraction. Lust. It was—

"I believe you, Naomi," Eb said.

The words pulled her eyes to him. Naomi found his gaze locked straight on her.

"I believe you," Eb repeated.

Those words sank into her. Poured through her.

"So after I fuck you at least twice more, how about we head out and hunt down the killer?"

Her heart raced. "Twice more?"

"Trying to make the apology good for you." But no humor lined his face now. He stopped right near the back door of the safe house. "I won't lie to you. Not ever again. Ask me anything. I'll give you the truth, no matter how dark or brutal. No matter if I think the truth will make you run from me, I'll give it to you."

She was almost afraid to ask the questions that swirled in her head.

"I'm gonna be on your side, Naomi."

"Why?"

His free hand lifted. Tucked a lock of hair behind her ear. "Because I believe you."

Her head turned. Brushing her lips against his palm felt like the most natural thing in the world. And, maybe it was crazy, but a part of her really, really hoped that one day, he'd tell her that he wanted to be at her side...

Because he loved her.

Chapter Twenty

"THIS IS BULLSHIT!" THE BELLOW COULD CLEARLY BE heard even through the closed hospital room door. "You can't do this to me! I want a lawyer! I know my freaking rights! *Bullshit!*"

Sighing, Madeline Desalt shoved open the door to hospital room 308. Inside, two agents were stationed on either side of the hospital bed. Lateisha Gray stood to the right, her shoulders straight, her dark hair pulled back, and her eyes on the patient. To the left of the bed, Colson Reid had his hands crossed in front of his body. His blue eyes were on the suspect in the bed, and his jaw had locked tight.

In the bed, their suspect twisted and heaved, as much as he could twist and heave with one hand being cuffed to the railing and with the other hand having recently been sewn up and bandaged.

"You're not breaking the cuffs," she said, annoyed as she approached Brock. Who did the guy think he was? Superman? "But you might rip out all the stitches that the doctor just put in your hand so I suggest you settle down."

At her voice, his head whipped toward her.

Madeline pasted a bright smile on her face. Time to play the game. "Hello, Brock."

"This is bullshit!" he cried.

"I believe you've noted that a few times, yes." She dipped her head forward in a commiserating nod. "However, it's technically not bullshit. This scene is about to be you...answering every single question that I have. Spoiler alert, I have lots of questions. About you. About your dead boss Ivan. About the woman you tried to burn alive."

He heaved up, dragging himself to a sitting position. The perp was bruised and battered, with scrapes all along his neck and arms.

"You look like you got the crap beaten out of you," she murmured. "And here you went in with your whole gang to take out Naomi Romano. Bet this is not the result you expected, is it?"

Colson snorted.

Lateisha didn't make a sound.

Fury twisted Brock's face. "I ain't telling you nothing!"

An annoyed sigh was her response. "Do I look like your local cops?"

"What?"

"Sorry, let me rephrase..." Her hands went to her hips. "Do I look like I'm going to give you an option on responding?"

He blinked.

"Colson, go stand outside by the door, will you? When he starts screaming again, I want to make sure we aren't disturbed."

Colson immediately double-timed it for the door.

"Wait!" Brock's voice broke. "I want a lawyer. I want a lawyer, *now!*"

Madeline rolled her eyes. "No."

His eyes practically bulged from his head. "You can't—"

"I can do anything I want. You see, I don't exist." She was not in the mood for this crap to continue. She had places to be. Other cases to work.

"The fuck you don't exist—"

"I have a fake name," Madeline cut through his snarling words. The man was giving her a headache. "I have a fake life. And I have the power to do anything to you that I want. You see, I'm not a cop. Told you that." She knew that she'd mentioned that important fact. The local cops had been the ones so dead set on getting the guy patched up. Frankly, she didn't give a real damn if he bled out or not. But she'd had to maintain the appearance of caring in front of them. Only, there were no more local police eyes on her. Time for her to get business handled. "I don't play by the rules that constrain local officers. In fact, I make my own rules." Something that brought her great pleasure in life. "You tried to attack a friend of mine last night. Granted, he pisses me off most days, but...I still like him. You went after Eb. You and your whole gang—"

He lunged forward.

Lateisha put a scalpel to his throat.

"*What the fuck?*" he breathed as he stiffened. "You can't do that—this is a hospital!"

"That's why I used a scalpel," Lateisha replied without any hesitation. "Seemed fitting. I do keep a knife strapped to my ankle, FYI. But this felt better. More in tune with the scene, you know."

Brock gasped like a fish tossed from the water onto a dock.

"Lateisha is very good at getting reluctant individuals to cooperate," Madeline said.

His still bulging eyes darted to Lateisha.

"Hi," she said, flashing him a sunny grin. "I like to excel at my job. I'm very goal-oriented."

"You're crazy." Those bulging eyes came back to Madeline. "You're both crazy."

"No, I'm impatient. Also bored." She also never enjoyed it when someone called her crazy. A real annoyance, that was. And Madeline had already been annoyed. She'd had to wait far too long for him to be patched up. "You tried to torch Naomi and my friend Eb hours ago."

"I—"

"Your prints are all over the gas containers. Plus, we have security footage from the scene. The property was wired like you wouldn't believe. So, yes, that means we have you on video. Every moment. So don't waste my time with denials. You and your gang were right there on the scene when I arrived. But I'm betting this wasn't your first fire, was it?" Though, in this particular instance, it had just been an *attempted* arson attack. Eb had stopped Brock from actually igniting the safe house. "You set the fire at Naomi's home."

His head jerked. The scalpel drew a drop of blood.

"So what?" Brock snapped.

Oh, damn. Okay, so he was just going to confess. Nice.

"Bitch had it coming," he grumbled.

Interesting response. "I did some digging while I was waiting on the docs to finish with you." Her head tilted. She'd always hated being idle, so Madeline had used the time to her advantage. "There have been quite a few fires in the area. Mostly—as odd as this sounds—targeting individuals who had lodged complaints against Ivan Sokolov. They'd said he trashed their businesses or extorted them or stole from them. So many complaints. So many fires. Weird, isn't it?"

He swallowed. The drop of blood that had been drawn tracked slowly down his thick neck.

"Let me see if I can guess what might have happened... when Ivan got angry, he liked to send a message to his enemies? And that message typically came via fire?"

No response. So annoying. Madeline continued, "Lateisha was going to be a doctor. Once upon a time. But I recruited her and convinced her that a job with me would be far more rewarding than she could ever imagine. However, she learned a great deal of helpful info from medical school. Picked up all kinds of handy skills. Fun fact, she can perform a perfect vivisection."

"What in the hell is a vivisection?"

"Oh, you don't know?" Madeline laughed. "If you don't know, then you really, really don't want to find out. You'll be alive during the process, you see. That's the whole point. You have to be alive when the cutting begins—"

"You can't do this! I know my rights!" He yanked hard against the cuff and his whole face flushed a dark red.

He seemed to miss the point that she didn't give a flying fuck about his rights. "You set the fire at Naomi's house. You took the bat from her truck, and you went back and you used it on Ivan, didn't you?" She strode to the left side of the bed, taking the spot that Colson had vacated.

He heaved out a breath and shook his head. "I ain't telling you—"

The scalpel dug deeper. "Whoops," Lateisha said. "My finger slipped."

Madeline caught Brock's chin in her hand. She turned his head fully toward her. Enough fun and games. "When I am done with you, I can have you dropped in the deepest, darkest prison in the world. No one will look for you, and I can assure you, no one will ever find you."

A tremor shook his body as he stared into her eyes. "I just—I wanted to be in charge, you know?"

"Um."

"Ivan always said...he said you had to scare your enemies. You had to make them fear you. I-I was just trying to—"

"Trying to take over?" Madeline cut in. "Trying to be the baddest bastard on the block?"

His breath sawed in and out. In and out. Finally, voice dropping, he rasped, "I know Ivan worked with you."

"Um."

"I know he made deals with Hudson."

"Ivan made deals because he had intel that was valuable to Hudson. To me. Contacts in Russia that were valuable. I don't see how you can offer me anything."

"I can!" Brock cried. "I can..." His voice trailed away.

Oh, no. He didn't get to stop. "Talk to me. Convince me. Tell me everything I want to know. Then I'll decide if what you have is good enough for me. Otherwise, get ready for a swift trip to hell and a drop in a prison hole so dark and deep that you will think you've been buried alive."

He blinked. Twice. Three times.

And, with minimal effort, with barely just a few drops of blood and just with the threat of a prison that didn't exist, she got her confession. She got exactly what she wanted. Pretty much in record time.

Because in her experience, the louder the bellows, the faster the prey broke. The toughest-looking criminals were often the ones who had the greatest fear buried in their hearts.

It's all show on the outside. When it comes right down to

it, the worst bullies are always the ones who are the most afraid.

A lesson she'd learned when she was just sixteen years old.

* * *

HER KNEES PRESSED into the mattress as Naomi straddled Eb's hips. They shouldn't be doing this. She knew it. They...

He surged up into her, his hips leaving the bed as he thrust hard and deep, and Naomi's eyes squeezed closed because Eb felt so insanely good in her.

Her hands fell against his chest. They'd gotten to her bedroom. They'd stripped. Then gone straight to fucking.

How can I want him this badly? This soon? "Are you..." *Don't ask. Don't ask.* She should not ask, not now because this was not the time or the place but... "Are you really an assassin?"

His hands bit into her hips. He lifted her up and down. Up and down. "Yes."

She had to bite her lip to hold back her cries. She didn't know where Hunter was, and the last thing Naomi wanted was for him to hear her.

Up and down.

Deeper. Wilder. Harder.

His gaze burned at her. "But they all...fucking deserved to die."

Her head shook. Her body shook.

His right hand moved to work her clit.

"I'm good at killing," Eb told her.

Can't be talking about this now. This can't be happening. Eb can't be saying—

"I'm even better at making you come." He squeezed her clit.

The orgasm detonated inside of her. Her inner muscles clamped hard around Eb's dick. Contracted and pulsed as the pleasure consumed her.

She would have fallen against his chest, but he rolled them. Twisted and turned, and she was on her back and he pounded into her until he came. Fast, driving thrusts.

He shouted her name when he erupted.

Didn't seem to give a damn if Hunter heard him or not.

She tried to catch her breath.

His hips ground against her.

Eb.

Her hands fluttered around his shoulders. Those strong, powerful shoulders. His eyes were on her. Seeing into her, and she shouldn't have said it, but the thought that she'd had—over and over—just wouldn't leave her alone. Naomi heard herself whisper, "I wish I'd met you first."

A growl broke from him.

But then he pulled away. Rose from the bed. Stalked to the bathroom, and she was left in the bed alone with a body that ached and goosebumps rising on her skin when she'd known such passion and pleasure just moments before. Suddenly too vulnerable, Naomi grabbed for the sheet.

He told me he was good at killing. I told him that I wished I'd met him first.

Probably not the right thing for either of them to say. Being *together* was probably not right for them.

So why did it feel like the best thing she'd ever had in her life? Why did he feel like the best thing?

Because I don't think he'll hurt me. Because I know he'd take on a whole biker gang to protect me. Because he doesn't hesitate to fight for me.

"I can't change the past."

At Eb's deep, growling voice, her head turned toward the open bathroom door.

"I can't change the things I've done. I can't change the person I am. Can't change the job that I had." Naked, he stalked toward her. Stopped right beside the bed. "But I can promise this. I might not have had you first, but I damn well will have you from here on out. You are mine, Naomi."

No, no, they weren't permanent. This was just—she didn't know what they were.

His hand rose toward her.

She sucked in a breath.

Eb's hand froze. "Do I scare you, Naomi?"

He'd confessed—during sex—to being a killer. No, an assassin. And then she'd exploded like a firework. She was so messed up. "I think I scare myself more than you ever could."

He climbed into the bed with her.

"Eb?"

His arms closed around her. He pulled her against him, and it seemed like the most natural thing in the world to rest her head against him. To exhale slowly. To feel safe.

I am so messed up.

"I can lie really well," he told her gruffly. "A talent I've had my whole life. My brother, Jake—with him, what you see is what you get. He's intense and dark and he...scared a lot of people away when we were younger. I saw how they all reacted, and I knew—hell, I knew I was so much worse than him. If they feared him, how would they feel about me?"

She could hear and feel the steady pounding of his heart.

"So I smiled when I didn't feel like smiling. I joked

when nothing made me laugh. I went to the parties and I drank the beers and I fit in with everyone else. I wore my camouflage like a second skin. I attracted the attention of the CIA after my stint in the military. I even convinced my brother to join me because do you know how excited the Agency was to have *twins*? We could be in two places at once. Talk about a real mind fuck to the enemy." He pressed a kiss to the top of her head. "I saw you dancing in the fountain that long ago day. I wanted to talk to you. I wanted to hear your laugh over and over. But my sister needed me. I left. I went to her."

She didn't speak. She wanted to see where his story went.

"I could have come back to you. Could have tried to win you away from Hudson. He was already telling me that he was falling for you and I was pissed and jealous—over a woman I'd never spoken to. Just a woman I'd seen dancing in a fountain." His heart continued to beat in its steady, deep rhythm. "But I am a vengeful bastard. It wasn't good enough for me that the man who'd hurt my sister was in prison. He'd been locked away when he hurt her. Marley— she'd wake up, screaming at night. He tried to shatter my sister, and no one shatters the things I love."

A hard chill skated over her body.

"So I made deals. Agreed to take more cases with the CIA even though I'd told them before that I was out. I went on my missions. Hudson got free of the Agency, but I was dragged in deeper, and then I was given the payoff that I wanted. Strings were pulled, and I camouflaged myself again. This time, I went in the prison as a criminal because I needed to get killing close to my prey."

Shock jolted her. "You lived in a prison in order to kill Sebastian Glass?"

"That was the goal. But my new brother-in-law beat me to the punch. Declan Flynn couldn't stand what Sebastian had done to Marley, and he eliminated the bastard with a few taps on his keyboard." Rough laughter. Mocking. "I was living in hell, and Declan took my prey right out from under me. I got out of that place, but still had to finish paying my CIA debts. I took hits." Flat. "But I swear, I never hurt an innocent. I read the files. I did my own intel gathering. I always made sure the targets were legitimate. And with every step I took, I lost more and more of my soul. Hell, some days, I'm not sure there is any real soul left in me."

She turned in his arms. "What's that mean? That you're the monster?" Is that what he was trying to tell her?

"I faked being a hero with you. I will never be the real deal."

He felt real enough to her. "Let me be the judge of that."

"*I didn't know that Hudson was evil.* I swear, I didn't. He was better than me when it came to wearing a mask because I didn't know. If I had known...if I'd realized..." The faint lines near his mouth deepened. "I would have killed him before I let him hurt you. You are my priority. *I believe you.*"

She lifted up. And pressed her mouth to his.

* * *

"Thanks for your assistance, Lateisha," Madeline murmured. "You can wait outside."

They'd gotten everything that was needed from Brock Arison.

The scalpel had vanished. Lateisha nodded and walked

270

calmly for the door. When she pulled it open, Colson stared inquisitively at her, then he glanced back at Madeline.

She nodded. "I'll be out in just a moment. Make sure no one interrupts."

Colson closed the door. He braced his legs apart, planted his feet firmly on that tiled floor, and whispered, "Vivisection?"

Lateisha grimaced. "You heard that part?"

"I've got exceptionally good hearing. Plus, I was eavesdropping for all that I was worth."

"I thought I'd faint when she said that." She balled her hands into fists so that Colson wouldn't see the trembling. She had *never* meant to accidentally scratch the guy with the scalpel, but he'd moved, and she'd nicked him. Twice. She'd been about to burst out with her apology and then Madeline had gotten all super scary on her.

"Thank Christ." He exhaled. Mock shuddered. "Because if you went around on the weekend slicing and dicing people, I'd be scared as hell of you."

Yeah, well, she was currently scared as hell of her new boss. "Is Madeline always that intense?"

He nodded. "Welcome to the Agency."

"Uh, thanks but—"

A scream erupted from inside the hospital room.

Lateisha stared at Colson. He stared at her. And then she shoved past him and thrust open the door and rushed into the hospital room where she saw—

Blood.

Blood-soaked sheets.

A blood-soaked gang member with a scalpel in his throat.

"He got out of the cuffs," Madeline gasped. She had one hand on the scalpel. One hand on Brock's throat. "Came at me..." She looked up at Lateisha and Colson. *"Get a doctor! If I move the scalpel, I'm scared he'll bleed out!"*

Uh, it already looked as if he was bleeding out.

Colson ran down the hallway, shouting for the doctors and nurses.

Lateisha ran to the bed. After all, Madeline hadn't been lying when she said that Lateisha had been in med school. She had. Madeline had told her before that all lies should have some truth buried in them.

I don't perform vivisections on suspects. Hell, no.

But...

She had been a med student.

And maybe, just maybe, she could save this jerk's life.

Chapter Twenty-One

"Declan got the files you needed."

Eb glanced over at Hunter's low voice. He and Naomi were in the kitchen—she'd been making eggs and grits, and he'd been trying to keep his hands off her so she could complete the task.

Hunter had just strode into the room.

Henry spared Hunter a brief glance and then went right back to watching Naomi. The Golden Retriever seemed to be hoping she might drop something delicious.

"He sent them to me a few minutes ago." Hunter held a laptop in his hand. "Didn't open them because they're both your former partner's files and your own files. Maybe I'm just an amazingly nice individual, but I don't like to just barge up in other people's business." His brows rose. "Even though other people clearly don't have a problem *screaming* shit for me to hear."

Eb could actually feel his cheeks heating.

Hunter placed the laptop on the table. "All you have to do is click the files." He turned toward Naomi. "Did you make enough for me? Tell me you did. Friends share food with friends."

"Of course, I made enough. You were fighting a biker gang for me last night. Did you seriously think I wouldn't give you breakfast?"

"It's lunch time," he corrected her.

"Breakfast for lunch. Whatever. Pretty sure that's called brunch. It's a thing the world understands. Besides, these will be the best grits you've ever had."

Eb headed for the laptop. He hauled out a chair and started to click Hudson's file. Then he glanced over at Naomi. "Don't you want to see what's on here?"

Her eyebrows did a fast and cute wiggle. "Thought I wouldn't have the government clearance for something like that."

Hunter snorted. "We got these files in a majorly less than legal way. Trust me, none of us have clearance."

"Then...hell, yes. Help yourself, Hunter. Everything is done." She tossed aside a spoon she'd just grabbed and rushed to huddle over Eb's shoulder.

He opened the files that Declan had obtained. Scrolled through them with his breath practically held. Psych evaluations that showed...

Nothing.

No red flags. No beige flags. No flags at all for Hudson. Nothing at all out of the ordinary. Just descriptors and notes indicating that Hudson was highly intelligent, that he had strong empathy traits. That he could promote team growth and had a positive mindset and a ton of potential and was leadership material.

"Well, that's a lot of absolute bullshit," Naomi muttered. "Either Hudson was conning the shrinks, too, or this is just straight lies."

Eb opened his own psych evals…

Narcissistic personality. Manipulative. Arrogant. Aggressive tendencies. Lack of empathy.

"I'm fucking charming," he growled.

"You are," she agreed. "And that's wrong."

No, he didn't think it was. But—

Hunter's phone beeped.

Eb glanced over in time to see Hunter check the screen.

"Company." A despondent sigh before Hunter shoveled grits and eggs into his mouth. "Of the police variety."

Great.

"Looks like our favorite detective is beelining fast for the front of the house." Hunter pocketed the phone. "I bet he's here to tell us all how wrong he was. To offer his deepest, most sincere apologies."

Eb highly doubted that and his snort said as much.

"By the way, the grits are fantastic," Hunter told Naomi.

But they left the breakfast and all hurried for the front door. They went outside and watched as the detective parked. Henry was right at Naomi's side, and her fingers stroked lightly over his forehead.

Eb and Hunter took up positions near her. Protective positions. Eb was not in the mood to play around with the detective. He had a brunch waiting. He hadn't even gotten to try the grits yet.

The detective slammed his car door. He advanced toward the porch. Paused and looked up at them all. His chin notched high as Clark announced, "We have a confession."

Eb blinked. Well, well, Madeline had certainly been working fast. He was surprised that she hadn't called to tell him the news. Why send the detective?

Clark exhaled heavily. He waved his hand toward Eb. "Brock Arison confessed earlier. Your, ah, former boss? Madeline Desalt got the confession from him." That hand angled toward Naomi. "He set the fire at your place. Brock swears he was acting on orders from Ivan. Only he got the idea that maybe he should stop taking orders once he was at your home. The man saw an opportunity. He took it. And by that, I mean...Brock took your bat. He attacked his boss. Killed him and then thought he could blame the death on you." His hand fell as he glanced around the yard. "Brock figured he could take you out. Act like he was getting vengeance. Then he'd walk away as the new leader of the gang." His attention shifted back to the front porch. "Madeline told me that Brock also...he confessed to killing Hudson."

Naomi bounded down the steps. "*What?*"

"I'm...sorry," Clark muttered.

"Holy shit." Hunter seemed stunned. "Can I predict the future now? Is that what's happening?"

Eb elbowed him.

"Ivan and Hudson were working some kind of deal. I don't have specifics on it." Clark sniffed. "According to Madeline, it's above my pay grade."

Yeah, that sounded like Madeline. And the details probably were above his pay grade. Classified CIA intel.

"Brock found out about it. Got pissed at being left out. So he knifed Hudson." His Adam's apple bobbed. "You're clear, Naomi. I'm sorry that I...hell, I'm just used to everyone being guilty. You see guilt day in and day out, and you forget that some people actually are innocent."

Naomi shook her head. "It's...I...are you saying...it's all over? Brock is being arrested and I'm...what? Clear? Safe now?" She snapped her fingers. "Like that?"

But Clark shook his head. "Brock isn't being arrested."

Eb's stomach twisted. "Why not?"

"Because Brock Arison is dead. Dead men can't go to jail." Clark took a step back. "Told Madeline I'd personally come and notify you while she's handling the mess at the hospital. You don't need to hide out any longer. No one is hunting you. The gang members who were part of the attack last night are being booked. You are free."

Naomi raked a hand through her hair. "I just..." She stopped. Spun around and ran back up the steps. She grabbed Eb and hugged him. *"I'm free!"*

He hugged her back. Held her close. Eb could feel her happiness but something just—hell, it wasn't sitting right with him.

Why was Hudson's psych profile so clean?

He peered over her shoulder at Clark. The detective's feet shuffled over the driveway.

Clark cleared his throat as he gestured vaguely toward his ride. "Gonna just need you to come down to the station and sign some paperwork, Naomi. Give official statements about what happened last night. You, ah, too, Eb. Will need you to both come."

Naomi pulled back. She beamed up at Eb. "I'm not a killer."

"No, baby." His fingers skimmed under her jaw.

"Everyone will know now. I can get my reputation back. My *life* back. I won't be the hated Wicked Widow any longer."

No, she wouldn't be. "You'll get every dream you ever wanted." Even as he said those words, Eb could hear Madeline like a ghost whispering in his mind...

Better get ready for her to leave you. It will happen as soon as she's cleared. We find the person who murdered

Hudson, we lock that individual away, and you will never see Naomi again. Sucks, I get it, but that's life. In particular, that's our life. You know no one at the Agency ever really gets a happy ending in this world. We lie to everyone, even the people we want to love.

He didn't expect a happy ending. Not for himself. But he absolutely wanted Naomi to be happy. Eb would do whatever it took in order to ensure her happiness.

"Naomi, why don't you ride in the car with me?" Clark offered. He moved back his hand, and the holster on his belt shifted slightly. Clark wore a wrinkled suit coat over a white polo. Khaki pants. It wasn't particularly hot—certainly not nearly as hot and humid as it could get in Baton Rouge—but Clark was definitely sweating. "Eb and his, uh, buddy over there can follow behind us."

"Name's Hunter," his *buddy* announced clearly. "Pretty sure I've told you that before, Detective Anderson."

Naomi edged away from Eb.

He caught her hand because she was not going to be edging too far away.

"I think Madeline wants to talk with you, Eb." Clark sniffed. His hands had fallen back to his sides. "You might want to put a call in to her. Like I said, I'll take Naomi into town and get her to fill out some paperwork. You can follow behind once you tie up your loose ends here."

Eb didn't move. "Naomi was in the middle of her meal. I'll drive her to the station when she's done eating."

Clark backed up a step. He squinted against the sunlight. "I have orders. I am supposed to bring her in to the station." He offered Naomi a weak smile. "They might not be the freshest donuts, but I can tell you we are well stocked at the station. You can get donuts and coffee, and we'll take care of closing this case. Giving you back your life."

Naomi nodded. She took a step toward him.

"Nope." Eb pulled her right back. Tension had crept through his veins. *I came out of the safe house without a weapon.* Because Hunter had only seen the detective approaching. It hadn't seemed like a situation where Eb would need to grab his gun. "I'll drive Naomi after we finish eating. Won't take long. We'll meet you at the station." Flat. "See you soon."

Clark's mouth tightened.

"I don't understand!" Naomi tilted her head to the right. "How exactly did Brock die? He didn't seem to have life-ending injuries when he was here."

"Just had a hole in his damn hand," Hunter added. "Shouldn't have killed him."

Clark swiped away the sweat on his brow. "He broke free of his cuffs. Tried to grab a scalpel and attack Madeline."

Sonofabitch.

"She stopped him." Fast words. They tumbled from Clark. "The scalpel wound up in his throat. Docs couldn't save him. But at least Madeline and her team got his confession first." Clark's stare darted over Naomi. "I can't give you that ride? Sure would make things easier if you just came with me."

The detective was trying way too hard to get Naomi in his car. Like that didn't set off alarm bells. Deliberately, Eb stepped in front of Naomi. "I have her."

Clark nodded. "Yeah, I see that." An exhale. "Sorry, again. Wish things could have been different..." He turned away. Shuffled for his car.

"Naomi, get inside," Eb ordered softly. He didn't take his gaze off the shuffling detective.

"What?" She seemed confused.

"Get *inside*," Eb barked.

Too late. The detective was already spinning around, and he'd snatched the gun from his holster. Eb knew the bastard was going to fire, and Eb didn't have a weapon. Eb couldn't throw his body to the side because he was the only thing standing between Naomi and the bullet.

At least it will hit me. She'll be safe. She'll be—

Boom.

Boom.

Two shots.

Eb was staring straight at Clark so he saw when the bullet slammed into the detective's chest. Blood seemed to explode from the guy, soaking the white shirt beneath his open coat, and Clark's whole body jolted. The gun he'd been aiming at Eb flew a few inches to the left, so when he fired, the bullet went wide and scraped a fiery path over Eb's upper arm.

Naomi screamed. Henry howled.

And the detective tumbled back and hit the ground.

Eb bounded down the porch steps. The gun had fallen, and he picked it up, aiming at it at the moaning cop. "You sonofabitch!" His hold tightened on the weapon. The detective's white shirt was almost completely red. That fast. *Shit.* "Call an ambulance!" he roared.

Footsteps pounded behind him. He looked back. Hunter was there, with his gun still gripped in his hand. Well, at least one of them had been prepared.

"Who's your best friend in the world?" Hunter demanded.

Obviously, it would be the brutal bastard who'd just saved his life—and Naomi's life. "Best friend forever," Eb promised.

"You can thank me later," Hunter told Eb.

Yeah, he would.

"Why the hell did you pull the gun on us?" Eb asked Clark.

But the detective wasn't talking. He was far too busy bleeding out.

Chapter Twenty-Two

T HEY'D SEPARATED HIM FROM N AOMI.

Fury heaved inside of Eb. He glared at the one-way mirror on the police station's dingy wall. *Back to this same freaking spot.* When they'd called nine-one-one, the safe house had been swarmed. Again. He'd eventually wound up at the station. So had Hunter. And Naomi. And Henry, of course. But at least Eb had been able to arrive under his own steam. He'd driven his Impala to the station, with Naomi and Henry tucked in his ride. A cop car had tailed him.

Hunter had been delivered *in* the back of a patrol car.

The detective had been rushed away in an ambulance. Though there had been no need for the rush. Clark Anderson had been dead even as the EMTs had worked feverishly on his body. Hunter and Eb had tried to help him, too.

There is no helping the dead.

Eb stared into that one-way glass. After arriving at the station, the cops had immediately separated him and Naomi. Why? They'd already talked plenty and if they had wanted to lie and collude, they would have already gotten their stories straight on the drive over. A separation now was just a pain in his ass. "I'm really getting pissed off," he announced deliberately. "A local cop just tried to kill me. I don't appreciate being treated like the bad guy. So how about you get your ass in here to—"

The door swung open. His head turned slowly toward it.

A local cop didn't greet him. Madeline filled the doorway. Dark shadows lined her eyes. Her skin seemed too pale, and her clothes were wrinkled. And, yep, he was pretty sure that was blood on her.

"Sorry," she said, voice brisk. "Busy day. Night. Whatever. Been dealing with a few things. Like...you know, a man trying to kill me in the hospital." She marched to the table. Hooked a chair leg with her foot, dragged the chair back, and flopped down. Hard. "I got the pleasure of dealing with all that red tape, and as I'm explaining what happened to my very displeased superiors, I receive word that you killed a local cop."

She'd gotten the wrong word. "I didn't fire the gun."

"Right. Sorry." She rubbed her forehead. "This stupid headache I have will not stop. Let me try again here. Your *friend* Hunter killed the cop." Her cheeks puffed up before she exhaled. "Why was the cop out there? Did you call him?"

"What? No." Eb shook his head. "Clark Anderson said you sent him. That Brock had confessed all to you. That Brock attacked you, and the perp died."

"True. He confessed. He attacked." She looked down. "I have his blood on me." Stilted. "It's on me." She kept looking at the blood.

The moments ticked past. Finally, Eb said, "I want to see Naomi."

Her head slowly lifted. Madeline blinked, as if waking from a fog. "I'm not usually in the field. I sit in my office. I plan the missions. Like chess, you know?"

Hell. Was his boss—former boss—in shock? Her pupils were pinpricks. Her tone way off. He was also pretty sure her fingers were quivering. "Madeline, are you okay?"

She blinked. Twice. "Of course." Her shoulders straightened. "He attacked me. I defended myself. I also got the confession. Like I said, I've been busy." She licked her lips. "Brock set the fire at Naomi's. He took the bat from her truck bed, and he killed Ivan. He...he'd been setting a lot of fires for Ivan in this town. No one crossed Ivan and got away scot-free." She swallowed. "I didn't send the detective to you."

He waited.

Silence filled the room. More moments ticked slowly past.

"There were a lot of fires," she repeated. "Someone else should have noticed that pattern. I noticed it after just minimal digging. People died in some of those fires. Homicides. But...no investigations. No links discovered. That's just piss-poor police work. Or else it was deliberate... as in, a dirty cop." Her head inclined. "Instead of figuring that everyone in the department was inept, my money was on a cop being involved and deliberately suppressing any investigations into the arsons and deaths."

"And I'm betting Clark Anderson was that cop." Adrenaline fueled his blood. *I want to see Naomi.* "When Clark showed up—you know, before he tried to kill me and Naomi—the detective said he was following your orders."

Another blink. A slow one. "The man was a liar."

"You didn't send him to the safe house." Just so they were clear.

"Why would I have done that? I was at the hospital. Brock attacked me." Her gaze fell to her blood-stained clothes once again. Not a lot of blood. Flecks. "But I have the confession. I got the confession. For Hudson's murder. For Ivan's. I did my job."

"*Madeline.*"

A shudder shook her. Her chin lifted. "Yes?"

He'd never seen her like this. He had the feeling his former boss was hanging on by a thread. "I think when you get your team to dig, you're going to see that Detective Clark Anderson was tangled up with Ivan. Clark was on the take. That's a conclusion you and I have both reached."

A slow nod.

But he continued, "I think that Ivan and Hudson and Clark were *all* working together. Hudson was not some good guy in this story. He hurt Naomi. He took away her seizure meds and replaced them with something else. Hudson hurt her. She had to fight him in order to survive on her wedding night."

Her breath came faster.

"I thought he was my friend," Eb added, voice grim. "But I didn't know him at all."

"Sometimes, we don't really know anyone." She tucked a lock of hair behind her left ear. "But to me, it only makes sense for the detective to go after Naomi if he believed she knew something that could implicate him. Otherwise, why not just leave her at the safe house? Why risk pulling a gun with you right there?"

Eb could only shake his head. He didn't get what factor had pushed Clark into taking such a drastic step. "Desperate people do desperate things." So what had made the detective desperate? What had finally made him decide he had to kill Naomi?

"What does Naomi know?" Madeline asked him.

Again, Eb shook his head.

"Come on, Eb." She reached out and touched his hand. "You seduced her. You gained her trust. Naomi must have told you every secret that she possessed. Did she say something that would make Clark think she had to die?"

His gaze cut to the one-way mirror.

"She's not behind the glass." Madeline sounded tired. "She's down the hallway, with Colson Reid. He's keeping an eye on her. At this point, I don't know if there are other dirty cops in the department or not, but giving her a guard seemed like a good plan."

His focus shifted back to Madeline.

"What else does Naomi know?" she asked again. She seemed so weary. The faint lines near her mouth cut deeper. Lines he had never seen before. "You told me that Hudson took away her seizure medicine. That he hurt her on her wedding night. That's intel I didn't have until now. Tell me more."

"She stabbed him twice on their wedding night."

Madeline leaned forward.

"Naomi did *not* kill him. She got away. Henry dragged her to safety. When Naomi came back to the guesthouse..."

"Yes? What did she see when she came back?"

"Hudson was dead. Naomi never saw the killer."

Madeline didn't move.

Eb raked a hand over his face. "But you said Brock confessed, so she didn't have to see him, did she? We know the identity of Hudson's killer now."

Her shoulders slumped a bit. "No, she didn't have to see him. We have the evidence that we need. Hudson's murder investigation will be closed. And as far as Detective Clark Anderson...well, I think the investigation into the corruption in this department may just be starting."

"If Hunter hadn't fired his weapon at the detective, I'd be dead now."

Her lips thinned. "The detective should never have gone after you. No one hurts my agents."

"I'm not an agent any longer."

One eyebrow lifted. "That debt you owe isn't quite paid in full. And once Naomi goes back to her old life in Vegas, I think you'll find that you want to keep busy." She rose. Stretched a little. "You'll know where to find me then."

He rose, too. "So can I leave this damn room? Because when I opened the door before, two uniformed cops told me to stay put." Fighting them had been tempting, but, in light of what had already gone down that day, probably not the best plan.

"A detective is dead. Try playing nicely for a bit while I straighten things out, will you? Dirty or clean, Clark was still one of their own. We need to make sure we're handling everything here just right. No sense in making unnecessary enemies." She rubbed her forehead once more. "Damn headache." Madeline turned away. "I'll go check on Naomi. And Hunter. Just try to not attack anyone while I'm gone, would you? I'd really appreciate that." She made her way to the door.

"Who was the serial killer?"

Her hand froze mid-air as she reached for the doorknob. "Excuse me?" Madeline didn't look back.

"The serial killer. Memphis thought it was Hudson. You said Memphis had it all wrong. But you told me that Hudson had stopped the real perp. Who was it? Was the killer Hudson's father?"

She turned her head. Just a few inches. Met his gaze. "Yes."

To be certain he had this right, Eb said, "Hudson's dad was responsible for the missing girls when Hudson was growing up. And responsible for Hudson's mother's death." Eb paused. "But what about the women who died while Hudson was an agent?" A deliberate question. He wanted to watch every moment of her reaction. "What about the women Memphis Camden believed had been murdered when Hudson was on international missions?"

She did not break eye contact. "What do you think happened to them?"

"I think they were ordered hits."

A slight movement of her head that *could* have been a nod. "Hudson was not his father. He didn't get off on torturing and killing innocent girls." Her head turned back toward the door.

"Mary."

She stiffened.

"Mary was the girl that Hudson loved and lost so long ago. He told me that she changed everything for him."

"Some people can do that." Her voice held a whisper of sadness. "They can change you for better or for worse." She still didn't open the door. Instead, her body turned toward him. "How will Naomi change you? For better? Or for worse?"

"Better." He was sure of it. "She makes me want to be *better*."

"Are you certain of that?"

Yes.

"I think she makes you want to destroy," Madeline stated softly. "She makes you want to destroy anyone who tries to hurt her. If Hunter hadn't pulled that trigger at the safe house, what would you have done? I heard the report from the officers who took your statement when they arrived on the scene. You were the person standing between Naomi and Clark. You had no weapon. If you had moved to the side, if you had protected yourself, she would have been shot."

Yes.

"Can't help but notice the bloody sleeve on your shirt. And that nice, new bandage you're sporting. The bullet grazed you. Not because you moved but because Clark did, am I right? When Hunter shot him, Clark's aim was thrown off. Otherwise, you'd be dead. We would not be having this conversation. You'd be dead. Maybe Naomi would be, too."

Eb's lips pressed together.

"Just so you understand what I'm saying here—you're not *better* if you're dead. Falling for the wrong person? It just makes you weaker. Not stronger. Remember that." She spun away. Opened the door.

Two uniformed officers still waited outside the interrogation room.

They glared at Eb.

She'd been right. Clean or dirty, Clark had been one of their own. And the detective was the dead one.

"Play nicely," Madeline threw over her shoulder at Eb.

Screw that. He wasn't in the mood to play at all.

The door closed.

He was already halfway across the room. He grabbed for the knob. Hauled the door open.

The cops immediately blocked his path.

* * *

Naomi couldn't believe that she was back in an interrogation room at the police station. But at least she wasn't alone this time.

Henry sat near her feet. Naomi perched at the small table, in a freakishly hard chair, but Henry's warm body pressed against her. He'd been with her every moment that she'd been at the station.

He'd been with her, and a blue-eyed, way too watchful man named Colson Reid had been her shadow. One glance, and she'd pegged him as CIA. Button-downed. Watchful eyes. Entirely too still and assessing. At this point, it was way easy to spot the agents.

A knock at the door had Colson rising. Leaving. Shutting that door behind him without any word to her. Figured. The agent hadn't seemed really big on friendliness.

Just leave me to sit and stew.

She wanted to see Eb.

He stood between me and a bullet.

She'd never forget the absolute terror she'd felt when the gunshots had blasted. Did Eb realize that she'd seen his blood splatter into the air? She hadn't realized that he'd been hit in the arm, not at first. She'd thought the bullet had gone into his chest. That he'd been lethally shot right in front of her. And a scream of pure terror and rage had erupted from her.

But Eb had been okay.

Okay. Eb is all right. He's safe. I'm safe. We are okay.

He'd bounded down the steps. And the person shot in the chest? It had been Clark. The detective who'd tried so hard to get her locked away. He'd been the one who tried to kill her.

The door to the interrogation room flew open.

Naomi jumped. It wasn't Colson returning to the small room that felt increasingly claustrophobic.

"Come with me," Madeline commanded as she stood on the threshold of the interrogation room.

Naomi frowned at her. "Where's Colson?"

"I sent him to hang with Hunter." Madeline glanced upward, as if seeking divine assistance. "Why does this have to be so hard?" A mutter. Then she extended her hand toward Naomi and motioned with her fingers. A come-on gesture. "Do you want to stay in this room for the next twenty-four hours or do you want to see Eb? I am trying to help you."

Naomi lunged out of the chair and was across the room in an instant. "I want to see Eb."

"That's what I thought." Madeline seemed pleased. "Come on, let's go."

And they did. They left with Henry. Through the maze of hallways, they twisted and turned. There weren't any cops around. Naomi wondered where all of the uniforms had gone. She and Madeline hurried to the back of the station, steered clear of holding, and Madeline shoved open a door that led—

Wait. Outside?

Naomi stopped as the sun hit her in the eyes. She lifted a hand to shield herself.

"Get in the car," Madeline told her. "*Now.*"

And...there was a car waiting. An old sedan, with its trunk up.

"The trunk," Madeline snapped. She even tried to push Naomi forward.

Naomi didn't move. The other woman could not be serious. *And I am not in the mood to be pushed.* "What is happening right now? Where is Eb?" She turned toward Madeline. "Where is—"

Gun. Madeline had a gun pointed right at her. Dammit, when would people *stop* doing that? "I am so over guns and them being aimed at me."

"You're getting in the back of the car. Now. Or else..." Madeline shifted the gun toward Henry. "Or else I'm shooting your dog."

Every muscle in Naomi's body locked down. "The hell you will!"

"I didn't want to do this here." An annoyed sigh. "But I can. I can come up with a story. You overpowered me. You forced me out here. Your dog attacked me. I had to shoot him...then you. I had to shoot you to save myself." She widened her eyes. "You think Eb will be sad when he finds your dead body? Or do you think he'll be a bit relieved to have you gone?"

Naomi gaped at her.

"It's your choice. I can kill the dog *and* you right now... or you can get your ass in the car. In the trunk." She looked over her shoulder, then back at Naomi. "*Now*."

No way did she want to get in that trunk. Naomi hesitated.

"Fine." Madeline nodded. "I sure as hell hope that old saying about all good dogs going to heaven is true because Henry is about to get a swift trip to the afterlife." She began to squeeze the trigger.

Naomi lunged for her. She grabbed Madeline's arm.

The gun fired.

Chapter Twenty-Three

HE HEARD THE DISTINCT BLAST OF A GUN EXPLODING just as Eb prepared to force his way past the cops who needed to get out of his way because he *was* seeing Naomi.

They heard the blast, too, because they both whirled. Ran toward the sound. Using their distraction to his advantage, Eb burst from the interrogation room after them. General chaos and confusion reigned in that station as everyone fought to get to the back of the building.

"Did a weapon discharge?"

"Who the hell fired?"

"Check holding! Make sure all the suspects are secure!"

He ignored the voices and the questions and, as the others flew toward the back doors at the station and snaked through the hallways, he stopped by the interrogation rooms.

Yeah, he knew where they were. Thanks to his last visit to the station.

Eb shoved open the door to the interrogation room on the left. It banged against the wall.

"What's happening?" Hunter was already on his feet. Hunter wasn't alone. Eb recognized Colson Reid. The CIA operative stood near Hunter. "This bozo..." Hunter jerked his thumb toward Colson. "Wasn't letting me leave! And I *know* I heard a gunshot!"

"You *shot* a detective! You killed him!" Colson huffed back.

"Because he was about to kill Eb!"

"I was making sure you didn't rush out and get caught in any crossfire," Colson snapped at him. "And—hey, hey, Eb! Where are you going?"

To the next interrogation room. Only when he shoved open that door, it was empty. He searched all the interrogation areas, but there was no sign of Naomi, and his heart just pounded faster and faster as cold, hard fear snaked through his veins.

Some of the cops had already filed back in the rear doors at the station. Others were still outside. They were talking and muttering and some were swearing, and he just pushed his way past them all as he headed out to fully survey the area behind the police station.

Naomi. Where the hell is Naomi?

"Could have been a car backfiring," one of the cops guessed. "Video cameras are down back here. Been telling the chief we need to get them fixed for weeks."

Uh, yeah, they did need to get them fixed.

Eb studied the scene. No blood. No sign of a struggle. No discarded weapons.

"Who'd be crazy enough to shoot behind a police station?" The question came from one of the female officers. "Probably was a backfire."

Eb searched more behind the building.

Then he heard the sound of a dog barking.

His head jerked to the right, and he took off running.

"Eb!" A shout from behind him. Hunter's shout.

Eb didn't slow down. He kept following that familiar barking, hauling ass, and then he saw Henry. The dog was on the edge of the sidewalk, about to launch into the street up ahead.

"*Henry, no!*" Eb roared. If that dog got hit, Naomi would lose her mind.

Henry stilled. After a brief moment, the dog looked back at Eb. But Henry's ears were flat, his tail thumped once against the sidewalk, and a whine broke from him.

Eb raced to him. "Henry, don't you dare go into that road!" He grabbed Henry's collar.

But Henry whined again and strained against his hold as his body turned and pointed to the left.

Cars whipped past them.

"What's the dog doing?" Hunter had arrived, slightly out of breath.

Colson was with him.

Another whine came from Henry. Eb crouched in front of him. Stared into those deep eyes. "Where is Naomi?"

"Oh, for fuck's sake!" An explosion of frustration from Colson. "That freaking dog is not Lassie! He's not about to tell you that some woman fell down a well. Can we all go back inside before Madeline finds us and chews my ass out? You're both still supposed to be in interrogation, and I am trying really hard not to get on that woman's bad side. Her bad side is scary as hell."

Madeline.

He hadn't seen Madeline when he'd been searching for Naomi. Madeline hadn't been in any of the interrogation rooms. She hadn't been outside with the local officers, either.

Henry whined. Turned his head to the left once more. The dog peered down the road and then...

Henry just flopped down. Fell against the sidewalk. Stared mournfully at the passing cars.

Fuck me. "Naomi is gone." Guttural.

Henry had lost her. Eb was certain the dog had been following Naomi. But she'd been taken away. The dog couldn't track her any longer. And Henry—the dog seemed to be grieving right there on the sidewalk.

We're not grieving. We're getting her back.

"Henry, come on. Now." He tapped his leg and whirled away from the busy road.

Hunter was right in his path. "What do you mean, she's gone?"

"She's been taken."

"Uh, excuse me." Colson cleared his throat. His blue eyes showed both his confusion and his worry. "Did you just say *taken*? How in the world did you reach that conclusion?"

He didn't have time to waste. Eb shouldered past both men. Henry was in perfect step with him, but the dog's head sagged forward. His tail was tucked between his legs.

We're getting her back, Henry. Drop that dejected shit. We are not losing Naomi.

He'd driven to the police station. Hunter had been taken in the back of a patrol car—something the guy had bitched and moaned about—but he'd been given no other option by the responders on the scene. Eb and Naomi and Henry had all followed in the Impala, with an additional police cruiser right behind them.

So when Eb got back to the station, he didn't go inside. He marched straight for his car.

Cops were still fanned out. Still searching and investigating the gunshot.

Eb stalked to the Impala.

Colson's hand closed around his arm. "You don't get to just drive away. I told you, Madeline will flip out. She gave orders that you and Hunter were to stay put at the station."

He looked down at the hand, then back at Colson. "Where is your boss right now?"

"Inside the station."

Eb didn't think so. "Call her."

"What?"

"Call. Her. Now."

Colson let go. Hauled out his phone. Called Madeline.

"Eb." Hunter's low voice. "What is going on right now?"

Eb cut his gaze to his friend. "Naomi is gone. Someone took her."

"Right. Yeah. I get that vibe. But you know who took her, don't you? Gonna share or keep me in suspense for shits and giggles?"

Colson shoved his phone back into his pocket. "Madeline isn't answering. She's probably talking to the cops."

No, he didn't think that was the case. At all. Unclenching his teeth, he growled, "Hunter, I'm gonna need Declan to do some of his usual illegal shit for me."

Hunter just nodded.

"Get him to trace Madeline Desalt's phone. It's gonna be hard because the CIA will have anti-tracking tech that he has to disable—"

"Say less, buddy," Hunter advised. "Declan made the tech that the Agency uses. I'm on it." He backed away.

Colson's jaw dropped. "Are you serious right now?" And he reached out for Eb once more, closing his hand around Eb's shoulder. "Look, just go in the station. Madeline is inside. Probably just busy and that's why she didn't take my call. You can talk to her in there. I'm sure that Naomi is inside, too. You're overreacting."

He wasn't. "Move the hand."

Colson did not move the hand. "And even if Naomi is gone...maybe the woman just left on her own. Did you consider that possibility? That she just walked away? She's clear now. Maybe she just wanted to get the hell away from all of this mess. Can't say I really blame her." Colson winced. "And, um, maybe she wants to get the hell away from, uh, you, man. Sorry to say it, but you're probably a bad reminder of a past that she is dying to forget. Sometimes people don't like saying stuff to your face, so they'll ghost you instead."

"Move the hand." The last warning.

Colson pulled back, slowly. But he positioned his body firmly between Eb and the Impala. "Madeline is inside the station," he said again. "She's my boss. She said you and your friend Hunter had to stay here. I can't let you leave. So let's both just take a breath and calm the—"

Footsteps rushed toward them.

Eb turned, body tense, as a woman in a light gray suit, with a holster under her right arm, ran from the station and right toward them.

"Lateisha!" Relief filled Colson's voice. "That's my partner, Lateisha Gray. She'll tell you that Madeline is inside and that you're overreacting. Look, I get it. I do. An attempted murder can put anyone on edge. But Madeline gave an order, and I have to follow it—"

"She's not inside," Lateisha cut in to say. Her gaze swept

over Eb. Head to toe, then back up. "She's gone. There is no sign of Naomi Romano in the police station, either."

"Well, maybe Madeline just got called back to the hospital," Colson offered by way of explanation. "She may need to do more paperwork after that creep tried to kill her with the scalpel."

Lateisha shook her head. Her gaze remained on Eb. "I was with Brock Arison when he died."

Eb didn't have time for this shit. Every moment that passed meant more time when Naomi was in danger. When she could be hurt.

"Brock was trying to talk. Hard to do with a scalpel shoved in his throat. But his lips were moving...and I swear, I swear...he kept trying to say..." An exhale from Lateisha. A long, hard exhale. "She did it."

Colson snorted. "Of course, Madeline did it. She defended herself!"

But Eb ignored him. His focus remained on Lateisha. "You're a new recruit, aren't you?" He'd seen her when he'd been rushing through the station.

"Yes, I am." Her chin notched up. "And I've heard plenty of stories about you. You're the boogeyman they send after some of the most high-profile targets."

Yes. Guilty.

"Brock confessed in his hospital room. I was right there. I heard everything. Said he killed Hudson. Said he'd beaten Ivan to death. He was talking fast and furiously. Just throwing things out." A quick breath. "Then Madeline sent me out of the room. It didn't make sense for her to send me out. I'd heard everything else. Why make me leave then? But I went out, and less than a minute later, she was yelling, saying he'd attacked her. The scalpel was in his throat."

"He *did* attack her," Colson argued. "Lateisha,

seriously, watch what you say. You don't want to get on her bad side. She will ruin you. I've seen her do it with other operatives. The woman is a master chess player. You don't go up against her and win."

But Lateisha's chin remained stubbornly notched. "Brock was trying to talk to me. Trying to tell me something. And the cuff was *unlocked*. He hadn't broken it. Hadn't broken the railing. Someone had unlocked the cuff. I think she did that after she shoved the scalpel into his throat."

"You're committing career suicide." Colson whistled. "Suicide."

Her head whipped toward him. "And I think our boss committed cold-blooded murder, so I have to say something!"

Hunter surged back to Eb's side, with the phone gripped in his right hand. "Got her."

The cops were rushing toward their little group. One shouted Hunter's name.

Hunter shoved his phone toward Eb. "This app will let you track her. It's a little something special Declan designed and gave to only a few, select individuals. Be warned. She's moving, and she's moving fast."

Then he needed to move faster. Eb didn't bother telling Colson to get out of his way. He just shoved the prick to the side. When Colson tried to fight, Hunter grabbed the agent and held him back.

"You're making a mistake!" Colson exploded.

No. Colson was. Sometimes, you had to stop following orders. Eb opened the car door. "Henry."

Henry jumped in the ride. Shotgun. Eb slid into the driver's seat. Cranked the car.

The cops were hurrying toward them. Calling Hunter's name. Hunter was fighting with Colson, still holding the agent back. Lateisha had retreated. Probably so she wouldn't get run over by the Impala. That agent showed definite promise.

Eb shifted the car into reverse. Rolled the wheel, spun the car around, and the motor roared as he fired off down the street.

Naomi, baby, hold on. I'm coming for you.

Chapter Twenty-Four

That bitch had threatened to shoot her dog.

No one—*no one*—threatened Henry.

The gunshot blast had missed Naomi. But before she could try to wrestle the gun from Madeline, the other woman had shoved the gun into Naomi's side. So Naomi had been given two new options. Either she could take a bullet to the gut or she could get her ass in the trunk of the car.

She'd gotten her ass in the trunk of the car even as she yelled for Henry to run.

The trunk release lever had been disabled. Naomi had tried to pull it over and over during the car ride from hell, but the crafty agent had obviously planned ahead.

She planned to take me from the station. And she's planning to kill me.

Didn't take a genius to realize how this little trip would end. There was no way that Madeline was just going to let Naomi walk away when this was all over.

Naomi had kicked at the trunk. She'd punched at the lid. She'd searched the back of the car, and she'd actually made one major score. Because Madeline hadn't been as thorough as she should have been.

After nearly dislocating her shoulder, Naomi had managed to pull up the flooring of the trunk. Beneath it, there had been a spare tire. And a heavy, wonderful torque wrench. Her fingers had fisted around the metal. Not quite as powerful as a bat, of course, but still better than nothing.

As soon as that trunk opened and she had the opportunity for a good hit, Naomi planned to swing for all she was worth.

The car was stopping. Naomi had no idea how long they'd been driving. But the tires ground slowly, and she knew they'd arrived at whatever the hell destination Madeline had picked.

A few more moments, and the car stopped completely. Naomi held her breath when she heard the driver's side door slam.

She'll still have the gun. You have to be ready.

When she strained, Naomi could make out the soft tread of Madeline's steps. And then—

The trunk opened. Sunlight fell into the car, momentarily blinding Naomi because it had been so dark in her little prison. Her eyes blinked quickly to adjust to the new light.

"Get out!"

She'd slid the torque wrench behind her body. Naomi didn't move to get out. Instead, she asked, "Why? Are you trying to avoid blood stains in your trunk?"

"Not my car. It belongs to Brock Arison."

Sure it did. Why not have a car tied to the gang member? The dead gang member?

"There are many ways this can end," Madeline informed Naomi as she pointed her gun in Naomi's direction and waved it in a little circle. "I can make this as painful as possible. I can shoot you in your legs. Your hands. Your face. Then eventually kill you. Or I can be merciful."

"Wow. You are quite the CIA torturer, aren't you? How about you just hold that trigger finger and pause with the threats for a moment? I'm getting out." She was. She just needed to get out slowly and keep her weapon hidden until the optimum time to use it. Carefully, knowing her halting movements made it look as if she was utterly terrified—*spoiler alert, I am*—Naomi angled her body out of the trunk. Then...

"*This* place?" Naomi exclaimed in shock. "You brought me back here?"

The guesthouse. They were right in front of the guesthouse.

Madeline smiled at her. "And who said you can't go home again?"

Disgusted, Naomi shook her head. "You brought me all the way out here to kill me? Why?" She truly did not get it. "I didn't kill Hudson." How many times did she have to say it? Naomi kept the wrench tucked behind her right leg. "Didn't Brock confess to the crime?"

"Brock was lying. He was saying anything and everything that he thought I wanted to hear. The fool believed that by taking the fall, I'd let him go."

Naomi stiffened. "I didn't kill Hudson."

"I know." Madeline smiled at her once again.

Naomi really, really hated that woman's smile. Far too creepy. It never reached Madeline's icy eyes.

"You didn't kill him because I did," Madeline confessed. "I saw you stumble outside of this place on your wedding night."

Naomi's gaze jerked to the guesthouse front door.

"Your dog was trying to pull you. You were falling. Crying. Your whole body was shaking. Seizures are a real bitch, aren't they?"

Yes, they were. *And so are you.* Naomi pulled in a deep breath as she peered back at her kidnapper. "He attacked me. I was defending myself when I fought back."

"Um. Yes. I'm sure you were." Madeline leaned forward, the movement almost conspiratorial. "He wasn't attacking me. I killed him because he deserved it."

How was she supposed to respond to that? "Aren't you like…supposed to be one of the good guys? You work for the CIA."

"I am good." Madeline straightened. "I've stopped more monsters than you can imagine. I've saved people from human trafficking. I've stopped arms deals. I've stopped wars. I've eliminated dictators. I've made the world better."

Naomi's left hand motioned to the gun pointed at her. "Not to be difficult or anything, but how will killing me make the world better?"

"Hudson should never have married you. I told him that you were a mistake. That you could never accept him—not who he really was. That the moment you saw the person he'd been hiding from you, the moment you saw the *real* him, you'd turn away in disgust." A bob of her head. "Only instead of turning away, I guess you decided to stab him first, huh?"

A lump rose in her throat, but Naomi swallowed it down. She could feel a faint tremble in her fingers, and she was terrified that a seizure would hit. *Not now. Not now.* She could not afford to be helpless. Stress could bring on seizures, she knew that. One of her doctors had told her that, ages ago, and, hell, yes, she currently felt stressed. Understatement of the century.

Not a seizure. Not a seizure. It's just fear making me tremble.

"He didn't belong with you," Madeline snarled at her. "Not after all I'd done for Hudson. Not after all I'd done to make sure we could be together. He didn't get to walk off with you. Didn't get to have a life with you and shut me out. I wasn't going to stay in the dark alone."

Okay. Her heart slammed into her chest. "You were in love with him."

"Since I was sixteen years old."

Naomi blinked. "What?"

Madeline peered over at the guesthouse. "Let's go inside."

Her feet remained rooted to the spot. "Why? If I'm going to die, why don't you just shoot me already?"

"Because I have plans."

So do I. The first part of her plan involved Madeline lowering the gun so Naomi didn't get shot when she attacked the other woman. "You knew Hudson when you were a teenager?" Maybe talking more would distract Madeline. "How? I thought back then he was hung up on Mary Fontenot. The girl who disappeared—" Naomi broke off.

Madeline's expression had turned smug.

"It's you," Naomi breathed.

"Fake name. Fake life." A shrug. "I'm not Madeline. I'm Mary. I've always been Mary."

"Hudson's father—I thought he killed you! There was a serial killer hunting back then. Memphis was sure you were one of the victims. You—Hudson never got over your death! He loved you!"

"*Loved.*" Her eyes glinted with fury. "He *loved* me when we were teenagers. Loved me and mourned me when

306

I vanished. And when I came back into his life, when I recruited him away from the FBI and got him to come and work for me, he swore that he still loved me. He went on all the missions I gave him, didn't question me but...he changed. Every trip he took away, *Hudson changed.* And then he met you. He saw you. He wanted you. He thought he could leave the life I'd made and take you instead."

The drumming of Naomi's heartbeat was way too loud. "This is...about you not getting over your ex?" Seriously?

"He didn't love you!" A shriek.

Naomi backed up. Her hip hit the side of the sedan.

"It was a game. *You* were a game at first. That's all you were. Nothing more. He wanted to take something away from Eb. Arrogant, perfect Eb. Eb who got everything he ever wanted while Hudson and I had both been to hell and back in our lives before we were even eighteen years old." Madeline took a surging step forward. "Hudson's father was a twisted bastard."

Twisted. Hadn't Naomi once described Hudson the very same way?

"He hurt Hudson. He tried to hurt me. But I got away from him. I knew exactly what Hudson's father was. I fled because I knew if I didn't vanish, I would be dead. His father *did* kill those other girls. *I got away.* I reinvented myself. I got the attention of the CIA. I showed them what I could do. My IQ is fucking off the charts! I survived. I thrived. I came back stronger, and when I told Hudson— when we found each other again, when I finally told him everything, we stopped his father together."

"Sounds like you two were a real killer couple. He should have married you."

Madeline raised the gun higher. Pointed it at Naomi's face. "Yes, yes, he should have. He didn't really love you. At least, that's what he said at the beginning. All a game. But then...then he started to tell me that life with you could be *normal*. That he could have a family. A new identity. I'd gotten to start over, and he said he wanted that chance, too."

"His fresh start really wasn't that stellar." The gun could stop pointing at her face any moment. "He switched out my seizure pills and attacked me on our wedding night."

"I took away the pills. Me. I replaced them with sugar pills. I wanted him to see just how weak you were. You were not a match for him. You never could be. Hudson didn't belong with someone who was weak. He belonged with me."

Had she just heard the growl of a motor, in the distance? *Maybe Eb is coming after me.* Surely someone had seen the abduction at the police station?

But...

I didn't see anyone else behind the station.

Henry had been left behind. Henry would bark. He'd alert someone.

I don't have a phone on me. No way to track me.

Unless...did Madeline have a phone? Could she be tracked?

"On your wedding night when I found him, Hudson was bleeding and he was going to kill you," Madeline revealed. A reveal that she seemed to relish. "When I came into the guest- house, he had a gun. He was going to chase you down and shoot you. I stopped him."

"You stabbed him in the heart."

"It seemed fitting. He'd broken my heart, after all."

Naomi had no response. But that was fine because Madeline seemed to have plenty she wanted to say.

"I trusted him. It wasn't just that he pissed me off by marrying you. He and Ivan were working together. Stealing.

Betraying *me*. Hudson was supposed to use Ivan to stop crimes. But he wasn't. They funneled so much money into offshore accounts. Hudson was neck-deep in sin with Ivan. Brock knew about it. He wanted a slice of the pie that they had. Brock is the one who came to me and told me what they were doing, before the wedding. So Brock is the one *I* partnered with. I took out Hudson. Brock killed Ivan. Brock was supposed to kill you, but Eb got in the way."

Naomi crept away from the sedan. Acted as if she was going to head to the entrance of the guesthouse. Naomi was seventy percent sure she'd heard a car engine. Not just any engine.

Hello, '68 Impala...I hear you growling for me.

Okay, fine, maybe her ear wasn't quite good enough to actually recognize the engine, but hope was keeping her going. She *hoped* that she heard that '68 Impala. "You killed Brock. To...to hide your involvement? To make sure your fall guy never changed his mind and turned on you?"

Madeline followed her. "I killed Brock because he could not be trusted. He would say anything when the pressure was right. I wasn't about to be implicated by him."

"Uh, I hate to point this out." She walked backwards, edging toward the guesthouse but keeping her eyes on Madeline and keeping the wrench concealed. "But you are about to be super implicated. You kidnapped me from a police station. Ballsy move, I'll give you that. But dangerously dumb."

"No one saw me take you! The security cameras in the back of the station don't work. Clark made sure they didn't work."

Clark? Her brows shot up.

Madeline laughed. "He was on the take with Ivan. That means he was part of Hudson's web. I knew it all along."

"You sent him to kill me, too."

"Um, I did. Told him that we couldn't have loose ends. Told him that Hudson had shared secrets with you and that you had to be eliminated. Clark was panicked and desperate. It was like pointing a loaded gun."

"You actually *are* pointing a loaded gun at me right now." Another step backwards.

"Indeed, I am."

She could feel sweat at the base of her back. "Even if there weren't cameras, Eb is going to realize something happened to me. Eb is going to come after me."

"You'll be dead when he arrives. A seizure that was too powerful for you. Such a shame. You fought them your whole life. But in the end, you just weren't strong enough."

Her knees locked. "I'm not having a seizure."

"You will when I'm done with you. Certain drug combinations will cause a seizure. A mix of stimulants and antidepressants, a lovely witch's brew that will boil in your veins. Something fun made up and used on a few of the CIA's enemies over the years."

Naomi shook her head. "No."

"Yes." Adamant. "It's easier, you'll see. I mean, torture would be terrible for you. This way, well, it will only be a few moments. I had intended for you to die in a fire. My original plan. Figured that would be a fun, full-circle bit for you, considering what happened to your parents."

Her hand tightened around the wrench. "Fun."

"Um. But Brock screwed that up—*twice*. He had two chances to make you burn, and he messed up both times. So now I'm improvising."

"So...Ivan didn't plan the fire at my home? You did?"

A shrug. "Brock was following my orders. But don't be

mistaken, Ivan wanted you dead, too. There was a line of people waiting for you to die."

How fantastic to know. Her breath panted out. "I'm no expert, but won't your little witch's brew show up in a tox screen after I'm dead?"

Madeline laughed at her. "Who will order the tox screen? You fled from the police station because you couldn't bear to be around Eb any longer. He was too much like your husband. A liar and a killer. You came here, and, overwhelmed, you suffered a life-ending seizure."

She had a death grip on the wrench. "And how did I get here?"

Madeline blinked.

"I rode with Eb to the police station," Naomi pointed out. "In that beautiful '68 Impala of his."

"I hate that car," Madeline gritted out.

"I happen to love it," Naomi returned. "And, speaking of my dream ride, it's right behind you."

Madeline spun around. The gun spun away, too. Shifted away from Naomi. "No, it's not! Eb isn't here!" Madeline cried.

No, he wasn't there. Not yet. But she definitely heard a fast-approaching engine, and she'd just gotten her perfect distraction. Naomi yanked up the wrench. "Batter up, bitch." She lunged for her prey.

Too late, Madeline tried to turn back for her.

Naomi slammed that wrench into Madeline's arm as hard as she could. The gun flew from Madeline's fingers. Naomi pulled back, and she swung again. This time, she slammed the wrench into the side of Madeline's head.

Madeline screamed even as blood arched into the air.

And a black Impala came hurtling toward them.

Yes! Yes!

Madeline fell to the ground. The gun had landed under the sedan. Eb was racing toward her in that beautiful Impala, and Naomi could even see Henry in the passenger seat.

I'm okay. I'm safe. We're all okay.

Gripping that wrench like the lifeline it was, Naomi surged toward the Impala. Eb was already out. Already shouting—

"Get down!" He had a gun aimed at her.

She dropped without hesitating. Because this was Eb. She trusted him.

She believed in him.

She loved him.

That certainty pierced through every cell of her body.

So she just fell.

Eb fired his gun, and she knew he'd hit his target when she heard the thud and grunt behind her. Pushing to her knees and pressing up on the palms of her hands, Naomi glanced back.

Madeline was on her feet. She'd gotten the gun from beneath the car. Or—no, maybe that was a secondary weapon? Didn't super spies always have second weapons? Madeline had a gun in her hand, but blood was on her body. Near her shoulder even as she tried to aim the gun and shoot at Naomi.

Eb fired again.

The second bullet had Madeline staggering back. *But still holding the gun.* That woman just would not stop.

But she didn't get to fire because Henry leapt at her. He slammed his paws into her chest and took Madeline down.

"Naomi!" Eb grabbed her. Pulled her to her feet. His hands bit hard into her shoulders. "Baby, baby, please, tell me you're okay."

She still had her wrench. "I heard you coming."

"I fucking love you."

She smiled. "Good, I love you—"

He shoved her behind him.

"Too," she finished. Naomi peeked over his shoulder.

Henry had his paws on Madeline's chest. Her blood stained his paws. Blood from the gunshots. But Madeline wasn't dead. Her eyes were open, and her hands pushed weakly at the Golden Retriever.

Eb stalked toward her. Scooped up the gun from the ground and tucked it in his waistband.

"Help..." Madeline whispered.

"Henry, back," Eb ordered.

Henry whined, but he moved back. Not to Eb's side. To Naomi's. That beautiful, fierce dog barreled right to her. He bumped into her legs. Sat on her feet. Hunched back and stared up at her with adoration on his face.

"I love you," she told him, and she dropped to her knees to hug him. "Who is the best boy ever?" The best, apparently blood-thirsty and vengeful boy.

That's what happens when you threaten to shoot my dog.

"Why the hell did you do this?" Eb asked Madeline. *"Why?"*

"Because she loved Hudson," Naomi replied.

His head turned toward her. Disbelief was clear to see in his expression.

"Because she loved him since she was sixteen years old." She held her dog tighter. In the distance, she could hear sirens. More cars approaching. Eb had apparently come charging in with a whole cavalry behind him. "And I think she loved you, too." Madeline had loved him. Hated him. Maybe both? Maybe love and hate all twisted together?

Maybe that was the way Madeline felt about both Hudson and Eb.

"The hell she did." His hands pressed to the wounds on Madeline's body. "You're not dying, you hear me? You're going to answer for what you've done. You'll *pay* for hurting Naomi. You will pay."

Then the other cars rushed onto the scene. Patrol cars. Unmarked vehicles. Hunter jumped from one. Colson Reid was right with him. A woman in a gray suit. So many cops.

"Put your hands up!" A fierce order from an older cop.

Eb raised his hands. His blood-covered hands. "I'm not the bad guy."

No, he wasn't.

Naomi rose. Moved to stand in front of him. "He's the hero." Henry bumped her. "They both are," Naomi corrected.

"Fuck that," Eb snapped from behind her. "*You are, slugger.*"

Aw, had he seen her killer swing?

"*Drop the wrench, ma'am!*" the cop blasted.

Oh, right.

She dropped the wrench. It clattered to the ground. "For the record, I didn't kill *anyone.*"

"I believe you," Eb said.

With her hands still up, she looked back at him.

"I believe you," he said.

I believe you.

Strange because it felt like...

I love you.

"Say it again," she whispered.

And he opened his mouth and said...

"I love you."

The best words she'd ever heard in her life.

Chapter Twenty-Five

"PEOPLE like us don't get happy endings. Pretty sure I warned you about that before."

Eb lifted his brows as he stared across the table at the prisoner. Her dark hair slid across her cheeks when she shook her head, and the garish orange uniform washed out her once vibrant skin.

"No one really wants to spend forever with a monster," Madeline continued in a musing tone. "We're fun in bed, at least at first. We have that dangerous edge. But over time, the monster loses its appeal. Ordinary people want safety. They want truth. They want the picket fences and the growing old together routine."

"You killed Hudson."

"Hudson was a traitor. To his country. To me." A pause. "To you. He only went after Naomi in the first place because he wanted to take something away from you. It took him a long time to woo her, but in the end—after he'd

315

learned her secrets and used them against her in order to make Naomi believe he was her perfect match—he got her to marry him."

"And that pissed you off."

She put her hands on top of the table. Her cuffed hands. And leaned toward him. "Yes. It pissed me off. So I stabbed him in the heart. I *told* him not to go through with the ceremony. But he—like you—thought he could pull off a happy ending. But as soon as Hudson showed her his true colors, it was over."

"He hurt her."

"Hudson hurt a lot of people."

"On *your* command. You're the one who gave him the missions at the CIA. The executions."

She shrugged one shoulder. The oversized uniform slid to the side, exposing more of her skin. "They were criminals. They had to be stopped."

"You turned him into a killer, just like his father."

"I'm pretty sure his father had already fucked with Hudson's head plenty. And maybe...well, I suppose that's just the old nature versus nurture debate, isn't it? Was poor Hudson a helpless victim of circumstance in all of this? Or was he always meant to be evil?" The cuffs clinked against the table. "I guess we'll never know."

"You got Brock to kill for you."

"Um, yes. Already made this confession. I get bored when I repeat myself endlessly." She turned toward the one-way mirror. "I cooperated, so I should have been rewarded."

There would be no rewards for her.

A long-suffering sigh escaped Madeline. "Brock overheard Ivan and Hudson. He learned about their deals. He reported to me. Brock became a useful tool for me, and yes, I got him to eliminate Ivan. Ivan was a national security threat, after all."

"Was he?"

She winked. A move that wouldn't be picked up by anyone on the other side of the one-way glass because Madeline had angled her head back toward him.

"Clark Anderson was on your payroll." A fact Eb already knew but he wanted her reaction.

"I don't think I'd say *payroll* exactly. But he did help when needed. And the man was buried up to his eyeballs in trouble because of his connections with Ivan and Hudson." Her nails began to tap on the top of the table. Short, unpainted nails. "I don't really get why you're here today. I mean, it's a pleasure to see an old friend, don't get me wrong. But...I thought you'd left the CIA. You quit, remember?"

"You're being charged by the state of Louisiana and by the federal government."

"Why are you here, Eb?" A ghost of a smile came and went on her lips. "Or could you just not stay away from me? Did you miss me?"

Not even a little. "What happened at the police station? What made you leave me and go after Naomi?"

"I planned to eliminate her all along. Couldn't risk that perhaps Hudson had let something important about me slip in the heat of the moment to her."

"Bullshit."

Soft laughter. Mocking. "I did plan to eliminate her before we spoke at the police station. I had Brock's old car ready and waiting behind the station. My plans were perfect. Though..." Her hand rose and brushed along her left temple. Brushed deliberately along the scar that raised her skin. "I should have made sure the trunk was completely empty. My mistake. I'll own up to that. I didn't think to look beneath the flooring of the trunk."

"Something happened. Something set you off while you and I were talking in the police station. Something made you act right then and there."

She rubbed the scar. "I'll say—yet again—people like us don't get happy endings."

He searched her gaze. "You didn't want me to be with her."

"I did so much for you, Eb. I helped to get vengeance for your sister—"

"You got me in the prison, but I didn't kill Sebastian Glass."

"I helped you. I liked you. With Hudson gone, I thought...maybe you could be the match for me. But you—you fucking shot me, Eb." Anger sharpened her words.

"Yeah. I did. Twice."

"For her."

He nodded. "For her."

Her lips pulled down in disgust. "And where is she now? Still in your life? Still willing to trust the man who has committed such violence in front of her? Who lied to her? Who wanted to seduce her and lock her away?" Madeline pointed to the observation window. "I don't think she's behind the glass. I don't think she's watching. You know what I *do* think?"

He waited.

"I think people like us don't get normal lives." Laughter. "I think you lost her. I think she ran away from you. And I think *you* will always be broken and lonely because you can't really feel. You can't really care. You don't have empathy. You don't enjoy real emotions. You don't know how to live like a *normal* man."

So many of those words were familiar. "You changed my psych profile, didn't you?"

Her lashes fluttered. "Who, me?"

"You switched my profile with Hudson's. You knew how dangerous he really was. You covered for him. You did it for years."

"Hudson's father twisted him. He got Hudson...he got him to watch so long ago. To watch terrible things. Hudson had to always be handled with care. He could be charming, but, when he saw weakness, when he got too much control... the beast inside came out. It was a hungry beast that liked giving pain too much."

"That's why you wanted Naomi to have a seizure in front of him? So he'd enjoy her fucking weakness?" His own rage slipped the leash for a moment.

She shrugged.

His right fist slammed into the table. "Naomi isn't weak. She will never be weak."

Madeline licked her lips. "She'll also never be yours, will she?"

His heart squeezed.

"Why are you really here, Eb?"

"I have a new job."

What *could* have been fear flickered in her eyes.

"You left a big mess at the CIA," he told her. Total truth. "Someone has to clean it up. Lucky me, I get to be that someone. Oh, by the way, the psych reports have all been sorted out. No worries on that score. Declan Flynn helped fix that, uh, technical glitch, shall we say? The glitch *you* caused."

Her lips pressed together.

"I got your old job. Well, with a few perks. Because I

don't come cheap, and you left one major clusterfuck in your wake. Every case you ever worked is compromised."

"You worked with me."

"Yeah, but I'm not the delusional psychopath. That would be you. I always vetted my cases on my own. I never believed you blindly." *Because I'm not Hudson.*

"But you...you believed Naomi. When she said she was innocent—"

"I believe Naomi. I don't believe you. I'm here today to let you know that the higher-ups are very, very unhappy with you. Lateisha told me that you once threatened to put Brock in a prison so deep and dark that he would think he'd found his way into hell."

She shook her head. "Eb..."

"You'll be going to hell soon. Hope you enjoy the trip." Now it was his turn to lean forward. "Told you...you'll pay for hurting Naomi. I don't make idle threats. I say what I mean. Always. And I get my payback. I'm a real vengeful bastard that way."

"No. *No!*"

"Enjoy hell. Hope it's worth the price you paid for admission."

* * *

VEGAS WAS...VEGAS. Beautiful. Glittering. Full of magic and sin. And everything in between.

Naomi slowly walked across the rooftop bar. Stars shone overhead, a band played soft jazz, and all of the richly dressed couples swayed and charmed and partied the night away. She'd taken the job at the hotel three weeks ago. After she'd fled from Baton Rouge. The fresh start she'd wanted down there?

Yeah, that was dead and buried.

Declan Flynn had pulled strings and gotten her the new gig in Vegas. Temporary, for now, while she tested things out. But, if she wanted, she could become the permanent manager of his new hotel.

Her head turned. Her gaze landed on the tall, broad-shouldered male who stood near the railing and stared out at the night. Thick hair. Dark, lustrous. A line of stubble on a powerful and stubborn jaw. A profile that was killer handsome.

A man she would know anywhere.

He wore a black tux that fit him like a second skin. She could see the edge of the crisp, white dress shirt he wore underneath it. She wore a strapless black dress. One that flared near her thighs so that if she were to spin, it would flutter in the air around her.

She hadn't been spinning anywhere.

She'd been walking through the hotel like a ghost. Barcly feeling. Her heart cold. Wishing that she could see him again.

Eb.

He'd gone dark on her. Been pulled back into the CIA's web. He'd rushed to the rescue with Henry and the man had said he loved her. She *knew* he'd said those precious words because they replayed through her head on a taunting loop.

And then reality had exploded around them. Cops. Agents. Powerful people in the government who'd needed to control a major scandal that could have international implications.

Eb had held her. Too briefly. Promised her that he would come back to her as soon as he could.

And...

There he was. On the rooftop. Waiting.

Her high heels raced toward him. She reached out. Touched his shoulder. "Eb!" Joy broke in his name.

His head turned toward her. Those familiar topaz eyes stared back at her.

But the smile on her mouth froze. Because he wasn't looking at her the right way. His stare—where was the hunger? The need? The craving? This man—this man looked at her like—

"You're not Eb," she said, definite, and she snatched her hand back from him.

His eyes narrowed. No warmth. He seemed cold. Calculating. Dangerous.

Naomi knew she wasn't staring at her Eb. "You're Jake."

"And you are my brother's obsession." His gaze slid over her. Assessed. "Did you enjoy breaking his heart?"

"What?" She took a hard step back. "You're mistaken."

"No. I'm never mistaken about my brother." Then he pursed his lips. "Okay, fine. Once I very much was. About something pretty big, but that was my own damn jealousy blinding me."

He'd lost her. "What is happening here?"

"I wanted to meet you. To see the woman who has obsessed Eb." He nodded. "Saw the dog a few moments ago. Cute bowtie on him. Guessing that was your idea, seeing as how he's your dog?"

She didn't glance to the right. Henry was, indeed, decked out in a bowtie. "Where is Eb? If he's so obsessed with me, shouldn't he be here?"

"Do you hate him?"

Her mouth opened. Then closed. Then... "You're a very direct individual."

"I have a zero-bullshit tolerance."

"Fair enough. So do I."

Interest gleamed in his eyes.

"I do not hate Eb." Those words needed to be stated, for the record.

"Even though he lied to you, betrayed you? Had sex with you while he was trying to wreck your world?"

Again, her mouth opened. Almost dropped to the floor. But Naomi recovered. "You don't bother at all with tact, do you?"

"Again, zero-bullshit tolerance."

"And do you also have a zero-manners tolerance? Because your questions—no, your *interrogation* is incredibly rude." A prim chastisement.

He shrugged. Not chastised at all. "Eb is the charmer. I'm the evil twin. Or haven't you heard?"

The man was a dead ringer for Eb. Same chin. Same forehead. Same thick, dark hair. Same gleaming eyes. Only —the *emotion* in the eyes was different. "I don't hate Eb." Deliberate words. "In fact, I told him that I loved him. He said the words back to me. After that, he pretty much packed me up and sent me here. Then he vanished." More than vanished. There had been no phone call. No text. *Nothing*.

"Uh. He sent you off to a penthouse that was ready and waiting for you."

Yes, a penthouse had been waiting for her.

"He lined you up with a dream job."

Her jaw firmed. The job was exquisite, but she hadn't asked for him to arrange it.

"And he sent you back to the city you specifically told him that you were already thinking of moving back to because Baton Rouge was a town of nightmares for you. He does all this, and you think he vanished?

Sounds to me like he was trying to give you the life you wanted."

"I want *him*." She didn't care about any of the other stuff.

"Do you? Do you truly want Eb?"

"Yes." A hiss.

"Maybe he wanted to make sure you had time to think. Time without him pressuring you. Time when you weren't worried about your basic survival and you could live without fear or adrenaline. Maybe he wanted to be certain that what you felt was real because it would gut him too much to love you and have you turn away just when he thought he had everything he ever wanted."

She sucked in a breath.

Again, he shrugged. A lazy roll of his broad shoulders. "I know my brother pretty well. I can tell what he's thinking because, not too long ago, I was afraid to hope that my obsession would really love me."

"I want Eb." How many times did she have to say those words? "I'm not going to change my mind about him. I won't be frightened off. I won't grow tired of him. I want to learn every secret he has. I want him to learn my secrets. I want him to know..." An exhale. "I believe in him."

His eyelashes flickered. "Maybe you should go tell him all that."

"I would if I could find the asshole."

He smiled at her. Naomi's breath caught because that smile—with the one dimple winking—was so much like Eb's.

"Do you really think he wouldn't be close?" His voice had *almost* softened. "It's your big night. The VIP reception here at the new hotel. Your moment to shine after the work you put in over the last few weeks. He would like to see you shine."

Goosebumps rose over her arms. "He's here."

Jake stared back at her.

Brisk now, she nodded. "It was...interesting meeting you, Jake." She extended her hand toward him.

He took the offered hand. Shook it. "Do you know my brother's middle name?"

"Of course, it's Dickens."

The cold seemed to thaw in his eyes. "He doesn't tell just anyone that name. Embarrasses the hell out of him."

She smiled at Eb's twin. "Because he can be a real dick?"

His laughter rang out. Warm and rich and it turned heads around them.

She let go of his hand and skirted away. She had another twin to find. A twin she needed to see desperately. And if the jerk even *thought* of ghosting her again, he would pay. Dearly.

But there was no quick exit. Too many people wanted to say hello. Including Hunter McQueen and Declan Flynn —her boss. Not like she could ignore him. Or his lovely bride, Marley. Eb's sister.

A sister who watched her with curious eyes. And a quick smile. And with a whole lot more warmth than Jake had displayed. Then Marley sidled close and whispered, "He just arrived. He's on the elevator and coming up to see you."

Her heart pounded far too quickly. Every sense suddenly seemed to be working at a fever pitch. "If you'll excuse me..." She didn't wait for a reply from the group. She turned on her heel. Marched past the crowd. Marched away from the party and the drinks and the laughter and the music in the night.

Henry darted forward to walk at her side.

They reached the elevator banks.

She looked down at him. "Give me a little time with him, would you?"

Henry—with his bowtie—sat down.

The elevator dinged. The doors opened just as her head turned back, and as those doors fully cleared, she saw him. An exact copy of the man she'd spoken with just moments before on that rooftop.

Tall. Broad shoulders. Strong jaw. Dangerous and menacing. Killer handsome. And with topaz eyes...

That seemed to eat her alive.

"There you are," she murmured.

He stepped toward her.

No. Naomi shook her head. She rushed onto that elevator. Pushed him back. Grabbed him and dragged his head down to her. Their lips met in a mad, frantic crush. She kissed him desperately. Wildly. Passionately. With every bit of need and desire that burned within her. And Eb met her. Need for need. Lust for lust. Craving. Taking.

His hands curled around her waist. He pulled her against him.

The doors dinged. She was pretty sure the elevator started moving.

Quickly, clumsily, Naomi broke from him. She pulled out her security card. Swiped it over the control panel. Typed in a code. The elevator stilled.

"Uh, Naomi?" Deep. Rumbling. "Did you just stop the elevator?"

Her heart raced so quickly. And the fingers that held the key card trembled. She dropped it back into her purse.

Tossed her small bag to the floor. Then confronted him. "You didn't call."

"I had to take over at the CIA." His eyes still drank her in. Stark hunger—need—hardened his features.

"You didn't text."

"You don't know the clusterfuck that Madeline left behind. I *wanted* to call, but they had me in level-nine clearance meetings because the people in charge were pretty afraid the world might just implode—the spy world, at least. Every move I made was monitored." Hard, rumbling words.

"You didn't tell me that you loved me."

His eyes narrowed. "Yes, I did." Adamant.

"Fine. You said it twice." A woman liked to hear certain things again and again. Especially when her heart—and her life—had been on the line.

But he shook his head. "Said it more than that."

She took another step toward him. "You did not."

"Baby, I did." A rough pause. "I believe you."

"Yes, you should believe me because you—" Naomi stopped. A shiver slid over her. Hadn't she thought before... when he said those words...

"I believe you," he repeated. "I love you. I'll love you until I die. There. Does that work for you?" He seemed to be holding his breath.

"You set me up here in Vegas. Gave me the perfect place to live. The perfect job."

His Adam's apple bobbed. His eyes *burned*. "I want you to have the perfect life."

Impossible. "I won't have that without you."

A shudder worked along his body. "You need to be sure. When you learn about all the dark spots inside of me or when you get tired of being with someone who committed so many sins in the past...you'll want to get away."

She was right in front of him again. Naomi reached out. Took his hands. Put them on her hips. "I want you. I don't care if you work for the CIA and you do your black ops work for the government. I don't care if you are scheming and charming and plotting to take over the world."

"That's *not* what I—"

She raised one hand and put her index finger against his lips. "It was a joke."

His tongue licked her finger.

She shivered.

He licked her again. Then he eased back. "I love you," Eb told her. "I...thought you might want time away from me. *Normalcy*. Time when you weren't threatened. When you weren't suspected of murder. When you could have time to think...to think and see if I was the man you wanted at your side."

"You are." Absolute certainty.

"We can try dating," he said. "I'll wine you, I'll dine you, I'll—"

"Fuck me right now?"

His eyes widened.

"Because that's what I'd really like. You and me. Here. I don't care about being wined and dined. Pretty sure my psycho ex did that. So I'd prefer to just be real with you. I want you. I missed you. I felt like you cut out my heart, and I was barely functioning without you. Don't do that again. Don't leave. *Stay*. I want you—"

His mouth was on hers. She was in his arms again. He'd lifted her up against him, and there were no more words. No more declarations, not from either of them. He kissed her as if he couldn't get enough of her. As if he'd been starving. His hands shoved up her dress, he yanked away her panties. Then he twisted. He pushed her against the wall of the elevator. Pinned her with his body and his power and that strength was so incredibly sexy.

She heard the hiss of a zipper. Felt the press of his cock against her. That broad head teased her.

"I...I don't have a condom. Dammit, I—"

Her hand feathered along his jaw. "I should tell you...I want kids. And I really think twins would be awesome."

He was staring at her. His pupils flared. His face turned utterly brutal with passion and a stark possessiveness. He drove into her.

That was it. *Done.* He pounded into her with a fierce, almost predatory lust. Again and again. One strong hand snaked between them. He stroked her clit just the way she liked. Over and over even as he took her body. The dress hiked up between them. His cock drove deep. Her nails bit into the tux.

Her whole body was bow tight. His mouth was on her neck. Licking. Biting. Sucking her skin in sensual torment.

She came for him. Screaming his name as her body bucked against his. She felt him come inside of her on a long, hot wave of release, and his orgasm just made her climax even *harder.*

When it was over, her legs slid limply down him. He withdrew, held her as her feet touched the floor. Then straightened their clothes.

But he didn't give her back the panties.

He pocketed those.

She tried to get her breathing under control. She should also, ah, unfreeze the elevator before security was called.

But Eb...he dropped to his knees before her.

"Eb?"

His head tilted back. "I want to spend my life with you. Sickness. Health. Darkness. Light. Lies. Truth. Every damn thing. I want to be there with you. I'll fight for you. I'll kill to protect you. And I will do my best to make you happy. You are it for me, Naomi."

She grabbed his hands and hauled him upward. "I'll fight for you. With a bat. With a wrench. With whatever is handy."

He smiled at her. That dimple winked. She was a sucker for his dimple.

"I'd kill to protect you." She would. Naomi knew it. "No hesitation. I'll be with you in the dark and the light and every shade of gray in between. You're mine, Eb. The person I always wanted to find, and now that I have you, I don't plan to let you go." Tears pricked her eyes. "Fight for me, and I'll fight for you. We'll fight for *us*."

"Damn straight, we will." His mouth came back to hers. He kissed her. A soft, sweet kiss after the explosion of passion. "*Always*."

* * *

THE ELEVATOR DINGED. The doors opened.

Hunter McQueen had been scratching Henry behind his ears, but when those doors opened, Henry jerked to instant attention.

"Come on, boy," Eb called out.

The dog rushed into the elevator. Bumped his head against a rather disheveled-looking Naomi—she'd been perfectly poised five minutes ago—and a smug Eb.

"Was wondering when you'd show up," Hunter said as he ambled closer to the elevator.

Eb and Naomi were holding hands.

"Coming to join the party?" Hunter asked them.

Eb looked down at Naomi. She smiled back at him. Smiled with absolute love.

Damn. That kind of love might just be worth killing for.

What would he do, Hunter wondered, for someone who looked at him that way?

"We have other plans," Eb announced.

Oh, yeah. He was sure Eb had plans. Plans to fuck Naomi all night long.

"After all," Eb continued as he brought Naomi's hand to his mouth and pressed a kiss to the back of her knuckles, "this *is* Vegas. And the place is full of twenty-four-hour wedding chapels."

It took a moment too long for those words to register.

"Besides," Eb added with a roll of one shoulder, "not like we should let Henry's bowtie go to waste. He's already fancy and clearly ready to be the ring bearer." The doors began to close.

"Wait!" Hunter lunged forward. "Are you getting *married* tonight? Those are your plans? Marriage?"

"Congratulate us," Eb said.

The doors closed.

Hunter gaped. Then he laughed and then...

Was that bastard serious?

He smiled. Yeah, Eb had probably been serious. Hunter whirled on his heel. No time to waste. He had to go tell the family, after all.

It was time to celebrate.

THE END

Want to read another sexy romantic suspense? Be sure and check out WHEN HE FIGHTS...

He saved her from a nightmare.

Once upon a time, Kane Harte rescued Anastasia Patrick from hell. He took her away from a killer, protected her, and maybe even came perilously close to loving her. But then she was given a new life. A new name. A new home. And there was no room for Kane or the darkness he carried in her new world. So he walked away. Didn't look back. Fine, maybe he looked back a little. Or a lot. Maybe he dreamed of her every time his eyes closed. Sue him.

She falls for bad guys. It's a quirk. A flaw? Whatever.

When her ex turned out to be a killer, Anastasia "Ana" Patrick knew she was in trouble. But enter the FBI—or rather, enter the super scary, slightly shady, and undeniably hot Kane Harte. He protected her, he gave her a new life—new name, new home, new *Ana*. And he also broke her heart. That would be the previously mentioned issue she had with bad guys. She fell for the dangerously secretive Kane, and he walked away.

He shattered her heart but gave her safety. Not exactly a fair exchange...

Now her safe world has been wrecked. Danger has found Anastasia—Ana—once again, and she has no choice but to flee on her own. The killer from her past has escaped prison, and he's coming after her. Ana runs, desperate to get away, and she finds herself barreling straight into the arms of the protector she never expected to see again.

Kane Harte can kill a man in a hundred different ways. He can also break a woman's heart without batting an eye.

She won't fall for him again. Absolutely, Ana will *not* make that mistake again. Once burned, twice super cautious. But she needs a hero, and Kane excels when it comes to handling deadly trouble. She will control herself around him—there will be no giving in to the crazy desire she still feels for Kane—and, uh, sure, when the Feds decide that she has to be the bait to lure in the killer, Ana will play by their rules. Not like she has a choice, not if she wants to stay alive...

He won't keep his control. He won't play by the rules. And he will take what he wants.

Kane is done. He did the whole good-guy routine once before and walked away from Ana. Not happening again. This time, he'll give in to his need, his obsession, and he will never, ever let go. The Feds want to trap the killer after Ana? Fine. He'll trap him, but Kane will be the one calling the shots and setting the stage. Kane and Ana will play lovers—they will *be* lovers—and they'll draw in the killer. Kane will eliminate the threat to Ana, and he will do whatever it takes to possess the woman who has haunted his dreams for far too long.

Kane made a mistake when he let her go the first time. Now, he's going to fight like hell for his second chance with Ana. Nothing will stop him from claiming Ana. Not the Feds. Not her killer ex. And not his own bloody and dark past. "Heartless" Kane Harte will put his life and heart on the line for his Ana. Touch what belongs to him? Try to hurt her? He will make you pay.

Author's Note

Thank you! Thank you for journeying into the Ice Breaker world and reading ICE COLD LIAR. I have loved writing the Ice Breaker books, and I hope that you enjoyed reading the story.

Henry was a particular delight to write in this book. He was inspired by my own Golden Retriever, Dash. Sadly, I lost Dash to cancer a few years ago, but that sweet, happy boy will always hold a giant piece of my heart. When I started researching service dogs and I learned just how often Golden Retrievers are used as Seizure Response Dogs—well, it just seemed to be fate...and Henry was born.

Our four-legged babies can be so important in our lives. Companions, family members, and even heroes to us.

If you have time, please consider leaving a review for ICE COLD LIAR. Reviews help readers to discover new books —and authors are definitely grateful for them! (Trust me— we are super, super grateful!)

If you'd like to stay updated on my releases and sales, please join my newsletter list. Did I mention that when you sign up, you get a FREE Cynthia Eden book? Because you do!

By the way, I'm also active on social media. You can find me chatting away on Instagram and Facebook.

Again, thank you for reading ICE COLD LIAR. May your days be filled with lots of great books and fabulous adventures.

Best,

Cynthia Eden

cynthiaeden.com

More Books By Cynthia Eden

Protector & Defender Romance
- When He Protects
- When He Hunts
- When He Fights

Ice Breaker Cold Case Romance
- Frozen In Ice (Book 1)
- Falling For The Ice Queen (Book 2)
- Ice Cold Saint (Book 3)
- Touched By Ice (Book 4)
- Trapped In Ice (Book 5)
- Forged From Ice (Book 6)
- Buried Under Ice (Book 7)
- Ice Cold Kiss (Book 8)
- Locked In Ice (Book 9)
- Savage Ice (Book 10)
- Brutal Ice (Book 11)
- Cruel Ice (Book 12)
- Forbidden Ice (Book 13)
- Ice Cold Liar (Book 14)

Wilde Ways

- Protecting Piper (Book 1)
- Guarding Gwen (Book 2)
- Before Ben (Book 3)
- The Heart You Break (Book 4)
- Fighting For Her (Book 5)
- Ghost Of A Chance (Book 6)
- Crossing The Line (Book 7)
- Counting On Cole (Book 8)
- Chase After Me (Book 9)
- Say I Do (Book 10)
- Roman Will Fall (Book 11)
- The One Who Got Away (Book 12)
- Pretend You Want Me (Book 13)
- Cross My Heart (Book 14)
- The Bodyguard Next Door (Book 15)
- Ex Marks The Perfect Spot (Book 16)
- The Thief Who Loved Me (Book 17)

The Fallen Series

- Angel Of Darkness (Book 1)
- Angel Betrayed (Book 2)
- Angel In Chains (Book 3)
- Avenging Angel (Book 4)

Wilde Ways: Gone Rogue

- How To Protect A Princess (Book 1)
- How To Heal A Heartbreak (Book 2)
- How To Con A Crime Boss (Book 3)

Night Watch Paranormal Romance

- Hunt Me Down (Book 1)
- Slay My Name (Book 2)

- Face Your Demon (Book 3)

Trouble For Hire

- No Escape From War (Book 1)
- Don't Play With Odin (Book 2)
- Jinx, You're It (Book 3)
- Remember Ramsey (Book 4)

Death and Moonlight Mystery

- Step Into My Web (Book 1)
- Save Me From The Dark (Book 2)

Phoenix Fury

- Hot Enough To Burn (Book 1)
- Slow Burn (Book 2)
- Burn It Down (Book 3)

Dark Sins

- Don't Trust A Killer (Book 1)
- Don't Love A Liar (Book 2)

Lazarus Rising

- Never Let Go (Book One)
- Keep Me Close (Book Two)
- Stay With Me (Book Three)
- Run To Me (Book Four)
- Lie Close To Me (Book Five)
- Hold On Tight (Book Six)

Bad Things

- The Devil In Disguise (Book 1)
- On The Prowl (Book 2)
- Undead Or Alive (Book 3)

- Broken Angel (Book 4)
- Heart Of Stone (Book 5)
- Tempted By Fate (Book 6)
- Wicked And Wild (Book 7)
- Saint Or Sinner (Book 8)

Bite Series
- Forbidden Bite (Bite Book 1)
- Mating Bite (Bite Book 2)

Blood and Moonlight Series
- Bite The Dust (Book 1)
- Better Off Undead (Book 2)
- Bitter Blood (Book 3)

Mine Series
- Mine To Take (Book 1)
- Mine To Keep (Book 2)
- Mine To Hold (Book 3)
- Mine To Crave (Book 4)
- Mine To Have (Book 5)
- Mine To Protect (Book 6)

Dark Obsession Series
- Watch Me (Book 1)
- Want Me (Book 2)
- Need Me (Book 3)
- Beware Of Me (Book 4)

Purgatory Series
- The Wolf Within (Book 1)
- Marked By The Vampire (Book 2)
- Charming The Beast (Book 3)

- Deal with the Devil (Book 4)

Bound Series
- Bound By Blood (Book 1)
- Bound In Darkness (Book 2)
- Bound In Sin (Book 3)
- Bound By The Night (Book 4)
- Bound in Death (Book 5)

Stand-Alone Romantic Suspense
- Waiting For Christmas
- Monster Without Mercy
- Kiss Me This Christmas
- It's A Wonderful Werewolf
- Never Cry Werewolf
- Immortal Danger
- Deck The Halls
- Come Back To Me
- Put A Spell On Me
- Never Gonna Happen
- One Hot Holiday
- Slay All Day
- Midnight Bite
- Secret Admirer
- Christmas With A Spy
- Femme Fatale
- Until Death
- Sinful Secrets
- First Taste of Darkness
- A Vampire's Christmas Carol

About the Author

Cynthia Eden loves romance books, chocolate, and going on semi-lazy adventures. She is a *New York Times*, *USA Today*, *Digital Book World*, and *IndieReader* best-seller. She writes romantic suspense, paranormal romance, and fun contemporary novels. You can find out more about her work at www.cynthiaeden.com.

If you want to stay updated on her new releases and books deals, be sure to join her newsletter group: cynthiaeden. com/newsletter. When new readers sign up for her newsletter, they are automatically given a free Cynthia Eden ebook.

9 781965 259344